WORTHY OF FATE

REALMS IN PERIL

A. N. CAUDLE

Book Cover by Covers by Jules www.coversbyjules.crd.co

Map by Cartographybird Maps

Developmental Editing by Kirsty McQuarrie - The Travelling Editor
Line Edits by Noah Sky

ISBN:

ebook: 979-8-9894445-0-2

Paperback: 979-8-9894445-1-9

Hardcover: 979-8-9894445-2-6

To my modern-day fairytale,
for giving me the inspiration.

Content Information

Worthy of Fate is a dark fantasy romance with some dark elements that may be triggering. For a list of trigger warnings, please refer to my website at www.ancaudle.com/content-information If you have any questions or concerns regarding this list, my DM's are always open or you can email me.

Your mental health matters.

THE
DRIFT
ISLANDS

JEHON

HELERIE

ULRIK

AHWEY
LAKE

TORX

NARH

GAOL

VOARA

SAABHA

ORYN

IHAB PASS

BORGARA

MIRREN

ATARA

BHARA

RIYAH

NAHALE
FOREST

ILREK

DUSAN

PLIYYA

THE DRIFT
ISLANDS

LUBLAD

THE GREAT LANDS OF
TAERALIA

Reference Guide

Characters

Kya: k-eye-uh

Ryker: riyk-er

Alo: all-oh
Asmen: as-men
Cade: k-aid
Daegel: day-gull
Deres: dare-ess
Fahmor: f-ah-more
Fyn: fin
Hamal: ha-maal
Hindella: hin-dell-uh
Kaan: khan
Lorotte: lore-aat
Mavris: ma-vr-iss
Nikan: ni-kaan
Odarum: oh-dar-um
Qaala: kah-la
Sora: sore-uh
Tsirra: t-seer-uh
Vicria: vik-ree-uh
Zana: zaan-uh

Arra: are-uh
Brynya: brin-ya
Cadoc: cad-ock
Dainos: day-no's
Eamon: eh-mon
Floria: floor-ee-uh
Hakoa: ha-koh-uh
Hanyo: haan-yo
Jymar: juh-maar
Leysa: lay-suh
Malina: ma-leen-uh
Nephin: neh-feen
Njall: n-jaal
Penny: peh-nee
Rolim: row-lim
Theron: therr-un
Umana: oo-mahn-uh
Voron: voor-on
Zeá: zay-uh

Gods

Kleio: k-lee-oh
Goddess of Silence
Mother of Atara

Xareus: zarr-ee-us
God of Chaos
Father of Oryn

Ayen: eeh-yin
Goddess of Obdience
Mother of Ulrik

Cethar: seth-are
God of Nature
Father of Torx

Noxelia: nox-ee-lee-uh
Goddess of Dreams
Mother of Gaol

Odes: oh-dis
God of Mercy
The Fallen God

Udon: oo-don
God of Mischief
Father of Dusan

Terms

Beira: beer-uh
Dauði: d-auw-thee
Fylgjur: fil-g-yur
Glaev: g-lay-v
Nagasai: naa-guh-sigh
Nex: necks
Onvera: on-ver-uh
Tanganats: tang-uh-nats
Waalu: wah-loo

Braegia: bur-eh-gee-uh
Demid: dee-mid
Galadynia:
gala-din-ee-uh
Lurvinea: lure-vin-ee-uh
Nailu: nye-loo
Noavo: no-aav-oh
Raith: rayth
Vaavi: vaa-vee

PLACES

Ahwey: ah-way

Bhara: baw-ruh

Dichara: dic-are-uh

Eckterre: ehk-tair

Halerie: ha-leer-ee

Ihab: ee-haab

Jehon: jay-own

Mirren: meer-in

Nahale: nah-ha-lay

Oryn: or-in

Riyah: ree-uh

Taeralia: terr-ay-lee-uh

Ulrik: ole-rick

Voltaryn: vul-tar-in

Atara: uh-tar-uh

Borgara: bore-gar-uh

Dusan: due-saan

Gaol: ga-ole

Hylithria: hi-lith-ree-uh

Ilrek: ill-rick

Lublad: lub-lad

Morah: more-uh

Narh: naar

Pliyya: p-lee-uh

Saabha: sob-uh

Torx: torks

Voara: voh-are-uh

Woltawa: wol-tah-wah

Chapter One

KYA

I didn't ask to be born into this life, to become who I was. Fate was a cruel force beyond my comprehension. Inescapable and ruthless, caring for nothing but its own will. I didn't fear death. I pressed against it, waiting to be pushed into the endless void of the After. I walked the shadowed line, always teetering on the edge of life. No, I didn't fear death. It had always followed me. What I did fear was life. However short it may be...

But the same could not be said for this male as he cowered against the stone wall, trying to dig out the poisoned arrow as the inky black liquid crawled its way toward his heart. The vibrations of his weakening heartbeat pulsed through the floor and to my feet just outside the cracked-open door. I could feel it in my bones as each beat became slower and slower, my own heart calm and steady. Brown eyes bored into me from across the bedchamber; a plea to spare him from this fate.

He would receive no mercy from me.

I had no intention of taking his life tonight, only to retrieve what was not his and getting out. But once I saw the monster within, the vile things he had done to those who didn't deserve it, I couldn't leave him to roam the world.

Eamon will not be pleased. Neither will Nik, for that matter.

This was supposed to be a simple job. Get the book. Get out. I wasn't supposed to take justice into my own hands. That wasn't what a Roav did. But it was what *I* did, when the opportunity presented itself.

And why shouldn't I? Shouldn't I leave this world better while I can?

Taking an unworthy life had never bothered me.

My nostrils flared at the pungent odor of fear as I lowered my wooden bow, squeezed through the opening of the door, and approached him. His eyes were trained on my hooded face as he slumped to his knees and braced an arm on the edge of the overly extravagant bed. Flame-lit sconces reflected off the gray stone walls in the large bedchamber, his body darkened by my shadow as I towered over him.

I reveled in the feeling of his thin body kneeling before me, heartbeat quivering through the stone of the room and humming up my skin. I bent down so my masked face was level with his, my dark brown braid falling over my shoulder.

I could sense the other figure shaking with terror in the corner. My eyes flicked to his battered victim as she fumbled to pull down the tattered remains of her gown back over her bruised hips. I would get to her later.

Holding the male's stare, a tiny bit of satisfaction filled me. He must have seen something in my eyes, for his own widened in horror and the color drained from his already pale face.

Good. He should fear me.

I relished his terror and felt no shame in doing so. He brought this upon himself. I wouldn't have interfered with him if he hadn't been such a fucked up bastard. If I hadn't found him over the female, laughing while she begged for him to stop.

"P-plea-se," he stuttered, his jaw clenched from the pain of the arrow embedded deep in his chest. Terror made his voice scratchy as he pleaded for his pathetic life. I rolled my eyes.

They always begged.

"I-I'll give you anything you want. I swear to the Gods," he gritted through yellow teeth. "Anything!"

I tilted my head toward him and narrowed my eyes, irritated with his bargaining. "Your life holds no value." My voice was cold and calm, concealing my rage.

His mouth turned into a sneer and he attempted to spit at me, but the blood-stained saliva just dribbled down his stubbly chin. He tried to throw a gust of wind to push me back, but with his air abilities weakened, it simply ruffled my cloak.

I chuckled at his feeble effort. Air wielders. Always so relentless.

"Roav bitch," he mumbled, fury etched on his face.

My eyes narrowed to slits. I leaned forward, close enough to his face that I could smell his rancid breath. He grunted and hunched over as I slowly pulled the arrow out of his chest, my gloved hand avoiding the tip. Even with the severity of this wound, he would heal quickly, as all fae do. However, my arrows were laced with the toxic oil from the stem of the Onyx Flower—a beautiful flower that only bloomed at night, with petals that glistened in the light of our two moons. Once it entered the bloodstream, the poison hardened the victim's veins, not stopping until it reached the heart. Anything it touched suffered a slow and painful death. It was called the Onyx Kiss for the black blood visible even through the thick flesh of fae, like the one before me. His skin was already tinted gray from the venom. It wouldn't be long now.

I left him to bleed. He didn't deserve a quick death—let him suffer for his repulsive pleasures.

I turned and carefully approached the other figure cowering in the corner of the room, wedged between the wall and a mahogany armoire. Her pulse raced with trepidation as I neared, and I flinched at her fear. I knew I wasn't exactly a welcome sight, with my tight black leathers and my face masked, but surely she understood that I wasn't her enemy—seeing as I had just sentenced her captor to death.

I squatted down and pulled my mask below my chin, smiling warmly at the captive. My eyes softened as I revealed a friendly face. She seemed taken aback by the change in my demeanor, but her shoulders fell with relief.

I gently reached out to the iron chains twisted around the girl's hands. She hissed as I removed them from her raw skin, then I set them aside and made quick work of the ones around her ankles.

"Are you alright?" I asked softly, while my eyes roamed over her, looking for any apparent injuries that could prevent her from moving. Thankfully, I only found a tiny cut already healing on her delicate cheek and slight burns on her wrists and ankles—that said nothing for the wounds she likely bore on the inside. We needed to get out of here quickly, and although she was petite, I wasn't sure I could carry her. She gave me a shaky nod, her dark brown eyes watering with tears.

Offering her my gloved hand, she took it as the tears began to fall, streaking down her dirt-smeared face. I carefully pulled her to her feet, noticing her torn dress and the filth coating her long golden hair. Her pointed ears peeked out from the tangles, framing her fair face. After making sure she could stand independently, I let go of her hand, and she wrapped her arms around herself, glancing down at the floor as if in shame.

"Can you walk?"

She nodded again.

"I'll lead you out of the estate and help you get home. Are you from Lublad?" I gave her a tight smile after the girl offered another silent nod. There was no time for pleasantries, as I was already behind schedule. The estate was just on the other side of the forest from the city, and while it wouldn't have taken long, it was more time than I had accounted for.

I should have been out of here by now.

I turned to walk away. "I just need to grab something before—" I stopped as she grabbed my forearm.

"They took me when I was asleep in my room. What's to stop those bastards from doing it again?" Her voice shook, though she was trying to mask it. Her fear was understandable—even I would be shaken up after being taken from my bed and forced into another's.

She had a good point, though. With the rising desperation for coin, thieves—of all kinds—had been getting bolder, selling their wares to the highest bidder without a care about the consequences. Not that there were many, anyway.

I glanced around the room, searching until my eyes landed on the glinting metal at the hip of the now-dead male. I walked over to his lifeless body, seeing blood trickling from beneath his untucked tunic and onto the exotic rug, soaking it in a crimson red with swirls of black from the poison. My boots squelched as I bent over and removed his sheathed dagger. I cringed at the mess I had caused—not from disgust. I just preferred to go unnoticed until I was well and far away.

I walked back over to the female. After getting a better look at her, I saw she was younger than I had initially thought. She looked to be in her late teens—barely older than a child, but not quite at the *staying* age of twenty where our fae bodies seemed to stop aging. We didn't stop, though; it was just that we aged at a much slower rate, making our lives ridiculously long. Having reached my staying age six summers ago, I didn't look much older than her, but I already felt protective over the young female.

I held out the dagger. "Learn to wield this, and you will be the one to stop them." My tone was firm yet warm. I desperately wanted her to take it. The world was only getting more dangerous, and I didn't have much longer to help those who needed it most. I needed her to learn to protect herself, but I kept my desperation from my expression.

Her mouth fell open, and she hesitated before taking the weapon. A slight sense of pride filled me as she studied the blade, testing it with her grip. After a few moments of silence, she glanced at me. I gave a slight nod as she straightened her spine, confidence written on her face and determination in those big brown eyes.

I walked back over to the dead bastard. His body had already begun withering to reflect his true age, and from the rapid rate of decomposition, I'd say he was at least in his third century. I fished through his blood-soaked clothing until I found a brass key tucked inside his jacket pocket.

Removing the key, I walked over to a wooden chest behind a chair next to the window. I jammed the key into the lock, opened the chest, and pulled out a dense object wrapped in thick cloth secured with a pin.

I beamed at the sight of the tome I had been tirelessly searching for these past few weeks. I quickly tucked the book underneath my cloak before returning to the female, who looked at me curiously. I didn't answer her stare, though she was clearly wondering why her savior was stealing from a thief. If she understood who I was, she'd fear me just as much as the others.

"Let's go." I motioned to the open doorway.

We left the room and entered the long, windowless hallway heading toward the south side of the estate.

"I think that's the way out," she whispered, pointing in the opposite direction. "That's where I was brought in."

I murmured over my shoulder, "Two guards are on the north side. I'd rather prevent more bloodshed." I continued walking, knowing she was following from the vibration of her steps.

"How do you know? I didn't see anyone there earlier, and that was just shortly before you showed up."

"I didn't *see* them either. I felt them. But trust me, they're there." It wasn't the time to explain.

"Felt them…" she mumbled, pondering to herself. "You have…*terbis* abilities?" She sounded surprised, which she shouldn't be. Elemental magic of ground wielding wasn't uncommon. Although having the finely honed skill to feel vibrations through terra, like rock and dirt, was. I turned my head and gave a quick nod, then put a finger to my closed lips.

We continued down the damp, dimly lit hallway until we came to an exterior door leading to the grounds outside. The estate was massive and not too far outside the city, but it was secluded enough that whatever went on inside was unknown to others.

I stopped at the door, and the female went to open it. I blocked her with my arm, then closed my eyes and bent down to place my now-ungloved hand on the stone floor. My bare skin was more sensitive to the vibrations. Once I was sure I didn't feel anyone near the door outside, I stood back up, placed my mask over my face and opened the door. Peeking my head out into the darkness, I glanced around, double-checking that no one was near where I couldn't feel. I flicked my head from the female to the tree line beyond, not waiting for her acknowledgment before I sprinted toward the forest.

I needed to get far away from here, and fast—it wouldn't take long for someone to find the male. The Onyx Kiss delivered by arrow was a signature only associated with the Roav on the rare occasions *I* used it, and I'd rather not have a hunting party after me until I was long gone.

Once we were far enough into the trees to keep from being seen, I slowed to a walk and allowed her to catch up, thankful for the fresh, crisp air compared to the stuffy, damp atmosphere of the estate.

I was no stranger to the forest, as I had navigated through it several times to stalk my targets. The trees weren't very dense here, so I could see the ground well enough with the *moons-light*—though I didn't need to rely on my eyesight. I couldn't say the same for my attendant, though.

With my terbis abilities, I could feel exactly where things were. I could feel where the trunks sprouted from the ground, the lurking creatures of the forest, and, in the distance, the city's buildings. I didn't know how others managed to rely on sight alone—I would feel blind if I couldn't *see* through the ground. I shuddered at the thought of losing half my senses. Though I knew it would happen eventually.

We would reach the city's edge in under an hour at this rate. I picked up the pace, eager to get back on schedule. I reveled in the quiet, closed my eyes briefly, and deeply inhaled the calming scent of the forest. We walked for a few more minutes in blissful silence before she spoke, her voice coming out in a rushed whisper.

"I'm Sora, by the way. I wanted to thank you. For before, I mean. With…you know. Him." She stumbled on her words. "I'm sure that wasn't easy." Sora's voice turned somber.

I shrugged my shoulders. "It wasn't difficult."

"Oh. Well, that's good…I suppose?" She paused for a moment. "So, you're a terbis wielder?" she asked again.

"I am." I didn't mean to be short. I just preferred solitude when working. The place I needed to go inside myself when I was playing the part of a Roav didn't make for great company.

"And your ability allows you to *feel* others?" Sora sounded as if she were in awe. She was a chatty one, but I'd bet she was trying to keep herself distracted with all that had happened to her. "How does that work?"

"I can't feel *them,* but I can feel their vibrations through anything made of land."

"I've never heard of that! Can you manipulate, too? Like the others."

"Yes, but it's not as strong as most. I can only move and shape small amounts." Sensing vibrations was an ability few possessed, so I had never felt I'd suffered from the lack of manipulation.

"That's fascinating!" she marveled.

Curiosity got the better of me, and I couldn't help myself. "What's yours?"

"Water," Sora said with a bit of pride.

"If you have water abilities, why didn't you use it to defend yourself?" I questioned, hoping it didn't come across as condescending.

"I'm not exactly a powerful wielder, and since there wasn't any water around, there wasn't anything I could do. I can't pull it from the air like the more powerful ones," she said shamefully before she continued. "I don't mind, though. Until…well, now, I've never really needed it for much other than simple manipulation. Filling basins, pushing it through the piping system. Basic stuff."

I hummed in understanding. It was practical. No shame should come from practicality.

As we approached the edge of the forest a while later, the city of Lublad came into view through the trees. Being the largest city in the Nation of Gaol, Lublad also had the highest crime rate. While murder wasn't as common, it was not for lack of trying—fae weren't easy to kill if you didn't know what you were doing. And it still had no shortage of smugglers, thieves, and traffickers. The kidnapping of another fae was a ruthless crime, usually selling their victims to rapers by subduing them with a drug that nullified their abilities. It was a deplorable trade, and one I wished to see put to an end.

We didn't speak as we reached the buildings on the outskirts, made our way through an alley, and came onto the street with flame-lit lanterns on stone pillars lining each side. I secured my bow to my back, hoping to look less threatening and not wanting to draw attention. It wasn't that weapons were uncommon here, but I didn't want more eyes on me than necessary. I kept my hand near the dagger at my thigh.

I turned to look at Sora. "Which way?"

"This way," she said with a nod, already stepping in that direction more hastily than she was walking before. "It's not far from here."

Our steps were quiet, muffled by the drunken laughter of passersby as we walked in the direction of her home before she jerked her thumb to the side and turned down another street.

"Why are you walking me back? Don't you need to get that…whatever you have, somewhere else? Seems important if you felt the need to take it while in such a hurry," she said as she turned her head to the side to look at me, although she couldn't see my face through the mask.

"I promised I would help you get back home," I replied sternly, conveying that I wouldn't elaborate on the book. I sympathized with her curiosity, but it was simply not her business. Her lips pursed at my response, and she faced forward.

Let her be displeased. I doubted we'd ever run into each other again. For her sake, I hoped not.

After two more turns, we arrived in front of a small stone house with a mud roof and an old wooden door. Most homes and buildings were constructed of stone or mud, erected by terbis wielders. I stopped as she started to approach. She turned to face me a few steps away from the covered entrance.

"Thank you again." She gave me a timid smile, then closed the distance and embraced me, which I awkwardly returned with an uncomfortable smile.

When we parted, she glanced down at my arm, and her face fell. I followed her eyes, curious to see what had caught her attention. I noticed my black sleeve had been pushed halfway up my forearm, revealing the unmistakable mark. I pushed my sleeve back down, and when I looked at her delicate face again, it held nothing but pity.

I kept it hidden for a reason.

I wasn't ashamed of it. Being born Marked, I became used to its constant reminder of my unavoidable fate. I gave her a shallow nod and began to turn to walk away, eager to get out of the area and back to my horse before the fae male was found, and people realized a Roav was in the area.

"Wait!" Sora blurted. "You never told me your name." Her eyes were hopeful for an answer, and though she couldn't see it, the side of my mouth turned up in a rueful smile. I answered with a name few knew.

"My name is Kya."

Chapter Two

KYA

After years of traveling for missions, I shouldn't have been as annoyed by the time it took to journey back to Ilrek as I was. Other than successfully retrieving the book, that whole mission was a disaster. None of it had gone to plan, from killing that piece of shit, to returning Sora, to how long it was taking to get back home. I was ready to get back and sleep on something other than dirt. And bathe. That was my priority.

While summer was ending, the constant heat hadn't shown signs of letting up, and I was tired of the grimy feel of being covered in sweat for days on end. My horse was exhausted. The chestnut mare was old and slow, contributing to the longevity of the trip. That, in addition to the fact that she was stubborn and refused to go any faster than a trot. But we were nearing the end of our travels and needing to pass through one more village before the final stretch. I sensed she knew it as well, as she bobbed her head with a snicker as the end of the forested path came into view.

"You and me both, mare," I chuckled under my breath, rubbing her long mane.

Coming out of the forest, we came to an open grass plain. The mare's head jerked up as she came to an abrupt halt. Ears pinned back, she stomped her hoof, refusing to move further even after giving her a kick. I looked to where her eyes were staring and saw the reason for her concern.

"Shit…" My stomach fell, and I felt the blood drain from my face.

The patch of land before me was scarred, black as night, as if scorched with fire. But it was not the work of flames. Fire would kill vegetation and destroy homes, but the plague that had infected this land consumed even life and magic, leaving nothing behind. Not even my terbis would have been able to pick up anything through the ravaged terra.

The Glaev.

Once the corruption had touched the land, nothing survived. Anything it came into contact with withered and turned to ash within minutes, if not seconds. No trees or grass, not even the buildings existed there anymore, and no matter how many years passed, it would never grow back and could never be touched. Not even magic could penetrate it. The Glaev completely consumed the land, wiping it from existence and leaving a dark, empty scar.

My breathing increased as I dismounted and slowly approached what was once the small village, my muscles tightening with each step. The magic under my skin felt agitated, like it wanted to pull me away from the proximity. I knew better than to get too close. But I wanted to examine it for a moment. It had been a while since I had seen the corruption and the first time I had seen it this close to Ilrek. My palms began to sweat with the realization. It had never appeared within the perimeters of the Riyah Nation, and this was damn near on the edge.

No one knew precisely what infected the land—or why Riyah had never had to suffer its intrusion—only that it was first noticed around one hundred years ago by some very unfortunate travelers when they reached their intended village. Some believed it was related to the War of the Gods and the division of the Nations—a theory of lingering rivalry. But the Gods couldn't interfere with our realm anymore. After the war, after the God Odes fell and died, the land was divided among the Gods, with Riyah being the neutral Nation belonging to none. That was why people assumed that Riyah was never a victim of the Glaev.

There weren't any indications of where it would have occurred or how large the infected area would be until after it had filled its voracious appetite. It was unclear if it indeed was a plague, and many of the Scholars of Morah had perished attempting to study it to determine its origin. Morah held the most extraordinary collection of knowledge in the entire world. Scholars from all over were constantly coming and going, adding to the vast array of information being poured into the great library.

Standing before the decimation, it was like my terbis met a wall. Or not a wall but a cliff? One that drops off the world and into an endless void. Even if I didn't see it with my own eyes, I would describe it exactly the same by feel. Absence.

Spirits lived in everything. They were life. And the scent of so much spiritual death put me in an uneasy state, and my head started to feel dizzy.

After a moment, I decided that there was nothing new to learn about this patch of plague, nothing I could have done, and I walked back to my horse. I pulled out a piece of parchment and a stick of lead and recorded the information. Where it was located, size and shape. I maintained as much detail as possible, including a rough sketch. I replaced the materials in my pack, mounted the mare, and continued on, praying to the Gods for anyone who was left to perish in that village.

Dark memories instantly flooded my mind, but before I let them do more damage than they already had, I pushed them back into the hole where they belonged.

Itching to get away from this place, I urged my horse into a trot, which she was more than happy to grant, most likely just as eager as I was to leave this corrupted land. Several hours later, with the sun highest in the sky, we crested over a grassy hill with a stone arch at the top. Marking the passage between the nations of Gaol into Riyah, the arch displayed symbols of both Nations, one on each side of their border. The City of Ilrek finally came into sight.

Colorful stone buildings lined the city's perimeter, consisting of three sets of rings separating the city in sections. The outer ring was for shops, markets, and inns. Being the closest to the edge, this made it easier for trade as well as travelers who needed to gather supplies and continue on their journey quickly. The secondary ring was for healers, apothecaries, and a few other trades and businesses. The inner ring contained the citizens' homes, spaced far enough apart that it didn't feel clustered, with small parks and gardens scattered throughout. The center of the city held Morah. It was also located directly in the middle of the continent, making it the most frequented library.

Morah was a beacon in the distance as I went through the city after leaving my horse at a stable on the outskirts. With its four towering spires, the obsidian building seemed to absorb light with its smooth, glassy texture. Each spire branched off more than halfway up the structure and reached into the sky with over thirty levels.

My heart swelled at the sight of the magnificent building as I reached the city's inner circle. I had finally reached the great library, where I lived, and it was time for my mission to be completed and deliver the news of another Glaev outbreak.

Chapter Three

KYA

"U don's balls, Kya. You look like shit," Malina greeted me as I entered the upper dormitory levels of Morah. She was sitting on a chair, picking at her long nails. She jumped up and approached me with a smirk on her olive-skinned face. Her black hair swayed behind her as she walked, stopping directly before me with her bare arms crossed over the low-cut top of her expansive chest.

"Nice to see you too, Mal," I replied dryly, unable to stop the corners of my mouth from lifting into an amused smile. I crossed my arms to match her stance. Being the same height, our eyes were level, and I raised a brow. "You know, one of these days, the God of Mischief is going to come down here and smack you in the face with those balls of his if you keep cursing them as much as you do."

She shrugged her shoulders. "Like I'd oppose a God's sack in my face."

I snorted and couldn't help my widening smile. I missed her snarky personality.

She smiled with a grimace. "I'd hug you after not seeing you for nearly a month, but you smell like horse shit and look like you've been lying in the dirt. And why is there blood on your leathers?" My sister—of a sort—never missed an opportunity to give me a hard time. While we had no familial relation, we were sisters of the heart. Just like Nikan was our brother. Where we came from, family was much more than blood.

"I have been lying in the dirt. And I'll explain the blood later. First, I need a hot bath." I realized I must have been quite the sight, with dried mud and blood on my clothes and my hair fraying out from my braid. Annoyed with the state of my hair, I reached up and attempted to pull a stick out of the tangles—a pointless effort until I could properly bathe.

Her smile fell, and she dropped her arms to her sides. "That'll have to wait. Eamon said he needs to see you once you arrive."

Disappointed, though not surprised, I nodded my head. My mission was only complete once I'd delivered his package, but usually, I had time to at least clean up.

"Alright. I'll at least change first. I'm not walking into a High Scholar's office with blood on my clothes."

"Probably a good idea." Malina laughed—a lighthearted sound like music to my ears. I began walking toward my room, and she stepped beside me.

"What are you doing?" My eyebrows bunched together as I looked at her while we walked to the hallway leading to the bedchambers.

"I'm bored. I don't have anyone to talk to, and I want to hear about the job," she said with a peppy tone and an innocent smile on her pink lips.

"Where's Nik? He should have been back by now. He left a week before I did." I glanced around the shared space with reading chairs and a hallway off the side leading to the small kitchen and dining area. My concern wasn't just for his well-being, but also because I wasn't exactly eager to face him again after our spat the last time we saw each other.

17

"Relax, Kya. He's in Bhara." Malina rolled her eyes, mistaking my concern for the missing male of our trio as we entered my room at the far end of the hall.

I put down my pack by the door, audibly sighing with relief, and walked across the sitting area into my bedroom. Malina plopped into a chair by the black glass wall overlooking the city, slumping against the cushioned arm.

"Why is he in Bhara?" I called out from my room.

The city of Bhara wasn't far from Ilrek, about two days' travel on foot to the other side of Riyah, but it wasn't a place wards of the Scholars frequently traveled to. The Central Temple, home of the Council of Sages, relied on the guidance of Spirits rather than knowledge written on parchment.

"Who knows. Some political issue between the Scholars and Sages. Knowledge versus faith and all that. More like a pissing contest if you ask me. Eamon thought it would be better if Nik went to deal with them rather than any of these stiff, old males." Malina stated, sounding utterly bored with the conversation, as I pulled clean clothes from the wardrobe.

"Fair point." I couldn't argue with that logic. Sages and Scholars rarely agreed on anything, but both were part of the Riyah government.

I removed my leathers and put on light-colored trousers and a matching sleeveless top, tying it at the bottom. I grabbed a pair of slippers, headed back into the sitting area, and put them on before I walked over to my pack to pull out the book.

"What's this one?" Malina stood up and gestured with a jerk of her chin to the wrapped book in my hands.

"Some history of the Hanyo family. It's old and brittle, so I didn't try to mess with it too much." With the book tucked into my side, I headed out the door, Malina following close behind.

"Hanyo? One of those old families of Ulrik?" Malina asked.

"Yep. Nou Hanyo was the first to be gifted with water abilities." It seemed fitting that he became Lord of Ulrik, half covered in ice and snow and with some of the coldest temperatures on the continent.

"Wonder how it got all the way to Lublad. What would anyone want with it? Is it really worth anything on the market?" she muttered as we went down to the lower levels, to Eamon's study. Our soft steps were quiet on the rugs covering the floor.

"I don't know." I pondered this as well, but after retrieving hundreds of lost or stolen books and tomes for years, I quit asking questions as to their value of thieves. All I knew was that the Lords and Ladies would rather start wars than see their Nation's histories in the hands of other rulers.

And the last thing we needed was another petty war.

As we approached the High Scholar's study on the fifth level, I turned my head to Malina. "I'll find you later and give you the details."

She nodded with a cheerful smile before heading back up the stairs. I took a deep breath and knocked twice on the thick wooden door, ready for this too-long mission to be over.

"Enter." Eamon's voice boomed from the other side, and I opened the large double doors.

Being a High Scholar, the overseer of the Morah Library, meant that Eamon had the largest study of the Scholars, the walls lined with shelves full of books and scrolls. A sitting area was positioned to one side with enough space for the entire council, all fourteen of them, with a sizeable plush rug in the center. The other side held a large table with documents and books scattered about for his research, and at the back of the room sat Eamon's sizeable mahogany desk with two upholstered chairs in front of it.

Eamon was hunched over on the other side, writing while deep in thought and glancing at his notes. I sat in one of the chairs, one leg crossed over the other and the wrapped book in my lap. I knew better than to interrupt him in the middle of his thoughts, so I waited patiently—giving him the respect he'd earned over the centuries. I forced myself to remain calm and rationalized that there was no chance that Eamon would have heard about the trafficker yet.

After a few moments, he looked up at me with big blue eyes. His lips widened into a warm smile, and his eyes softened. A hint of wrinkles was forming around his eyes and mouth with his age. He stood and walked around the desk, his arms opening for an embrace as I stood from the chair, placing the book on the desk and accepting a welcoming hug, a smile of mine forming on my lips. I missed him as much as I missed Malina.

His usual scent of parchment and ink, mixed with the musty smell of books, flooded my nose.

"Kya," Eamon breathed with a sound of relief. He stepped back, his hands on my shoulders, looking me up and down. "You look well! And I see that you were successful in your journey as always," he beamed with pride.

"I was. The book was in Gaol, as I suspected," I said with a nod.

Gaol, the Nation located at the southern end of the continent, was known for its dark market of smuggled items. His eyes glinted excitedly as he released me and turned to grab the book, unwrapping it from the cloth.

"Magnificent," he said in awe. "Ulrik has paid a handsome price for its retrieval. To stay here, of course." He huffed a small laugh. "Lord Hamal tried to get out of that particular condition, but ultimately conceded once they realized it wasn't a negotiation. If they want to see it, they are welcome to come here, as all are."

People contracted jobs through Morah to retrieve items of knowledge lost or stolen. Payment was given to the High Scholar for the item, which was then used as part of the income to run the place. The other condition was that the item had to remain at Morah. The Scholars believed that Nations shouldn't hoard knowledge and it should be available to all, kept in a neutral location.

The Roav—Malina, Nikan, and myself—were given the jobs and paid a percentage from the Scholars. And we did whatever was necessary to be successful in our missions, and no one questioned us. Regardless of getting paid, it was the least we could do for Morah. We owed the Scholars our lives.

How Eamon was able to let us stay here without swearing citizenship to Riyah was a question that had never been answered.

The Riyah Nation was a neutral House located in the continent's center, bordered by the other six nations—well, five now. Riyah was the only Nation that a Lord or Lady didn't run. In place of one leader, Riyah was governed by multiple, consisting of the Sages and Scholars. The Sages were spiritually enhanced, swearing their life to obeying them and upholding the balance of the realm. The Scholars were dedicated to keeping record of unbiased knowledge, and educating. Sages and Scholars held no allegiance to any other Nation. Both of which had to make great sacrifices to obtain their title, giving up any abilities by going through a ritual, as well as never bearing children.

And the sacrifices extended to the citizens as well. It was the reason Riyah's housing ring in Ilrek was so small. Few lived in the city permanently, but many frequented for travel. You could only reside in the Nation if you became a citizen. In order to do that, you had to have never declared citizenship anywhere else, and only then could you request the Council of Sages to take away your ability to bear children. It was a brutal decision and one that someone didn't take lightly. Unlike the Sages and Scholars, the citizens themselves were able to keep their abilities.

"I apologize, but I'm spent from my travels and would like to rest." He turned to me, and I didn't bother trying to hide my exhaustion from showing. All I could think about was my bathing tub waiting for me.

"Of course, child." His face portrayed understanding with a soft smile. While Eamon was not my father, he was my guardian and had practically raised me here at Morah with Malina and Nikan, giving us a better life than we would have had without him.

"Oh, and before you go," Eamon spoke again. "A Roav is needed. Since you just returned and Nikan is away, I'll be sending Malina. Inform her when you see her and take a few days to rest."

"Thank you, Eamon."

With a wave, I left the study and rushed to my bedchamber. After running my hot bath, I stripped my clothes off and threw them on the floor, pouring in the eucalyptus oil I had gotten from a trader in the outer ring.

I cringed slightly at the sight of my grime-covered body, skinnier than I remembered. The toned muscles of my torso and arms were less defined without the usual daily training sessions. Displeased with how weak I looked, I made a mental note to double my sessions for the next few weeks. At least my thighs and calves were still up to my standards—all thanks to having to kick the mare into motion as well as the constant walking when I wasn't on horseback. I eased my way into the steaming water, hissing at the heat. A pleased sigh escaped my lips.

The large tub allowed me to submerge up to my neck as I rested the back of my head on the edge. As with every room with an exterior wall, the bathing room was lit up by the light coming through the tinted glass. I closed my eyes and inhaled the steam, the eucalyptus scent relaxing me further, and I could feel the tension falling from my muscles. I sat in the water for a few minutes, and just as I began to drift off, the door burst open.

I didn't bother opening my eyes to see who it was, as I already knew. I heard footsteps thumping on the hard floor as a sweet, melodic voice began to speak.

"Ugh!" Malina scoffed in mock exasperation. I failed to hide my smile at her irritation. "You were supposed to find me after your meeting, but you seem to think a bath with your weird-ass oils is more pressing than me!"

I couldn't help a little laugh from escaping. I opened my eyes and saw Malina standing over me with her hands on her hips and a dramatic scowl.

"You were the one who said I smelt of horse shit. I figured you'd appreciate my *weird-ass oil* scent over that," I teased with raised eyebrows.

"Yeah, alright. But you promised details of the mission, and I want to hear them now." She pulled up a vanity chair to the side of the tub and plopped down on it, propping her elbows on her toned thighs and her chin on her fists. Her hair fell around her face, her sweet, innocent look reflecting nothing of what she was truly capable of.

I slid down to dip my head below the water and quickly unbraided my long brown hair, the water making it a bit easier with the tangles. I resurfaced and grabbed my lavender-scented shampoo.

I began to wash my hair and body as I recalled the mission's events to her. I explained that I had connected with my usual black market contacts to learn of the book and who had it last. Once I knew, I had found the male in Gaol at his estate in Lublad, retrieved the stolen book, and began my journey home.

"Sounds like every other job. But that doesn't explain the blood all over your clothes. From the scent, it wasn't yours," she probed, visibly irritated.

"It was his, actually," I said matter-of-factly. While I preferred to complete my missions less violently, killing a target wasn't entirely unusual.

Malina's lips lifted to one side, and her eyes narrowed in amusement. "So what did this one do to deserve the wrath of a Hunter of Morah?"

"He was a fae trafficker." My face portrayed no emotions as I finished rinsing. "He had a young water-wielding female…"

I didn't mention that I returned the female to her home after killing her captor, not wanting Nikan to find out. I wasn't in the mood to get berated for my *reckless* actions again.

Malina's face fell. "They're getting bolder," she bit out with frustration. "If the Worthy would just assign a few of the Watch on their streets, most of them would be too scared to do shit like this. Yet the pretty Lords and Ladies can't be bothered, only doing the bare minimum to appease their God." She paused. "Still, Eamon won't be pleased to hear that you took justice into your own hands. Again."

I ignored her retort about Eamon, "They're busy worrying about the Glaev. More locations are showing up faster than it ever has before. They're concentrating their forces to evacuate the people in the smaller towns." I stood in the tub, water dripping down my bare skin, making to get out as Malina handed me a towel. Being raised as sisters alongside one another had removed the usual self-consciousness over seeing each other's naked bodies.

"In Gaol?" Her face was a mask of indifference.

I wrapped the towel around me and stepped out of the tub, my long hair trickling water down my back as I went to the vanity, where my clean clothes lay folded.

"Yeah," I said, trying to hide any worry in my voice but turned solemn despite my attempt. "Along the border, about a half-day's ride from here. It was a small village, but still…"

I unwrapped my towel, patting myself dry while taking a glance at my round ass and modestly firm breasts, grateful that they didn't suffer the same fate as my withering muscles. I bit my lower lip, thinking of who else would appreciate them tonight.

"It's getting closer." Fear laced her voice, jostling me from my thoughts before they could go any further. "What if it reaches here? What if it gets to Morah? We can't go through that again—"

"Stop," I said firmly as I quickly threw on my clothes and crossed the room to put my hands on her shoulders. My voice softened to a whisper, "It has never been within the borders of Riyah."

"There's nothing to say that it won't, though. You know that."

"There's nothing to say that it will." I chuckled in an attempt to ease her worries. "We can't worry about it if it's not here. And right now, it's not."

Malina took a deep breath to center herself, visibly relaxing. Not much worried her, but after what happened to us when we were younger, the Glaev certainly did.

She shook her head. "You're right. And besides, I don't want to think about that now. Let's go out tonight!" She beamed with no trace of worry, like it was never there. "I heard there are some soldiers from Oryn staying at the inn tonight on the east side of the city. You know they never turn down a good time." She playfully wiggled her eyebrows, making me laugh.

The Oryn Nation was known for forcing their recruits into rigorous training for decades. The results were prominent, hardened soldiers capable of defending their Nation. But they tended to unleash themselves once they were finally released into the world. Usually, by drinking as much ale as they could and fucking anyone willing.

"No, I'm good. I have a few errands to run, then I'm going to bed," I said.

Malina rolled her eyes. "Uh-huh. We all know it won't be your bed though." I shoved her lightly as we walked into my sitting area.

"I don't know what you mean," I said with a look of feigned innocence.

"You do realize that the walls are made of glass? We can see you when you sneak out." I ignored her retort and changed the subject back to her.

"It's nearly sundown. Shouldn't you be headed to your Oryn males that you're pining for?" I said teasingly.

She flashed me a mocking look of shock. "You're missing out if you've never fucked an Oryn. They've got endurance." She winked at me before heading for the door. "And who said they were all male?"

I rolled my eyes and failed to hide a smile. Malina had never shied away from someone because of their sex or identity. She opened the door to leave and called over her shoulder. "Training tomorrow. Sunrise." Not a request.

The door slammed shut behind her, and I dashed back to the vanity in the bathing room to finish getting ready, replacing my undergarments with something a little more desirable. While I was more relaxed after the bath, I still had some tension that I planned to relieve.

Chapter Four

KYA

As soon as the sun set, I left Morah under the cover of darkness and headed to the residential ring of Ilrek. My hood cloaked my face as I passed the few remaining fae still wandering the streets. The Roav—the *Hunters of Morah*—had a reputation for being formidable and ruthless. To stave off the wary looks, it was best that I kept hidden when possible. Not that I minded. I preferred the shadows.

The streets were illuminated in a soft glow from the lanterns sparsely lining the edges of the streets. Fire wielders kept them lit throughout the night.

I made my way to the door of one of the small cottages and walked up the steps. Excitement coursed through me, knowing what awaited on the other side. Releasing a shuddering breath, I pushed back my hood just enough for my face to be seen, then lightly tapped on the door in a specific pattern.

Tap, tap, tap. Tap tap.

It took only moments before the locks unlatched, and it was thrown open.

Cade stood before me. And Gods, was he a sight to behold.

Shirtless, the rippling muscles of his chest and abdomen contracted with each breath, and I couldn't tear my eyes away. His cropped dirty blond hair, showcasing his pointed ears, was the same as always—a cut favored by the fire wielders as longer hair tended to catch from the flames. And how I'd missed the heat in his amber-colored eyes as they slowly traveled up the length of my body until finally meeting mine. A warm feeling pooled in my lower stomach.

"About fucking time." His voice was low and guttural.

His nostrils flared slightly, scenting my arousal. A broad grin crossed his sultry lips as he stepped to the side and gestured for me to come in. He closed the door behind me before he grabbed my waist, pushed me against it, and took my mouth with his. A groan rumbled in his chest when I returned his kiss and placed my hands on his shoulders. He yanked the hood from my head and pushed his body against mine.

His eyebrows scrunched together when I suddenly pushed him off me. I gave a playful smile and winked before darting around him. Mismatched furniture cluttered the small living space as I hurriedly made my way to the bedroom down the narrow hallway at the back of the residence, Cade right on my heels with eager steps. The playful chase excited me further.

We made our way into his small, cozy room, and I headed straight toward the bed we had shared many times before. Barely having crossed the threshold into the room, he grabbed my wrist and twisted me to face him. His other hand came to the back of my head and grabbed a handful of hair at the base, tilting my face up. His warm, soft lips were on mine instantly, voracious and desperate. I quietly moaned as he dug his fingers into my waist, resting my arms around his shoulders as my hands fisted his hair and pulled my body in to meet his—the already hardened length of him pressing against my stomach.

The kiss was rough and hurried, desperate—like we had been starved. His tongue thrust and tangled with mine in a skillful way that electrified all the way down between my legs.

He removed my shirt, our lips parting only briefly, before pushing me backward until the backs of my knees hit the edge of the bed. My hands ran across his broad shoulders and down the sculpted muscles of his torso until they met the lining of his loose-fitting pants and untied them. I bit my lip, glancing up at him as his darkened eyes watched my hands and moisture pooled between my thighs.

The tips of my fingers moved to the band of his pants but stopped when he pushed me back onto the bed. He made quick work of my pants, my slippers already discarded on the floor beneath me. He groaned at the sight of me lying before him in nothing but my lacy undergarments.

"Did you wear this just for me?" Cade asked in a low, husky voice as his fingers traced the lace at my hips, his eyes growing hungry. Goosebumps pebbled across my sensitive skin, and I gasped at his touch, wanting more.

I nodded, and a whimper escaped my lips when his fingers trailed further down, my heart racing in anticipation. I knew what lace did for him, and I got the reaction I'd hoped for. His eyes fluttered closed momentarily before they shot up to meet mine.

Cade was instantly on top of me and his mouth on mine as he quickly removed his pants. One of his large hands grasped my breast, kneading the soft flesh with his fingers—the other wound around the lace on my hip. I silently thanked the Gods as he ripped the undergarments down to my ankles. I kicked them off somewhere across the room.

My hands were all over his body. I wanted to touch him all at once, but it still wasn't enough. I felt his back flex under my fingertips as he moved to position himself.

My thighs parted, and he settled himself between them just before he placed the tip of his finger at my entrance, circling there. My back arched at his touch. His mouth spread into a rueful smirk. He knew what he did to me, how his touch affected me. And he was damn good at it.

His finger slowly entered my already slick core, his thumb pressing down on the bud of nerves I was so desperate for him to touch. My body jerked and writhed as he circled slowly with his thumb, and his finger pulled in and out of me several times before adding another.

"Oh…Gods," I breathed. My pleasure was building and already threatening to crash over me. I began to shamelessly press into his hand, desperate for more.

He hummed a pleased chuckle at my desire for him.

"The *Gods* aren't the names I want coming from your lips tonight. Only mine." He whispered, his lips brushing my ear.

He pulled back, removing his fingers—but thankfully not his thumb—and I groaned in protest at the loss. His other hand aligned the tip of his cock with my core, lubricating himself with my arousal. His dark eyes gazed down at my face the entire time. He was taking his time. Teasing me. Knowing exactly what drives me wild.

As much as I appreciated his playfulness, I was getting impatient. Drunk with pleasure, I wrapped my legs around his waist and slammed him into me, overcome with the need to be filled. His pleasured grunt was met with a moan of my own.

Cade paused, allowing me to adjust to his size—not that I wasn't used to it, but it had been a while—before pushing himself in fully.

I released a breathy moan at the fullness of him, and his thumb resumed circling the bud at the apex of my thighs. My hands flew up to his back, and I dug my nails in as he began pushing in and out of me, his thumb circling faster in time with his thrusts.

Cade's free hand grabbed my hip as his movements became more brutal, and the tension was building inside me even faster.

My eyes rolled to the back of my head as I arched farther off the bed—my pleasure near the point of no return.

Stars filled my vision, and intoxication flooded my veins as my core pulsed, squeezing around him. Cade's climax followed immediately, and I could feel him spilling into me. We carefully rode each other through our euphoria.

I didn't have to worry about getting pregnant with him. Since he was an initiated citizen, he had sacrificed his ability to bear children. Not to mention, I still took yearly tonics to prevent it anyway.

Sated and covered in sweat, Cade removed his thumb, gently pulling out of me. He got off the bed, briefly leaving the room before returning with a damp cloth and cleaning himself. All I could do was lay there as my body recovered from the overwhelming sensation.

Cade pulled his pants back on and retrieved his discarded clothes before returning to sit on the bed.

"I missed you," he said with a smile that would make females grovel.

"Only for that, though, right?" I pressed.

He rolled his eyes and sighed. "Yeah. Only for that."

"Good," I stated firmly. I cleaned myself off as well, and got dressed.

Cade and I had come to the mutual understanding that our relationship was strictly physical. We'd tried to pursue an actual relationship once before, but it didn't work out. We weren't compatible and didn't want the same things. Not emotionally anyway.

Being in a romantic relationship wasn't easy when I sporadically had to leave for unknown periods of time on jobs. It didn't help that he had no idea what I did or where I went. What I was capable of.

He wanted to know everything when I couldn't tell him anything, which strained the emotional state of things. So, we decided to stick to just the physical aspect. Using each other as an outlet for sexual release. As awkward as it was at the time, we sat down and discussed rules and conditions. No staying over, no cuddling, and we would stop when one of us wanted to stop.

That was a little over two years ago, and it worked well for us both—for the most part, with the exception of his occasional request to further our relationship again, more so recently. He was a good male, but I had never felt anything for him. Not to mention, I had the constant reminder of my impending fate embedded in my skin. I glanced down at my mark—the only thing he really knew about me, seeing as it wasn't something I could hide from him.

"So…where did you go this time? Must have been far for how long you were gone." He said in an attempt to extract information from me as he had many times over the years.

"Cade," I said in warning. "I won't give you the details. You know that. It's better this way."

Cade likely suspected I was one of the Roav but knew better than to straight-up ask. Our tight-knit unit wasn't a secret, but what and how we found and reclaimed, how we hunted, was information that no one other than ourselves and the Scholars were privy to. Even our names had been concealed—only a few knew them. It was imperative that we kept the details of our operation confidential to maintain the reputation we had earned.

He scoffed as he rose to a stand and headed for the door. "Yeah, yeah. I know. It's just… How would I know if something happened to you?" He turned to look at me.

"You wouldn't." It was the truth.

He pursed his lips, then walked into the sitting room down the hall, and I followed. He leaned against the wall, and as I made to leave he held his arm out to block me.

"I don't like your *job*." His lips curled up over his teeth.

My eyebrows raised.

Again, with this? I was really hoping he'd be used to this by now but here lately he has been pushing more and more.

"That's unfortunate for you, but I do. You don't get a choice in the matter." I tried to push his arm out of the way, but he grabbed my shoulder. I slowly lifted my narrowed eyes to him.

"You need to stay here with me," he demanded. My blood began to boil. "I've got a good job, and you could stay here and be safe, or we could find you work that is more suitable to your...abilities."

I knew what he was insinuating. Since I couldn't manipulate much, my particular set of skills wasn't useful to anyone other than me. What I saw as a unique strength was seen by others as a weakness.

"You don't need to be going off to who-the-fuck-knows-where on your own when you can't defend yourself. Stop being so Gods-damned reckless when you don't need to be."

The audacity!

Typical arrogant male, wanting to assert dominance and save the weak little female.

I was anything but weak. He just didn't know that—yet. I yanked my shoulder from his grasp and took a step back. My voice turned cold.

"Who are you to try to make decisions for me? We're not together. I like my life just the way it is. And I want to keep it this way as long as I still have one."

"Exactly!" he yelled. "You don't have much time left, and you're risking what little you do. And for what?"

"Back off Cade. I'm not quitting my job, and I'm not going to be with you. Now drop it."

"Kya, I've waited two years. My patience is running thin," he spat. "What if we were mates? Would you still deny me then?"

I shook my head and stepped around him, but he grabbed my arm tightly and jerked me back. I ripped my arm from his grasp and spun around to face him, hooking my foot around the back of his ankle and pulling it forward while pushing against his chest with my hand. He fell flat on his back, and the impact knocked the wind out of him. My other hand, already holding the dagger hidden in my clothes, came down to hold the blade to his throat.

"No. But we're not mates. We had a deal. And this is exactly why we couldn't work. I don't want what you want for me. I only wanted you for the piece of meat between your legs." I leaned close to whisper into his ear, "And it would quite literally take the divines intervention to make me want you in any other way." I raised my head so he could see the seriousness in my eyes as I continued. "This was my mistake. I've let this go on too long. It's obvious that your expectations for this," I gestured between us, "were more than I agreed to. This was exactly what I wanted to avoid."

I stood and left him lying there, eyes wide with fury and breathing heavily. I wrenched the door open and looked back at him over my shoulder.

"You don't have to wait anymore," I said before slamming the door shut behind me.

Fuming, I decided to walk off my frustration before returning to Morah. I was angry that he had to go and ruin the good thing that we had going. It was supposed to be light and fun.

He had seen my mark and knew what it meant. He should have known that I didn't want a romantic relationship. Not when my future was so uncertain. Not with him. Not with anyone. Not when my hopeless romantic fantasies craved a mate with a non-existent happily-ever-after.

By the stroke of fate alone, there were the rare occasions—so rare that I'd never seen it—that two fae were bonded through their souls. According to what I had read, mostly from the romantic novels I devoured at night, it was an unbreakable bond of near-primal instinct. And some instances on record stated they could be horrendously unpleasant and violent, especially for the mated female. Regardless, it was still highly desired. Children grew up being told stories of mates and their unconditional and unbreakable connection to each other. It was made to seem like the ultimate goal in life: to find your mate. And for most, it was.

Just not for me...

I walked around for a time before I quietly made my way back to Morah in the shadows. Once back in my room, I settled on my bed, not bothering to put on a nightgown. I was too exhausted.

I lay in the darkness, with only the soft light from the moons illuminating my room, processing all that had occurred. But my mind couldn't stop the nagging thought of mates and bonds. It was childish to hope and dream that I could have such a thing, especially given what fate already had in store for me. But here, in the late hours of the night, alone in the darkness and with no one to judge my thoughts, I let my mind blissfully wander as I quickly fell into a fitful sleep.

Chapter Five

KYA

*T*he smell of fire was what first woke me from my sleep. The thickness of the air burnt my nose with each breath I took and I wrinkled it against the strange stench. Propping myself up, my blankets slipped down to my waist, pooling heavily in my lap.

"Mama?" I sucked in a breath and rubbed the sleep from my eyes, blinking through the blackness that still surrounded me. My eyes adjusted quickly to the faint beams of moonslight that lit my small room.

A muffled roaring registered in my ears. My brows furrowed. I didn't know what it was, but the sound made my heartbeat quicken and my chest tighten. Slipping out of bed, I shivered against the unnatural cold, watching as my breath puffed out in a white cloud in front of my face.

Something was wrong, it shouldn't have been that cold in the summer months. I nibbled my lip, a nervous energy filling my body and chasing away any lingering sleepiness.

The roaring sound got closer. Swallowing my fear, I carefully stepped over to the window, straining to make out where the noise was coming from. With the increased volume, I could make out individual voices, each making panicked screams which continued to rise in pitch as they grew closer. The cries pierced my mind, their strained wails turning my blood to ice and twisting something inside me.

A hoarse scream sounded just outside my window, making me jump back in fright, a whimper clawing it's way up my dry throat. I wanted mama, but fear had my feet rooted in place. Tears began to prickle at the corners of my eyes as I grew desperate for comfort.

The screaming continued to grow closer just as the wooden door to my room crashed open. I swung around, breath catching in terror, only to droop in relief when mama rushed in. I stepped toward her, gulping past the lump in my throat.

Ignoring my distress, she snatched my arm, making me cry out in shock. Her large hand wrapped easily around my wrist and she gripped it tightly, tugging me toward the door.

"Come Kya, quickly!" she choked out, her voice scratchy. She pulled me into a run behind her, looking back at me with panic-filled eyes that did nothing to dispel my rising fear.

I tripped over my bare feet as she dragged me through the house, her frantic pace making me whimper. I pulled back against her as she raced to our front door.

I didn't want to go out there. That's where the screams were. But I couldn't stop her from throwing open the door to our home and sweeping me out behind her.

Fear and horror flooded my body. The night was ablaze with the rush of chaotic activity. The screams rang louder in my ears as mama dragged me into the river of people. Everyone from the village was running toward something—no, not toward something, but away. It was like a stampede as we tried to flee. Large bodies pressed against me and in my terror, my arm was ripped from my mothers grip.

"Mama!" I cried, freezing in place as my eyes darted around to find her.

Someone shoved into my shoulder, knocking me to my hands and knees. I closed my eyes as so many feet began to stomp all over my body, pinning me to the wet ground. I tried to cover my head with *my arms but I couldn't move them in time before another foot forced it back down into the mud. My chest grew tight and I tried to draw enough breath to scream for help.*

"Ma—"

My cry was drowned out when a boot slammed my head face-first into the mud. I choked on the bitter sludge, a high-pitched ringing filled my ears.

I couldn't breathe.

I forced open my mouth to gasp in a breath but only mud seeped in. I couldn't lift my head or move my arms and legs to push myself up. My body began to shake, my mind shutting down from the shock and pain and cold.

Over the roar of the crowd, I heard a sharp crack in my body—then the excruciating pain started.

I couldn't think about anything but the agony. The searing sensation in my leg overwhelmed all else.

I choked and whimpered for what felt like eternity, until my battered body and confused mind registered that the bodies crushing me had gone. I pulled my head up to finally draw air into my aching lungs, the mud squelching as I pried my face from its grasp. I winced with each breath, a sharp pain piercing my ribs. I managed to look back to check if more feet were coming before I tried to get up to continue to run and find my mother.

A pained cry escaped my mud-covered lips as I attempted to stand. I glanced at my leg and saw something white and dripping with blood. My stomach churned violently and I felt a burning in the back of my throat at the sight. I looked away, breathing heavily to calm the rising hysteria building in my body.

A movement behind me had my eyes widening. My breath escaped me in an icy rush.

Darkness, only a stones-throw away, crawled its way forward, looking for its next victim. Me.

A blood-curdling scream ripped through the night air, "KYA—"

"Ghah!" I jerked up in bed. Sweat was dripping down my heaving chest and I looked around the room frantically, not immediately realizing where I was. I hadn't dreamt of that night in a long time. But the terror of the Glaev coming still lived with me. I was fortunate to be alive, unlike so many others…

A searing pain drew my gaze to my body. It felt like fire scorching my skin. I lifted the sweat-soaked sheet from my right arm and grunted through clenched teeth.

My breathing came to an abrupt stop and I was almost certain my heart did too. The normally black mark on my arm glowed with soft white light. It was faint and eerily beautiful—despite the burning sensation that accompanied it.

No. No, no, no. Not yet.

The mark was given as a *blessing* from the Gods—or so it was said. It was more reminiscent of a curse.

During the War of the Gods, they gave nearly every fae unnatural amounts of magic so that they could use them as soldiers for their cause. If the fae didn't die from the magic overwhelming their mortal bodies, they died fighting for the Gods. After the war, there was too much unbalance as the amount of magic had gotten out of control, threatening to tear the world apart. At least more than it already had been. The Gods were forced to stop gifting the fae with so much magic.

The six remaining Gods came together and decided to gift only a select few so that the balance could be kept while still giving thanks to our race for dying during the war. The Spirits conceded to this, but under a stipulation that only the Worthy could be granted such divine gifts. And so the Gods and Spirits resolved to holding a Trial to determine who would be deemed Worthy. The mark—an intricate design of swirls and divine symbols—indicated the chosen few who were forced to participate in the Trial.

Approximately every one hundred years, a new Trial began, providing the Gods an opportunity to each choose one victor that they deemed Worthy. Any God could choose any Marked from any Nation. But not all Gods chose. And not all contestants survived.

My time has come.

The glow was the sign that the Trial was approaching for its contestants—the burning, a warning of what would happen if we did not attend. It seemed to realize that I acknowledged it because the burning began to lessen until it stopped entirely. I took this opportunity to touch my Trial mark. It didn't feel any different. The slightly raised skin was the same as always, but the glowing remained.

I knew that the marks were given at random, even before birth, but I couldn't help but wonder: *why me?*

According to what I had read, it always started ten days after it…woke up? Called? I didn't know what to name it. But I did know that I wasn't going back to sleep, despite the late hour. My heart raced from the adrenaline coursing through my veins. Whether it was present due to the realization of the Trial approaching or from my nightmare—or both—I didn't know. And it didn't matter.

I didn't have time to dwell on the dream and why my past was coming back to haunt me tonight. I had more pressing worries.

My mind wandered the possibilities of the upcoming Trial for hours. I tried distracting myself with formulating a plan, something I thoroughly enjoyed doing. But how could I plan for something when I didn't even know what to expect? The tasks in the Trial were always different each time and given in the form of a riddle, some sort of sick entertainment for the Gods.

Knowing what my future held, I studied the recounts of the contestants that made it out alive. I memorized the complex riddles, all so vastly unique to each Trial. I understood that the Gods chose based on not only who completed the task but also those who had some unknown quality that they desired.

What qualities? Would I have them? Do I even want to be chosen? Would I make it out alive?

I shook my head, willing my mind to stop. I didn't have time to fret over the dreadful possibilities. Worrying wouldn't help me survive the Trial. My mark, and therefore my future, had never scared me until now. I supposed since I was born with it and I knew what to expect, I had just accepted it. My scars defined my past and my mark defined my future. Both were equally a part of what made me, me.

So why was I questioning it now?

I needed to do something, anything other than pacing my room and leaving my thoughts to spiral in anxiety.

"Get ahold of yourself, Kya," I whispered to myself.

And now that the Trial mark was glowing, it was more easily seen. I would have to be more careful of going outside the protected walls of Morah. Those that are Marked risk being killed by the Lords and Ladies, the Worthy, of the Nations—they're a direct threat to them. If there weren't any contestants for the Trial, then there wasn't anyone who could possibly be deemed Worthy and challenge them for their position.

That was just one threat. Not to mention the Trial itself.

"Breathe. Just breathe," I said to myself. "You've prepared for this. You've read every document, every recorded word, of the Trials and you've trained your body to handle this."

I walked over to the glass wall facing east, facing the Temple of Odes.

41

"Gods, please let it be enough. I just need to survive." Praying to the Gods, I could only hope that they would listen.

I paced back and forth in my room, recalling everything I had learned, every minute detail that I could remember so I knew what to expect. The only thing I could expect was the unexpected. No Trial was ever the same.

At dawn, I went to my bathing room to bathe and get ready for my training with Malina. I was glad that I was about to relieve some frustration and pent-up anxiety. And hopefully training would help wear me down so I could get some rest tonight. Or maybe that was a bad thing.

I stopped halfway down a step, my chest tightened as my breathing increased when I realized that I might only have ten days left to live. My vision blurred with unshed tears as I ground my teeth in anger.

I don't fear death.

Did I want to sleep off that precious time? Did I want to even go and die a gruesome death rather than defy the Gods and have them take my life right then and there?

No.

NO!

My fists clenched and my eyes hardened.

I could do this. I *would* do this. Even if I only had a few days left, I refused to spend it as a coward, giving in to my panicked thoughts. I pushed the fear to the recesses of my mind, then continued down the stairs with determination in its place, and anger.

I don't fear death. But I will not die.

I would survive the Trial of the Gods.

Chapter Six

KYA

I arrived at the training grounds just moments before Malina walked in. Dark circles were already outlining my eyes from my lack of sleep last night. The grounds were originally a part of the gardens on the south side of Morah, but were modified for the Roav to use for training. Stone walls, nearly two stories high, were erected into an oval-shaped arena, lined with exercise equipment, weapons, and smaller confined sparring areas.

Malina was chipper as usual, waking in a good mood—unlike myself most mornings. She skipped over and sat with her legs crossed on the thin mat beside me with a bright smile on her face. She reveled in how her perky mood annoyed me in the early hours of the day.

"Morning!" I winced at the high pitch of her voice. "You look like you didn't sleep at all. Cade keep you up all night?" She wiggled her eyebrows.

"No. Not that it's any of your business anyway."

She raised her eyebrows in challenge.

I rolled my eyes and moved the topic to her. "What about you? I would have thought you'd still be in bed with a hulky Oryn soldier." I batted my eyelashes mockingly, our usual banter lifting my Spirits.

"Oh I had my fair share, don't you worry," she said with a grin.

I shook my head and chuckled. "You ready?"

Malina stood and extended a hand to me. "Let's do it!"

I took her hand and stood, then walked over to one of the weapon racks and picked out four daggers. I turned and handed two of them to Malina. She held out a blindfold but I shook my head, refusing it.

"No wielding today?"

I avoided her eyes as I began to take off my jacket that concealed my mark.

"Not today." After tossing my jacket onto a bench, I turned back to her and squared my shoulders, bracing for her reaction.

"What the fuck happened to your arm?!" Her voice was nearly screeching.

Yeah, that's how I thought she would react.

"The Trial has been called. I am to report to the Temple of the Fallen God in ten days," I stated, my voice firm and devoid of emotion.

Malina's face fell and her spine straightened. My heart sank seeing her big brown eyes filled with dread.

"Kya… I…" Her voice was soft and quiet, "Are you okay?"

"I'm fine. It is what it is. I've known this was coming for a long time now. We all did." The side of my mouth tilted up.

"So… you're not scared of the Trial?" She said each word slowly, her eyebrows raised.

"Not anymore." The truth—mostly. Of course I was scared, but I wasn't about to admit that to Malina. It would only make her worry more and there was nothing that I could do about it anyway. I had to compete in the Trial. I didn't have a choice and I refused to cower in fear over a fate I couldn't control.

"Did you have another one of your internal temper tantrums with yourself?" she deadpanned, tossing the blindfold aside.

"I do not have *temper tantrums*. It's called thinking. You should try it sometime," I scoffed.

"Uh-huh. Whatever you say." Her mouth turned into an amused smile. She always had a way of lightening the mood.

We stepped into the sparring ring and took our stances, when she continued, "So why the daggers? Shouldn't we be working on your manipulation with the Trial coming up?" She lunged without warning.

I grunted and blocked. "No. Our magic is nullified during the Trial." I brought up my other dagger in a sideswipe.

Malina dodged the blade and spun around. "How many contestants are there?" She kicked a leg out, aiming for my ribs. I leaned back just enough for her to miss.

I knew what she was doing. She was having me work through it mentally while I was distracted physically. Not giving me the chance to mull over anything other than the facts.

"I don't know. The number of Marked varies from century to century—" I spun, my braid whipping around my neck, and lunged. "And not all survive from birth so there's no way to tell. Especially given that the Marked are generally hidden from society as much as possible."

We sparred for several more minutes until we came to a draw and went to the water station for a break. Malina was silent, her eyes distant in thought. I stayed quiet, giving her the time to take everything in.

Even knowing this was coming, it felt different now that it was actually here.

"How do you get to the Woltawa Forest?" she asked.

"That's the first task. The Sages will give us an elixir, blessed by the Spirits, and then we're…transferred. No one really knows how it works exactly."

"Then the second task."

"Yep," I said with a pop of my lips.

"Get back in the ring and work it out with me. Brains and brawn at the same time." She smiled, walking over to the mat and discarding her weapons.

Hand to hand it is.

"You've lived with me for twenty years. I've told you every-thing I know."

"It's not like *I* have the mark." She paused, "You've got it all wrapped up in your head. Now get over here and try to hit me. If you can."

My lips thinned and I nodded. I stepped into the ring.

"The Trial consists of three tests," I said as we circled each other. "The task of each test is unknown until the Sages call upon the Spirits in a ritual at the Temple. The first test—"

Malina suddenly dropped to a crouch and kicked her leg out, nearly knocking me on my ass. I stumbled back, recovering.

"The Test of Loyalty," she grunted, flipping back as I swung at her and narrowly avoiding my jab.

"The second is a Test of Strength." I blocked her punch to my throat with my forearm, and thrust my knee up to hit her in the ribs. "The third, a Test of Fate. That much has always remained the same, but the details of each test varies."

We continued to hit, jab, and kick, blocking each other's attempts at contact. We were equally matched, having trained with each other for years, but each of us would land a blow now and then.

"And in the second test, you'll be given your task in the form of a riddle. The same as everyone else, right?"

I inhaled sharply when she managed to square me in the jaw.

"Right. And it's different every century and varies with the required task." I stretched out my jaw, feeling it pop.

"This is the one where everyone dies?" Malina didn't give me the chance to recover, lunging at me once again with her other hand.

"Not all die. But yes, most of the deaths in the Trial occur during the second test." I caught her fist and pushed her forward to my side, throwing off her form.

"If a contestant completes the first two tests, one of two things can happen," I continued as our sparring resumed. "They will either be deemed Worthy by one of the Gods, gifted with great magic and allowed to proceed to the third test, or they will be sent back to the temple with nothing to show for their victory other than their life."

"And how many are chosen? Can the Gods choose more than one?"

"No. They can only choose one, but they also don't have to choose at all. At most, only six can be chosen during each Trial since there are only six Gods left."

Odes, the Fallen God, was destroyed during the war. When he fell, it caused the world to become unbalanced and the land tore itself apart. *The Rip*—a literal tear in the world—rested within the Dusan Nation and was known as Odes's Grave. A temple was built in honor of the Fallen God, and it was there that the initiation of the Trial was held.

"Tell me about the third test," she said, spinning and kicking near my face as I ducked.

"The third test is a mystery. All we know is that when the Worthy return from the third test, they are accompanied by a Spirit animal."

"And those that don't make it through the second test?"

"Those who fail are considered dishonorable and are sent back with the others. However, as a punishment, the Gods will strip them of their life's memories, leaving only their worst nightmares and greatest fears for the rest of their lives. I'd rather die in the Trial."

She paused and stared wide-eyed at me with a look of disbelief and ferocity. She unleashed herself upon me, attacking me relentlessly.

Apparently, I had pissed her off.

"Why would the Gods do that?"

"Because of the pact with the Spirits, they can't kill a fae. So they found a way around that." She landed a blow directly to my chest, nearly knocking the wind out of me.

Malina's eyes narrowed. "How is that a way around it? They're still killing them." She didn't let up.

"The dishonorable are driven mad with horror and eventually take their own lives. Either way, they die. So let's hope I don't fail." Tears threatened to fall down my face but I willed them away. I would not cry. And I would not fail. Malina's own eyes mirrored mine, and I could see the muscle in her jaw clench.

"So what are you going to do?"

"I don't know," I said, exasperated.

She tackled me then, slamming me to the ground and pinning my throat under her forearm.

"What are you going to do!" She screamed in my face with a fury few saw and lived to tell.

I reversed our positions and pulled a knife from my boot, putting the tip of the blade under her chin. She smiled, regardless of me 'cheating' during the spar. This was what she wanted. She wanted me to break the rules and do whatever was necessary.

"I am going to survive."

Chapter Seven

KYA

E amon was in his bedchamber on the upper residential levels of Morah. The High Scholar had an entire floor to himself, while the other Scholars who resided in the library had bedchambers similar to my own. From the dark disheveled hair on top of his pale head and the hands rubbing the sleep from his eyes, he must have been asleep when I knocked. But even in his sleepy state, he immediately noticed my mark, still glowing, though more faint than before. With a sad smile, he escorted me to his sitting room. He listened intently as I recalled the events of the night, taking in every word.

"Kya, I know I don't need to remind you that it's imperative for you to stay here until you have to leave for the Trial. Once the Nations' rulers find out the Trial has been initiated, they will be even more desperate to eliminate any threat to them. At least until you are all within the grounds of the Temple of Odes," Eamon said.

"I know. Mal will gather supplies for me. I'll remain on the upper floors until my departure." I pulled my sleeve down, covering my mark.

Eamon eyed the motion. "You don't need to hide your mark here. I'll inform the Scholars that no one is to enter for the next few days."

"No, it's fine. Some of the topographers are having an assembly to update the cartography from the erosion of the coastline. They've been looking forward to it for months. I don't want to take that from them." I smiled, thinking of the enthusiasm.

He chuckled. "They have been anticipating this for a while. They're quite excited. But I'm sure they would be more than willing to postpone for your sake. Let me know if you change your mind."

I gave a subtle nod. I knew they would, but it would break their little scholarly hearts to do so. I could easily remain hidden so it wasn't much of an inconvenience to me.

Eamon smiled but didn't reach his eyes. These were likely our last days together. One scenario resulted in me having the ability to return here after the Trial. But then, it was likely my identity would be known. I couldn't be a Roav anymore.

"I don't want to go." My voice was barely a whisper as I bowed my head, holding back tears trying to escape. I just wanted everything to remain as it was. I was happy there.

"What is it that you fear? You've trained your body and your mind far beyond anyone's expectations. You're stronger than you think. Trust yourself that you can do this." I looked up at him, this male that has already given me so much and continued to do so. "I trust that you can. And I trust that you will be chosen."

My eyebrows creased. "You want me to be chosen? To be Worthy? I would have to leave here. I would have to leave *you*." His smile spread, this time reaching his eyes.

"It is your fate, Kya, to obtain spiritual enhancement and powers beyond what you can comprehend right now."

"But what's the purpose? Those that are Worthy are meant to defend and protect their lands and use that power to help it thrive and prosper. Yet they are defenseless against the Glaev that would destroy it all. No one can stop it, Worthy or not." Tears began to streak down my cheeks as guilt and sorrow overwhelmed me. I quickly wiped them away, irritated that I couldn't hold them in.

Eamon cocked his head to the side. "Do you think that is the purpose of being Worthy? From all your years of research, I would have thought that you knew the true meaning by now."

I shrunk inwardly at that and scoffed. "What else could it possibly be? Everything I've read about, and every story I've heard explained it pretty well. The Worthy are measured against the current Lord or Lady of that Gods' Nation, whoever is more powerful takes over, and then they are burdened with the duty of protecting the lands of their Nation."

He grinned. "Come with me."

By the time we entered his study on the lower levels, the rising sun had illuminated the large space in morning light through the tinted glass. I closed the door behind me as Eamon walked over to one of the floor-to-ceiling bookcases along the inner walls and searched the titles of the tomes.

"Do you remember when you came here, to Ilrek? You were so young, I would be surprised if you did." My guardian said while he continued his search, not looking at me as he spoke.

I shook my head. "No, not really. Just bits and pieces." Images of standing in front of the doors of the Morah library flashed through my head.

He moved to the next bookcase. "One of your elders, Hindella I believe, traveled here with you, Malina, and Nikan, each of you too young to be initiated as citizens of any Nation, even yours." I nodded my head even though he couldn't see. "Your elder knew of the old laws and asked for refuge for you three, for you to stay here. No other Nation would take your people,

51

but she knew that Riyah could take only the young that had not been initiated. I took you three to live here in Ilrek and reside with me inside of Morah and train to be its Roav. But after what happened to Atara, the rest of your people would have been left to find refuge on the Drift Islands, as you know."

We were the only Roav at Morah. Protectors of knowledge, and hunters. There used to be more of us, but they had either left or been killed, and Morah went many years without any until Eamon took us in.

"I do know this," I said, not sure what his point was.

Eamon pulled a dusty leather book down from the bookcase and turned to me. "Then you also know that without lands, they cannot return to the continent. The Drift Islands suppress their magic and they suffer for it. Their Spirit suffers too."

I knew that magic had to be used or else it drained the Spirit of the wielder. I hated knowing that my people, my mother and father, suffered that fate, that there was nothing I could have done to save them. It was one of the reasons I tried to block it from my mind. The constant guilt would have consumed me.

Eamon placed the book on a table and began flipping through old brittle pages. He gestured for me to come over as he pointed to a passage. It was written in an ancient language and I couldn't understand what it said.

"This was written by Lord Alo, the first wielder of air." His finger traced the lines of text as he read. "'Those that are deemed Worthy to receive the gifts of the Gods are entrusted to preserve the spiritual balance of the land and its people…' It's *people*, Kya. The Spirits care nothing of the imaginary lines that our ancestors drew through the land to separate us. Being Worthy is about protecting the balance of both."

I lifted my eyes to him and found that he was already looking at me. An emotion splayed across his face that made my heart clench. Pride.

"*This* is your fate." He leaned forward and whispered, "You are the only survivor of Atara that bears the Trial mark. If you are chosen, you can bring your people back. You can give them a new home."

Determination and will seeped back into my veins at his words, his belief in me was something I didn't know I needed. But still, I doubted.

The tasks of the Trial were ruthless. There was a reason that so few had been honored with the title of Worthy. Most contestants didn't survive long enough to complete the second test, whether they were killed by something in the Woltawa Forest or by *someone*.

It wasn't uncommon for contestants to kill each other, even before the Trial started—another one of the many reasons I kept my mark concealed. Contestants would take down anyone they saw marked if it meant less competition later. The fewer there were left alive at the time of the Trial, the more of a chance they had at being chosen. It was vile, yet the Gods allowed it. Not only did I have to keep my eye on the task ahead, but I also had to watch my back.

Eamon and I continued conversing even through lunch, which was served in his study. After I inquired about Nikan, wanting to see him before I left for the Trial, Eamon informed me that Nikan wouldn't be back in time before I had to leave even if he found out now. Nikan was sent to take care of additional business with the Lord of Oryn.

I hated that I wouldn't see Nikan before I left for the Trial, knowing that I wasn't able to say goodbye. If our last encounter was the last time I ever saw him... I didn't want that to be our last memory together. He was my brother and I loved him. I didn't want to leave things the way we had. I could have hoped and prayed all day long that I would survive but there was no guarantee.

Afterwards, I headed back to my rooms and grabbed a stack of books on past Trials on my way. I'd already read everything I needed to know about the Trials—but I needed to do something. I needed some tangible task to make me believe I was helping my chances of not only surviving but also winning. So I reviewed the material until the sun set and the moonslight shone through the obsidian walls.

Another light came from behind me. I turned to find a small, delicate orb of light hovering in front of my door, and I couldn't help the smile that spread across my lips.

Always so subtle.

I reached out my hand and gently touched the orb with my finger. The light recognized my touch and slowly drifted through the wooden door. I followed the sphere out of my rooms and toward the staircase, until it led me to the top level of the third spire of Morah and across a walkway that overlooked the great library below. I stopped at the railing and looked down, taking in what was likely my last time seeing this wondrous place. The orb stopped a few steps ahead of me, waiting, until I followed it again out a set of hidden doors that lead to a ledge.

Malina sat on the edge, her feet dangling as she watched the stars appear in the darkening sky. I joined her without saying a word, and she looked at me as I gestured to the orb with a smile. She grinned as she made it disappear between us.

"Your light wielding is improving. It didn't flicker this time, even being so far away from you."

Malina was able to not only manipulate light, but to also create it—a rare form of wielding. Wielding light was rare in and of itself.

Every fae was born with some kind of elemental ability—usually ground, water, air, and fire. Light and shadow wielding were extremely rare, while mind and blood wielding were forbidden—a fae discovered with it met an unfortunate end. There didn't seem to be any way to determine what kind of ability they would have when born. Their abilities generally manifested around puberty.

"I've been working with one of the Scholars who studies it. He's been really helpful in guiding me on holding it at longer distances. It's different from manipulating, that has always come so easily to me. But producing it takes a lot of concentration and feels harder to control, unnatural even." Malina spoke with a soft smile on her lips as she lifted her hand in front of her, producing another soft light over her palm. I knew she was proud, she had been working hard on the creation aspect of her abilities and it was paying off. She let the light go out, then dropped her arm when she finally looked at me.

"Do you want to see what I've been working on?" she asked.

I nodded. Malina's face lit up with a bright smile that showed her teeth. She raised her head and threw her hand out in a sweeping motion that I followed with my eyes.

Hundreds of dots of lights twinkled around us, like the distant stars had fallen to surround us on that ledge. It felt like we were inside of the gleaming sky for a brief moment before they went out. It was beautiful, unlike anything she'd conjured before. I turned to her with a look of astonishment.

"It's something new. I can't hold them all for long but even I was impressed." She shrugged.

"I'm impressed too. That was beautiful." I sighed. "How long have you been out here?" I laid on my back and looked at the stars shimmering in the black, inky sky.

"Not long." Malina laid down next to me, her black hair haloed around her head. "I just miss coming out here like we used to."

A few years after being taken in by Eamon, Nikan used his terbis abilities—since I couldn't manipulate as well—to create the ledge on the side of Morah and Malina bent the light so that it wouldn't be visible from below. Out on the ledge, it was like we were floating above the world, leaving all our troubles and our past below us. Our secret place, just for the three of us. Not even Eamon knew.

"Yeah, I miss it too." And I wondered if—no, when—I would be able to be here again.

We sat there under the stars in silence for several minutes, taking in the breathtaking view of the night sky. I had always loved gazing at the stars, a passion of mine. As a child, I spent the better part of a year staring up at them and reading every book I could find about the different stars and galaxies and constellations. I was fascinated—near to the point of obsession. By the time I had turned twelve, I had them all committed to memory, and every time I came out here, I would point them out to Malina or Nikan.

"Where do you think they are?" Malina asked after a few moments.

I didn't need to ask who *they* were, I knew she meant our parents. "I don't know. I'm not even sure that they do."

Malina and I were lucky to live in a small village on the border of Atara and our families survived the Glaev, just barely escaping death that night—except Nikan's. His family lived farther inland, and he lost his parents and his little sister while he was traveling. He came back to a nightmare. With the Atara Nation destroyed, our people no longer had a home, nowhere to go except the Drift Islands. Both of our parents sacrificed being with us so that we wouldn't have to live a life on the islands with no abilities, suffering day after day. They wanted us to have a better life here in Ilrek. I understood that. Malina did too. But it didn't mean we were happy about it. We missed our parents.

For a long time, I hated the Lords and Ladies of the other Nations. I hated the laws of Riyah. No one would take in my people. Few Atarans had survived and I didn't understand how the Worthy could be so heartless. They knew what had happened, they had to. An entire Nation was completely decimated. I understood the laws, but I still hated them for it.

True to their name, the islands drifted in the sea, with no attachment to the seabed below. No one fully understood how it worked, but Sages said that the Spirits of the sea drew them near when they were needed most, only to be lost over the horizon once again.

I missed my home, I missed my parents. I would do just about anything to see them again. And if I were to be Worthy, I could bring them back. I pondered on telling Malina my plan but I ultimately decided against it, not wanting to give her uncertain hope.

"Well, that's enough of that." Malina sat up and grabbed my hand to pull me up to sit with her. "Let's get on to the real concern: we have to get you laid as much as possible between now and when you leave." Her face was completely serious and I gawked at her.

Laughter erupted out of me, then her, tears springing from our eyes.

"That's your biggest concern? Not to spend quality time with me and make long lasting memories before my departure?"

She placed her hand over her heart. "I would think that you would have been corrupted by me enough by now to realize where your priorities should lie."

After a moment she added, "I wonder what it's like to bone a Worthy."

My mouth fell open.

I can't believe she just said that.

Malina looked confused at my shocked expression. "What? I'm just saying—I mean, think about it." Her eyes lit with excitement. "They get all that non-elemental magic, it has to show for *something* other than power."

"Oh my Gods, they don't get magical dicks Mal. That's not how it works!" I huffed a laugh, still in disbelief.

She shrugged her shoulders. After a few moments we fell into a comfortable silence, soaking in each other's presence before finally going back to our rooms.

I struggled to clear my mind, thinking of the Trial. It consumed my thoughts. Staring at my ceiling while lying in bed, I realized what I could do to distract myself so I could sleep. A cunning smile crossed my lips.

One last time.

I stood on the obsidian floor of my room, closed my eyes in concentration, and lifted to my toes before slamming my heels back down. I felt the slight rumble of the floor as it shifted down the hall. I wasn't able to manipulate much, but I had spent years perfecting this one particular skill.

"Ah! Kya, enough of that shit! You sunk my bed completely into the floor this time." I heard Mal scream from her bedchamber.

I giggled and pictured her pissed off face level with the glass floor. I felt her steps coming from down the hall and rushed to lock my door just before she started banging on it. I quickly jumped back into bed and closed my eyes, a smile on my face as I heard her grumbling from the other side of the door. I swiftly fell into a dreamless sleep, with no thoughts of the Trial worrying my mind.

The next few days seemed to pass in a blur. I occupied myself by training with Malina—delayed in her mission, no doubt because of me—and going over and over the books about the

Trial. Malina had gathered the needed supplies for my journey from the tradespeople of Ilrek.

It was my last night before departure, and I hated goodbyes. I always left under the cover of darkness while everyone slept, and this time was no different.

After assembling my pack with weapons, clothing, books, and a few rations of food and water, I drafted three letters at my small wooden desk by the window. I dressed in my leathers, braided my hair behind my back, and grabbed my now-filled pack and the letters before leaving my bedchamber for what was likely the last time. I slid each letter under the doors of their receiver. Malina would be pissed I didn't say goodbye, but she was used to it by now, and I knew that Eamon understood.

I only hoped that my letter to Nikan would patch things up as best it could. But ink on a piece of parchment could only do so much. It was my only regret as I left Morah.

If I survive, I'll make things right.

Chapter Eight

RYKER

Blood drained from my face and dread settled as I saw my Worthy mark, faintly glowing an angry red—a warning of my eventual doom. The intense visceral reaction never eased with each initiation of a Trial. For the third time, my status as Lord, my life, was threatened.

I may have been a powerful Worthy, protector of my Nation, but all that power couldn't stop the undeniable fear coursing through my veins.

Keeping my features neutral, I quickly masked my scent before it reached the diplomats sitting around the table during the meeting. Unfolding my rolled-up sleeve and pushing it down to cover the flowing swirls and symbols of Xareus, I struggled to pay attention to the conversation—my thoughts flooding with memories of past challenges and worries of another to come.

Maybe Xareus would get rid of me and choose someone from Dusan, Gaol, or Torx. Perhaps he'd be a bastard and select someone from our rival Nation, Ulrik. Or maybe he'd replace me with someone from my own Nation. Now that would have been fucking cruel—to force me to fight for my life against someone I had sworn to protect.

But the Gods were ruthless. I wouldn't have put it past them.

A throat cleared, and I glanced up from my covered arm to find the room looking at me expectantly. Mavris narrowed his eyes questioningly. I subtly shook my head. It wasn't the time or place to discuss what was occurring.

"I apologize," I said to the room. "Something has come up. Continue to coordinate with Mavris. He will see that your concerns are dealt with. Excuse me."

I stood from my chair at the head of the long table and left the hall as wide, shocked eyes followed me. In the three hundred years since I was initiated as Lord, I had never left in the middle of an assembly. But I couldn't think. I wasn't able to give their words the consideration they deserved.

Ten days.

Time was conditional upon the one perceiving it. Ten days of suffering felt comparative to that of a lifetime. Yet, having the awareness that you may have only ten days left until you were challenged for a life you could very well lose seemed so limited. It was the only thought consuming my mind.

I went upstairs, down the dim corridor, through the doors, and onto the balcony. The chilled wind instantly cooled my heated skin. I inhaled deeply, filling my lungs with the crisp air and willing myself to calm. Though I had been through this before, and came out victorious each time, the foreboding left me anxious that this time would be different. I leaned on my forearms against the railing, looking down at the city below and the people I had defended for centuries. The streets I walked, the shops I visited, the memories I had created—all of it could be taken away.

Ten days.

What if that was all that was left?

"Ryk, what's gotten into you?" Mavris asked as he stepped onto the balcony behind me.

I didn't speak, too lost in my thoughts to explain to my brother that, once again, I would be leaving and may never come back. He wouldn't even know until the new Worthy appeared on the palace doorstep to take my place as ruler.

Resting against the railing next to me, his eyes grew concerned.

"What is it?" Mavris' voice was stern.

I rolled up my sleeve and presented my glowing arm.

He drew in a sharp breath. "Well, I mean, it's not like you weren't expecting it. We all knew it would be sometime before Nailu."

"I know." I nodded slowly.

He was quiet for several moments, following my gaze over the city. "It'll be fine. You'll be back."

I huffed a humorless laugh. "And if I'm not?" I turned to face him with raised eyebrows.

"You will. Or else, I'll piss right off the edge of the Rip all over your corpse," he said with a straight face.

The side of my mouth twitched up. "That's a pretty cruel way to treat your only brother."

"Then I suggest you ensure you get your ass back here." He clapped me on the shoulder. "We need you."

"Thanks, Mav."

I spent the next few days trying to get everything ready. I knew that Mavris hated it, but I refused to be less than fully prepared. While I hoped to return, I wanted to ensure my people were cared for if I didn't. I took my duty as protector seriously, and I continued to do so even considering my death.

Getting a new Worthy was a rough adjustment for a Nation. It could have been someone they knew, or some stranger from another Nation. Regardless, a time of acclimation was required for everyone, and I would make damn sure that they had the smoothest transition possible.

"Ryk?" Mavris rapped on my study door as he opened it.

I glanced up from the papers I was signing while sitting behind my desk. He approached and sat on the chair opposite with his arms resting on the sides.

"Is this about the assembly with Hamal?" I leaned back in my seat.

The Lord of Ulrik was the most considerable pain in my ass. With his ability to replicate himself, as well as heal others, he was a burdensome opponent to deal with on the field. I secretly hoped Ayen would choose for him to be challenged by someone who could defeat him, and I could finally try to end this rivalry with the neighboring Nation. Someone new and fresh. The fucker didn't even have to challenge in the last Trial.

Mavris nodded. "All the diplomats will return to their posts in a few days. The one from Ulrik says he's concerned with the rising tension there. We previously arranged for the Riyah Scholar and Sage representatives to come to discuss the new border issues. Ulrik remains wary about citizens trespassing and is looking to increase security. Riyah wants them to back off and allow for more open passage and trade."

I shook my head and forced myself not to roll my eyes at the absurdity of Hamal's paranoia. "I leave in two days. I'll already be at the Temple by the time the representatives arrive."

"I know. I'm just keeping you informed. I'll deal with it as best as I can until you return, and at least make sure their Watch doesn't start an all-out war. But is there anything you'd like me to say on your behalf?"

"I'd appreciate that. And, yes, tell Riyah we'll cooperate. I'm tired of Ulrik's petty demands preventing us from having a treaty." I was tired of a lot of things.

"But if Hamal is challenged, that could solve a lot of issues."

"And if he's not and I am, and defeated, that will leave the Nation vulnerable. It needs to be laid out before then. I'll write up an outline of my new offer. Hopefully, Hamal's advisor will consider it."

With that, Mavris bowed his head and left.

At dusk, the night before the Trial, I stood on the palace roof, looking down at the city again, next to Mavris, who was waiting for me when I arrived.

"You'll help the next Worthy should it be needed," I commanded.

"Ryk—"

"Don't start, Mav," I clipped. "If I'm challenged, I will fight with everything I have, but realistically, I may not survive. And if that's the case, you will do what is best for the Nation and assist the new Worthy." I placed my hand on his shoulder. "Let's just hope it doesn't come to that. I'd hate to get pissed on in the Rip."

The side of his lip twitched up briefly before his eyes flicked over my shoulder. I turned to follow his gaze to find Theron waiting.

It was time.

With a pat on Mavris's shoulder, I stepped back and walked to Theron. With what may have been my last glance at my brother, I nodded and placed my hand on Theron's side.

"Goodbye Ryk."

"Goodbye Mav."

Chapter Nine

KYA

The morning of the Trial, I maneuvered my weary horse through a forest at the southern end of Dusan and beyond the treeline at the base of a grassy hill. We kept off the common path to avoid passersby and any possible adversaries. I rode for three days straight, stopping only to eat and rest for a few hours at night. I probably pushed the old mare more laboriously than I should have, but I wanted to spend as much time as I possibly could at Morah before I had to leave. And we arrived right when I intended.

"Well done mare. We made it," I sighed.

We came upon monumental boulders that were scattered along the hill—a result of the formation of the Rip—indicating the grounds of the temple. At the top of the hill sat the square-shaped Temple of Odes. The back side of the temple rested directly at the edge of the Rip.

An enormous, jagged chasm cut through the land, so wide that you couldn't see the other side with your naked eye. This was where Odes fell. It was a sight unlike any other. Black mists swirled just beneath the cliff's edge and down into the bottomless abyss of the Rip. The sight was ethereal and unsettling. No matter how many times I laid my eyes on the chasm, I still found myself overwhelmed with astonishment at the world's scar.

My horse nickered as we made our way up the hill and navigated through the various tents on the grounds, some cloth and others made of rock protruding from the land. The Lord or Lady of each Nation were required to attend the Trial as well. They were forced to engage in a challenge with the emerging Worthy to keep their title or lose their life. It was a cruel but necessary system, and was sanctioned by the Sages. With the use of an elixir, the current Lords and Ladies would have their magic temporarily nullified since the new Worthy were untrained with their new magic.

At least they somewhat leveled out the field.

In order to keep the magical balance, there *could* only be six Worthy alive at one time—one for each of the remaining Gods and their Nations. The Worthy of Gaol was chosen by Noxelia. Dusan was loyal to Udon. Torx, Cethar. Oryn, Xareus. And Ulrik, Ayen.

However, there had only ever been five Worthy at one given time. One of the Goddesses, Kleio, had never chosen a contestant. Not once in the past few millennia of Trials, and no one knew why. She was known as the Silent God. Her land was Atara, and the only Nation with a Lady that was chosen not by the Gods, but by the people.

Maybe that's why it was destroyed, it angered the Gods that a non-Worthy was the Lady of a Nation.

I made my way to the towering square monument built of white stone. Its roof, five stories above the ground, was a dome made of one continuous piece of glass. It was breathtaking to stand at the base and look upon the sacred temple. I tied my chestnut horse to a post at a trough with other horses of all colors and sizes, then took off her saddle and pitched my tent closer to the trees, away from the Rip.

I patted her sweat-covered neck. "I *will* see you soon." I hoped that I wasn't lying to her.

The contestants had until the sun was at its peak to report to the temple, so I stayed in the shade of my tent, preparing the necessary mentality—going to the dark recesses within my mind, that of a Roav. The cloth doors were tied open to let the breeze cool the sweat dripping down my body as I sat with my legs folded beneath me and performed a series of breathing exercises. The breeze brought with it a faint, appealing scent of cedar and bergamot, and something else I couldn't place. I closed my eyes and inhaled deeper, the scent seemed to reach my core as I instantly felt heat of another kind.

This is not the time to get turned on.

I must have been losing my mind. The stress from the impending Trial was getting to me, I was sure of it. I shook my head, trying to clear my mind of inappropriate thoughts, and concentrated once again.

I looked at my Trial mark, the glow from the swirls and symbols had grown more faint during my travels the closer I got to the temple, and was nearly gone now.

I stayed in my tent for the rest of the morning, until the sun rose to midday, when some of the contestants started heading into the temple. I quickly strapped my thighs with a pair of daggers, my bow and quiver across my back, and another set of daggers concealed at the small of my back, the holster already underneath my leathers. Lengths of rope and a canteen with water were attached to my belt. The only thing the contestants were allowed to bring to the Trial was what we could carry on our bodies, nothing more. I shrugged to myself.

No matter. I don't need anything more.

I exited the tent and made my way to the temple. Squaring my shoulders, I held my chin high, portraying confidence to those around me. Yet, I felt a hole form in the pit of my stomach and my palms began to sweat as I ascended the marble stairs and crossed the threshold into the Odes's Temple.

The glow of my mark finally winked out. The Trial had begun.

Chapter Ten

KYA

The Worthy of each Nation lined the inside perimeter of the temple along the marble walls. Each was identically cloaked in dark ceremonial robes so no one could tell them apart. If I were chosen, I would be challenging one of them. And thank the Gods that they couldn't use abilities or magic during the engagement. While some wouldn't have been so difficult to battle against, most had terrifying power that seemed impossible to win against.

Jymar, the Lord of Gaol, had the ability to negate our natural elemental abilities if close enough. Zana, Lady of Dusan, was an empath who could use others' emotions against them, and it was rumored that she could breathe under water. Dainos, Lord of Torx, could manipulate sound—matching the frequency of an object in order to obliterate it. Hamal, Lord of Ulrik, could replicate himself, so instead of fighting one of him, you fought several. And then there was Ryker, Lord of Oryn, who had shadows that could kill a person without him so much as moving.

As I stood amongst the contestants, I wondered which would be challenging the Worthy. Which would walk away with their unmarked lives. Which wouldn't return.

At one end of the temple, the Sages were gathered upon the dais, spanning the length of one whole side, looming over the contestants.

Nineteen contestants were gathered in the large expanse. Significantly less than the last century. Though there was no way of knowing just how many were born with the mark between each Trial or even if it were a consistent amount. So either there were considerably less fae born with the mark, or a vast amount of them had been killed since the last Trial. Anyone who was past the Staying age of twenty and who bore the mark was forced to enter the next Trial. The ages of the contestants could vary anywhere from one hundred and twenty to twenty years old.

Since they had all passed their Staying age, it was impossible to tell their true age. The older contestants would be a more formidable threat, as some could have had a century or more to train. I would have liked to have that bit of information as I glanced around at the other Marked around me—which ones were the biggest threat.

I was jolted from my thoughts as the large marble doors behind me slammed shut, and I heard the latching of a bolt lock. My heart pounded in my chest so violently I was certain others could hear it. Sweat licked my brow and my palms felt clammy. I had a feeling that the other contestants were thinking the same thing I was, as their faces paled.

This is it. No turning back now. Survive or die.

I squeezed my eyes shut and inhaled deeply through my nose. The scent of dread was thick in the large expanse of the temple, wafting off of all of us.

I can do this. I can do this. I CAN do this. I have no choice…

Initiation into the Trial had begun. No one was allowed in and no one was allowed out. Immediately after they closed, muffled banging came from the doors then abruptly stopped moments later.

Likely a late contestant.

We were to be inside of the temple at the exact time that the sun was highest in the sky. Any marked contestant who didn't make it was dead in seconds, their own markings consuming them.

The Sages were huddled in a circle, and began their ritual—a low recitative chant. The unison of their voices filled the temple. It felt ghoulish and transcendent all at once.

No one dared to breathe a word or even make the slightest sound as the Sages called upon the Spirits. They spoke in the ancient words of the Gods. The foreboding created a wave of unease that swept across the room as the temple darkened and became so cold that I could see my breath clouding in front of me. The tension in the air was like a thread pulled, so tight I thought it would snap at any moment.

Keeping my head facing forward, I trained my eyes on the other contestants, trying to get a read on them. While faint, I could feel each of them through the marble floor. The vibrations of rapid heartbeats, the shaking, the tremors.

And something else.

Moving only my eyes, I looked around the room and tried to examine each face that I could see. Someone was *excited*. I could feel the electricity thrumming from them, though it was muffled, and I couldn't place who it was coming from. Then it just…stopped.

I shook my head slightly, brushing off that eerie feeling, and resumed studying the males and females around me. While differing physical features played no role in discerning their nationality, their cultural appearance did. I tried to get a read on a few of the others, sizing up who could possibly be a threat.

Out of the nineteen contestants, including myself, there were twelve males and seven females. Some had the half-shaved heads representative of Ulrik, while others had the intricate designs inked onto their skin like those of Oryn, the clean and pristine look of Dusan, the long dreadlocks and muscular bodies of Torx, or the pierced faces of Gaol. I couldn't help but notice that no one had donned the painted face and feathers braided into the hair like those of Atara—myself included, not having gone through the citizen initiation after my Staying age, I hadn't earned that honor.

Then, my spine straightened and the hairs on the back of my neck stood.

Someone is watching me.

Which wouldn't be surprising, as I was doing the same, but it felt...different. It didn't feel like eyes were skimming over me, but solely trained on me. I glanced around, careful not to turn my head too much to make it noticeable, but no one was being obvious in their stare.

I scanned the contestants and the Sages. Then the hooded Lords and Ladies, moving only my eyes while my body was as still as the stone beneath me. Their faces were concealed in shadow, heads all bowed slightly. Almost directly to my left, I thought I saw a flash of silver from underneath one of the hoods. It was gone in an instant.

As the Sages finished their recitation, the magic in the air became thick. In the blink of an eye, the braziers lining the walls filled with a dark red flame. All of our heads bent in submission to the Spirits' emergence. A loud groan sounded as the walls behind the dais began to part, the grating of stone against stone. A harsh, whispering wind entered the temple through the opening wall, carrying a foul scent and made the loose strands of my hair sway around my face. Then just as quickly as it started, the grinding came to a halt, leaving one side of the temple open.

After a few moments of silence, the Sages turned to face us, their expressions blank. A Sage with gold rope around his waist stepped forward.

"The Spirits have spoken." His thunderous voice cut through the silence as he motioned to the tables lined with small glass vials at the bottom of the dias. "While in the past, contestants were to drink the elixir to gain access to the Woltawa Forest, they have chosen another passage. This shall be your first task. A Test of Loyalty to the Gods. If your heart is truly loyal, you'll pass, if not, you'll fall to your death in the depths of Odes's grave." His voice, cold and hard, rang through the temple.

He paused momentarily. The contestants around me shared a look of concern, uncertainty and distress written on their faces.

"Submit yourself to the Rip." His deep voice boomed across the temple with a firmness that left no room for question.

My breathing hitched, and my heart stopped for a beat. The scent of fear seeped into the room from the contestants. No one knew what was at the bottom of the Rip. Any fae who ventured inside never returned.

What did they expect us to do? Willingly fall into the chasm? Of course they did. It was blind faith. A willingness to die at the command of the Gods.

All at once, we stepped forward, making our way up the dais. The sounds of heavy boots scuffing against stone echoed off the walls of the temple. Standing where the walls parted, we all stopped at the edge of the Rip, so wide that I couldn't see the other side, and glanced down into the abyss. Wind ripped through the air and I widened my stance for balance.

A darkness so absolute that it felt as if light could not escape filled the void to unknown depths. Dark mists swirled around just below the edge of the cliff. The air around it was stark, cold, stale, and devoid of all life. Only those who had little care for their own life would dare to venture this close to the Rip. One slip and you were never seen again.

In the past, either out of curiosity or stupidity, several had tried entering with ropes to rappel into it or climb down using long thin axes that hooked into crevices of the rock. Anyone who entered the mists never returned—either having silently fallen to their death or something else. Some, driven by their curiosity but not courageous enough to venture inside the chasm, braved its ragged edges and threw their magic inside to try to clear the mists. But it was soon discovered that the mists seem to devour magic. Like a starved beast, it craved more and pulled the magic from its wielder. One such case that I came upon, while studying about the Rip during my free time in the Morah library, the wielder wasn't strong enough to stop the mists from pulling his magic until it ultimately pulled him in with it.

One of the contestants, a female with more than a dozen piercings on her face, stepped closer to the Rip.

"It's just a fucking hole. What's so intimidating about that?" She threw out her hand—

"I wouldn't do that if I were you." A smooth deep voice came from inside the temple, one of the Lords.

A cold chill snaked down my spine at the voice. I didn't turn to see which Lord it was, my eyes were locked on the female. I wanted to see what she was planning to do. Our wielding didn't work in Odes's grave. Surely she knew that. Everyone did.

The female gave a mocking smirk just as fire streamed out of her palm and into the chasm. She began to scream as her body started to twitch, the black mists crawled up the fire she was conjuring. She couldn't let go; she couldn't even *move*. The mist reached up and surrounded her before it yanked her body into the chasm, her screams echoing off the cliffs.

No one said a word, not even the Lord who spoke before. It happened so fast, it would have been unbelievable if I hadn't seen it with my own eyes as I stared in abject horror.

I guess she wasn't strong enough either.

No one was certain what happened to the wielded elements that went in there. Our ability to manipulate the elements, funneled by the Spirits, was energy manifested in different forms. The wielder did just that, they wielded the energy in the way that their abilities allowed them to influence it. But none of that mattered at that moment. From what I knew, magic wouldn't have helped me to survive the fall into the chasm. And it certainly wouldn't have helped me in Woltawa Forest.

"So what, we just…jump in?" A male with curly red hair down to his chin on one side and half a shaved head called over the gusts of wind. I followed his line of sight to the Sages who ignored him and walked back into the temple.

As if in answer, all our marks glowed again, burning the skin to a sharp stinging sensation. A push from the Spirits. Looking down at the chasm, my breathing came faster, and my heart raced.

The dark-haired male with dreadlocks down the line, a few paces to my right, spoke up, "Let's see if the Fallen God can kill from the grave." He stepped off the ledge falling into the black mists.

Another male, shirtless and covered in tattoos, stepped forward, his toes stopped just over the edge briefly, and didn't say a word as he followed.

Closing my eyes, I took a deep breath through my nose to center myself while sending a silent prayer to the Gods. Clearing my mind of any thoughts, any fears.

I will not die.

I opened my eyes, and without thinking I stepped out into nothing, falling into the abyss of the Rip.

The rocky cliffs quickly disappeared from sight as I fell farther and farther into the deep mists, everything around me growing darker. At first, the air was rushing past so quickly that it stung my eyes. My stomach lurched into my throat at the sensation, not knowing when it would end. Then, there was nothing but blackness all around me for a long while. Either my body had turned numb or I had gotten used to the stinging air.

I wasn't sure if minutes or hours passed as I continued to fall. At least, I thought I was still falling. I couldn't see or hear anything. I wondered if the Gods would let me fall to my death after I'd trusted them with my life.

Am I still alive?

I blinked several times to make sure my eyes were actually open. Then I bit my cheek and the metallic taste of blood pooled in my mouth. I was still alive. But I couldn't feel the air on my face, and my hair was still, almost like I was floating. My head spun, disoriented. It was as if I were suspended in time.

Blinding light suddenly filled the space below me, and I slammed my eyes shut. Wincing at the brightness, I put my arm over my eyes to shield them from the agonizing luminosity. Then, I slowly blinked my eyes open and removed my arm after a few moments of adjustment. Underneath my floating body was a large island, covered in trees of every shade of green and of all sizes—some so large they had to be taller than Morah.

The Woltawa Forest.

My breath caught and I couldn't tear my eyes away from the sight. I had never seen land from above like this before, like I was in the clouds. It was magnificent. Birds that I had never seen were gliding around the island. In the treetops, creatures lurked that were unknown to my world. On the west side of the island, a single extraordinary mountain protruded from the land, its peak not coming to a point but a crater.

I got lost in the view when a celestial blend of voices spoke. The voices were all around me. A shiver crept across my body at the otherworldly sound, goosebumps prickling along my skin.

The Gods.

"You have trusted us with your life to see you through the Rip. We have seen your soul and your intentions. Your loyalty is true. We shall allow you passage into the Woltawa Forest until the third dawn."

I passed the first test.

I quietly breathed a sigh of relief as the voices continued.

"Your task is this: Where the land reaches the sky, you shall find what light brings to life, yet dies in darkness. Only its death will bring forth the path, guided by what has a river that does not flow." The voice was gone.

What?

My mind couldn't focus, so I repeated the riddle to myself over and over and over. The Woltawa Forest began to disappear as the darkness enveloped me once again.

Chapter Eleven

Kya

My head felt dazed after I landed on the hard ground flat on my back. I hadn't fallen far apparently, or at least the Gods' magic had protected me. I wasn't injured, just a pounding headache and a few bruises. I peeled my eyes open, squinting past the sunlight shining through the canopy of trees and sat up, bracing myself on my hands. Several hours must have passed because the sun was lower in the sky than when I went into the Rip.

I was in the Woltawa Forest.

Colossal trees surrounded me, reddish-brown trunks as wide as ten males towered above me. My mouth fell open in awe. Small animals that I had never seen skittered across—

I gasped as reality came crashing back into me, interrupting my thoughts.

Where the land reaches the sky—

I scrambled up and patted my leathers for anything I could use to write.

You shall find what light brings to life—

I cursed myself for not thinking to bring any parchment or ink to jot down the riddle. I was so concerned with my weapons that it hadn't even crossed my mind. In all my careful planning and preparation, I foolishly didn't think to bring something to fucking write with. Stupid, stupid, stupid.

Yet dies in darkness—

I grinned as an idea came to mind. I grabbed the dagger from my thigh and sliced down the pad of my finger. I dropped my dagger onto the moss-covered forest floor and pushed up my sleeve. With my finger now covered in my blood, I wrote the riddle on my forearm.

Once I finished, I grabbed a blade of grass and wrapped it around my still bleeding finger. It probably wasn't the smartest idea to cut myself in a place with unknown creatures lurking about with the chance that they could smell blood, but I would worry about that later. I glanced at my forearm, now covered in scribbles of blood, still dripping.

The writing extended from the inside of my elbow down to my wrist. It wasn't ideal, but it would do. I kept my sleeve up so that it wouldn't smear the blood. I shifted to my knees and returned the dagger to my thigh, placing my hand on the ground to feel for vibrations.

Nothing.

Even knowing that my abilities didn't work here, I had still doubted that I wouldn't be able to feel through the land. It was like I had lost one of my senses—I felt blind in a way. Stifled. As if a part of me was gone.

I glanced around at the trees, knowing that I needed to get to higher ground in order to get a bearing on my location, looking for low-hanging limbs to climb. No one knew where the Woltawa Forest was. Some thought that it was on one of the drift islands, but no one other than the contestants had ever seen it. It was massive, nearly half the size of some of the Nations on the continent.

I spotted a climbable-looking tree in the distance, up a small hill. Pulling out my bow and drawing an arrow from the quiver, I trekked my way through the underbrush of the forest.

The snapping of a limb had me whipping my head around, bow drawn taut with an arrow pointed in the direction of the sound. My eyes narrowed, looking for the source. After a few moments of not detecting any movement, I let out the breath and turned back to head towards the tree at the top of the hill, keeping my steps light and silent through the forest and my bow loosely drawn.

I heard another snap, and before I could turn around or raise my bow, something large and hard slammed into me from behind. Thrown flat on my stomach, I threw my elbow back into whatever had tackled me, a low growl rumbled behind me. I arched my back and flipped forward, causing the attacker to stumble off me. I quickly stood and drew my bow, now aimed at the *male* standing a few steps away with his hand holding his bleeding nose.

I remembered him from the temple. He was one of the Gaol contestants with his nose, eyebrows, lips, cheeks and ears pierced with metal bars and rings. Dark brown eyes cut into me like my own daggers.

The sound of shuffling footsteps informed me that at least two others were quickly approaching. I didn't turn to look at them. The male in front of me lowered his hand to display a wicked smile covered in blood.

"Mmm. I hate to see a pretty thing like you to go to waste." He licked his bloody lip. "The things we could do to you if we only had the time."

Then he lunged for me. I released my arrow but narrowly missed his shoulder just before he tackled me again. His large body crushing my legs, I couldn't reach the daggers at my thighs. The two others rushed forward.

Feeling weak and disoriented, I tried to grab one of the daggers at my back, but two sets of hands grabbed my wrists and slammed them onto the ground. My bow became dislodged from my grip. The male on top of me shifted his body so that his knees pinned my thighs to either side. I thrashed, attempting to kick or hit, to free myself from their hold.

"Grab the blades," one of the males holding my wrists said.

The other one tried to hold me down with one arm while reaching for my leg but I thrashed harder, forcing him to hold me with both hands to keep me immobile.

The male on top of me leaned down, his stubbled face hovered over mine and that wicked smile still on his arrogant pierced lips, as I scowled at him. His light brown hair hung down past his chin, tickling my cheeks. I continued to thrash as they tightened their grip on my wrists and moved my arms above my head. The male on top of me reached to my thigh, pulled out my dagger, and held it to my throat.

"Nothing personal. Just increasing our chances of being chosen," he sneered.

He was wrong. The Gods didn't choose based on who was left. Even if only one contestant completed the Trial, the Gods could still find them unworthy and choose no one at all.

I felt the blade press against my neck and my body tensed as I squeezed my eyes shut. I silently prayed to the Gods as tears welled beneath my lids.

This can't be happening. I can't die this soon. I'm not done yet. I'm not done yet!

I gasped as I felt warm blood spray over my face. I cracked my eyes open to see a sword protruding from the chest of the male straddling me, the tip grazing my breast with each panicked breath. A scream caught in my throat, and for a moment I was frozen in place.

The two other males let go of my wrists and drew their swords. I heard the clashing of metal a moment later. I shook away the shock and shoved the male off me, and he slumped to the ground, the blade still embedded in his chest.

Another male was fighting against the two that had held me. I ripped my dagger from the injured male next to me and the other from my thigh, and immediately jumped to my feet when one of the males came at me with a crazed look in his eye. He wasn't very large, but he was fast. I ducked at the last second, avoiding the slash for my throat, and pushed my body toward him. He grabbed my arm with one hand as I aimed my dagger for his chest. I released the blade and grabbed the arm that was holding me, locking them together, and pulled him toward me so that our chests were touching.

At this proximity, he had to take the time to stretch his other arm out so his sword could extend far enough to reach me. While it was only a fraction of a second, that was just enough of a delay for me to reach around and stab him in the back, right where his kidneys were.

Always go for the vitals.

He howled, and his sword arm jerked back. I let go of the dagger, but he still had a firm grip on my other arm. I twisted my body around behind him, contorting his arm into an unfavorable position as I yanked and dislocated his shoulder to break his hold. He didn't have time to scream before I extracted my blade from his back and slit his throat.

The male dropped his sword and grabbed his neck as the blood gushed from the wound. I planted my booted foot between his shoulder blades and he fell forward. Our bodies didn't heal as quickly here. I turned around and left him to bleed out on the forest floor.

The fourth male, who had stabbed the one on top of me, had effectively taken out the third male and was standing right in front of me. I recognized him as having jumped into the Rip right before me. He was shirtless, a head taller than me, and his impressively muscled body was covered in tattoos from the base of his neck all the way down his torso—most likely an Orynian. He had dark brown hair that came to the bottom of his ears, his honey-colored skin that contrasted his light blue eyes.

He opened his mouth to speak but I kicked him at his torso, which felt solid beneath my boot, and caused him to stumble back with a grunt. Regardless of having helped me, he was still a threat. I lunged for him with my dagger out to my side. His eyes widened, his sword fell, and he raised his palms up in submission. I stopped, looking at him through narrowed eyes.

"Easy now. I don't intend to harm you," he said slowly, as if I would spook.

I wasn't buying it.

He went to take a step, but I crouched down and spun, kicking his unbalanced legs out from underneath him. He hit the ground hard, knocking the wind out of him. I was on top of him before he could cough out a wheeze, the tip of my blade underneath his chin as I straddled his muscular torso. My heart raced as I reveled in the adrenaline.

My lips thinned into a straight line when he raised his arms up next to his head. A bad move on his part. I took advantage of his vulnerable position, exposing the softer side of his torso, and pressed the tip of another blade I had taken from my back between his ribs.

I should kill him. He'll probably come for me later anyway.

No. He saved me. A life for a life. I have a debt to pay.

I growled at my inner turmoil. The Gaolin male with the sword in his back gurgled a cough behind me.

I would feel no conflict about killing him.

My body rose and fell with the Orynian's heavy breaths. I leaned down so that my face was a mere breath away from his.

"I will spare you now for saving my life, but if you so much as cross my path again I will not hesitate to slit your throat," I warned through gritted teeth.

Keeping my blades in their positions, I maneuvered myself off him and backed away. Even with his large frame, he seemed non-threatening. His eyes were soft, and his body was surprisingly relaxed despite the situation.

I lowered my blades, still eyeing him with suspicion, before deeming him not enough of a concern at that moment. I turned and approached the other male on the ground, still bleeding, to finish him so he wouldn't come back for me later. Fae were difficult to kill, but we were mortal after all. If one were to lose their head, heart, or enough blood, they wouldn't be able to heal. Especially during the Trial.

I bent down to inspect the barely conscious male, leaning back on my heels, careful to avoid stepping in his blood. I watched him struggle against his labored breathing.

"Our bodies don't heal as quickly here." I turned my head to look at the shirtless male now sitting with his forearms resting on his bent knees as he continued. "It has to do with the nullification."

"I know. I'm pretty sure the Gods want us to be easily killed."

I set down one of my daggers and pulled up the hem of my shirt, exposing my torso. My skin was already turning a bluish tint from where the male's thighs had crushed my sides. Out of the corner of my eye, I saw the Oryn male's cheeks turn a shade of red behind me as he looked away. One side of my mouth turned up in an amused grin. I wouldn't have expected someone who looked like him to blush at the sight of a little skin, especially seeing how much he exposed himself.

The male next to me groaned, and I let my shirt fall as I grabbed for my dagger, the other one already trained at the vein pulsing in his neck.

"If only I had the time," I mocked his previous words. I leaned down so my head was next to his, my lips brushing his ear as I spoke. "Nothing personal. Just increasing my chances of *survival*."

With his own words thrown back at him, his eyes widened just before my blade sliced across his throat, blood gushing out of the wound. I replaced my three daggers before I stood and turned, removing the sword from his chest and walking back to the other male. I held the sword out to him as he stood, and he hesitantly took it. I held his stare for a moment and he nodded once in understanding—a truce.

He reached for my arm as I began to walk toward my discarded bow. "So look, um…" He dropped his arm and rubbed the back of his neck, avoiding eye contact.

"Kya."

"Kya. I'm Njall." He glanced at me and grinned. "So look, *Kya*, I was thinking that we could help each other out."

Does he think I'm an idiot?

"And what makes you think I need your help, *Njall*," I said with a raised brow. If he noticed my mocking tone, he didn't show it.

"I'm going to be honest, I just want to get out of this place alive. And with my mind intact. Obviously, you can handle yourself, but it's also evident that my presence could be beneficial to you." His hands gestured to the other males as he spoke, and I bristled in irritation at his truth. Without my abilities, I couldn't easily evade attacks here.

I leaned away slightly and my eyes locked with his, distrusting of his motives.

"And how exactly do you expect *my* presence to be beneficial to *you*?" I wasn't ignorant to the ways of males.

Njall leaned forward and lowered his voice. "I'm betting that you're decent at deciphering riddles, Roav." He smirked.

"What led you to think that?" I wasn't going to confirm the title, but I sure-as-shit wanted to know where he got that information.

"Well, you're from Morah, aren't you?" He shifted on his feet.

"You know who I am?" I asked more defensively than I intended.

"No one knows who *any* of you are, or even *how* many," he huffed. I gave him a suspicious look as he continued, "Your blades. They're from Ilrek." He gestured to my daggers with a gentle smile.

I raised an eyebrow, still not understanding.

"Those blades were forged by a blacksmith I know. I recognized his signature on the hilt when you held it to my throat." His hand touched the nick on his neck. "No one in Ilrek, besides a Roav, would be *that* skilled with a dagger."

I couldn't help the small swell of pride in my chest at the compliment. I nodded my head in admission.

"How do you know the blacksmith?" I asked.

"I'm a blacksmith too. I apprenticed under him, for a time, several decades ago." Njall's smile nearly beamed.

"I take it you're a fire wielder, then?" It was common for blacksmiths to be fire wielders, having to work with the element in order to forge the metal. It was how I met Cade a few years back.

Njall nodded.

That explained the lack of clothing. Fire wielders ran hot, but without his fire I wondered if he'd regret his lack of clothing once night fell.

He cleared his throat. "Anyway, I figured we could work together, help each other out." He must have sensed my lingering apprehension. "I won't hurt you."

"You said you only wanted to get out here alive. You don't want to be Worthy?" I cocked my head to the side. I didn't believe that he wasn't interested in being powerful with the way he honed his body.

"No. I'd rather not." He shook his head.

"Why not? Don't you want to be spiritually enhanced and be granted powerful magic?" My curiosity got the better of me.

"I really don't. I have no desire to become a Lord, let alone fight one. I just want to survive so I can go home and live out my life in peace."

I didn't expect that. I hadn't even considered that another contestant wouldn't want to be Worthy, to be granted such great power. But I understood it. Fighting a standing Worthy, one of the five most powerful fae in the world, was no easy task.

I had almost forgotten about the challenges. The Worthy had to continually prove themselves every century, even after their own Trials ended, until they died or were defeated. People were fools to think that being chosen was the end to this.

I eyed Njall carefully.

He wasn't wrong that we could help each other, and without my terbis, I could use the help. I promised Malina I'd do whatever was necessary to survive.

I released a sigh. "Alright. We can work together. But remember my warning, if you ever attempt to betray me in any way."

I would keep an eye on him. If he did anything questionable, I'd just kill him. String him up with my rope and leave him for the creatures of the forest.

I replaced my bow across my back, then walked over to the dead male and started rummaging through his pockets for anything useful. I took the matches, dried meat, and a canteen of water.

"We need to get higher to get an idea of where we are." I turned back to Njall and motioned to the top of the hill.

Njall smiled, his arms crossed across his chest. "I'm on it. See? I can be helpful."

I rolled my eyes. It wasn't like I couldn't have climbed the damned tree myself.

He walked to the nearest tree, hoisted himself up the trunk, and climbed to the lowest branch. My mouth fell open at the ease with which he moved up through the branches—and the impressive view I had from below. I kept watch on the ground while he made his assent. His large body was hidden by the leaves as he continued to the top. I leaned against the base, propping one foot on the trunk with my knee bent, and waited for him to climb back down.

After several minutes, I heard him descending the massive tree, branches groaning under his weight. He jumped down from the lowest branch and I could feel his body land—even without my abilities. I pushed off the trunk and approached him as he bent down and pulled out a knife. He brushed away fallen leaves and began carving in the dirt with the blade.

"It looks like we're near the south side of the Woltawa Forest, here." He circled an area where he drew a bunch of symbols for trees. "It ends just at the base of the mountain, on the northern end of the island. I couldn't see a water source from the tree but from the aerial view I saw before I landed here, I noticed one cutting through here." He pointed to a squiggly line in the dirt map. "I'd guess it would take us a few hours to walk there. As long as we don't run into trouble along the way."

"Let's hope we don't," I said, extending a hand to Njall which he took with a smile as he stood. Not that I could actually help him up with how big he was. "I suggest we get moving. I don't want to be wandering around at night with the nocturnal beasts out."

"Agreed," he replied hastily and pointed in the direction of the river.

Watching him from the corner of my eye, we walked side-by-side in silence for several minutes, taking in our surroundings and looking for threats, winding through the forest. I was grateful for the pleasant temperature. I listened to the wind as it rustled the leaves above us and the birds' songs as they echoed through the trees. I loved being amongst the trees, the smell of the bark and the moss-covered ground calmed me, even in my unnerving situation.

"That was smart of you to write down the riddle. But whose blood is that?" His voice lowered to a hush as he gestured to my blood-covered arm. His face had contorted into a grimace.

"Don't worry, it's mine. I didn't want to forget it. One missed word could change the entire meaning."

"Good thinking," he smiled again. I found it odd that he smiled so much given our current circumstance. But I returned a tight smile of my own.

"I think I figured out the first part. It seemed somewhat obvious to me at least," he continued.

"'Where the land reaches the sky', do you think it's referring to the mountain?" I had thought of this while I was…suspended? Over the Woltawa Forest. It made sense, it was the highest point on the island.

"Exactly," his deep voice confirmed. "We can rest at the river tonight and head toward the mountain at daybreak. That will at least give us time to figure out the rest along the way and hopefully have it solved by the time we get there."

"*If* we get there. I'm not so naive to think that we won't have other encounters such as before, with fae or beast."

Not all contestants died from rivals during the Trial. The creatures that lived here were known to hunt the invaders that appeared in their territories, and other terrors inhabited the island.

"Don't think like that! You have to think positive," Njall said cheerfully and I looked at him in astonishment.

"You're awfully confident for a contestant," I chuckled, his unusual optimism was infectious and I couldn't help but smile widely. It reminded me of Malina a bit.

"And you know the other contestants well enough to make an accurate comparison?" he asked teasingly.

"No, I suppose not." I shrugged.

It was a rare occurrence that contestants met with one another before the Trial. Even if they did, most kept their Trial mark hidden, the only indication that they were a contestant. Being Marked wasn't something that most boasted about.

We came across a fallen tree, the trunk taller than my head, and we had to climb over it. Njall climbed to the top first, his muscles bulging with the effort, and I stared longer than I probably should have before he helped hoist me up. He jumped down to the other side and I followed. My joints ached with the impact. Healing slower took some getting used to.

"Any ideas on the second part?" he asked.

I debated for a moment if I should really be working with him. He could double-cross me and I was never quite a team-player. But this was a life-or-death situation. At least for the time being, it would benefit me just as much as it would him. It was worth the risk.

I looked at my arm and studied the riddle, analyzing each word.

I have no idea.

"No. I can't think of 'what light brings to life yet dies in darkness' could be. Maybe plants? They need sunlight to live."

I silently cursed the Gods. Why did it have to be a riddle? I hated riddles. Yes, I studied the ones from the past Trials, but that didn't mean that I liked them.

"Could be. However, that could prove to be difficult if it is." He swept his arm out in front of him as we started walking again. "Seeing as there's no shortage of plants in the *forest*."

"I wouldn't exactly expect any of this to be easy. The Trial is meant to be difficult, testing us in more ways than one." I huffed.

"Then I certainly hope you researched botany in that great library of yours." He smiled sweetly down at me, and I returned the sentiment.

As the sun lowered in the sky, its warm light cast long shadows from the trees over the forest floor as we walked in and out of the rays. Njall's breathing was loud in the quiet of the forest, and it was getting on my nerves. I wasn't accustomed to traveling with someone, but at least the view was nice out of the corner of my eye.

We didn't speak for most of the trek to the river, which didn't take as long as expected. I heard the rushing water before I saw it, and the sound grew louder as we neared. The trees cleared and, as I looked down the river, I could see that the sun was beginning to set, a soft hue of orange and violet staining the sky. We came upon a part of the river that was rapidly moving, the sound almost deafening as we stood on the bank.

"We should rest here for the night. It might get cold, but I can make a fire," Njall stated as he looked around the area.

My brow lifted. "You know that you can't wield fire here, right?"

He chuckled, "Yes, Roav, I know. But I also know that you took matches from that male earlier."

"Oh. Right." I reached into my pocket and handed him the small box of matches.

"Good. I'll collect some kindling, if you want to scout out the best place to bed down for the night." His voice raised over the sound of the river as he backed away into the trees, still holding one of his swords while the other remained sheathed.

I gave him a quick nod and turned to survey the area. Having the river at our backs was an advantage in the event of something—or someone—approaching us in the night. But that still didn't ease my worries.

I looked up, and grinned. I had found the best place to rest.

When Njall returned, arms piled with sticks, he dropped them on the ground and furrowed his brow when he noticed me laying out lengths of rope I had brought with me.

"What's the rope for?"

"It'll help hold us so we don't fall in our sleep," I said without looking up at him.

"And why do we need to be concerned with falling in our sleep?"

I looked at him and gave an innocent smile. "Because the best place to sleep is up there."

I pointed to the limbs above me. I wasn't particularly pleased with the idea and I generally avoided being in places, like trees, where I wasn't able to feel with my terbis. But seeing as I couldn't use it anyway, it seemed like the most logical place to be while we were vulnerable during sleep.

Njall pursed his lips and blinked slowly, looking to the branches above.

"Don't tell me you're afraid of heights? You had no problem of climbing that tree earlier," I said playfully.

"Just because I can climb a tree doesn't mean I want to sleep in one. And I'm *not* afraid of heights, I'm afraid of falling from them," he stated defensively.

"Hence the rope." I gestured to the lengths on the ground.

He didn't argue any further. He simply nodded and walked over to the base of the tree. He intertwined his fingers together and held his hands low, palms splayed out, and grumbled something about the pointless task of gathering kindling. I slung the rope over my shoulder as I stepped into his hands and he pushed me up the tree.

It took some effort, but I was able grip the grooves of the bark and climb up the trunk until I reached the thick limbs. I settled onto a branch as wide as my body and tossed a length of rope down to Njall, who was resting on a thicker branch below me. We tied ourselves to the branches, and I tried not to think of how high up I was. I laid my head back and took in the night sky through the canopy. Stars began to twinkle as the sun's final rays faded into darkness. The sound of the river drowned out the noises of the forest, and the gentle breeze cooled the sweat on my brow from the climb.

I prayed that nothing would come for us in the night as I closed my eyes, exhaustion finding me quickly as I began to drift to sleep under the star-filled sky with my hands resting on my daggers.

Chapter Twelve

KYA

I woke to a hand clasping over my mouth. My first instinct was to struggle and fight, but when my eyes snapped open, Njall was hovering over me with wide eyes and heavy breathing. He put a finger up to his lips and nodded down below. He released my face and I took a silent breath before turning to look at the ground beneath us, trying not to think about the fact that he was so close—and still shirtless.

A monstrous creature, bigger than any animal I had ever seen, stalked through the darkness toward the tree we were perched in. I had to squint to just barely make out its silhouette against the blackness around it. The river drowned out the sound of the beast's steps as it grew closer and closer. My chest rose with rapid breaths and I couldn't tear my gaze away from it.

I had read about the creatures of the Woltawa Forest, and even saw a few drawings, but it was nothing compared to reality. The beast walked on all fours and was covered in thick mangy fur. Black eyes glowed with the reflection from the water. It had small stunted ears on top of its large head, and a gaping hole where a nose would be at the end of its fanged snout—a living nightmare that I knew would haunt my dreams. Its claws, each as long as my hand, dug into the ground as it moved past our tree and to the river.

I craned my neck to watch it drink from the bank of the river. Njall leaned in closer to get a better look, and I could have sworn he didn't even blink, never taking his eyes off the threat for a second. I twisted to get into a better position and my boot scraped against the bark.

The beast's ear twitched and it slowly lifted its head, sniffing the air before whipping around toward our tree. Njall ducked and pushed my head down with his hand, keeping us out of sight from the creature.

It can hear well. Better than us. Good to know.

I hadn't noticed until now that Njall was breathing just as hard as I was, fear in his eyes as we listened for the slightest sounds. We couldn't hear anything over the roaring water, and I prayed that its hearing wasn't sensitive enough to hear our heavy breaths.

We waited and waited, too terrified to move to see if the beast was still there. Panic settled in my chest and I began to shake. Njall held me tighter. I was so used to being able to detect movements, and not knowing where it was filled me with an unfamiliar feeling of anxiety. But without my abilities in this place, I was grateful to be away from that thing. If it had snuck up on us while we slept on the ground… I wasn't sure we would have been able to run away or fight it off.

Njall took a deep breath and slowly raised his head to the side to look around the branch. He released his breath and his shoulders relaxed. Curious, I twisted my neck and my own tension eased as I watched the beast walking back the way it came.

After the creature was out of sight, Njall sat back on his heels and helped me untie myself from the wide limb. At least he was decent enough to warn me. That could have gone a lot worse if he had chosen to look out for only himself.

"What the fuck was that thing?" His voice was barely a whisper as he took the rope and placed it over his shoulder.

"A beira. Very territorial and temperamental. Its claws are sharp enough to shred through bones. We're lucky it didn't choose to investigate because it can climb trees just as fast as it can run." I mentally recalled the details of my readings. We had indeed been lucky. While they didn't have good eyesight, they had an incredible sense of smell.

"How do you know that?" he asked.

"I live in a giant library with the greatest collection of knowledge in the realm. How do you think I know that?" I retorted.

"Right. Well, regardless of their climbing ability, I feel much better about being up here now. I vote we sleep in trees *every* night. I do not want to wake up to that thing in my face." He shuddered.

"How did you know it was there? I didn't hear anything." I swung my legs over so he could sit beside me, his back against the trunk and one leg bent up.

"I had to take a piss. Just happened to see it in the distance as I was laying back down, then climbed up here to wake you." He wasn't boasting. He spoke as if it was the normal thing to do—to look out for me.

I dipped my head in thanks and gave a tight smile. Not sure how to feel about having someone around, even someone as helpful as Njall, but grateful for it nonetheless. We sat in silence with our legs hanging over the edge of the branch until the sun began to rise before we made our way down the tree and continued toward the mountain.

The first dawn.
After finding a spot up the river that wasn't moving as rapidly, we swam across. The bottom was deep, too deep to see or touch. Njall had to help me through the water, keeping my

blood-covered arm above the surface so the riddle didn't wash away.

"We should refill the canteens before continuing. I'll go see if I can find anything edible in those bushes if you want to take care of the water." Njall said, handing me his canteen from a pocket on the side of his pants.

"Alright. But watch out for tanganats. They look like little orange balls hanging from bush leaves mimicking berries," I warned while removing the canteen from my dripping belt.

Njall blanched. "Do they bite?"

"Not your skin. But they're venomous parasites that will chew through your intestines if you consume them."

"Right," he squeaked out before slowly walking away.

I chuckled as I made my way back down to the bank of the river. I would check whatever he brought back before we ate anything.

Opening the canteens, I bent down to submerge them in the cold water one at a time. I did my best to hurry. With the rapids, I couldn't hear if Njall shouted for me.

I didn't see the dark shadow moving through the water. I didn't hear the thrashing of the tail on the surface as it came in my direction. It wasn't until a long snout full of serrated teeth burst out of the water that I realized the river contained monsters.

Within a fraction of a second, the creature broke through the surface of the water and wrapped its teeth around my leg. I barely had time to comprehend what was happening, let alone scream before it dragged me from the bank, slamming my head against the ground, and pulled me under the water.

I had the good sense to expel my lungs before being submerged but aside from that, I couldn't think outside of the pain searing my leg while the creature carried me further down. Twisting and kicking did nothing but tear my wounds more.

The creature's bite was firm—there was no chance of pulling myself free. My lungs were aching. With my instincts finally functioning, I pulled a dagger from my back. I bent forward against the swift current and stabbed the black, gaping holes in the creature's face where its eyes should be.

My blood clouded the water when the creature released its hold on me and pushed myself to the surface as fast as I could with my arms and uninjured leg, leaving a trail of red in the wake behind me. The moment I felt myself breach the surface, I gulped down air into my burning lungs. I scrambled to the bank, grappling with the dirt to pull myself out of the water.

The creature burst from the river again, snapping its jaws. I rolled out of the way just in time and screamed. Ignoring the pain in my leg, I quickly got to my feet and backed away, arming my other hand with a dagger from my thigh. I couldn't run. At least not fast enough to get away, and I was not turning my back on the beast before me. Hopefully, it couldn't walk on land. Otherwise, I would have to fight it. Or perhaps it couldn't breathe air and would have to return to the river soon. Maybe I just needed to get far enough away before it gave up.

As if hearing my thoughts and taking it as a challenge, the creature slowly emerged from the water. Its head was half the size of me, and its skin was covered in a slimy-looking substance. Its body was long with a pointed tail flicking at the end of it and was carried by two legs with claws at the end of webbed feet.

I had never seen nor read about any type of water creature in the Trials. I had no idea what I was up against. I did know that it could be wounded, as blood seeped from its eye sockets.

It stalked toward me as I slowly backed away before it came at me again with a strike so fast I barely escaped its jaws once again. Its head landed next to me and I drove both daggers into its skull. It was then that I learned that the translucent, slimy substance was acidic, and burnt my skin as my wrists touched the top of its head.

The creature hissed and thrashed its head from side to side. I was flung down the bank from the force and landed painfully on the side with my injured leg. I grunted from the impact but never took my eyes off the beast. I watched with wide eyes, as it continued to hiss and screech and claw at itself, trying to dislodge the blades anchored in its skull, tail lashing from side to side in an attempt to remove them.

I heard the clamor of metal dropping to the ground a mere second before hands hooked underneath my arms and pulled me away. I grabbed his discarded sword and whipped my head up to look at Njall. The color had drained from his face as he watched the dying creature in horror.

I gritted through my teeth as he sat me up against the trunk of a tree, far enough away from the water and the beast.

He took his sword from me, while his eyes remained trained on the creature until it finally stopped thrashing a few moments later. He sheathed his sword and dropped to my side. His eyes roamed over my body, taking in my injuries as I tore off a strip of my shirt. They were hard and cold, so unlike what I had seen so far even when he was taking on those Gaolin males. I started to shiver, and I wasn't sure if it was from the chill of the water, my nerves, or the pain.

"Shit..." Njall whispered.

He took the makeshift bandage from me and rolled up my pant leg to expose my shredded calf. I couldn't tell where the wounds were underneath all the blood coating my skin. I removed my soaked jacket and winced as the leather ripped at the skin it was seared onto from the acidic slime.

Without asking, I dried my arm on Njall's pants. They were still damp but at least more dry than mine. Then I reached down and gathered blood from my leg onto my fingertip. His brows scrunched, but he didn't question me as I re-wrote the washed-away riddle on my forearm. He corrected me on one word, but didn't say anything else as I finished and slumped back against the tree.

Njall took my jacket and gently wiped away as much blood as he could before he wrapped my leg with the scraps of my shirt.

"We shouldn't have separated," he said in a low voice. His face was tense.

"Don't worry about it," I grunted. "I've never read of anything like that before. You?"

"No." He shook his head and lifted my hands, careful not to touch the burns on my wrists or the drying blood on my arm. "Does this hurt?"

"Stings. It's fine. My leg is the biggest concern. We need to get moving." I made to stand with his help.

"Can you walk?"

"I think so. It may be slow going though. Look… I appreciate you helping me and all but I'm a liability now and I'll only slow you down. Go on without me." It would have been the smart thing to do. My wounds would likely attract more predators, and I couldn't outrun anything with this injury.

"Not gonna happen, Roav. We had an agreement." The side of his mouth lifted into a smirk.

I let out a breath of relief. There was no way I could have made it on my own. And if I was able to solve the riddle, then maybe this symbiotic relationship really would have been worth it for both of us.

I put my jacket back on while he went to snatch up the canteens that were laid by the river, and we started walking north again. Njall supported me for the first few steps until I got to a steady limp. I left my daggers in the river creature's head. I wasn't risking getting burned again to retrieve them.

"Where's the food?" I asked after a few moments.

"Well, while you were fighting for your life against some water-lizard-thing, I was busy being scared of parasitic insects, so I didn't get any," Njall said sheepishly. "But thankfully the dried meat wasn't ruined!"

He passed me some as we walked. He walked, I limped. I knew that he was slowing his pace so that I could keep up.

"Alright, let's work out this riddle," he practically chirped with a mouth full of meat. "I estimate it will take about two days to walk to the base of the mountain. And then we'll have an entire night to do whatever else we need to do."

I glanced down at my arm and read it several times, '*you shall find what light brings to life yet dies in darkness*'. I mumbled it under my breath over and over and over, until I had it committed to memory. At least it gave me something to think about other than my injuries.

"You still think it's about the plants?" He gestured to my arm.

I shook my head. "No. Maybe? It could be." I struggled with deciphering it. "I mean, if it is plants or *a* plant, then you're right, that doesn't narrow it down. And here." I pointed to the next part on my arm, Njall bending over me to get a better look, a scent of iron and leather filled my nose. "'*Only its death will bring forth the path*'. What if that means it can only be seen at night, since it dies in darkness?"

Njall ran a hand through his damp brown hair and seemed to contemplate my theory. "But how do we know which one or ones? We're in a forest for Nox's sake," he said, beseeching the Goddess of Gaol.

I stopped and looked around. The moss and trees and bushes looked average, nothing seemed particularly different. If I could just get a better look—

My gaze snapped up. Between the trees, I could just barely make out the concave tip of the mountain.

"What if we just can't tell from down here? Maybe we'll be able to see it from up there." I pointed toward the mountain peak. It made perfect sense. The riddle was leading us to the mountain so that we could see the path. "We have to climb to the top of the mountain."

Njall let out a sharp breath. "At night."

"What?" My confusion was written all over my face.

"'*Dies in darkness*'. We have to climb the mountain at night. And since it'll take us two full days to get there, that only leaves us a few hours to find what we're looking for before the third dawn."

Njall was right. If we had the riddle correct, we would only be able to see the answer from the mountain in the darkness. With the slopes completely barren of any trees, we would be completely exposed, unable to hide from the beasts that dwelled in the forest. Something neither of us looked forward to.

We trekked through the forest for an entire day, and thankfully, we hadn't run into any additional unsavory creatures.

Njall talked. A lot. I listened. He revealed that he was indeed from Oryn, and he told me all about his life as a blacksmith. He rambled on and on about the metals he forged, his favorite weapons he had been commissioned to make, and how much he loathed forging horseshoes—which he apparently did often. And, how excited he was to finally work without long sleeves that had to cover his mark. To my surprise, I found myself actually enjoying the sound of his voice, appreciative for the distraction of his stories as we walked for hours.

At some point, I tuned out his words, my mind trying to figure out the rest of the riddle. My eyes glazed over in thought, and my legs moved automatically. I couldn't make sense of the words, and it bothered me to the point of frustration.

'*What has a river that does not flow*'

I really didn't want to think about any fucking rivers. But I repeated it in my head over and over and—

"Kya?" Njall brought me back from my thoughts, looking at me expectantly.

I shook my head. "Sorry. What?"

"I said, 'What is it like being a Roav?'"

"Oh. Well, I like it. But I suppose I don't really have anything to compare it to. It's all I've ever done." I shrugged.

"How many Roav are there?" His eyes sparkled with curiosity as he moved a low hanging branch out of the way for me.

"How many do you think?"

Njall shook his head and sighed. "Gods, I don't know. From the stories I've heard, there have to be dozens, if not more. The Hunters of Morah are legendary."

"There are less than you think, I'll tell you that. But our vast resources make up for what we lack in numbers. Not to mention, we train rigorously."

Being a Roav was our entire life, and everything we did revolved around making us better equipped to do our job. Morah used to have other Roav before us but they had died long ago and the Scholars had used mercenaries until Nikan, Malina, and I came along—now, we did it all.

His jaw dropped. "There is no way there are less than twenty. You guys infiltrated and took out that clan of pillagers who ransacked all those towns in Torx." He gaped at me.

"I can tell you that it is definitely less than twenty." I thought about the bet that Mal and I lost against Nik. We bet he couldn't handle them all on his own, and suggested that Malina go with him. He came back after only a month, and we each owed him a new weapon of his choice. The specifics of how he did it remained a mystery, as he refused to talk about it.

"Damn. That's impressive." He seemed to speak more to himself than to me.

The sun was lowering in the sky as we scouted out a tree to rest in for the night. While Njall worked on building a fire, I prepared to go out to hunt for food, but he stopped me as I turned to walk away.

"Maybe I should come?" he suggested.

"No river in sight. I think I'll be okay. And I won't go far."

He nodded but was clearly unhappy about the decision. "If you get lost, just use the shadows of the trees to get a bearing on your direction. Just don't stay gone past sunset or you'll lose them." He stood, wringing his hands.

Was he worried *about me?*

"I'll be fine. I'm a Roav. Remember?" I could swear I saw a hint of pink on his cheeks as I slipped into the thicket of the forest—staying mindful of the shadows.

Njall was sitting next to a small fire, when I emerged holding a small animal by the tail—similar to that of a rabbit and was big enough for the two of us. We cooked the meat over the fire and ate as much as we could before burying the rest away from our tree, so we didn't attract hungry predators in the night.

I walked over to the base of the tree and looked up to the branches—which were higher up than the last one. I rubbed my aching fingers together and worried about my leg.

So much for the Test of Strength. I was probably one of the weakest ones here.

"Let me help." Njall came to stand beside me.

He smiled and tucked a loose strand of my hair from my braid behind my ear. I didn't know what to think of the gesture, and I gave an awkward smile in return before he pushed me farther up the tree and I climbed to a branch wide enough to lay on. My calf throbbed from the exertion, and I was thankful to be able to finally rest it. Njall followed after me and took a branch next to mine, as we tied the ropes around our waists, securing ourselves to the tree.

We decided to take shifts sleeping while the other kept a lookout for beasts—Njall taking the first shift. I stared up at the night sky, watching the stars and constellations twinkle in the inky blackness. My mind began to wander back to the riddle, bothering me that we hadn't figured it out, and I knew it was bothering Njall too.

"So what *does* have a river that does not flow?" I asked, still looking to the sky.

"I've been thinking about that all day," he sighed. I turned to him, his light blue eyes finding mine. "I think maybe it's not so obvious as a river of water, but perhaps a river of something else?"

"Could be. But we need to figure out what it is before we reach the mountain."

He hummed in agreement.

"Let's lay it out," I said. Njall turned to face me as I continued. "At the mountain, we can find what dies in the darkness."

"Which is why we have to go at night. So that in the dark, we can find the path." He nodded.

"Not exactly. This thing that has a river that does not flow will *reveal* the path. That's what we have to find. I just don't know what that is. And I'm worried we won't find it, since we don't even know what we're looking for." I hated having a half-assed plan but I supposed it wasn't any different from my job as a Roav, not knowing where I was going until I had worked through my resources. My lips pursed, and my eyebrows creased in thought.

"Let's hope that it'll be obvious once we're there and this...thing that has a non-flowing river will just...appear," Njall stammered, his hands moving as he talked. He did that a lot.

"I feel like the answer is right in front of us. Maybe I'm overthinking and it's simpler than it seems." I shook my head.

"Which part?"

"All of it."

"Look, this Trial is supposed to test us in more ways than one. It's meant to push us to the edge and set us apart from all the others. Trust yourself. Don't doubt now," he uttered softly.

"It's testing my patience for sure," I huffed, my irritation earning me a quiet chuckle from him.

"Let's just get to the mountain and see what the night reveals. Then we—"

A horrifying wail echoed through the forest. I whipped my head in the direction of the sound and my breathing stopped as my eyes widened.

That was a contestant.

I quickly untied myself and sat up, panic and fear taking over. For the first time, I didn't want to be alone. I made to move to Njall's branch, but he was already next to me, his sword drawn. I pulled out my bow and nocked an arrow. I looked to Njall, his tattooed chest rising up and down with his quickened breaths, and his eyes met mine. Adrenaline coursed through me as the spine-chilling wails continued for what felt like hours.

Njall settled with his back against the tree, legs hanging off due to the lack of room. His eyes were hard and searching the surrounding forest. He touched my back then quietly patted his chest, pointed to me then pointed his finger in a sweeping motion to the right. I nodded in understanding. Keeping my gaze to the right side of the tree while he kept his to the left. I rested my back against his chest, surprised that I felt comfortable in this proximity. This forest had my skin crawling. Both of our weapons were drawn as we waited, hoping we would make it through the night.

Chapter Thirteen

KYA

"Wake up, Roav."

Hot breath ruffled my hair as a calloused hand brushed down my arm. I stirred against something soft, nestling farther into the warmth against my face. A throat cleared and my eyes flew open.

The second dawn.

Daylight was just starting to appear through the trees. I moved to sit up more and hissed at the soreness of my muscles. My ass was killing me but at least my leg felt better. I was leaning against Njall's chest, his sword resting beside him. We had stayed up for most of the night, listening to the sounds of the beasts prowling and the squelching of their meals.

Mercifully, the wailing had stopped after a while. I spent the night thinking about the task over and over, trying to crack the riddle. I must have dozed off at some point.

"How long was I out?" I rubbed the sleep from my eyes as I stretched my back, my bow resting on my thighs. My leg really did feel much better. Maybe our healing wasn't completely gone, just delayed.

"Not long. Maybe an hour," he yawned.

"We should get moving."

I grunted as I made to stand, balancing on the branch. Njall stood as well and stretched his arms above his head. My eyes widened as I noticed the bulge in his pants and I snapped my head to the side, looking away.

"What's wro—" He stopped, presumably noticing what I had. "Fuck. No. Trust me, it wasn't you. It's morning."

I slowly turned around, making an effort to stare him in the face, which paled when I lifted my eyebrows at him.

"I mean…not that you couldn't. You're beautiful. But you didn't…ugh," he groaned as he ran his hands down his face.

I laughed, truly laughed. This brute of a male stammering over a little erection—okay, big—had me laughing so hard I had to cover my mouth to quiet myself. Njall laughed with me.

After our fit of amusement, we climbed down the tree and continued our slight uphill trek toward the mountain—and the source of the wailing from last night.

We could see the crater at the top of the mountain clearly now, being so close. Its steep grassy slopes, barren of trees, were covered in large jagged rocks halfway to the top. I hadn't anticipated that it would be an easy ascent, but the rocks would make it more difficult. I didn't even know how high we would have to climb to see what we needed to—or if we even would.

I still doubted my solution to the riddle. Something at the back of my mind told me that we were wrong, a feeling in the pit of my stomach. I just… *knew.* But without an alternative, we had to work with what we had. And what we had right now was telling us to climb the mountain.

We continued to walk in silence, still apprehensive of our surroundings and keeping a sharp eye on the woods around us. I surveyed the right, he surveyed the left. I glanced around a large tree to the side and did a double take.

"Njall." My hushed voice broke the silence.

I crouched and drew back my arrow, Njall raised his sword as he quietly walked to me. I flicked my eyes to the tree then back to him. He nodded in understanding and took a protective step in front of me. We naturally worked well together. Even in such a short amount of time, subtle gestures were enough.

I didn't know what I saw exactly, but it had a body, and that alone was threat enough in a place like this. We took a stance on either side of the tree and carefully craned our necks to look around the trunk before we leapt out with weapons raised.

Dangling from the tree was the gruesome sight of a male with the lower half of his body missing. His wrists were impaled with blades that held him up the tree. Blood pooled beneath him, with shreds of skin and muscle littering the ground.

I closed my eyes and took a deep breath, calming my racing heart. I turned around just as I heard Njall vomiting behind me.

"This has to be who we heard last night," I said as I tossed Njall a canteen of water. He poured the water in his mouth before spitting it back out. My own stomach churned. I had thought it was from one of the beasts in the forest, but this was fae…"You alright?"

"Better than him." He nodded. He wiped his mouth and tucked the canteen in his side pocket.

I took one last look at the male and shuddered before turning around to face Njall.

Gods, that could have been either one of us.

I jutted my chin. "Let's get out of here."

He nodded as we both turned to go back around the tree before Njall was tackled to the ground. An arrow was aimed at my face before I could react, and a sword at Njall's neck held by a brawny male on top of him.

"Move and she dies," the male spat.

Njall growled, bearing his teeth.

"Well if it isn't the lovebirds, finally down from their perch," a silky voice said venomously. The female was tall, taller than me, and dressed in sleeveless leathers showing her muscular arms. Her dreadlocked blond hair hung loosely down her back to her waist. "We saw you two cuddled up in that tree of yours." Her eyes flicked to Njall. "What, you couldn't go a few days without a piece of ass?" She aimed a smug smile and winked.

This Torx bitch was delusional, and I wanted to smack the look right off her face. The male let Njall stand, the tip of his blade still pressing into the skin of his neck—a small amount of blood dripping down the length of it. The female stepped closer, the arrow aimed at my eye and so close that I could see the string of the bow fraying from lack of care. I smiled inwardly.

Big mistake.

"We couldn't get close enough without you noticing us, and thought maybe you'd come running to this one's rescue once you heard the screams. Seems our bait took a little longer than expected to catch its prey." My eyes snapped to the burly male standing in front of Njall, both staring each other down with rage rippling off them. The scent of their fury was stifling.

"What do you want?" Njall's voice was low as he seethed through clenched teeth. I swore that if he had his fire, his burning look would have melted the male's pale skin right off his bones.

"Why don't you tell us what you know of the riddle, and *maybe* I'll let one of you live," the female said, glaring at me.

Njall's eyes narrowed on her. "We don't have it solved."

She scoffed. "Liar. You've been traveling together since the first day, with purpose. Looks like you two have it all figured out."

The male stepped forward, pressing the tip of his blade harder into Njall's neck. I gritted my teeth. I wouldn't have been able to move fast enough to get to him without her killing me first.

But I knew they weren't going to let us go until they got what they wanted. And even then, they would have still killed us so we didn't get in their way.

Neither of us spoke. We both knew they wouldn't let us live, so why make it easier for them.

"Kill her. Maybe it'll loosen his tongue," the male suggested.

The female shrugged and pulled back the arrow—

"You don't want to do that," Njall said quickly.

"Oh? Why is that?" she asked.

My fingers twitched, itching to reach for my blades.

Njall paused for a moment, then sighed. "She's my mate." Completely forgetting about the arrow, I snapped my head to him with wide eyes. "I felt the bond when we arrived and she was in distress."

What?!

My heart sank, and I felt the color drain from my face.

No. This couldn't be happening. It didn't feel right. I hadn't felt anything. I should have felt something, right?

He has to be mistaken.

"So?" the male snorted.

Njall didn't even look at me. "You think the Gods will deem you Worthy by destroying a mating bond? A direct gift from *them*?"

The female tilted her head and pursed her lips. "Perhaps not." Her lips turned up into a rueful smile. "But I guess we'll find out."

He looked at me, his eyes spoke where his mouth couldn't, and I understood.

In an instant, Njall leaned back and kicked the male square in the chest. At the same moment, I let go of my bow and grabbed hers just below the arrow, pointing it up, and kicked back her hand holding the string. The already frayed fiber easily snapped, and the arrow shot off behind me. I yanked the wood from her hand and whipped her across the face. In the span of a heartbeat, I grabbed the dagger at my back and launched at the female. Pinning her hand to the tree with my blade and my other hand around her throat, she screamed. I tightened my hold on her as she clawed at my arm, gasping for breath. I didn't let go until she fell still, and her body went limp.

Njall had the male held firmly to the ground. The male's own sword was embedded in his shoulder. Njall's eyes were filled with hatred as he looked down at the male below him. I breathed a sigh of momentary relief.

We tied each of them up to a tree next to the male they had used as bait, a sacrifice to the beasts. We didn't linger, running hard and fast toward the mountain, not wanting to get caught by whatever would feast on them later. I pushed through the pain shooting up my leg.

Once we were far enough away that we couldn't hear their pleading cries, we came to a stop. My hands braced on my knees as I caught my breath, Njall's words ringing in my head.

'She's my mate.'

I glared at him as I walked to his hunched over body, heaving heavy breaths. He straightened, sorrow filling his eyes right before I swung up and punched him in the side of his face.

He grabbed his cheek as I turned and stormed off. He tried to grab my arm but I yanked it out, spinning to face him.

"What the fuck, Njall?" I yelled as I shoved his muscled chest as hard as I could, but his large body didn't even move with the effort. "Mate? You're lying!"

He has to be.

My hands shook and my heart raced. I would have felt something. That's how it worked. Two souls bound together for eternity. Even after death. I would have never admitted it out loud but a part of me wanted the mating bond that I had read stories about. I wanted that unbreakable connection, the love and passion that blossomed from it. My mind spiraled in a split second. Fear and anger filled me. Tears threatened to escape.

Was something wrong with me?

I inhaled sharply as Njall grabbed my face. "I *was* lying."

"What?" My shoulders dropped as I reared my head back away from him. "Why would you do that? Why would you *lie* about something like that?" I shoved him again, and he released my face but still didn't move.

"I panicked, alright." He ran a hand through his hair, tugging at the roots. "I'm sorry. I just needed to stall them. I don't know why that was the first thing to come to mind but thank the Gods it worked."

"So...we're not mates?" I breathed.

He huffed. "No, Roav. Trust me, if we were mates, we'd be marked. There's no way I would have been able to hold back from sealing the bond with being so close to you in that tree last night."

My gaze briefly flicked to my unmarked arm, the one I had secretly hoped would be marked one day.

A childish dream.

The mark was a symbol of the mating bond—a gift from the Gods, a sacred one. The mating bond was divine, a connection of two souls, and it drove them to each other. As much as I was relieved, a small part of me was also disappointed.

"Well next time, try not scaring the shit out of me without warning."

"I'll do my best," he sighed and visibly relaxed.

"How did you know all of that about the mating bond anyway?" I asked suspiciously. Not many did, seeing as it was so rare and very few records of it.

"Oryn has libraries too, you know." He smirked.

We walked in awkward silence, avoiding eye contact for the next several hours. The mountain had started obstructing our view of the sky through the trees as we drew nearer. Being this close, we were able to see the northern side of the mountain, darkened by constant shadow and completely devoid of vegetation all the way to the base.

"We should reach the base soon. Do you think we can make it to the peak by nightfall?" I glanced at him, finally breaking the silence.

He tilted his head and pursed his lips for a moment. "I think so. We'll have to be quick. Those rocks will slow us down, and I don't want to be up there long. We'd be too visible out in the open, and we don't know what, or who, will be watching."

"Let's plan to head back down the same way we came so we'll be somewhat familiar with the path—"

My voice was cut off when large thorny vines sprang out through the trees toward us. I dropped to my stomach with a gasp as the air whooshed from my lungs, narrowly evading the thick plant.

Njall wasn't so lucky.

As I looked behind me, the vines from a Lurvinea plant quickly wound their way up Njall's body as he struggled to free himself. The thorns dug into his flesh while squeezing around him. Once it got to his waist, it pulled him across the forest floor as he roared.

I jumped up and chased after him, grabbing the sword that he dropped along the way. I needed something bigger than a dagger with the vines being nearly as wide as my body.

The vines were pulling him faster than I could run and I pushed myself to the point that everything around me passed in a blur. I could hear him bellow even as he was out of sight. I followed the sound along with the trail of his blood left behind through the forest.

I'm coming Njall.

Adrenaline filled my veins as I continued to run faster and faster. I could barely see where I was going as the trees rushed by me.

I was gaining on him.

Within my distorted vision, I hadn't noticed that I had entered into a much darker place where the air was thick with a smoke-like substance. It took only moments for the cloudy air to enter my lungs and its effects began to sink into my bloodstream.

Dizziness. Blurred vision. Headache. Nausea. Suffocation.

It was so much. Too much.

This was what the Trial did. It took out those that couldn't survive, couldn't endure. That was the purpose. To fight against all odds for only a fraction of a chance to survive. And even then, that didn't guarantee being deemed Worthy. And everything here was meant to kill. Gods was I sick of everything trying to kill me. It was already midday and the mountain would still take us until nightfall. There was no time for additional shit to deal with.

I want out of this place.

If I were smart, I would have turned around and left Njall to his fate. I would have only worried about my own survival. I barely knew the male anyway.

I guess I was stupid.

I held my breath and ran harder than I thought my body could handle. The vines seemed to slow down and I could see Njall gasping and coughing from the poisonous air. My lungs ached and pleaded for oxygen, but I knew that the more toxic air that I breathed, the faster it would kill me. I got closer and closer as I had to keep telling myself *just a little farther.*

I was finally close enough to see Njall thrashing and clawing at the ground in a desperate attempt to escape the clutches of the carnivorous plant. Pushing my body to its limit, I thrust myself through the air, Njall's sword over my head, and stabbed it into the vine below his body. It writhed, finally stopping. With all my weight behind it, I pushed down on the blade, slicing through the dark green appendage as an opaque liquid oozed out of it. I lifted the blade and chopped through the rest of the vine, effectively severing it. The vine trembled, but ultimately retreated farther into the murky forest.

I didn't have time to think as I pried the remaining vine from Njall's suffocating body. My vision filled with spots of black as I struggled for air. Njall's eyes closed as he fell unconscious. I couldn't scream and waste the last remnants of oxygen.

Pulling his arm with all my might, I wrenched him through the smoky air until we were clear of the poisonous gas. I collapsed on my hands and knees and sucked the fresh oxygen into my lungs. After a few minutes and half a canteen of water, when I could finally see clearly and breathe normally, I went to Njall. His body was covered in blood from waist down.

"Njall." My voice was scratchy. "Njall, I need you to wake up because I can't drag your big ass all the way to the mountain." I shook his shoulder until he stirred.

I offered him the canteen, which he drank deeply from. He coughed and sputtered for a second before finally opening his eyes and looking up at me.

"Been looking at my ass, Roav?" he wheezed.

"It's hard to miss." I huffed a laugh. My face fell as I observed his wounds. "Do you think you can walk?"

"It's mostly superficial cuts. I'll make it." He gritted his teeth as he stood. "And I don't want to stick around here any longer. That Lurvinea could come back. Let's go."

Chapter Fourteen

KYA

S tanding at the edge of the tree line, hidden amongst the shadows, the mountain loomed above us, stretching toward the stars that were beginning to twinkle in the fading sunlight. Between Njall's injuries and mine, it took us longer to trek to the end of the forest than we had originally anticipated. My body ached and I was sure that Njall's did too but thankfully his wounds had stopped bleeding after wrapping them with large leaves and securing them with the rope. My stomach was in knots as I looked at the mountain towering above us. We would be completely out in the open on the slopes.

The peak of the mountain was our target—it gave us the best advantage for spotting whatever it was that we were to look for. Hopefully it would be obvious, like a trail of dead trees that we could easily follow. It had to be. We were out of ideas. And out of time.

On the far side of the mountain, up on the slopes, I saw five contestants. Three were fighting each other while the other two were scrambling to get away from a Beira.

Looks like we aren't the only ones to figure out the first part of the riddle.

Those five plus Njall and I made seven. I knew that another seven were dead. Which meant that there were still five unaccounted for, either dead or still in the forest somewhere.

I was startled when Njall pulled me back farther into the trees and led me away from the other contestants, our weapons drawn and ready. We tucked ourselves behind thick bushes, scanning the slopes for the best path to the top. The other contestants put a damper in our original plans.

Njall's voice was a whisper. "Why is there no grass on the shadowed side?" He tilted his head.

An odd question for a time like this.

"The island is probably farther north than our continent. The sun's light can't reach the other side, so the plants can't survive when always cast in shadow." I wasn't sure what he was getting at, but I could tell that he was contemplating a new plan.

Njall squinted at the mountain. "I think we should stay on the shadowed side during our assent. It'll be harder to climb up with the loose rock rather than the grass, but it'll also be harder for the others to spot us. The last thing we want is to have to fight anyone off under time constraints."

"Agreed. We can stick to the edge of the shadows, using it as our guide. And once night falls, we can make our way to the other side."

He shook his head. "No. We should use markers of some kind, sticks perhaps. Once the light dies out, the shadow goes with it. We won't be able to see our path if we rely on the edge of the shadow as a guide."

I stilled.

'*Once the light dies out, the shadow goes with it*'
His words rang through my head.

I gasped. "That's it." I glanced at my arm, the smeared words were faded from sweat and dirt but still somewhat legible.

What light brings to life yet dies in darkness.

Always cast in shadow.

Once the light dies out, the shadow goes with it.

I dropped my bow and grabbed his face, his eyes widened with an incredulous look. "Njall, it's the shadow of the mountain."

He arched a brow. "Yeah," he drawled.

I released his face. "No, you don't understand." I grinned, my voice a raised whisper. "The riddle! You have to have light to see shadows and they disappear in darkness. It's not plants, it's the mountain's shadow."

I shook my head, I couldn't believe I didn't think of this sooner. It made perfect sense.

Njall looked at me like I was crazy. Perhaps I was, but this whole godsdamn thing was crazy.

"Think about it, something that reveals a path is on the dark side of the mountain and can only be seen in darkness." I was practically beaming. "Trust me. Please."

Njall hesitated for a moment before nodding. "I trust you."

We waited in the forest until darkness fell before we made our way around to the other side of the mountain. The base was so large that it took a couple hours of non-stop running. We didn't know where we were supposed to go. And we still didn't even know what we were looking for. Njall was taking a big risk, blindly following me.

We were running so hard that my legs felt numb, and my side was cramping. Sweat trickled down my back and I regretted wearing thick, leather pants. I couldn't think of anything, my concentration solely on keeping my legs moving.

"Kya," Njall whisper-yelled from behind, and I skidded to a stop on loose gravel.

Panting, I looked back to him and raised my bow, ready for whatever would come. But Njall wasn't in a fighting stance. He was staring at the mountain, his mouth gaping.

"Look," he breathed.

My gaze drifted to the towering rock. My mouth gaped and I nearly fell backwards. The entire side of the mountain was covered in soft, gold glowing swirls and lines embedded in the rock—not all that different from our marks. A triangular shape at the top came to a point, the bottom section was covered with crosses, a curving line through it. All of it encircled in a familiar shape.

The island.

"I think I know 'what has a river that does not flow'," Njall breathed.

I marveled at the glowing shapes above us. One in particular caught my eye. The side of my lips curved up into a smile. "A map."

Chapter Fifteen

KYA

We saw it at the same time. The map showed a path leading from the backside of the mountain, down to the beach and along the perimeter of the island where it ended at a crescent shaped symbol. We shared a hopeful look with each other before we sprinted down to the sandy beach.

After a few more minutes, we came upon cliffs, separating the lapping waves of the ocean from the land above. Up ahead, I heard the groans of what sounded like a male. Njall and I pressed our bodies flush to the cliffside and crept our way around the bend of the beach.

A male, trailing blood and holding his side with one arm, a sword in the other, limped his way to what the crescent symbol on the map referenced. An arch. A tall stone arch that was filled with the same soft glow as the map on the mountain, stood at the base of the cliff facing the water. It glistened in the darkness, like an ethereal beacon.

I recognized the contestant from the temple, but I didn't remember seeing him on the mountain slopes. His shoulder-length hair was as dark as his tattoo-covered skin, tangled in his torn and bloodied clothing. The Ulriktin looked like he had been through hell. Then again, I was pretty sure that was where we were, and I knew I didn't look any better. The male slowly limped his way toward the arch, briefly pausing under it to study the looming architecture, before he took a final step through and…vanished.

My eyes widened. The arch was some kind of gateway.

That's how we would get out of here. This was it. The way out of the Woltawa Forest and off this godsforsaken island. We had made it.

My heart pounded in my chest with anticipation and the unfamiliar feeling of hope.

Njall and I stepped out from around the cliff and sheathed our weapons, our feet sinking slightly into the damp sand, leaving footprints behind us. I didn't know what to expect on the other side of the arch and my heart raced at the thought, but I held my chin up anyway. I would not cower before the Gods. I had solved their damned riddle.

A growing whistle sounded before it abruptly ended with a fleshy thump. I knew that sound. I'd been the cause of it countless times before. Njall grunted, dropping to his side and holding his leg—an arrow sticking out of it. The hair on the back of my neck stood as instinct overtook me.

In one swift motion, I whirled around, grabbing for my daggers behind my back, and threw them toward the sound of quickly approaching feet slapping on the sand. I wasn't quick enough. Just as the blades left my fingertips, a male tackled me to the ground. The air left my lungs as my back was slammed onto the grainy sand, my wooden bow snapping underneath me and splintering into my skin. Pushing with all my strength, I tried to scramble from underneath him. The male grabbed daggers from his thighs, and held one to my neck while plunging the other through my hand.

A pained scream ripped from my throat. Njall roared, spewing curses at the male. I couldn't think, the pain in my palm blinding my mind. I barely registered the weight lifting off me as Njall crashed into the male, pulling him off—the muted sound of sand scattering from their tussle.

The sound of grunts and flesh striking flesh was insignificant to the ringing in my ears as I rolled over and yanked the blade from my hand. I knew it was foolish to remove the blade, the bleeding would only worsen, but I couldn't function without it. I whimpered through my tightly pressed lips as tears escaped. A glint of light caught my eye as a sword was hurled into the deep ocean waters.

I jumped to my feet, holding my bleeding hand to my chest and the dagger in the other. Njall's body was against the rocky cliff to my side, blood running down his face and dripping onto his rapidly moving chest. The sound of creaking wood and taunt string had my head snapping in the other direction to the male who had his bow aimed for Njall.

I can't let this happen. Njall doesn't deserve this.

Time slowed to a near stop as the arrow was released at the same time as my blade, while I dove between the arrow and Njall.

Everything went white, and then a deep otherworldly voice rang out all around me. "It's her."

I waited for the pain in my chest, but it never came. There was no sound of the waves, or Njall's labored breathing. I couldn't see past the blindingly bright light all around me. It only lasted for a moment but, I wondered if this was what it was like to finally greet death.

The light faded, and the sound of leaves rustling in a breeze had my eyelids slowly prying apart, blinking several times to adjust. When I could focus again, my breath caught in my throat and my mouth fell open.

Luscious green grass gently swayed in a vast field with large trees spaced throughout. Somehow, it felt ancient here. The air was warm with a gentle wind blowing through my hair. Everything was bathed in soft light, yet the sky held no sun. There were so many colors all around me. It was beautiful. A sense of tranquility and peace washed over me as all of my worries melted away—a contentment I had never known. I didn't think of the Glaev or the Trial or the beasts or the contestants or my bleeding hand. Not even of Njall. All of it was gone. I prayed this was the afterlife, and I never wanted to leave.

Maybe I did die.

I slowly spun to take in my surroundings and when I made a full circle, a radiant figure stood before me.

Draped in white silk, the female—more beautiful than any I had ever seen—glowed with ethereal elegance and might. She had black hair cascading around her slender body. She was tall, more than a head taller than me, and her delicate feet hovered just above the ground. Not a female. No.

A Goddess.

A voice of silk and honey glided through the air. "Hello Kya. I am Kleio."

Kleio. The Silent God. The Mother and Goddess of Atara, my homeland.

"It is an honor to be in your presence." And I meant it. Being born of Atara, she was the Mother of my people, having blessed each child with life. I bowed deeply at the waist then rose to face her again.

"The honor is mine." She smiled softly. I tentatively smiled back before she continued. "Walk with me. I am sure that you have questions. You may ask them during this limited time, if you wish."

I fell into step next to her as we walked—well, I walked, she...glided—through the field.

"Thank you, Mother." I bowed my head slightly.

Limited time. In other words, choose my questions wisely.

"Where are we? What is this place?"

"Hylithria. A name in a language unknown to those in your realm of Taeralia. It is the birthplace of the Spirits. This is their realm." She spoke gently.

"How did I get here?" I shook my head. I could barely wrap my mind around it.

I had to tilt my head back as the Goddess turned to me and colorless eyes locked onto mine. "I brought you here. You have been chosen, my child." She laid her long delicate fingers against my chest. "You have been deemed Worthy."

Worthy.

I had actually done it. But it was hard to believe. Kleio, the Goddess who had never chosen a contestant from the Trial, chose me.

"Why?" I breathed. "Why did you choose *me*?" It came out in more of a whimper than a demand. I didn't feel like I had done anything extraordinary to deserve being Worthy. I survived but nothing was overly...significant.

And why her of all the Gods?

"Because I deemed it so. You were continually willing to sacrifice yourself for another. And you have trusted yourself to seek the truth. I have no doubt you will continue to do so," she said.

I didn't understand what that meant. Her answer only added to my endless list of questions in my mind. One in particular bothered me most.

"I still don't understand. This was a Test of Strength. I'm nowhere near as strong as many of the others." Though I had trained my body and was able to take care of myself, I was still small in comparison to those like Njall.

"There are some strengths more valuable than physical abilities."

"But…you've never chosen. In thousands of years, not once have you chosen. Why now?"

I inwardly kicked myself for daring to question a Goddess, let alone the one who only just named me Worthy. But damn her for choosing me. How was I to save my people when I still wouldn't have lands?

Her eyes flickered with something I couldn't read. "Things have changed. And no one was worth being chosen and granted my gifts before now, before you. I have standards that are not easily met."

The gifts. Magical abilities beyond anything in the natural world were granted to the Worthy. Each God granted their chosen Worthy a different, new ability, usually one that benefited them in some way, and the Worthy would have to work on mastering their newfound power.

I opened my mouth to ask about the gifts, but she continued, "I have chosen you to be Worthy and serve my Nation."

I huffed in a single breath, "How can I be of worth to Atara? There's nothing left. The Glaev—"

"Is not what it seems." Her voice grew cold and dark, and I swore the realm around us did as well.

I instinctively lowered my head in submission to my Goddess. She may have been lenient with my questioning, but I would have done well to remember that she was, in fact, a Goddess and possessed great power.

"What do you wish for me to do, Mother?" My voice was barely a whisper.

She hooked a finger under my chin and lifted my head until I met her eyes. "Restore the balance so they may return." A command.

Awfully vague one.

"How?" My eyebrows furrowed.

Kleio leaned in close, our noses nearly touching. "Listen and you shall learn. Seek the truth, Kya." She leaned back and stood to her full height.

This was sounding more like another riddle to solve.

"How do I find it?"

"You already know." She started walking again, a clear sign that our conversation was complete.

"Where are we going?" I rushed to catch up with her.

She looked down at me. "The final test." My eyes widened as she placed her hand on my shoulder.

Suddenly, everything sped past us in streaks of color before leaving us standing at the base of a small mountain. I bent over and hurled the contents of my stomach onto the grass.

"What was that?" I coughed before spitting out the remnants of vomit from my mouth.

"Traveling," Kleio said with a shrug.

She turned her attention up the slope of the mountain. My gaze followed, and I noticed a large, flat section of rock about halfway up the side of it, shimmering with light. I had never seen rock like that. The section was at least thirty paces high and spanned the length of Morah. Before it was a flat expanse of stone, like a dais.

"The Galadynia." She raised her chin toward the flat stone. "A Test of Fate. The Galadynia will pass judgment, your fate will be sealed, and you will have completed the Trial of the Gods."

My fate. So uncertain.

"And Kya." She turned her head toward me. "Save the blood-line from peril."

I stepped onto the flat stone after climbing up the mountain. After Kleio had informed me of my task, she vanished. Leaving me to complete the final test. It dawned on me then. I was alone.

Where are the other contestants? Am I the only one?

I glanced behind me down to the open slopes of the mountain. No one was around. I turned back to the flat rock, only to realize it wasn't rock at all. It was made entirely of glass, and reflected the landscape in front of it. A mirror.

I slowly approached the Galadynia. It was built into the side of the mountain—no, part of the mountain. The edges of the mirror blended seamlessly with the surrounding rock. I stood before it and saw gentle swirls of light and darkness within it, like thick black smoke fighting against the rays of the sun. It was enchanting and captivating.

Once I approached, only myself was reflected, nothing of the landscape around me. My clothes were torn, burned, and covered with dirt and blood. My hair was a tangled mess and nearly unbound from the tie I had around it. Dark circles outlined my green eyes, and my face was more hollow than I remembered. I barely recognized myself.

I leaned closer and pressed the wounded palm of my hand, free of pain in this wondrous place, against the mirror—the wound I had forgotten about. The swirls inside the mirror slowed and seemed to part as images of people appeared. I turned around, no one was there. It was coming from inside the glass. I squinted at the figures and realized that I knew them as they came into focus. Nikan and Malina were standing between rows of books in Morah. It looked like they were having a heated discussion, but I couldn't hear anything. Nikan was holding up a piece of parchment. I could barely make out the words I had written a few days ago.

'Dear Nik,
By the time you…'
"What is this?" I whispered.

In the blink of an eye, another image appeared. A small village of beautifully crafted homes that I would always recognize. My home in Atara before it was destroyed by the Glaev. The house to the left was mine. It had been twenty years since I had seen my house but I could still feel the cracks in the foundation beneath my feet, the smell of dinner cooking on the kitchen stove, the sound of laughter within the walls.

In the mirror, a horse-drawn cart on the street next to my house toppled to the side when the wheel fell off. Before it happened, I knew that children would rush up to it to gather the tarts that had fallen from it—Malina and I amongst them. I remembered. I knew who was about to come out my front door to hurry off the children from the baker's cart.

A tear escaped down my cheek and my lip quivered.

This is a memory.

It was gone in an instant and replaced with another image.

"Wait! Let me see them!" My voice was hoarse as tears streamed down my cheeks and I banged on the glass with my fist.

Eamon was sitting in his study, hunched over books on his desk. But it seemed wrong. His hair was white, and he looked frail with wrinkles etched over his usually smooth face. That wasn't a memory.

"This hasn't happened yet," I gasped a sob.

More images flashed from the mirror. Memories from my past, vague and obscure visions of my future, streaked across the glass. The people I had killed, wars that I had no memory of, flashes of my childhood, a male in the shadows, previous lovers, hooded cobalt eyes, beings I didn't understand. Darkness, love, pain. My enemies, my worst past nightmares and ones that had yet to come, every mistake I had ever made stared back at me. It was too much, and it was terrifying. Tears blurred my vision and I wanted to look away but I knew I shouldn't. The Galadynia was measuring me. This was the test.

A Test of Fate.

The mirror was judging my past, present, and future.

After what felt like a lifetime, the images, familiar and unfamiliar, finally stopped. The swirls didn't return and the Galadynia remained blank, not even reflecting me. I was emotionally drained. And I was pissed too. Of all the memories that it showed me, it wouldn't give me the satisfaction of seeing my mother and father again. I glared at the mirror as another image came into view after a few moments.

My glare fell as I curiously stared into the eyes of a magnificent black horse. It tilted its head and I could have sworn that it was studying me, judging me. Like it was seeing right into me with its charcoal-colored eyes.

It reared its massive head and my reflection came back into view below it. In front of it. Gods, it was enormous in comparison. It snorted, and my heart dropped when I felt its hot breath on the back of my head. This wasn't part of my future projected through the mirror...the horse was standing behind me.

Slowly, I turned around and came face to face with the biggest horse I had ever seen—except it wasn't *just* a horse. It was a Spirit. An actual Spirit was standing before me. I had never seen one.

Its body was as black as the night itself, its forelock and mane long and wavy. Its hooves, each the size of my head, were covered in the same hair and supported long muscular legs. At the back of its hindquarters, a thick wavy tail brushed the stone beneath it. The Spirit horse's withers were well above my head. And just behind the shoulders were two tremendous wings. Covered in black feathers, they were folded and tucked to the sides of its body.

I couldn't breathe. I couldn't speak. I couldn't do anything other than gape and marvel at the remarkable being before me.

After a moment, it stretched its neck and extended its muzzle until it touched my chest. An electric shock tore through me and I winced at the sensation. The Spirit pinned its ears back and flared out its wings before it reared up off its front hooves slightly and slammed back down.

I shrieked and ducked, covering my head with my arms. The entire mountain shook when its front hooves landed. The rumble filled my ears and I felt it in my bones, my soul. I gasped when I felt a pulsing flare in my chest. I looked at the winged horse when it took a step back and bobbed its head for me to stand.

We stood there for several moments staring at each other. When nothing else happened, I broke the silence.

"H-Hi. I'm Kya."

"*I know who you are,*" a low deep voice sounded, coming from no particular direction. I glanced around, searching for the source.

"*What are you looking for?*"
I slowly returned my gaze back to the Spirit.

"*Kya, I am Odarum. A Spirit of this realm. A Spirit now bound to you, and you to me.*" His mouth didn't move. My eyebrows rose and my mouth fell open.

He can talk!
"You can...speak?"

"*I can communicate with you, and you me, through our bond.*"

"You can understand what I'm saying and speak back to me in my mind?"

131

"*You may speak to me through the bond as well. Feel for it within you.*"

I could already feel it. That pang in my chest was like a tether to him. I closed my eyes and reached for it in my mind but was met with a thick haze. It was like soft mist, soothing yet unbound. I tried to grapple for it, to push it back together but to no avail. There, through the haze I saw it, the thread. It was like a beam of light.

I held on to it and attempted to send a thought, "*Hello, Odarum.*"

"*Hello, again.*"

I opened my eyes. "I don't understand." I spoke out loud. Speaking through the bond would take some getting used to. "Why are we bonded? What does that mean?" I knew that the third task was getting a Spirit animal, but I had never heard of them being *bonded* to the Worthy.

"*Those that are deemed Worthy by the Gods are gifted by them. But the Trial is not just for the Gods. It is also for the Spirits. The Worthy are gifted with a bond of one of the Spirits from this realm. The third task of the Trial is being judged by your fate, and a Spirit choosing you. They bind themselves to you for the remainder of your life.*"

"Why have I never heard of this? It isn't written anywhere." I ran my hands over my hair and blew out a sharp breath.

"*It is forbidden to speak of the Spirit bond. Only the Worthy know of it. Not even your Sages.*" His tail swished behind him.

"Why? What does it matter if anyone knows?"

Odarum snorted. "*We do not wish it to be known. We have our reasons.*"

I nodded, still in disbelief that Spirits have been roaming the world bonded with the Worthy all this time and no one knew.

"Okay. So what now? How do I, or we, get back?"

"*I can take us back to the Temple of Odes.*"

"Will you be with me all of the time?" I narrowed my eyes. I didn't necessarily like the idea of a Spirit being around me constantly. It would feel like I was being watched.

"Not all of the time. But a lot of it, yes. Especially until the bond is complete." His wings flared out slightly before tucking back in. I felt a little relief at that but only a little.

"What does that mean, 'until the bond is complete'?" I leaned my back against the mirror behind me, my legs tiring from standing still for so long.

"We are connected in more ways than one, Kya. We are a part of each other. You will need time to adjust to the magic you have gained from me."

I pushed off the glass. "You share magic with me? I thought only the Gods did that. What magic?" The pitch of my voice raised an octave.

"They will manifest as our bond strengthens. You will need to train with it, and me."

I let out a long exhale. "Alright."

Odarum dipped his head. *"It is time to return."*

Before I could say anything, he touched my chest with his muzzle and stomped his heavy hoof against the stone. Everything went black and cold, as we left the Spirit realm of Hylithria.

Chapter Sixteen

RYKER

The feeling was undeniable—a weak-yet-sharp throbbing in my chest that electrified my entire body, causing me to grunt as I jerked back in my seat. After so many years, I had started to doubt it would ever happen. Tears pricked at the back of my eyes at the overwhelming sensation. I felt the connection snap into place like it was always meant to be there, a perfect fit to a piece of my soul that I never realized was missing. Until now. And now that it was suddenly ingrained into everything that I was, I couldn't imagine living without it. The bond.

My mate.

And I knew, with absolute certainty, who she was. It was one of the contestants. The precious little beauty with long brown hair and eyes a striking color of pine green.

When I saw her for the first time in the temple, I couldn't tear my gaze from her. Her lightly freckled face and those plump pink lips had been at the forefront of my mind for days. And now I knew why.

She must have been chosen. That was the only thing that would explain the sudden surge of connection in a mating bond. She had become bound to one of the Spirits. That was how I was able to feel her from another realm. It also explained why the bond was so unsure before—her fate had yet to be sealed.

Like all those born Marked of the Trial, their fates were not known until they competed. She would return soon, and I prayed to Xareus that he did not betray me and choose my mate. If I was forced to challenge her, I'd throw myself into the Rip willingly. I didn't even know the female, but the thought of having to fight someone who was now a part of me felt wrong and vile.

I had remained in my tent for days, pacing back and forth as I waited and waited for a Sage to collect me to challenge one of the Worthy. But they never came. Perhaps Xareus hadn't chosen anyone, and if that was the case, I wanted to leave before the Challenges began. I had no interest in watching someone succumb to being thrown into the Rip—yet now, I needed to stay to make sure my mate survived.

The Sages forced the duelers to drink an elixir to temporarily nullify their abilities during the challenge. The goal during the challenge was simple: throw your opponent into the Rip and claim your right as Lord or Lady. Something I never wished to do again.

I grew tired of waiting for the Sages. I needed to be there when my mate returned. I needed to make sure she would survive whoever she had to challenge and hopefully it wasn't me.

I stood from the chair in my tent and shook my head to clear my mind of her, taking a deep breath to gather myself before stepping back into the mask of a Lord—fearsome and powerful. I threw open the flap of my tent and stepped outside. Large tents of cloth and stone littered the grounds around the temple. I wove my way through them to the temple steps where the Sages were standing in a line like a barrier. No one was allowed back inside until all of the contestants—the ones who survived at least—returned. How the Sages knew was beyond me.

I placed my hands behind my back and raised my chin as a female Sage broke away from the line and met me at the bottom of the marble steps. She was in her ceremonial robes, the thin material doing little to hide the tall slender body beneath it, and it swayed in the warm wind as she descended. I had to fight to keep from rolling my eyes as she approached.

Of course she *had to approach me.*

"Lord Ryker," Vicria greeted with a sultry tone, bowing at the waist before rising. I didn't return the gesture. She deserved no respect from me. "I'm surprised to see that you're still here."

My eyebrows rose. "Why would I not still be here? I have yet to be informed that I am not due to challenge."

The female batted her long eyelashes at me. "My apologies, Lord Ryker." She blushed and placed her hand on her chest. "I had assumed that you had been told." While Sages were forbidden from taking lovers, this one was often known to disregard her vows to get her way. I despised it, and I despised her. She was a disgrace to the Sages.

"Told me what?" My words were clipped and my lips curved into a sneer.

"Your presence is no longer required. The Gods have chosen. You will not be challenged."

I kept the relief from my features and silently sent thanks to Xareus that he did not choose the contestant who was fated to me. Even though the Gods bestowed the mating bond, I wouldn't have put it past them to have a pair duel to the death for the sake of entertainment.

But I couldn't leave yet, I needed to see my mate.

"I will remain until the contestants return. Have one of the other Sages come to my tent when they have." My voice was cold, demanding.

Vicria stepped closer, our bodies nearly touching, and I resisted the urge to retreat. "I'm afraid I must insist. Return to your home, you are no longer needed."

"Enough." I pushed past her and stormed my way up the temple steps, Vicria followed with a huff. "Sages." I greeted them with a slight bow of my head.

"Lord Ryker." A tall male, Zareb, spoke after bowing in return, "I hope you have not been waiting to be challenged. The Worthy have been chosen, and Xareus did not select a contestant. You may return to your Nation."

"As I have told Vicria, I will stay. The bond of my mate has been enacted, a Worthy."

Elated gasps broke out amongst the group. The mating bond was a sacred gift from the Gods, one cherished deeply by the Sages. The female beside me fumed with rage while holding her composure in front of her brethren.

"An unfortunate situation," she shouted over the gleeful chatting of the other Sages and I couldn't help but notice the slight scent of nervousness from her. "This could cause a great imbalance in power."

I glared at her from the corner of my eye as she gave an innocent looking smile.

Always the manipulator.

"How do you mean?" another male asked.

"Two Worthy being mated? This is unheard of. Even if they are both from different Nations, they would be a formidable pair," she stated, with a fake worried expression plastered across her face

Damn right we would be.

"That does not guarantee an imbalance." I didn't bother hiding the annoyance from my voice.

Vicria ignored me as she continued. "We've all heard the rumors of Lord Rykers insatiable greed, and I don't need to remind you of the Battle of Red Waters, named for his bloodlust."

Absurd. That battle was won before it ever began and it wouldn't have even begun if not for the tyrannical appetite of Hamal and his ignorance of just how far I would go to protect my Nation. Ulrik's blatant disregard of our peace laws brought it upon themselves when they attacked my borders from the sea.

"What's to say that he would not seal the bond and use this female to overrule another Nation, or all of them? If they *mated*," Vicria spat the word as if it were rancid. "They could be unstoppable."

The group of Sages began quietly muttering to themselves. Vicria swept out her arm, gesturing to the tents of the other Lords and Ladies.

"Do you not think they would feel threatened by this union of power?" She continued to feign innocence and righteousness. I wanted to beat her face in, but I would not be sentenced to death over that low-life excuse for a Sage.

"This needs to be discussed, immediately." Zareb stepped forward. He turned to one of the Sages next to him. "Call the Lords and Ladies. This matter must be handled before the Worthy return."

Chaos erupted outside the temple after the Lords and Ladies were summoned and informed of the situation. I remained still, refusing to engage in this ridiculous debacle.

She's my mate and I will have her. No Sage or Worthy will stop me.

Practically in unison, the Lords and Ladies collectively demanded that I deny the sacred bond, arguing back and forth on how to deal with the situation. I finally grew tired of listening to their bickering about *my* mating bond.

"The Gods granted this bond. My mate has been fated to me. I will not deny them, nor her. I can guarantee that I have no interest in seizing other Nations."

The shouting grew louder, Sages and Worthy alike pressing for retribution for my denial of their proposal and voicing their distrust. Vicria smiled maliciously as she stepped into the center of the horde circled around me. I narrowed my eyes. She was the one who was not to be trusted.

"I believe that there can be an alternate solution, one in which the two Worthy may be together without contest." The crowd quieted, giving her their full attention with wary looks. She turned to face me. "Undergo the Raith. Forfeit your wielding, your magic, your bonds, and your Worthy status. Both of you. You and your mate would no longer be a threat."

My teeth clenched. I fought to keep my magic contained as it begged to eliminate the true threat standing before me.

What is her problem?

The mass of fae bristled around me in agreement with her.

"No," I snapped.

The Raith was a gruesome ritual that stripped any and all bonds to the world. The Sages and Scholars made such a sacrifice to gain their positions, but to take away the power and status of one that was Worthy was worse than death, leaving them weak with no contribution to the world. A shameful life that I would not allow myself or my mate to endure. I wouldn't let her succumb to that fate.

"Lord Ryker," Zareb interjected. "If you cannot agree to either of these terms, a formal panel will be convened, consisting of the Council of Sages as well as all of the Worthy. Is this what you wish for?"

They wanted to put her through another fucking trial after having just completed one.

"I will not deny the bond of my mate. And I will not put either of us through the Raith."

The male bowed in respect for my decision. "Very well then. The panel regarding the mating of the two Worthy will be held one month after the Nailu at the Sages Temple in Bhara. This will allow the new Worthy, victorious in the Challenge, to be sworn in as Lords or Ladies and establish their ruling."

The grumbling crowd reluctantly dispersed and resumed their duties. I turned back to head for my tent to wait for my mate to return.

My mate.

Nailu, the Night of No Moons. It was a highly celebrated night, filled with music and dancing, all over the continent. And it was less than three months away.

Before I made it back to my tent, Vicria stepped in front of me.

"I will continue to insist that you return home. Being near your mate once she returns will not be beneficial for either of you if you can't control yourself and try to claim her." She placed a hand on my chest as she looked up at me from underneath her lashes. "Return now, and I could help you. Help relieve some of this tension. Seeing as your mate can't."

I grabbed her wrist and she winced, her eyes widening as I lightly burned her wrist, pulling it away from my chest. My nostrils flared, menace lacing my words, "You would do well to remember who I am, *Sage*. You do not command me. And if you dare to touch me again, I will burn your hand from your body." I released her wrist, now scorched raw where I had held it.

Vicria cradled her burned wrist. Her eyes turned cold as she leaned forward and whispered, "If you do not deny the bond of the Riyite female, your Nation will suffer more than it already is."

"What are you talking about?" My eyebrows furrowed and a pit formed in my stomach.

"I suggest you go home and find out, *Lord* Ryker." Her lips curved into a depraved grin and she walked back up the steps of the temple.

Fury erupted in my chest at the threat to my lands and my people. I stormed off down the hill, past the encampment and into the wooded area north of the temple. I couldn't risk that Vicria was lying just to get me to leave. That would be a mistake. My duty was to my Nation.

Damn her.

Every step was a painstaking effort as I moved away from where I knew my mate would return to. The bond was driving me to be with her no matter what. I would find her—nothing would stop me from finding her. But I had to go back.

"Theron, take me home. Now."

Chapter Seventeen

KYA

My head was spinning, and I felt disoriented once Odarum brought us back to the Temple of the Fallen God. My legs wobbled and I stumbled, holding a hand over my mouth in an attempt to fight back the nausea. I never wanted to travel like that again.

I instantly breathed a sigh of relief as my magic returned, and I could feel the muted vibrations through the soles of my boots. The aches in my body returned but thankfully, I felt my wounds already healing. Yet something inside had an unfamiliar burn that I couldn't place, and it wasn't diminishing. I shook it off as a result of the Spirit Travel.

I instantly thought of Njall. I wanted to curse Kleio for taking me before I could save him. I should have known better than to get close to a contestant. To care.

After a moment, my focus came back and I realized we weren't alone. Standing near the other side of the temple between the outer pillars was another contestant, a Worthy female with black hair, shaved on one side, and rich, dark skin. Her hair was a clear indication that she was from Ulrik, and I wondered if it would be her own Lord that she would have to challenge.

Next to her was a wolf. Its back was nearly as high as my shoulders. Covered in pure white fur, it seemed to glow in the dawning sunlight shining from the glass dome above. The wolf's tail swished, sweeping the marble floor. Her Spirit... companion? Animal?

Now that I thought about it, I didn't know what they were to us. I didn't know what to call them other than animal, but that seemed too mortal of a word for Spirits.

I whispered to Odarum, "What are you to me?"

"*Learn to speak through the bond.*"

"Do I have to?" It took a lot of concentration to speak through our minds, and I just didn't have the energy for it.

He gave me a look. I would have to learn the expressions of Spirit horses because I couldn't read him.

"*Fine,*" I grumbled through the bond. "*Are you my Spirit animal? Match? Friend? Don't you have a special name for what you are?*"

"*Fylgjur is what we are called.*"

My lips pursed, "*Felgej—I can't even think it let alone say it. Is there a translation?*"

He huffed, "*Guardian of the Worthy.*"

The Worthy female and her Spirit *Guardian* made to leave the temple and I realized that, even though I could see the wolf, I couldn't feel it through my terbis. I couldn't feel Odarum either. I found that curious and I saved that bit of information to ask Odarum later.

The female turned her head to look at me and raised her chin in acknowledgment. I returned the gesture. No matter where we came from before, we had both gone through the Trial and were deemed Worthy. A title deserving of respect.

When the doors opened, I could see a glimpse of the Sages lining the top of the steps outside, facing the temple where two other returned contestants stood before them. Both with

Spirit animals. A slight breeze entered the temple and with it, an intoxicating but faint scent of cedar, bergamot, and something else that nearly had my eyes rolling into the back of my head. I rapidly blinked away the intrusive thoughts.

Odarum bobbed his head and nudged me toward the doors, ruffling his feathers as we exited Odes's Temple and stepped up with the others. I stood next to the female with the wolf. Next to her were two males, one with a Spirit that had a lion's body and a bird's head and wings, and the other with a large snake, bigger than I had ever seen, with fangs so long that they rested outside its mouth and past its jaw. I shuddered. These creatures were the things of nightmares.

One of the male Sages, the same one who spoke upon the dais inside just days ago, stepped forward. He made a long look up and down the line of the four contestants who had returned and were all in some way battered and beaten. When his gaze landed on me, his eyes widened and flicked between Odarum and I before turning forward again.

"Returned Worthy." He bowed his head quickly. "You have completed the Trial of the Gods. We give thanks to—"

"*Where is everyone else? The others who completed the Trial?*" I said to Odarum through the bond, not paying attention to the Sage. I quite liked speaking through my mind without anyone else hearing.

"*They were brought back once the Gods refused them. Plus one other.*"

A failed contestant.

"—only three of you will challenge, being that one of you has been chosen by *Kleio*." The male Sage, as well as everyone else, looked directly at me, followed by whispered murmurs from the Sages and the Worthy alike. One Sage in particular, a female with white hair, glared at me with malice in her eyes. I ignored her.

"Worthy Kya," the male continued. "You have no challenger, as your God has never before chosen. You and your Spirit are free to go." He turned away from me and addressed the other Worthy. "As for the rest of you, your challenges will take place immediately. Please make your way to the rings along the edge of the Rip. The sitting Worthy are waiting for you."

In one swift motion, all of the Sages turned on their heels and made their way down the steps with the Worthy following behind. I hesitantly walked down the marble steps, making to head to my tent and retrieve my horse to go home. Odarum walked beside me.

When I reached the bottom and stepped onto the grass, some of the Sages gathered around me. They crowded and bombarded me with questions I had no answers to.

"What was Kleio like?"

"Did she say why she chose you?"

"Was she magnificent?"

"What gifts did she grant you?"

"Did she speak or is she actually silent?"

The sound of all their voices rose to a dull roar and blended together. My breathing quickened. I didn't like the attention. I didn't like being in the spotlight when I was so used to staying in the shadows. Is this what the rest of my life would be like as a Worthy? Never again invisible to the world as I had grown so accustomed to?

"Enough," the male Sage that had spoken before commanded. The Sages reluctantly dispersed back with the others up ahead. Once they all left, he offered a tight-lipped smile before turning and joining them. The sorrowful expression on his face left me confused and uneasy.

I released a shaky breath, grateful to be left alone, then continued to my tent. Their questions bounced in my head. Kleios' gifts. I would need to work on discovering what they were and train in order to master them. I had a feeling I would need all the help I could get to complete the Goddess's task.

Everyone stopped in their tracks as a female around the side of the temple began to scream. Running around frantically, her fingers were pulling at the roots of her hair. Her skin was completely covered in marks, even her face. It was the mark of a failure of the Trial—one of the Gods' punishments. Most of her screaming was incoherent but I could make out one phrase she repeatedly shrieked at the top of her lungs.

"MAKE IT STOP."

I recognized that voice. It was the Torx female who had strung up that male to the tree. The one who tried to kill Njall and I. I had thought she died.

"*The failure,*" Odarum said beside me, watching the female.

We remained frozen as we watched the torture tear her mind apart. I couldn't fathom what she was seeing as she hallucinated her worst nightmares and greatest fears—a punishment from the Gods that would last for the rest of her life.

She won't last long. They never do.

I was right. Unable to bear the torment any longer, the female ran straight for the edge of the Rip and gave her soul back to the Gods. I looked away just before I felt her step off the edge of the world. Even though the female was vile, no one deserved that kind of death. The sentence for failure in something we had no say in competing in in the first place never sat well with me. This was their own form of damnation.

One thing still bothered me that I couldn't let go. I ran ahead, Odarum staying behind, and approached one of the Sages at the end of the group. I was glad to be able to run again without panting for air or the pain in my leg.

"Sage, if I may have a word," I said to the pale male. He stopped and turned to face me as he offered a bright, toothy smile.

"Of course! What can I do for you?"

"The other contestants, the ones who returned, was Njall of Oryn one of them?" I needed to know. The last time I saw Njall he was badly injured, and an arrow was headed straight for him before I was taken from the Woltawa Forest.

"I'm afraid that I don't know their names. The Spirits tell us only of those that are Worthy. We don't even know who all perished in the Trial." He placed a hand on my shoulder.

"You mean to tell me that the Sages don't even bother to take record of who entered the Trial?" I crossed my arms and offered a stern look.

Absurd. Absolutely absurd. Scholars would never be so negligent as to not even document the names of the contestants.

"It does not matter to the Sages who enter the Trial. Only the Worthy who return." His voice was apologetic.

I took a deep breath. "How many returned?"

His face turned downcast. "Not counting the Worthy, such as yourself, five completed the Trial. Plus the…failure."

I huffed in disbelief.

Only five out of nineteen.

In the shape he was in, it was unlikely that Njall was one of them.

"And where are the returned now?" There was still a chance, and I'd like to see for myself.

"After their marks were removed, they departed."

It was the one thing that I couldn't decide how I felt about. Most of the Trial made me furious—but, at least, not all the contestants shared the same fate as those who failed. If you passed but weren't deemed Worthy, you were still allowed to live. Growing up, I couldn't decide what I wanted more. If I wanted to make it out alive and be able to live a normal life, or if I wanted to be Worthy. Most saw the removal of their marks as cruel. They believed it was their own form of punishment for not being chosen—having them removed hid the evidence of what we were forced to endure. It was as if the Gods were ashamed and wanted nothing more to do with us, and now that the Sage admitted to not even bothering to record everyone's names, I was starting to agree.

"How long ago?" Frustration was beginning to seep out of me.

"I beg your pardon?"

"How long ago did they leave?"

The Sage swallowed. "Last night. Before dusk."

"We were still in the forest last night." I shook my head.

He gave that sad smile again. "They arrived nearly a day before you."

My mouth fell open and I whipped my head to Odarum.

"*I was in Hylithria for an entire day?*" My mental voice screeched down the bond. It had only felt like a few hours in the Spirit realm.

"*Time is perceived differently in different realms. This should not be surprising.*"

"*Right. Because fae know so much about time in other realms.*" If he noticed my sarcasm, he didn't show it, and he didn't respond to my retort.

I turned back to the male.

"Is there anything else I can help you with, Lady Kya?"

"She is no Lady," a female Sage, the same one who was glaring at me earlier, said before I could respond as she walked up from behind the male. "She was chosen by Kleio, and therefore has neither lands nor people. As for your friend, I personally removed the marks of the returned and there was no one by the name of Njall."

Her voice was light and sweet, but I could hear the mocking tone hidden underneath it. I wanted to punch her petite little nose and watch the blood stain her white robes.

I looked her slim body up and down, from her white hair to the odd burn on her dainty wrist. A slight hint of cedar and bergamot scented off of her, and my vision turned red with fury. I took a step back and shook my head, trying to gather myself.

What is it with this smell that has such a strong effect on me?

"You may return with the others now. I'll handle this," she said to the male before turning back to me as he scurried off.

I scowled at her. I didn't know why, but I did not like her.

"An honorable feat, becoming Worthy. And a greater one at that, being chosen by Kleio." Her fake admiration was getting under my skin and pissing me off.

"What do you want?" I said coldly.

"You may be revered for being the first to be chosen by the Silent God, but I would advise that you keep a low profile and steer clear of the other Lords and Ladies. Never before has there been a Worthy with no Nation to rule. They'll see you as a threat, and won't hesitate to eliminate it."

I opened my mouth to tell her to go fuck herself, but she turned and walked away before I had the chance.

The Sage's words weren't wrong. I hadn't ever thought about what would happen if Kleio chose a contestant to be Worthy, and what would happen to them if she did. I was a Worthy with no lands. I had no home to protect and rule. But I still had a purpose. I had a task to complete.

Restore the balance so they may return.

I added that to the things I needed to ask Odarum about later. I was too tired to think about it at that moment. I wanted a bed and a bath. And I desperately needed to clean my teeth as I could feel grime all over the inside of my mouth.

Once I was back at my tent, I replaced my dirty, torn clothing with a clean set but stopped when I saw my mark. It was different from before. Having memorized every line and swirl on my forearm, the mark now extended up to my shoulder and a display of symbols was now entwined throughout the black design. It was meant to separate those newly born with the mark and those who completed the Trial and were deemed Worthy. Your original mark remained, but the God or Goddess that chose you added more. It was an extension of Kleio. For several minutes, I stared at the new symbols, completely mesmerized, before I finally finished getting dressed. I stepped out of the tent just as I was putting on my long sleeve jacket.

"Do not hide your Worthy marking. Display it with pride." Odarum tilted his head at me.

I paused, contemplating taking the advice of my guardian and showing the symbols of my triumph—which I was proud of—or heeding the warning of the female Sage and hiding it. The side of my lips tilted up slightly and I removed the jacket.

Shouts and grunts, coming from the other side of the compound, caught my attention and my face fell. A sick feeling twisted in my stomach, accompanied by the burning in my chest. The challenges had started.

I couldn't help myself as my feet made their way through the tents, just close enough so that I could see from a distance. All three challenges were occurring at the same time. Why? I had no idea.

There were three semi-circle rings, each ending at the edge of the Rip. A Sage announced each one and I was finally able to put a face with the name of each Worthy. The one on the left had the Lord of Gaol, Jymar, pitted against one of the male contestants from Torx, the one with the serpent Spirit and who was clearly outmatched. I recognized him as the first jumper into the Rip.

The middle challenge ring had the Lady of Dusan, Zana, the oldest Worthy in the realm, challenging against the female contestant. I found it curious that both were female.

Perhaps Udon prefers a Lady to rule his Nation.

The ring on the right had the Lord of Ulrik, Hamal, fighting poorly against the other male contestant from Oryn that had the lion-bird Spirit, which Odarum had explained was called a griffin.

Neither of the challenges took long, a few minutes at most, and each one was a testament to the strength of the winner, with the exception of one. Lord Jymar beat his contestant incessantly, showing no mercy, even as the Torx male begged, before he shoved him over the edge.

The hissing screech of his bonded Spirit serpent ripped through the air before it disappeared. I didn't know what it was like for the Worthy and their Spirit to have their bond broken. But surely, with something so transcendently seared into their soul, it felt like death itself.

"Qaala will live. It is a tragic loss once your Worthy dies as it shreds the bond, but that is why the challenge occurs so soon after the Trial. The bond is still weak and does not harm the Spirit too greatly," Odarum said. It eased my heartbreak for the serpent but only a fraction.

Jymar, stalked out of the ring, still Lord of Gaol.

The challenge that earned my respect the most was the one between Lady Zana and the female contestant. Zana didn't fight. She didn't even try. Perhaps it was due to the fact that she was older in age or perhaps it was due to something else, but she held out her arms, palms facing the sky. With a prayer to Udon, she willingly forfeited by walking over the edge of the Rip of her own volition, with a smile on her face. While it was uncommon, occasionally a Lord or Lady would forfeit their challenge and fall to their death. Returning their magic, their soul, to the realms and keeping the balance.

"Lady Asmen of Dusan," one of the Sages announced. Asmen looked shocked, relieved, and saddened all at the same time as tears streaked down her face.

I turned away, I didn't need to see the rest. I had already witnessed enough death for one day. As I walked back to my tent, I felt the opponents of the other challenge. I felt the male contestant as he kicked Lord Hamal so hard that it sent him skidding across the ground to the edge. I felt him dangle by the tips of his fingers before he fell into the void of Odes's grave before I heard the announcement of the new Lord Voron of Ulrik.

I gathered my belongings, packed up my tent, and saddled my horse. Odarum stayed beside me the entire time. We left and headed to the only home I knew—the burning inside of me remained.

Chapter Eighteen

RYKER

Theron Traveled us back just inside the gates of the Oryn Palace in the capital Voara, the glow of the setting sun illuminating the gray stone walls. We appeared on the lawn and I immediately stormed up the steps through the crowds of my people, frantic and scared. They bowed as I passed by. I never closed the gates on them. The palace belonged to the citizens just as much as it belonged to me.

A female gently brushed her fingers against my arm. "Lord Ryker, please, my family. They were in the village—" she said between soft sobs. My chest tightened.

I placed my hand on her shoulder. "I'm sorry, Nephin. I've only just arrived. Please, come inside, and after I speak with my advisor, I'll come and find you." I had to figure out what in the After happened first, but I didn't want to tell her that I had no idea.

She nodded quickly, tears still streaming heavily down her face as she started making her way through the crowded palace doors. There were too many people I ruled over to know everyone by name, but I made it a point to not forget someone once I met them. I remembered meeting Nephin and her husband several years back with their two small children. A pit formed in my stomach thinking of what could have happened to them…

Pushing open the double doors to the palace, I went inside. People were everywhere in the great hall. Citizens were sitting all along the perimeter of the expansive room while volunteers were assisting them with injuries and giving out blankets.

What is happening?
I gazed around the room, searching for my advisor and second in command. I spotted him talking with a group on the other end of the hall near the stone staircase and made my way over to him.

"Mavris." My deep voice boomed over the commotion. His head shot up and he briskly walked over to me, weaving between people.

He bowed at the waist. "Lord Ryker."

I nearly rolled my eyes at the formal greeting, but I kept my face hard. "Care to tell me what is happening?"

He squared his shoulders. "Of course my Lord. Although it may be best to do it in private." Mavris kept his face stoic while his silver eyes bored into mine with concern. Not for me, but for the people. His light brown hair was tied at the back of his neck and his court attire was in pristine condition. While he looked stately and kempt, his eyes reflected his exhaustion and distress.

I nodded before turning and made my way up the stairs, Mavris following behind closely. On the second level, we walked down the long corridor, lined with sconces that I lit with my flames before reaching the wooden double doors to my formal study.

Mavris had barely closed the doors behind him before I spun on my heel to face him.

"Mav, what the fuck is going on? Why is half of Voara in the palace?" My mask having fallen, I could finally be myself—I always could be with him.

He leaned his back against the door and his head made a light thump against it as he ran his hand over his face.

He let out a sharp exhale. "It's bad, Ryk. Really fucking bad."

I took a breath and mentally braced myself. *If he thinks it's bad…*

"The southern village of Mirren is gone," he said in a pained sigh. I closed my eyes, knowing what he was about to say next. "It was destroyed by the Glaev."

I walked over to a cushioned sitting chair by the fireplace and slumped down into it, my elbows rested on my knees and my face in my hands.

"Holy Cethar. How many were lost?" My voice was solemn.

"Almost all of them. The only remaining survivors are downstairs. The rest are family or friends looking for information from those still…missing." Mavris sat in the matching chair across from mine.

I removed my hands from my face and snapped my head up to him, my eyes wide with horror.

"When did this happen?" I demanded.

"Yesterday."

The day my mate was chosen.

We stayed quiet for a few moments as I took this all in. Hundreds of males, females, and children…gone. My lands had several areas of decimation from the Glaev, but never a loss so great. My eyes narrowed as the words of Vicria repeated in my mind.

"…your Nation will suffer more than it already is."

"She knew," I snarled as I stood, the fireplace igniting instantly with my temper. For years, Nations blamed other Nations for the plague—claimed it was some kind of rival attack and had resulted in many conflicts and wars between them.

Mavris squinted. "Who?"

"Vicria. She told me that Oryn was suffering and that I needed to return." I wanted nothing more in this moment than to burn her alive, but I knew that would only cause more disruption to the balance.

Sages had a heightened spiritual link to the realm, giving up their magical abilities in sacrifice for the connection. Killing a Sage was a horrendous crime, resulting in the murderous fae being given back to the Gods, given that both the Spirits and Gods have such a symbiotic relationship. There must always be balance. But at that moment, I was questioning whether or not the consequences would be worth it.

"How…how would she know? Wasn't she there the entire time?" Mavris's eyes tracked me as I paced back and forth.

"I don't know. But she knew. She was adamant about me leaving and…" I shook my head.

My mate.

I hadn't yet told my brother that the mating bond had enacted and that I knew who it was—sort of—and that we had been threatened with yet another trial to take it away. I felt for it, the bond, just to make sure that it was still there. I needed to be sure that it was. Now that I had it, I never wanted to let it go. And I wanted *more*. It was faint, too faint. But it was there. I was certain.

"And what?"

I contemplated telling him for a moment, but ultimately decided against it. "Nothing we need to worry about right now." My people needed me and there was nothing I could do when she was in another realm. "Give the survivors anything they need. Anything at all. Redirect all workers in the palace to assist them. Bring in as many healers as you can for the injured. If they're not too traumatized, ask them for a recount of the event. The people can remain in the palace as long as they need."

Mavris stood as I continued, "And send a team to the perimeter of the Glaev to search for more survivors in the area. Where is Hakoa?" I paced to my desk in front of the windows, the morning light reflecting off the mountains.

"He's already there with several Noavo warriors."

"Good." I stood at my desk and studied the map of the continent laid out on top of the wood. From Voara, the southeastern village of Mirren was a two days' journey. Hakoa was the leader of my army, the Noavo warriors, and my oldest friend. He and the warriors were a force to be reckoned with their vast numbers and brute strength, not to mention fiercely loyal. But they were slow in traveling.

"I'll go down and assist with the survivors. We have plenty of resources to accommodate all of them and anyone else Hakoa finds." He headed for the door but stopped just before opening it. "Will there be anything else, Lord Ryker?"

This time I didn't hide my eye roll. "Yes." I had another task in mind, one I had put off for too long, and I needed someone swift and agile. The Noavo warriors wouldn't do. "Send for Arra."

He gave a knowing smile and bowed before leaving me alone in my study.

What good did it do being a powerful Worthy, a Lord, if my greatest enemy was something intangible and had been a mystery for a hundred years? I ran my hands through my hair, pulling at the roots. I shook it off, hoping I would have answers soon.

Bending over the desk, I jotted down instructions on a piece of parchment. It was detailed enough so that I would get what I needed, yet open enough so that Arra could complete the task without much restriction. I finished and folded the paper right before the doors opened again.

When Arra came in, I gestured for her to sit across from me.

"Glad to see you're not dead. Did you challenge?" she asked.

"Not this time." I blew out a breath and leaned forward. "I can go into details later but right now, I have a mission for you."

I handed her the parchment. She opened it and read it quickly before folding it again and placing it in her lap.

"We'll need a few weeks," she said with a nod.

"That's fine. Anything else?"

"Can you make Theron come with us?" she asked jokingly.

The side of my lip twitched. "Highly unlikely."

"Worth a shot." She shrugged and stood to leave.

"Arra," I said just before she reached the door. "I don't think I need to stress to you just how important this is. Lives depend on it. The Nation depends on it."

"I understand," she replied with a curt nod before walking out and shutting the door behind her.

She could do it. I knew she could.

I worked late into the night, helping gather and disperse supplies to the survivors and planning for further fallout from the Glaev, before I went to my rooms on the top level of the palace. My mate haunted my mind along with everything else. But a hint of the bond tugged at my soul for her, clouding my thoughts of anything else.

I ran a cold bath to clear my head and shock the hardness from my cock—not that it helped much. Even realms away, the bond enacted my primal drive to be with her and claim her.

Sleeping was a troublesome task. I couldn't help but think of those pine green eyes looking up at me with those plump lips wrapped around me. Wondering what my name from those lips would sound like, with my face buried in her, ravaging and ruining her.

Fuck this is wrong.

But I couldn't help it. I closed my eyes and pulled on myself as I imagined her head bobbing up and down between my legs.

I imagined the feel of her hair between my fingers as I held the back of her head and pushed her down to take me to the back of her throat until I came.

I cleaned myself up and lay back down with my arms behind my head. Staring at the ceiling, I wondered what my mate was like. I wanted to know everything about her, besides what I already did. My thoughts drifted aimlessly, but eventually I drifted off into a fitful slumber.

Mine.

I woke instantly, my heart beating heavily in my chest and a burn from the newly formed bond searing inside of me. Father had said that the sensation was unmistakable and he was right. The feeling was embedded in my soul.

I didn't need a mirror to know that the usually muted silver of my eyes was now glowing, and tendrils of my shadows drifted across the floor. The smell of char filled my nose. I released my grip from the sheets to find them scorched where I tightly held them.

I shook my head and internally scowled at myself. I refused to become like the other mated males and turn into some feral animal. That wasn't what I wanted. That wasn't what she deserved.

Inconveniently timed, there was a knock at my bedroom door. I took a few deep breaths, composing myself so that my eyes would dim back to their original state, just before Mavris opened the door. He paused as he made to enter, looking at the shadows blanketing the floor. He glanced at me, his eyes eyebrows raised in question.

I withdrew them. "What is it, Mav?" My words were clipped and my tone irritated.

"I was only coming to tell you that the Vaavi have been dispatched. Arra is personally overseeing the unit," Mavris said as he walked to the end of the bed. I threw off the covers and swung my legs over the edge before walking over to my wardrobe. "Ryk, what's going on? Your sheets… Your shadows."

I pulled my arms through the sleeves of my shirt and sighed as I began working the buttons. "My mate has just returned from Hylithria. She's a Worthy."

"Oh shit," he breathed. He paused for a moment. "When did the bond enact?"

I closed my eyes for a moment and breathed deeply. "Yesterday. Before Theron brought me back."

"Why the fuck didn't you say anything last night?"

I turned to face him. "Because I was dealing with the Mirren survivors. It was more pressing at the time." I had wanted to tell him last night—I told him nearly everything about my life.

"You don't think that your *mate* is pressing?" His mouth fell open in shock.

"Do *not* speak of her," I snarled at him for mentioning her and insinuating that she wasn't already important to me. I cringed at myself for getting so furious. I knew that it was the unsealed-bond causing me to be temperamental and possessive, just due to the fact that Mavris was a male.

I pinched the bridge of my nose and sighed. "Of course she is. But she was not in our realm when I first felt the bond. And there is still no guarantee that she will pass the challenge—if she's challenged. I didn't see the purpose in mentioning her until I was certain."

He gave me a mocking smirk. "She's on the other side of the continent and you're already losing it." He paused and tilted his head to the side. "How do you know who she is?"

"I saw her," I said softly.

I recalled the events of my time at the Temple of Odes. About how I had a feeling about the female but didn't understand it at first.

"Why didn't the bond snap into place when you first saw her?"

"She hadn't yet passed the Test of Fate." It was undecided by the Gods until Galadynia had seen into her soul, until her fate had been sealed.

Does she understand what is happening? Did she feel it just as intensely as I had? Does she even want this…

Mavris watched as my mind started to spiral and his smile fell. "You're going to have to find her before the bond takes over and you have no control left. From the looks of it, sooner rather than later."

I shook my head. "I need to be here. I need to help my people to get through this tragedy." Gods, this couldn't have come at a worse time.

He huffed a humorless laugh. "You aren't going to be helpful to anyone if the mating bond hasn't been initiated and you damn well know it. Would it be beneficial for you to relieve some of the…urges you're having, with someone else?"

The low growl that emanated from my chest made him flinch.

"Forget I suggested that." He held up his hands and took a step back.

Mavris was right. The bond would take over more and more until it would completely control me, forcing me to find my mate. I needed to be here but I also needed to find her, and quickly. She would have the chance to reject me, to deny the bond if she chose, if the Sages convinced her to do so. But it wouldn't be easy. Denying the bond meant denying the Gods—it was damn near impossible. And if she didn't want it, I wouldn't force it.

My mate.

I met Mavris's stare. "You're right. But there's more to it."

Mavris listened intently, and his face fell further and further until it morphed into outrage as I told him of the panel to decide the outcome of our mating. He didn't speak for several moments after I finished relaying the demands of the Worthy and Sages.

"This is bad. If one of you doesn't deny the bond, do you understand what they'll do if you don't accept the Raith and they forbid your mating?"

"Nothing good," I laughed humorlessly.

"They'll order the *Nex.*"

I closed my eyes and sighed. "I know."

The Nex—execution by a blood wielder, and a horrendous death. I would rather throw both of us off the edge of the Rip than for either one of us to endure that excruciating end.

"Ryker," Mavris said sternly. I opened my eyes to look at my brother. "Go find her."

Without arguing, I pulled an emergency pack from the bottom of my wardrobe. "You'll have to take care of things here while I'm away." I slipped on my boots and laced them. "I'll begin formulating preliminary treaties for the new Worthy once I confirm who they are. In the mean time, I want you to identify all of the areas that have the capacity to take refugees and compile a list. When I return, we'll go over it and begin discussions with any that wish to relocate and provide them the assistance to do so."

Mavris nodded and crossed his arms. He could handle it, I had no worries about that.

"*Theron.*"

Silence passed for a few moments before he grunted in response in my mind.

"*I need you to Travel me somewhere.*"

"*I am busy. I will find you when I return. Do not bother me before then,*" he snapped. He was always a temperamental bastard. That or he just didn't like me.

My mate would not stay at the Rip long after she challenged—if she survived. But I would know it if she hadn't. I would have felt it. I needed to travel quickly, and I had a means to do so. Not as fast as Theron but fast enough.

I stood and walked out of my room, heading down the long hall. Mavris bowed as I left. I rounded the corner and nearly bumped into Fahmor, one of the administrators that worked in the palace.

"Lord Ryker! So sorry. I was just looking for you. Some of the—" He stopped when I put my hand up, smiling warmly.

"Forgive me Fahmor, but I must leave." His eyes noted the pack in my hand. "Mavris will be tending to my affairs until I return. He is in my bedchamber if you need to speak with him. I will return soon."

He followed as I continued down the stone hallway, bright with the light from the many large windows along the walls, to the glass doors at the end, leading out to a balcony. I opened the double doors and was met with the chilled breeze from the mountains. Even in the summer months, Oryn never got hot.

"Where are you going?" he asked, his eyes wide.

I walked to the end of the balcony, where there was a gap in the stone railing and turned to face him, my heels just over the edge. At this distance, the trees on the ground below seemed like nothing more than sticks.

A dark smile crossed my lips. "Hunting," I said, before I leaned backwards and fell over the edge.

Chapter Nineteen

KYA

"Look, the mare's old. She doesn't need to be making such a long journey. Let me free her and relieve her from having to carry me back to Ilrek." I jutted out my bottom lip into a dramatic pout.

"*You are the one who brought her, are you not? If she was too old, you should not have made such a decision.*" Odarum wasn't budging on the subject, no matter how hard I pushed.

I groaned as I leaned back in the saddle atop the chestnut mare. It would be much faster if he would have just Traveled us to Ilrek or even let me ride him as he flew. The prospect of flying was something that sounded both exhilarating and terrifying. But after practically begging him for the past day, he still wouldn't agree to it. Odarum walked next to me and the mare, his wings folded to his sides. He was almost twice as big as my horse and I knew that his long legs had to shorten their strides in order to keep her stubbornly slow pace. The trip back was taking nearly twice as long as when we had traveled to Dusan for the Trial. Perhaps I had pushed her too hard on the journey and even a few days' rest wasn't enough.

"Wouldn't you rather get there sooner? At this rate, it'll take four more days just to reach the Riyah border." I was becoming irritated with both of them. The mare, for refusing to go any faster, and Odarum for not helping.

"I am in no rush. And I enjoy the pace of a walk. Have you not given her a name?"

"No. Just...mare."

"You should name her. It is the respect and honor of a rider."

I pondered for a moment. I had thought of naming her, but with everything that had happened lately it wasn't exactly at the forefront of my mind.

"Quilla," I said, patting the horse on the neck over her long mane. She perked up and even quickened her step at the sound of her new name.

"Good. And you should speak through your mind. You need to work to build upon the bond with me," Odarum said.

I mumbled a curse under my breath.

"There. Happy now, you stubborn ass?"

He jerked his head up and looked at me in what I assumed was offense to my retort. *"I am no ass. My form is that of a horse...with wings."* He added on that last bit.

I chuckled, and he turned his head forward again. I thought of what he had said to me yesterday before we left the temple grounds, that I needed to work on discovering the magic granted to me by Kleio. And that by working with him, his gifts to me would begin to manifest.

I didn't understand how I was supposed to discover them. I didn't feel any different, besides the burning in my chest, and nothing unexplainable had occurred. I had doubted that Kleio had gifted me anything, though I also had no idea how to tell. My terbis felt the same, I couldn't move things with my mind, and as far as I was aware, I didn't have unfathomable strength. The Worthy were all granted different magical abilities, and it wasn't the same from each God every time. With each new Worthy, they had new and different magic.

On top of my newly gifted magic from Kleio, I also had my gift from Odarum to figure out. With every Spirit animal, the Worthy was able to partially shift into their form. It was a lot and almost overwhelming to think about.

And I needed to figure out mine.

"Do you already know what magic I'll get from you? Or what I'll be able to shift?" I asked as we walked through the grassy field.

"*I do not know what you will shift from me. I have never been a Fylgjur and it could be different with each one anyway.*" I nodded as he continued. "*The Spiritual magic you received from me will manifest once you are ready.*"

"Why can't you just tell me what it is? I don't understand the purpose of keeping this information from me." His vague answers were becoming increasingly frustrating.

He stopped and turned to me. I pulled on the reins to bring Quilla to a stop as well. "*You are correct, you do not understand. You must discover it for yourself. I do not have a choice in what I have given you, and I do not know which you will receive. It is a manifestation of myself just as it is with the shifts.*" I recoiled at his harsh tone, his deep voice thundering down the bond through my head. "*Obviously you have not gained my patience,*" he grumbled, with what I assumed was a glare, before continuing to walk again.

I deflated inwardly as I nudged my horse to walk as well. Odarum was right, I was being impatient. But I couldn't help feeling like I was running out of time. I had a feeling like something was coming. Something big. I couldn't explain it. And I could still feel the burning inside of me and it was really starting to piss me off that it hadn't lessened.

Despite having completed the Trial—what I had always seen as my end—I still felt like something was coming. I had thought, perhaps, that the feeling of death shadowing me would have ended when I was chosen. But it hadn't. I could still feel it licking at my heels, sitting just at the edge of my peripheral.

We continued to walk for hours until we came upon a small lake on the outskirts of a forest. We decided to rest there, allowing my horse to graze and drink after I dismounted and removed her saddle. I set up my tent underneath a large tree and sat against the trunk with my palms against the ground, eyes closed in concentration.

I felt Quilla's hooves as she walked through the tall grass. Deer and other animals were in the distance, deep within the woods behind me. Thankfully, I didn't feel any large creatures or fae around and I opened my eyes to the field and lake before me. I still didn't feel Odarum through the ground, just like the other Spirits from the Temple. They were huge in comparison to their mortal counterparts, and it made me curious as to other Spirits.

"What other species of Spirits are there? I've seen descriptions of some of the Worthy's Spirit guardians and I know about you and the big wolf, the griffin, and the serpent, but are they all similar to the animals in this realm, Taeralia? It's so different. I can feel the Spirits in the living things around us, but those don't have a physical form." I spoke through the bond, hoping that would please him enough to answer me.

Many Spirit animals have been recorded, but most were never actually seen unless they were with their Worthy. Until I met Odarum, I had never personally seen one. He turned to look at me from the other side of the small lake between us.

"No. Spirits have the bodies of creatures that are not of this realm. Though many of the animals here have a similar likeness to a few of them. Such as a horse does to myself, a pegasus, but without wings. When this realm was formed, they were made in some aspect after us."

"A few of them?" I played with the grass beneath me.

"*Yes. The Spirits have many forms that are unknown to your world. Forms that your kind could not imagine.*" He turned and walked away before disappearing altogether. I took that as a sign that our conversation was over.

I pondered his words, only made more curious about the mysterious beings and their realm. As dusk arrived, I remained by my tent thinking over all that had occurred with the Trial and the Silent Goddess, and her task for me—what it meant. I replayed our conversation in my head over and over.

Restore the balance so they may return.

How?

Listen and you shall learn. Seek the truth.

How do I find it?

You already know.

Except I didn't know. And restore the balance? Of what? The realm? How the fuck was I supposed to do that? I had assumed she was referring to the Glaev, but Kleio said that it was not what it seemed. And they could return... The people of Atara.

I needed to get back to Morah and start furthering my research and talk to the Scholars who specialized in studying it. I waited for him long into the night before falling asleep.

I woke the next morning to find that Odarum still hadn't returned. Quilla stood nearby, sleeping, and I was slightly relieved that I was alone, yet disappointed since he had said he would be with me until the bond was complete.

"*We need to get moving. Where are you?*" I asked through our bond.

"*I apologize, but I cannot return right now. Continue your journey and I will find you when I can.*" His voice was like a soft whisper and I thought that he must be far away for how distant it sounded, possibly not even in this realm. I gathered my things and continued on to Ilrek.

I guess it was a good thing I didn't let Quilla go like I originally wanted.

Three days had passed and Odarum still hadn't come back. I tried to reach out to him several times, but he only told me that he was busy. To keep myself occupied, I attempted to discover my new magic when I rested at night—but nothing came of it. How was I supposed to try to make something happen when I didn't even know what *could* happen?

The fourth morning, Quilla and I crested over a hill and I could just make out the towering spires of Morah in the distance. I smiled widely, elated to be so close. As if she could sense that the end of our journey was near, the old mare finally picked up the pace into a smooth canter until we reached the outer ring of Ilrek. I deposited her at the stables and briskly made my way to the great library.

I immediately noticed the wary looks of the people in the peaceful streets. My brows furrowed. They knew who I was. Yes, I usually kept my mask up to hide my face, but it wasn't completely unusual for me to walk around without it. But I quickly realized it wasn't my face they were staring at—it was my arm.

Other than those closest to me, no one knew I was Marked. The design, now extending from my wrist to my shoulder, was unique and unmistakable. And with it now up to my shoulder and embedded with the symbol of my God, everyone would understand that I was now Worthy. The only way the citizens even knew that the Trial had begun was from the Sages or from announcements of a new Lord or Lady. Now that I was Worthy, I didn't have to worry about covering my mark anymore.

I held my head high and kept my eyes forward as I made my way to Morah. I would not cower in fear of the Lords and Ladies. I would not hide what I had accomplished.

Let them see that I am Worthy.

I had never heard so much noise within the walls of Morah. Scholars surrounded me the moment I entered, congratulating me and asking question after question. I tried to walk further into the library but they wouldn't let me pass, the excitement at one of their Roav having returned Worthy consuming them and causing them to forget their usual calm disposition. I smiled and returned their loving gestures of greeting, appeasing their questions as best I could.

I was leaning forward, trying to listen to one of the young Scholars asking about the geographical details of the Woltawa Forest, when the crowd began to part down the middle. Eamon emerged from between the Scholars, grinning from ear to ear, and he swept me into an embrace, lifting me to the tips of my toes. He set me down and released me, his eyes glistening with unshed tears of joy.

He looked at the crowd around us. "Please, everyone. I know we are all eager to speak with Kya and learn from her. I can assure you that each of the field chiefs will get the information and will relay it to you for your work through our proper protocol. But for now, let this Roav have a moment to catch her breath."

They all bowed their heads in respect before dispersing back to their sections throughout the library. Eamon turned to me and grabbed my hands, squeezing them firmly between us, his smile so wide that his eyes squinted.

"Kya…you did it. I knew you would. I am so proud of you, child."

I was smiling just as wide. "Thank you, Eamon. I'm glad to be back."

"Come, come! I will gather the field chiefs. I know you must be exhausted, but we need to debrief you while it's still fresh in your memory." He threw out his arm, gesturing toward the stairs leading to his study.

Not that I could forget so soon.

I nodded and followed but quickly stopped as my eyes caught sight of a dark-skinned male at the base of the staircase rushing toward me. My breath caught in my throat as he approached and I let out a squeal of delight as Nikan lifted me into his broad arms and spun, his face buried in the crook of my neck.

"I'll meet you in my office soon." Eamon called over his shoulder as he ascended the stairs, leaving Nikan and I to reunite.

Nikan set me down and brought his calloused hands to my face. I tilted my head to look up at his striking blue eyes. His curly black hair was shorter than the last time I saw him, now close-cropped to his head. His tall form held me close as he smiled down at me.

"I'm sorry, Kya. We left things on such bad terms, and I hated myself for it. I had to go to Bhara before you returned from your last mission then it was straight to Oryn from there. I didn't get the chance to make things right before you went into the Trial."

My brother moved his hands to my shoulders and held me at arms length. "And look at you!" He looked at my arm and beamed. "You're a Worthy! And all in one piece, thank the Gods."

Tears threatened to spill, and I blinked rapidly to keep them away. I missed him desperately and I had been worried that he would still be upset with me. Relief flooded through me, and it was almost too much to bear.

I laughed a sob, "I'm sorry too, Nik. But I'm so happy to see you."

He brought me into a warm hug and I returned it, wrapping my arms around his muscled torso. I was feeling so much. Too much. The Trial, Njall, becoming Worthy, magic I was unsure about, Kleio's demand, Nikan's forgiveness. I couldn't hold it in anymore.

Gripping the back of his shirt tightly, I buried my face in my brother's shoulder and quietly sobbed. He tensed for a second before realizing what was happening, then relaxed, brushing the back of my head with his hand. He had always been my anchor, the one that would be there to comfort and protect me, to help me pick up the pieces of myself. Though he was only thirteen years older than me, he took it upon himself to care for Malina and I like a parental figure, having lost his own parents as well as his little sister to the Glaev.

He continued his soothing strokes until I fully released my emotions, soaking his beige shirt. I released him and wiped the wetness from my face.

He gave me a soft smile. "It'll be okay. You're not alone." His repeated words from when I would cry as a child warmed my heart and I smiled again.

"I know. Thank you." I released a shaky breath.

He nodded once. "We should go to Eamon now. He'll be anxious to hear all about the Trial. Hasn't stopped talking about it since I got back." He huffed a laugh at the last part.

I could picture Eamon going on and on about what he thought was happening as he paced back and forth in his study.

"When did you get back?" We walked side-by-side toward the stone staircase.

"The day after you left for the Temple of Odes." We ascended the stairs to the level that held the High Scholar's study. "I was in Oryn and planned to meet with Lord Ryker, with the Sage and Scholar that traveled with me, but when we arrived, we were told that he had departed for the Trial initiation. I knew that meant you would be leaving soon as well…" He paused for a moment. "I was so angry with you before that moment, but once I realized you'd be going to the Trial before I could see you, I regretted our last conversation and wished I could have taken it back."

I looked to the floor and muttered, "I shouldn't have said that to you. You were right to call me out. I know you were just trying to look out for me."

Nikan and I had argued before he left on a mission, about me always going off on jobs alone and being reckless with my actions, taking justice into my own hands. He was right of course, I cared little for my safety then. Not when I had thought I might die during the Trial anyway, and I wanted to rid the world of at least some of its filth before I did.

Nikan had told me I was too brash and reckless, and I told him that he was too controlling, too uptight, and that he would never have the right to tell me what to do—but I did it in a degrading way. I was in the wrong with how I approached it and I knew it. I overreacted and regretted it the moment the words came out, but I was also too stubborn to admit that at the time. I knew that he wasn't being controlling, just protective, as always. It was something that he had never seen as an issue when it came to me and Malina. He had taken it upon himself to be responsible for us but he often took it too far. But other times, he was right. We were the only ones he had left, and he wanted to protect us—even if it was from ourselves.

"I got your letter. We were both on edge and were too harsh in the moment. You obviously don't need me to look out for you. You are more than capable of taking care of yourself." He jutted his chin out, gesturing to my Worthy mark.

"I didn't do it alone." My lips thinned into a sad smile.

My voice was solemn, thinking of Njall. Nikan nodded but he didn't say any more on the subject as we slipped through the open door to the study and were ushered to the sitting area where Eamon waited.

Nikan and I sat across from the High Scholar. I relaxed into the tufted chair and relished in the familiar smell of the study and the sounds of rustling paper of books from the Scholars working in the library. Eamon waved the waiting field chiefs, head Scholars of their sections, into the room. They each sat at the large table on the other side of the room and laid out parchment and paper. They knew not to speak or ask questions, as not to influence my recollection, and to only take notes as I disclosed the events of the Trial. I didn't know how to feel about now being a part of the history that I had read so much about. But I knew that this was important and I would do it no matter what, for them.

Eamon leaned forward and rested his elbows on his knees with a soft smile. "So, tell us. How did Kya, the daughter of no Nation, become *Worthy* of the Gods?"

Chapter Twenty

KYA

E amon, Nikan, and the Scholars quietly listened as I told them of everything that had taken place during the Trial. I started from when I arrived at the Temple grounds, describing all who were in attendance as best as I could. I summarized the first task, the Test of Loyalty, detailing notable contestants and what I saw, heard, and felt inside the Rip as well as the riddle and how I had written it on my arm in my blood—though now permanently committed to my memory.

A few of the Scholars gasped as I told of the brutal attack from the males when I first arrived. I told them of working with Njall—skipping over the moments of sharing a branch together. Once I had told them of the river creature that attacked me, they informed me that it was a newly discovered beast and as its unfortunate discoverer, I was allowed to name it—Nagasai. A few of them tensed when I relayed the attack of the Lurvinea, the thorned vines, and how it dragged Njall into suffocating mists. I told them of the male that was used as bait by the failed female and assumed dead male.

Dinner had been served in the study and I continued while we ate—I nearly inhaled it, completely famished. Eamon's eyes reflected pride when I briefed them on how we solved the riddle and found the map glowing within the side of the mountain. I went into as much detail on the map as I remembered, drawing it as best as I could. The Scholars and Eamon copied it down once I was finished. I blinked back tears as I told of the male attacking Njall and I. And when I was taken by Kleio just as I had leapt in front of the arrow, and the voice that spoke.

Confused looks passed around the room, but still no one uttered a single word while I finished telling them of Hylithria, Kleio's task, the Test of Fate at the Galadynia mirror, and Odarum, my Spirit animal. I kept the bond to myself, knowing it was to be unknown to those that were not Worthy. Though I wanted to tell them, it didn't feel right. I finished off describing the challenges and the new Worthy that were announced.

I let out a sigh of relief when Eamon dismissed the Scholars and we were alone with Nikan. I slouched in my seat, my arms hanging over the side, and I looked up to the ceiling.

"I don't think I've ever spoken that much at one time. My face hurts." I stretched out my jaw.

"I don't think you've spoken that much, period," Nikan huffed, his arms were crossed over his chest, leaning against the back of the chair.

I glanced at Eamon, whose face was pinched in thought and staring in the distance.

"Eamon? Are you alright?" It was unlike him not to join in our banter.

He blinked rapidly before meeting my stare. "Apologies. I just can't stop thinking about what Kleio said to you." My previously good mood dampened as the worries of reality rushed back into me.

"It can't be a coincidence," Eamon whispered, seemingly more to himself than to us.

"What isn't a coincidence?" Nikan's eyes narrowed as we both sat up.

Eamon shook his head. "Kleio said that the Glaev is not what it seems. Correct?"

I nodded.

"We have never known what the Glaev truly is, but the most common theory, from those that have studied it, is that it's some kind of unexplainable disease. However, there was one earlier theory several decades ago from a Scholar named Rolim Fawarin in Torx, that the Glaev was the result of a kind of magic not of this realm."

My eyebrows raised. "Like magic from the Gods? Or Spirits? What made him think it was magic and not a disease?"

"I don't know, and no one else knows the full extent of the theory either. He died and, we had thought that the information had died with him."

"*Had* thought? You no longer think this?" I tilted my head slightly.

Eamon grinned widely. "Yes."

He stood and retrieved a scroll of parchment from his desk before returning and laying it out on the table between us.

"A few weeks ago, we received word that a book in an unknown language *mysteriously* appeared, and that this anonymous founder was willing to sell it to Morah." We all knew that was code for 'most likely stolen' and Nikan and I gave Eamon a knowing look that he didn't seem to notice.

"The interesting part was that when it was examined for authenticity, there were pages of notes tucked into the creases written in the common tongue."

"What does any of this have to do with Kya finding out the truth of the Glaev?" Nikan interrupted. I understood his impatience, the High Scholar had a habit of rambling.

"I was getting to that," Eamon scoffed then cleared his throat to continue. "Several of the inserted pieces of parchment were inscribed with the author's initials: R.F." He pointed to the intake record in front of him, detailing the notes within the book.

My mouth fell open when I realized what he was insinuating, and Eamon smiled, noting my expression.

"Would you like to take a guess on *where* the book was found?" he prodded.

"Torx," I muttered.

"Exactly." He leaned back and crossed his arms with a pleased expression on his face.

"And the notes in this book contain Rolim's theory about the Glaev?" Nikan asked skeptically.

"Erm, well, we're not entirely sure. That was the next part I was getting to."

"Please do."

"Right. Well, the book arrived at Morah only a few days ago, and it had not yet had the chance to be properly examined. It was placed in the linguists' department initially to see if they could decipher the language, they didn't recognize it."

"So we need to examine it," I said. Seemed simple enough and I understood then why Eamon thought all this a coincidence.

"We can't." Eamon sighed heavily. "The book, and the notes within it, were stolen last night."

I flinched when Nikan jumped out of his seat.

"What?" he yelled. "Why didn't you tell me immediately? I could have tracked them down." The stone hearth next to us cracked when Nikan hands curled into fists.

"Nik," I warned.

"It's alright, Kya." Eamon held up his hand and Nikan sat down, his breathing heavy, I could scent the rage emitting from him. "The Scholars didn't realize it until this morning and told me shortly after they confirmed it was missing. And before you ask, yes, they were certain that it was in its proper place when they left it last night. I didn't have the chance to tell you before Kya arrived."

"I'm sorry, Eamon." Nikan bowed his head.

A moment passed as we took in this information. My mind was reeling. I couldn't understand how anyone could have done this or why. Not to mention how they knew about the book when it hadn't even been fully cataloged yet. It had to be because of the seller. No Scholar would have given out this information without understanding the full extent of the book's contents.

"How do you know the notes are about the Glaev being a magic theory? You said that it hadn't been fully processed," I questioned.

"One of the intake Scholars flipped through the notes to try to see if they could find a translation for the title, and he noticed a phrase that was mentioned several times: dark magic."

"'Dark magic'? What is that?"

"I have no idea. However, I do plan to look into it tomorrow, but we need that book back. It would help you discover the truth behind the Glaev, if this theory has any merit whatsoever," Eamon said, shaking his head.

"Alright, let me rest for the night and I'll start tracking it down in the morning at first light." I sighed. I so desperately wanted more than a single night to recuperate, but the longer I waited, the harder it would be to find. This was my job as a Roav.

"I'm coming with you," Nikan demanded.

"Excuse me? No. Out of the question," I snapped.

"Kya, obviously it was someone extremely skilled. And most likely a team. They were able to enter Morah, take the book, and leave completely undetected. That's never happened before."

"For the love of Nox, Nik, I can handle them. I'm a Worthy for fuck's sake." I stuck out my arm, gesturing to the mark extending up to my shoulder. "You just want to get your hands on the little bastards." I crossed my arms and glared at him.

"You're damn right I do. And you're out of your mind if you think I'm not coming along."

"Enough." Eamon's deep voice rumbled.

I stuck my tongue out at Nikan and he rolled his eyes.

"Kya," The High Scholar warned. "Nikan will be accompanying you. You can use all the help you can get. Not to mention, you're more recognizable now. If Nations learn that another Worthy is sneaking around on their lands, they'll think the worst and likely react to it as a threat. Nikan is going with you. End of discussion."

I groaned and rubbed my temple with my fingertips. I hadn't thought of that. Eamon's warning paired with the Sage's left my stomach feeling uneasy. If I were discovered in another Nation, they wouldn't see me as just a Roav working for Morah, but as a Worthy.

"Nikan," Eamon continued. "You are going to be there to *assist* Kya. This is her mission and she will be the lead Roav."

"Ha!" I pointed to Nikan and he slapped my hand playfully.

While I wasn't particularly excited that my brother would be joining me, Eamon was right. I also wasn't completely upset that I would get to spend some time with him. And the thought of getting to annoy him for days or weeks on end was more than appealing.

I gave him a mocking smile, and he rolled his eyes again. I could see that he was fighting a smile himself.

"I also want you to find Malina and recruit her. If she hasn't already completed her mission, she may continue it after you have completed yours." Nikan and I nodded. "Now leave, both of you. This old male has had enough excitement for one day," he said through a grin. The demanding voice of the High Scholar now replaced with the warmth of our patriarch.

One of these days, I will finally find out just how old he is. One of his many mysteries.

We stood to leave, and Eamon brought me into a firm embrace and whispered into my ear, "You are worthy in more ways than one. This title does not define you. It describes you."

I smiled up at him as he pulled away and nodded in thanks before Nikan and I both left the study. Tears pricked the back of my eyes, but I shook them away. I had already cried enough for one day.

I went to my rooms while Nikan took care of the preparations for our morning departure. My bath was hot and long, my skin pruned and the water was cold by the time I got out. I dressed in loose clothing and went out to the library to grab a few books for our journey. I hadn't read at all since I was here last, not wanting to risk the chance that I wouldn't come back to return them. I stuffed them into my pack once I got back to my rooms. I audibly sighed as I finally laid in my soft bed and snuggled into the warm blankets. My mind was too exhausted to dwell on worries weighing down on me, the light pattering of the rain against the glass walls causing my eyelids to feel too heavy to hold open. Sleep took me quickly.

Wind rushed past me, a deafening howl in my ears. Rain was stinging my face as it pelted my skin and I squinted to keep the water from my eyes. I could feel my soaked clothes weighing me down as my back muscles ached from working tirelessly to keep me above the ground. I could scarcely make out the black outline of a towering structure, reflecting the flashes of light from the storm.

Morah.

I drew closer and closer, soaring over the sleeping city below. Another flash of light. A creature with leathery appendages, as dark as the night, was coming toward me. Yet I still thrust myself closer.

The sky was illuminated with streaks of blue light violently piercing the darkness. My reflection in the inky black glass revealed that I was the creature. But where there should have been the sight of my body, it was instead that of a male carried by wings, his silver eyes flashing through the darkness.

A crackling sound startled me awake with a gasp. I clutched my chest and blinked the sleep from my eyes, perplexed by the strange dream. The male with wings and silver eyes. I had seen those eyes before from underneath a hood at the temple—a Lord.

I should have felt scared. I should have been petrified. Yet I felt oddly calm, which only added to my confusion.

Why would I dream of a Lord with wings?

I realized then that the burning sensation inside of me had started to recede, like a fire that had sated its voracious appetite, and left a swirling of smoke that was soothing and comforting. I didn't know what to make of it, but at least it was better than the continuous inferno in my chest I'd had since returning from Hylithria.

I didn't go back to sleep, too curious to stop my mind from wandering, and remained awake for the next few hours. Then dawn came, and I met with Nikan outside the doors of Morah, thankful that the storm's intensity had lessened to a downpour, then we mounted our horses and left Ilrek.

Chapter Twenty-One

RYKER

The bond did exactly what I hoped it would do—what I needed it to do.

After leaving the palace in Voara, I let the bond guide me to my mate. That constant pressure inside of me pulled me toward her, a constant nagging stretched taut that couldn't be ignored and edged on the side of pain.

Whenever I would veer off course, it would tug me back in the right direction, to Riyah. The bond was desperate to be with its other half. Nothing would stop it—would stop me. I could feel myself getting closer. The connection calmed as I closed the distance between us.

For days, I didn't stop. I couldn't. Every muscle in my body ached in protest as I pushed myself harder and farther. Until, finally, that unbearable pull eased, and I knew that I had found her.

She's here.

I dropped down, mud squelching beneath my boots. Rain poured from the storm above. My hair whipped wildly in the harsh wind as thunder rumbled. I looked up at the monumental tower before me as I stood at its base, silhouetted against the night sky with streaks of lightning to illuminate it briefly.

She's in Morah.

She couldn't have been native to Riyah, no one was born there. But even Vicria mentioned she was from Riyah. She must have abdicated her citizenship from another Nation to come here. And of all places, she had to be so close to the central location of the Sages. Though being in Morah, where no Sage would go, they wouldn't find her.

I waited atop a house across from the doors of Morah. Lying in wait, like a hunter stalking its prey. The storm had let up, but left a constant downpour that had begun to piss me off. I heated my body to keep warm, the water steaming off me. I kept hidden behind a stone chimney, peeking out to keep an eye on who came and went from the library on the other side of the gravel street. A few Scholars came and went, shielding their books rather than their heads from the rain. A hooded male exited and rushed down the street, leaving the inner ring of Ilrek.

The sky brightened the slightest bit, noting dawn had arrived. But with the cloud cover, it was still dark enough to stay concealed. I could mask my body with shadows if needed anyway. The male who had left before returned a while later with two horses and waited outside Morah. Not long after he arrived, the doors opened. Someone, cloaked and hooded, exited the library.

My heart instantly raced. My body felt electrified and my cock hardened.

It was her. My mate.

Seeing her was breathtaking. It was like finding a precious gem I'd been searching for—shining amongst the dullness of the world.

She mounted one of the horses, and the male the other. A growl rumbled in my chest, and my lips curved into a vicious sneer at the thought of another male with her. I shook my head, trying to stave off the possessive feeling the bond was forcing upon me. I braced myself against the chimney, so that I wouldn't go to her.

That wasn't what I had imagined. I thought that I could find her and control myself long enough to talk to her. But it hadn't occurred to me that she would be with another male. And why wouldn't she have been? She was fucking gorgeous *and* a Worthy.

Seeing her here in Riyah and not in one of the other Nations meant that she hadn't challenged. And the only God that could have chosen her that didn't already have a Worthy was…shit. Kleio. I released a shaky exhale.

My mate was chosen by the Silent Goddess. The mate to mine.

It didn't make sense. Why would Kleio choose a contestant? Her lands and her people were destroyed by the Glaev. She had never chosen before when she had a Nation, but she decided to choose when she didn't? And she chose my mate, when her own mate was the God that chose me.

They had to have known. Did they do it on purpose just for that reason alone? There had never been two Worthy alive that were mates. Or was it something else?

She started riding off on her horse. With the male… She wouldn't have wanted this. She had to have felt the bond once it snapped into place. Yet she was still with someone else.

Gods, this is not how I thought this would go.

I thought for a few moments, contemplating what I needed to do next as they rode off out of sight. It took everything in me not to charge after her and claim what was rightfully mine.

Mine!

But I couldn't do that to her. I refused to force the bond on her. I wanted this to be her choice. Perhaps it was for the best. For her and for Oryn. My Nation, my people, had been threatened if I bonded to my mate. I needed her to deny it. But I didn't want

185

her to… I had wanted this for so long and it was finally within my reach. There had to be another way.

I stood facing the direction she rode. Even now as she was getting farther away, I could feel the bond urging me to go to her.

I would find another way. I had to. If she wanted this, we would find a way.

Chapter Twenty-Two

KYA

Normally, it would have taken Nikan and I two days to get to the city of Narh in Torx, but part of that journey required us to cross the Ahwey Lake. I hated water. Especially after my encounter with the Nagasai in the river during the Trial. And even though it would add additional days to travel around it, I refused to cross it.

Nikan knew this and tried to convince me that I should confront my fear to get to Narh faster. But this wasn't something that I would budge on. Unless it was my bath, I began avoiding the element at all costs. Even then, I wouldn't fully submerge myself.

Between his grumbling, he told me his recent assignment of working with the Sages and Scholars and traveling to Oryn. I tried to listen, but half of the time my mind was elsewhere. There was too much to think about. Too much to process. And I was getting increasingly irritable. I wanted to go back. I thought perhaps I was simply just tired and I needed a long rest, but it felt different. It was something I didn't know how to explain. It felt like when Odarum called to me through our minds, yet different.

I had reached out through that light inside me and tried to talk to him but he remained silent. I tried not to worry about it. He said that he would find me when he returned. And I wasn't sure if this was normal of him to just up and disappear like this for days on end. I assumed it was but it still bothered me that he wasn't around like he had assured me he would be.

Nikan and I talked about what gifts I could have. I wished that I could have had some sort of guidance on how to even approach it. I tried everything to manifest my magic, but I didn't understand how it worked. It wasn't like my terbis where it came naturally. Other than bed-sinking-pranks, I had very little manipulation abilities, and I had to use an extreme amount of concentration and exert myself in order to do it. Moving and shaping…wasn't my greatest strength.

I would have liked to have had something tangible and useful to others rather than just myself. That's what the purpose of the magic was, right? So that I could have used it to protect a Nation.

I knew of no one alive that had honed the ability to feel vibrations through the ground. Though there had been records of past wielders having such abilities, none were alive that we knew of—besides me. Without a master to teach me, I had to teach myself. Over the years, Nikan and I would train with what little manipulation abilities I did possess. I could never do anything more than a novice, and people seemed to think that I was just cursed with weak abilities. But I never saw it that way.

Nikan and I had stopped for the night on the eastern side of the Nahale Forest just before dusk. As we unsaddled our horses, I told him of my concerns about manifesting my new magic. He knew nothing of the topic but offered to help.

"Let's start with the basics of manipulation to see if you can access it that way and we can go from there," Nikan said after leaving our horses under the shade of the trees. "Manipulation is different from sensation. Both take great amounts of concentration, but I'm guessing that it's a different form of concentration. How do you hone into the vibrations?"

I thought for a moment, thinking of how to explain it. "I don't know honestly. I just do. I can feel a vibration and focus to make the sensation more intense, so that's what my main focus is on, while dulling other sensations if needed. It just comes naturally to me." I shrugged.

"Manipulation is definitely different. It takes full, uninterrupted concentration. At first. The more you practice, the easier it comes and eventually becomes second nature. Like wielding weapons, with time, it feels like it's a part of you," he said.

At that, I took my dagger from my thigh and threw it as it spun end over end until it embedded itself into the tree, narrowly missing the top of Nikan's head. It was second nature to me. I barely had to think about it anymore.

"Exactly." He smiled.

Nikan was the one to train Malina and me with both our weapons and our wielding. He would push us harder and harder, no matter how skilled we were. And after years of training, finally mastering our particular abilities, we would all push each other. Even though Nikan and Malina didn't need the training for the Trial, they needed to be able to protect themselves, myself, and each other. Without having the people of a Nation, we only had one another to rely on.

"Try to feel for it, whatever it is, and concentrate on that. Does anything seem different for you since you were deemed Worthy?" he asked.

"Sort of. I can feel…something. But I can't quite grasp that feeling. I don't know how to explain it."

"Good. Just try to center yourself with that feeling, even if you can't grasp it yet. I don't know how magic from the Gods works exactly, but it's a start," he said.

I nodded as I took a deep breath in and slowly let it out, feeling for the wispy lights inside me. But after a few hours and multiple attempts, nothing happened.

"Don't worry about it. You'll get there. All the Worthy do eventually. There's a reason they wait for their magic to manifest before being sworn in as Lord or Lady," he said with an encouraging smile.

"*That's* why they wait?" I asked.

"Well yeah. They can't exactly protect and rule over their Nation much without it."

"So…who rules until then?" I sat down by our packs, resting my forearms on my knees.

"Technically they still rule, but the Nations are vulnerable until then at least." He sat down beside me. "That's why, even in times of peace, their forces remain active. Especially when they get a new Worthy."

"Because if their Worthy dies, their Nation is susceptible to being overthrown by another."

"Precisely. Unless they get a new ruler."

"One voted in like Atara," I added.

Nik nodded. His eyes went distant, staring at the grass.

"Brynya was a good choice for Atara. Uncontested for what? Four hundred years?" I smiled at the memory of our passed Lady.

"Nearly half a millennium," he corrected. "People stopped challenging her after she was powerful enough to create a vortex that could level entire cities. The Atarans had finally accepted that she was the best choice as a protector with no Worthy." His smile faltered. "But she still wasn't powerful enough to save them…"

We fell into silence. Nikan and I rarely talked about Atara. Even after twenty years, it was painful to remember. His sister by blood, Tsirra, was also an air wielder, and aspired to be just like

Brynya when she was older. Every time Brynya was brought up, he thought of her. I had never met her, but I wondered what her life would have been like if it weren't cut so short.

Nikan got up and walked away, erected two tents, and went into one—where he remained. I tended to the horses and waited.

Once darkness fell, I went out into the trees to forage for the Onyx flower, finding one just as it was unfurling in the moonslight at the base of a bur oak. While I still had a surplus of the lethal liquid back at Morah, I made it a point to always gather more whenever I was traveling. Pulling on gloves, I carefully extracted the delicate petals and placed them in a glass container.

Returning to my tent, I put the filled container back in the pack with the rest of the materials in my Onyx Kiss kit. Not bothering to reach out to Odarum again, I settled in for the night, sleeping with my head sticking out of the stone tent so I could see the stars as I fell asleep.

The following morning, we trekked through the Nahale Forest along the top of the cliff over the Ahwey Lake. I rode atop a sound gelding. He was calm, responsive, and had a nice gait. Yet, I kind of missed that old mare, Quilla, and her stubbornness. I had grown rather fond of her.

Nikan and I only spoke to each other when needed and in hushed tones, not wanting to be heard from by creatures that lurked in the dense canopy and remaining on alert. But perhaps we weren't quiet enough.

There was a reason people took passage over the lake rather than around it, and it wasn't just for the convenience of getting to their destination faster. Predators lived in these woods. Territorial bears that could match a horse in speed. Wolves that hunted in packs, always hungry for their next meal. There had also been stories about large cats with fangs, too large to fit within their mouths. While nothing about them had ever been confirmed, it was said that they remained perched in the trees, stalking their prey from above.

It was confirmed now as a nightmarish, carnivorous feline dropped down between our horses.

My horse reared up on its hind legs, and Nikan's bucked and ran off into the distance. But that was a poor choice. The fanged cat became intrigued by the retreat and engaged in a chase, leaving the one who had shown a hint of defense. It snarled as it ran after them.

I kicked my horse into a sprint after Nikan. The fanged cat was incredibly fast and quickly caught up to Nikan and his horse. He drew his sword and leapt off his horse to swing at the cat when it neared, trying to pass around him to go for his horse. The horse continued to gallop through the trees away from the predator. Nikan missed the cat and compensated by quickly shifting the ground beneath it to turn it away from his horse and direct it at himself.

The fanged cat hadn't seemed interested in Nikan and attempted to pursue the larger prey of the horse, but once Nikan was between them, it switched its focus. My horse halted as we approached, and I jumped off, pulling out my daggers as I landed. My horse trotted away, but surprisingly didn't go far.

At the sound of my steps toward Nikan, the cat whipped around and turned sideways, allowing it to look at the both of us as I came up on Nikan's side, caging it in with the cliff at its back. The cat crouched down and curled its lips back, revealing a mouth full of sharp teeth. My mind flashed back to the Trial.

Just another fucking beast waiting to devour me.

Nikan stomped the ground to raise a large boulder in front of him before he thrust out his free hand in a fist. The boulder flew through the air toward the cat but it jumped, avoiding the rock and latching onto the trunk of a tree, then pushing off down on us.

Nikan and I lurched in opposite directions, rolling to a stop as the cat landed right where we were standing. I leapt to my feet and realized that I hadn't rolled far, while I could feel that Nikan had stumbled over the cliff's edge and into the lake below.

The cat was stalking toward me. Its body came up to my chest. I pulled my arm back to throw my dagger but before I could release it, Odarum appeared in front of me. Wings splayed out, Odarum looked colossal and far more intimidating than myself.

Of course it took a life-threatening situation for him to return. He was my guardian and vowed to protect me.

The cat growled and lunged for Odarum, but he didn't move. Not a single muscle twitched. My heart stopped and my breath caught. Before I could even blink, roots from the surrounding trees burst from the soil and wrapped around the cat, catching it in mid-air and suspending it above the ground in front of Odarum.

"Gods…" I breathed. My eyes bulged at the powerful magic displayed. It had to be one of Odarum's abilities. I had never seen anything like it before.

The cat yowled and thrashed against the roots, but was unable to free itself as they tightened around it. Odarum lowered his wings, the threat neutralized. He turned around to face me.

"You have not been harmed?" Odarum asked.

I shook my head, still marveling and unable to speak. I felt Nikan manipulating back up the cliff to get back to me.

"Are you going to kill it, or should I?" I asked.

"This being has done nothing to deserve death. You will not kill it," Odarum ordered.

"If you let it go, it'll just come after us again."

"It will continue to be restrained until you have safely left the forest," Odarum said.

"Thanks," I replied.

"I cannot stay. But I will return."

Seriously?

I sighed and nodded once. *"Fine."*

He stomped his hoof once and just stood there. After several moments, our horses came back, seemingly unbothered by the suspended predator who was still clawing and biting at the roots. Once the horses approached, Odarum vanished without another word.

"Good to know he'll show up when needed," I grumbled to myself and mounted my horse. I grabbed the reins of the other horse and led them toward Nikan.

"What happened?" he asked, looking around for the cat.

"Odarum showed up and took care of it. Trapped, not dead." I handed over the reins before he mounted his horse. "Let's get out of here before he releases it."

"Don't have to tell me twice." He kicked his horse and we galloped off through the trees.

It took nearly the entire day to pass through the Nahale Forest and cross into the great plains of Torx. We rested that night in the grass. Nikan erected a triangular stone shelter, and we hung the cloth to act as a door. We decided against building a fire for fear of the dry grass catching fire and spreading. We ate from the rations of dried meats and berries that we had brought in our packs, and had water from the canteens that were beginning to run low. It would last us until we could resupply in Narh, before we tracked down the seller of the ancient book.

I told Nikan more about the Trial, and I opened up about Njall and what the Sage said about me being in danger from the other Worthy—something I neglected to mention to the Scholars. I told him everything that I didn't tell them. Except for the dream of the winged Lord with silver eyes.

And why should I have mentioned it? Yet, dream or no, it still bothered me and I had thought of it often over the past few days as we rode. I felt as if I knew who it was. And those eyes. The silver eyes that saw right into me.

No. It didn't need to be mentioned until I knew what it meant.

We eventually retreated to our shelter for the night. I lay there and tried to clear my mind, but failed. The Trial. Kleio. The Glaev. Njall. Seeking the truth. My magic. Odarum. A dagger through my hand. Silver eyes. Rolim the Scholar. The soothing swirls inside of me.

I stood up and left the tent, needing the fresh air and not wanting Nikan to realize what was going on. Once I was far enough away, I fell hard to my knees, squeezing my eyes shut as I hung my head, shaking it from side to side. Pleading and desperate to stop the maddening thoughts that continued to invade my mind, I took a deep, shuddering breath, clenching my hands into the soft grass. I forced my focus to feel the thin blades of vegetation and the moisture clinging to each strand, pressing deeper until my nails dug into the rich soil underneath. A soft sob escaped from between my trembling lips. The pressure in my mind was too great to suppress and, as the tightness in my chest grew, so did the wetness behind my eyes until a tear emerged, rolling down my cheek and falling to the dew-soaked dirt.

Beneath my fingertips I felt a thump in the distance with my terbis. It felt large and heavy, but didn't move. It was far enough away that I wasn't able to tell what it was exactly but it was undeniably there. I stood and faced that direction. I couldn't see anything.

Even in the dark, I could see well. But it seemed darker in the distance, obscuring my view. I stepped forward, the grass lightly tickling my bare feet. A chill ran down my spine when all of a sudden, whatever it was simply vanished.

Chapter Twenty-Three

RYKER

I had stayed far away from my mate and the male she traveled with. I couldn't actually see them, but I could feel through the bond where she was. Occasionally drifting to nearby towns, I was able to discover which of the Nations had gained a new Worthy—not at all disappointed to discover Hamal failed his challenge—and drafted rough agreements between our Nations in the evening while my mate and the male stopped.

They had slept on the outskirts of the Nahale Forest the first night. And thank the Gods they were smart enough to not stay within the trees. Being on the forest floor was the most vulnerable place during the night.

I found it curious that they decided to go around Ahwey Lake, and not cross it. The large barges, propelled by water wielders, were built in order to allow safe passage to the other side for travelers. It took great ingenuity from terbis and air wielders to create the porous material of the barge, similar to that of pumice. Not only was it out of harm's way, it was also faster. Journeying around the lake and through the deepest parts of the Nahale Forest was reckless. But perhaps it was for a purpose.

They made their way through the dense woods on horseback. I stayed out of sight as I followed, the trees allowing me to be closer without being seen, and when they thinned I had to stay back a little farther. And I hated every minute of it. Too cowardly to approach, but also too desperate to be near my mate.

I was a Lord. I had survived the Trial of the Gods and was deemed Worthy. I had led a great Nation into prosperity, protecting them in times of war. Yet, I couldn't build the courage to even engage with that strikingly beautiful female who already held a piece of my soul.

I wanted to talk to her. To touch her.

Nearing the treeline at the end of the forest, I waited to see what direction they would go. Once they left the forest, I had to fall back farther to remain out of sight. I watched from high up in a tree, using my shadows to conceal myself until darkness fell and I could close more distance between us.

In the dead of night, the feeling of torment washed through me. And it wasn't mine.

My mate.

Unable to hold back, I had made sure to stay far enough away in that open field that neither of them would be able to see through the shadows around me. Remaining concealed, I dropped to the ground, desperate to go to her but refusing to go farther.

I was losing control of myself.

I reached for her mind. I hated violating her like this, but I needed to know that she was okay. What I found was beautiful and terrifying, so much confidence and strength it was intimidating. But it was also anguished. Then, suddenly, the flow of feelings stopped. Her focus shifted. She could sense something.

Me.

My heart swelled in my chest with hope that my mate recognized this for what it was, until I heard that she could *physically* feel me somehow. I let go of her mind as she stood and took a step toward me. I hesitated, thinking that this would be when I finally got to meet her. But it wasn't the moment I wanted. Not with her in such an emotional state. I left before I could change my mind, but I didn't go far.

I couldn't.

I retreated back to my perch in the tree, far enough that I couldn't be seen but close enough that the bond felt content enough. Closing my eyes and resting my back against the rough bark, I let my imagination wander to the possible future I could have if my mate accepted me. I wanted to learn everything about her. What her favorite things were, or what she feared. What made her laugh and smile, or what made those gorgeous green eyes glare. I wondered if she loved the mountains or the ocean or caves. I needed to know.

Theron's voice interrupted my dreams, eliciting a scowl from me.

"You have been summoned by the Sages."

I sighed and pinched the bridge of my nose. I knew that Theron was near me, and could feel his presence. *"When?"* I bit out.

"They wait for you now at the Oryn Palace."

"And you suddenly have become their messenger?"

"The Sages have spiritual enhancement, Worthy. They have spoken to me to request your presence. I would advise that you heed their call," he snapped.

Grumpy fucker.

Regardless of his temper, he was my Spirit Guardian and I respected him. I went to where he was waiting, and agreed to have him Travel me back to Oryn. Taking only seconds to get there, we appeared on the roof of the palace. Theron stayed behind while I made my way down to my bedchamber to change into my black suit and Lord's Circlet. Mavris met me in the corridor outside the great hall. Also dressed in formal attire, the stern look on my brother's face told me that I would not be pleased with this meeting.

Taking a deep breath through my nose, I stepped into the mask of the Lord of Oryn and proceeded into the great hall, taking my seat and gesturing to the steward to open the large double doors.

My lips curled into a sneer as one of the high Sages of Bhara, Zareb, and Vicria entered the room. I had no issues with Zareb. From what I knew of him, he was a good and honorable Sage who was dedicated to the Spirits and the balance they demanded. It was the female Sage he was traveling with that repulsed me. Mavris tensed. He knew of Vicria and her vile ways, having personally known good males to fall for her seductive tactics and be ruined afterwards.

The Sages approached and bowed their heads.

"Good evening, Lord Ryker. Thank you for seeing us. I hope you are well," Zareb greeted.

"It is well past evening, and I do not wish to exchange useless pleasantries. Get to the point and tell me what it is that you want." My snarl echoed against the stone walls. I didn't care that he was a high Sage, and I wanted her out of my Nation.

He nodded. "We wanted to plead with you again to stop this panel from happening and deny the bond between you and your mate. The other Worthy have expressed their rejection of this divine union between two Worthy. As a Lord yourself, I would personally find it to be a great shame for either of you to endure the Raith."

"Your concern for both me and my mate's well-being is noted, but irrelevant. I will not leave our fate up to you or the council. And you should be ashamed. The bond of mates is one you should hold in the highest regard, *especially* between two Worthy. The bond was granted to us by the Gods, and it will be our decision. Not yours." I stood, my shadows creeping along the floor around me, streaked with heat, and their spines straightened. "Will that be all or did you have any other pointless purpose for traveling all this way?"

The arrogance of these Sages, coming to my home in the middle of the night, summoning me and making demands, had wrath burning through my veins.

"Please, Lord Ryker, I strongly urge you to reconsider. It's not solely our function to favor the bond, but also to ensure the balance of peace between the Nations. This will not end well, you know the laws. The Council's decisions will be absolute."

My eyes narrowed. "Leave," I commanded with a lethal calm. My hands vibrated with energy.

Mavris cleared his throat. "I'll escort you outside the palace." He stepped from the dais and the Sages followed him out of the hall. I turned to leave as well, recalling my shadows and ready to put as much distance between us as possible, but stopped when I heard the unpleasant sound of Vicria's voice right behind me.

"Lord Ryker," she said with her sultry tone. I turned to face her. Her white hair cascaded over her shoulders and down her robes as she approached with heavy-lidded eyes. "I can see that the bond is paining you. You desire to have her. My offer still stands. There are many ways to lessen the urges, and I can help with that. It's late, but we could start right now."

She lifted her hand as if to touch me, but my shadows erupted forth and pinned her to the wall. She writhed and snarled, trying to escape the grasp of my shadows.

I huffed a humorless laugh. "You're a fool for not remembering my warning during our last encounter. And you're utterly deranged if you think I would accept *help* from you." I leaned in close, my shadows tightening around her and heating, not enough to burn her but enough to cause her to wince from the sensation. "Enter Oryn again and I will burn you alive, consequences be damned. So long as the realm is rid of your filth—"

"Lord Ryker," Mavris snapped from behind me.

I slowly turned to face him, letting Vicria fall to the floor. "Get her out of my Nation."

"Talk some sense to your Lord before you all regret it." I heard Vicria say to Mavris as I rounded the corner.

I stormed back up to the roof and paced back and forth. The bond burned in my soul, displeased with the distance, making my skin crawl with unnatural discomfort. Theron didn't say a word as I mumbled curses to myself. A few minutes later, Mavris walked up to the roof.

"They're gone. I had three Noavo warriors escort them to the borders through the Ihab pass," he said as he approached me. "So, you're not going to do it?"

"Do what?" I bit out.

"Deny the bond."

I blew out a breath and stopped pacing. I tossed him my circlet and ran my hand through my hair.

"No," I whispered. "I won't. But I'll give her the chance to. She has the right to make this decision herself."

"Well hurry up. You don't have much time left. And I'd like to know in advance if we're going to war with every other Nation on the godsdamned continent, or if you're going to become unruly and brooding for the rest of your life," he said with a smirk. "Whatever happens brother, I stand behind you. Fuck the world."

"Thanks, Mav." The side of my mouth twitched up.

We talked for a bit longer about the state of the border as well as what I had drafted up for treaties with Dusan and, thanks to Ayen, Ulrik. Then we went over his list of potential towns and villages for the refugees and made adjustments, taking into account their available resources. After a farewell, Mavris returned to the palace.

I looked to Theron, and he nodded before he Traveled us back to the patch of forest near my mate. Relief flooded me instantaneously, the piercing intensity of the bond reduced to that of a slight irritation.

"A word of advice," Theron said.

"Of course." He rarely gave any, and I had always listened to what he had to say.

"Claim your mate. It is your duty and your right," he growled. Then he was gone.

Chapter Twenty-Four

KYA

"**K**ya."

"Hmm," I mumbled.

Nikan's voice stirred me awake, and with it came that burning sensation once again. But at least it wasn't as intense. I gripped my shirt tightly in my fist over my chest, unable to ignore it.

"Kya, wake your ass up and get out here." Nikan sounded like he wasn't in a particularly good mood that morning.

This should be fun.

I crawled off the warm furs I slept on and left the shelter, shielding my eyes from the sunlight cresting over the hill as I emerged.

Nikan was standing with his legs braced firmly on the ground. His eyes were nearly bulging out of their sockets, and he was breathing heavily out of his nose. I could feel the tension of the rock beneath us as he had a hold on it with his terbis, ready to use it to strike. My hands immediately grabbed for my daggers, my bow and quiver still on the ground inside the stone tent, before I saw what had Nikan so worked up.

Odarum was standing in front of him. His pitch-black mane and tail swaying gently in the breeze. His wings were spread wide and they were captivating, each black feather glistening in the morning's rays.

I released my breath, my shoulders slumping in relief, and I put my daggers away.

"Congratulations. You've gotten my brother on edge. Not much can do that to him," I said to Odarum.

"This mindless oaf threatens me with harm, holding the terra such as he is. Does he not know what I am? Tell him to release his terbis," Odarum said. He glared at Nikan with his ears flattened back against his neck. His hoof stomped against the grass and he snorted heavily through his muzzle in warning.

"Nik, stand down. This is my Spirit guardian." I gestured to the pegasus in front of me before walking between them. "Nik, Odarum. Odarum, my brother and fellow Roav, Nikan," I introduced and looked at Nikan pointedly. "Odarum is no threat."

I felt as Nikan released his hold on the ground. Odarum's ears shifted forward and became relaxed. He ruffled his feathers and pulled them to rest against his sides. I lifted to my toes and smacked the back of Nikan's head with my palm.

"Ow. What was that for?" he said, rubbing the back of his head.

"What were you planning to do? Throw some dirt at a Spirit?" I whispered loudly.

"He startled me. I came out and he was just…there, all menacing-like," he said defensively as he threw his hand up toward Odarum.

"Menacing? I was simply standing here," Odarum said. I ignored him.

"And you should have expected it. I told you my Spirit *horse* would return at some point. What, did you expect him to announce himself or something?"

205

"Yeah, I expected a *horse*. You failed to mention just how fucking big he is and that he has *wings*." Nikan was shouting now.

"You described me improperly?" Odarum asked.

I turned to Odarum and said out loud, "Stop talking." Then I turned back to Nikan. His face was scrunched in confusion, his eyes darting between me and Odarum.

I sighed, "Odarum, who's a *pegasus* by the way, and I can speak to each other through our minds. It's part of the—"

Odarum growled through our minds.

"Calm down. I'm not going to say anything about the bond," I said to him, and it was then that I noticed that communicating with him had become easier.

"It's part of the Spirit guardian and Worthy deal."

"See?" I said in a mocking tone.

"Very well," the Spirit grumbled.

Nikan pursed his lips and I could tell that he was holding back a smile. "You're hearing voices in your head?" I gave him a deadpan look when he placed his hand on my shoulder with a teasing smile. "Don't worry. I know a great healer who can help."

I pushed his hand off me and punched him in the shoulder. "Shut up."

"But seriously, Kya. I wouldn't go around talking about that. People will think you're insane."

"Trust me, it is insane," I chuckled.

"Alright. I guess I better get used to having a Spirit around then. But we need to head out and get to Narh," Nikan said before turning and walking to the horses. Which got me thinking.

"Why aren't the horses afraid of you and your wings? And they came when you stomped yesterday," I asked Odarum. It had just occurred to me that they didn't seem startled at all.

"They recognize what I am and know that they do not have to fear me. I would not harm an innocent life," Odarum said softly.

"I gathered that from yesterday's encounter. Speaking of, what was that? How did you do that with the roots?"

"I have the power to manipulate life."

I paused and stared at him for a moment. *"Like control it? Could you take it away if you wanted to?"*

"No. Manipulate. Not destroy," he stated firmly.

"Well, what you did was really magnificent. Is that the gift I gained from you?" I couldn't help but ask.

"I won't know which one you have received until it has manifested."

I wondered what his other abilities were.

After gathering our things, Nikan put the rock of the tent back into the ground and I re-fastened my hair into a braid before we mounted our respective horses. Odarum still wouldn't let me ride him.

Ass.

It took only a few hours to travel to the city of Narh in the Torx Nation. During our ride, my thoughts were consumed with our mission of tracking down the anonymous seller in Narh. Questions plagued my mind.

How did it come into his possession? Why didn't he sell it on the black market? How long did he have it? Why didn't someone take it from him rather than from Morah?

Odarum had followed quietly behind the entire way, seeming content to stay on the ground. I had yet to see him fly, and I wanted to. I also wanted to ride him while he did, just to experience it for myself. When we approached the city, Odarum stopped in the grassy field. I halted my gelding and turned to face him.

"Are you not coming?" I asked.

He remained quiet for a moment, his eyes seemed distant, before answering, *"Another Spirit wishes to speak with me."* My eyebrows furrowed in question. *"I will come back and wait here when I return."*

Odarum was gone in the blink of an eye. I glared at where he had just stood and released a frustrated huff.

Again with the disappearing. He's supposed to be with me, helping me.

I rolled my eyes and turned back around to catch up to Nikan. At least the burning feeling inside of me had stopped, the soothing swirls having taken its place. I thought that perhaps it was correlated to Odarum's proximity, but then that didn't explain when it stopped the first time in Morah or why it stopped again *before* he left just then. Maybe it had to do with my unmanifested magic.

Nikan and I pulled up our masks as we rode our horses into the city. People parted for us in the street, giving us a wide berth out of fear for the Roav, identifiable by the broach attached to each of our cloaks. An unprovoked reputation from those that were innocent. We had never harmed anyone who didn't deserve it. Even the soldiers that we passed remained wary of us. Cowards.

We wove our way through the busy streets to the northern side of the city, where Nikan dismounted and entered one of the buildings. I remained outside on my horse and held the reins of Nikan's as I kept watch.

The hair on the back of my neck rose with the feeling of being watched. I searched the faces and stone buildings for any threat but found nothing of real merit, and most averted their eyes.

After a few minutes, Nikan came out of the building and nodded to me, then led us to another location. We tied our horses to a post outside a run-down building with several small residences within. The stone building was cracked in multiple places, with broken windows and painted vulgarity on the outside. The smell was horrible. The residents' excrement puddled in the alley next to the building, likely because the building didn't have a water system and they dumped their waste out the windows.

I still had the feeling of being watched, and that meant they were also following. Training my eyes all around me and feeling for anyone coming closer, I searched for who it was. Nikan silently waited, sensing my apprehension, and looked around on alert.

After a couple of minutes, I turned to Nikan and shrugged, unable to detect anything substantial. We made our way to the revolting building.

My nose crinkled in disgust. I pitied anyone who had to live next to this putrid aroma. We entered the building and I followed Nikan up the dim, narrow staircase. A man lay unconscious on the stairs inside, and we had to step over him. We made our way up to the fourth floor before Nikan kicked in one of the wooden doors in the hallway. A rancid scent flooded my nose and stung my eyes. I had to cover my masked face to keep from vomiting.

A mattress on the other end of the room sat on the bare floor, stained and reeking due to the dead male atop it. I closed the splintered door behind me and walked over to the corpse. He was small in stature and completely naked, giving a full view of the Onyx-colored veins webbing over his pale skin.

"It's the Onyx Kiss." I bent down to inspect the body closer. There was a small puncture wound in his shoulder. That's all it would take to poison the blood and with a small amount, it would have taken longer to fully kill him rather than the amount I use on the tips of my arrows. "From the smell and discoloration, I'd say he's been dead for at least a week."

"Discoloration?" Nikan bent down next to me.

"Yeah. The black color in the veins begins to fade over time. Usually around a week. See here?" I pointed to the male's fingertips, the veins taking on a charcoal gray tint.

His eyes narrowed at me. "How do you know that?"

I fidgeted with my fingers and refused to meet his stare. "I may have conducted an experiment on one of my victims a few years back for a toxicology Scholar." I tilted my head and gazed up at Nikan with an innocent look.

His eyes widened in horror.

"For the love of Xar, it wasn't that bad. It was for knowledge."

"I'm sure it was." Nikan stood and shook his head. He gestured to the dead male. "This is bad. Really bad." Nikan said as he walked over to the small, rickety desk. "No one uses the Onyx's poison as a weapon besides you. It makes it look like you did it."

"My work doesn't look like this. Anyone who knows it well enough to recognize it would realize the differences. I'm much more merciful, opting for a quick death rather than dragging it out, where they would have time to get help. Not to mention, no one knows it's *me* who uses it. They just know it's a Roav thing. I doubt they even know it's only a single person." I stood to face Nikan. He was rummaging through the papers on the desk.

"He's definitely our anonymous seller," he said holding up a sheet of paper with the Morah emblem stamped at the bottom. "This is the proof of purchase and payment from the intake Scholar."

"Is there anything else in there? Anything at all about where he got the book in the first place?"

"No. I don't see anything indicating that. But I think his name was Moury," Nikan said, looking down at me with a worrisome expression.

"We need to figure out who else knew about the book. It's likely that wherever it came from was also who took it from Morah. They probably came for him first, extracted the location, then killed him," I stated.

Something so big and so threatening to our realm lay within the pages of a single book. I wanted to curse the Spirits for keeping the Gods from interfering.

"That leaves us with no leads," Nikan sighed.

I nodded slowly as I contemplated this information.

"Meet me on the outskirts of the city in an hour," I said as I turned to leave. I didn't give Nikan the chance to speak before I slammed the door behind me and left.

I stopped my horse in front of a small, quaint home on the western end of the city. I had always adored that house. Its lime-stone walls gave it a pleasing milky color that felt homey and welcoming. Large bushes of flowers lined the base all around the exterior, and the door was dark cedar that gave a striking contrast to the brightness of the stone around it. I tied up the gelding to the porch post and knocked on the wooden door after removing my mask, taking in a deep breath of that cedar scent.

I love that smell.

After a few moments, the door creaked open slightly. Through the crack a pair of emerald-green eyes shone back at me, squinting in a smile before the door opened fully. I grinned widely as Umana pulled me inside her home and embraced me.

Umana was a small female, shorter than me even. She was plump and kept herself and her clothes pristine. I wasn't sure how old she was exactly, but I knew that she had to be close to a thousand. The surface of her skin was wrinkled, and she had trouble getting around. But her mind was sharp.

"Kya. My, it has been too long. Come in, come in." She stepped aside and shut the door.

The inside was bright and warm. Umana didn't clutter her home and had little in terms of furniture. She preferred to keep her possessions to a minimum. A small table for two in the kitchen and two comfortable chairs in the sitting area where I sat. I glanced around and nothing seemed different from my last visit. Few items decorated the shelves mounted to the walls and she had no paintings or drawings. She lived a very simple life—or so it seemed.

"Now, what can I do for you, Kya the Worthy?" she said while offering me a hot cup of tea.

My eyebrows raised. "How did you know?" I had never allowed Umana to see my mark, and I had never told her. I told her a lot but never that. I wanted to have someone in my life that didn't know. But I was surprised word had gotten out so soon.

"I may be old, but I'm no fool. I've known for years now that you bore the mark of the Trial." She leaned back in her chair and took a sip of her tea before continuing, "And since you're here now, that means you survived. And the Gods would be fools for not deeming you Worthy."

Ah, so she didn't hear it from anyone in particular. The wise old hag was usually always right. I half removed my jacket to display the mark all the way up my shoulder. Umana leaned forward to examine it, taking my arm in her hands and turning it to get a better look at the whole design. She hummed to herself the entire time and I smiled with contentment.

"I've seen many marks in my lifetime but none such as this. Who chose you?" She lifted her eyes to meet mine.

"Kleio."

Umana made a sound like she wasn't surprised. She released my arm and sat back in her chair. I gave her a questioning look, but she ignored it.

"So, I'll ask again. What brings you here?"

"I need information about a book. A male named Moury had it and sold it to Morah."

Umana may look like a sweet elderly female, but she was known for her knowledge. She was my contact here in Torx. She knew everything about everyone, it seemed. How she knew such things was anybody's guess.

"If it's already in the great library, why are you asking about it?" she asked over the lip of her cup.

"It was stolen. And I would like to know how Moury came into possession of it, so I can track down who might have taken it back."

"Moury was a troubled male," Umana sighed. "He became dependent upon the demid elixir and lost everything to it. He had a good heart and meant well but his mind was constantly fixed on how he could get more of the substance."

A wretched concoction, demid was originally made by healers to help with a disease that made some lose their memories, but it was altered by those in the black market to cause a state of artificial euphoria. If used long term, fae became highly addicted and nearly reliant on it. More and more fae were falling to the elixir.

"As far as the book, all I know is that supposedly Moury found it on the beach at the northern end of Dusan," she said.

"At the *northern* end of Dusan?" There wasn't even a coastline at the northern end. Not since the Rip's formation anyway.

"Apparently. But it was undamaged from the water."

"What was he doing there? How do you know?" I questioned.

"I saw it, of course. Moury brought it here to see if I knew anyone who would buy such a book and I informed him that

Morah was his best choice. I don't know much outside of that, and I didn't ask why he was in Dusan."

"Hmm. Alright, thank you Umana." I started to stand but stopped when she spoke again.

"Something else troubles you. What is it?"

I hesitated a moment, debating on if I should tell her of everything that was going on. I decided against it. She didn't need to carry the weight of it as well.

I stood and offered a small smile. "Nothing I can't handle."

I had just stepped through the door when she called out from behind me, "Let that feeling inside lead you, Kya. It will bring you your fate."

I shook my head and smiled as I closed the door and replaced my mask.

Crazy old dame.

The city center of Narh was busy in the evening. Crowds of people filled the streets and I wove my way through as people bumped into my horse. The gelding nickered when a child ran underneath him, giggling and squealing with delight. Merchants sold cooked meats and fresh produce, nourishing the air with savory and sweet aromas. Instruments sang melodic tunes, filling the atmosphere as people danced and spun to the music. Apparently there was a celebration for their God, Cethar, who had not chosen a Worthy during the Trial, and Lord Dainos remaining their ruler.

I hid the Roav pin on my cloak and pulled my hood farther over my head, so that I could leisurely move my way through without being spotted. I didn't want to interrupt the blissful feel of the lively city. The sun was setting, and a crisp breeze blew leaves across the stone road, heralding the approaching autumn season and promising cooler temperatures from summer's heat. I slowed my horse, wanting to absorb the joyful contentment of the night for just a little longer before returning to the grimness of reality. Even with so much corruption in the world, there was still the promise of life.

I slowly made my way to the other end of the street. The crowds started to dissipate the farther away I got. The noise of the people chatting and the music grew faint.

It was too quiet.

I wasn't that far from the celebration, and there were people still around me. But everything slowly went silent. I got off my horse and stood on the street. I didn't even hear my boots hitting the stone, and I felt nothing with my terbis—except something in the distance. Then I noticed that I could no longer scent the food or the sweat of my horse.

What is happening?

I looked around at the people passing, seemingly unaffected. Their mouths were moving but I heard nothing. Steam and smoke rose into the air from the merchants cooking, but I couldn't smell it. My braid blew over my shoulder and my horse's mane swayed in the breeze, but I couldn't feel the bite of the crisp wind on my face.

My breathing quickened, and my heart began to race. I could hear slow thumping in my ears. I placed my hand over my chest, now burning unbearably, and felt fast beats opposite of the slow thuds pulsing in my head.

Deep, even breaths sounded, not at all like my panicked ones. My skin felt energized, as if electricity was flowing through me. I started to smell something faint and familiar—cedar and bergamot and something else. The breaths I could hear and the

215

heartbeats I could feel were getting louder and faster, nearly matching mine. It was calling to me.

Driven by another force, I wove my way through the street, abandoning my horse and ignoring the crowd. I didn't know where I was going, but somehow, I knew exactly how to get there. I couldn't stop, the force inside, luring me to where I was going like a rope pulling me through the water. I couldn't stop it.

I started running, the beating in my head getting louder and louder, more erratic. Compelled by the burning inside of me, I needed to find what it was drawing me toward. I turned down an alley filled with shadows, too dark for the night not yet reached.

Suddenly, the burning stopped.

My eyes locked onto another's, ones of bright silver that seemed to glow. It was like I knew exactly where to look in the inky blackness that now opened and consumed me as I stepped closer.

As if the world around me fell away, all I could see was *him*, and my breathing stopped.

The male was tall, my head not high enough to come over his shoulders. His murky black hair was ruffled against the tanned skin of his forehead and fell just above his thick eyebrows. His broad frame was donned in black leathers that were tight against his muscular body.

"It's you…" His voice was a strained whisper. But it was as soothing as the shadows around us, speaking to my very soul.

My breath rushed back into me at the sound. That scent of cedar and bergamot exuded from him and invaded my nostrils, causing my eyes to roll in the back of my head. Heat pooled in my lower belly. The urge to be even closer to him was overwhelming and irresistible.

I took a step forward but stopped suddenly when he braced an arm against the stone wall of the building and his nostrils flared.

His other hand was clenched into a fist. His eyes were locked on mine and his face looked pained. As if he were holding himself back.

A moment of clarity hit me and my eyes widened.

He's the Lord from the Trial.

I felt it then. It all made sense, the burning, the drive, the dream, the intoxicating scent…of him. My body trembled, and my breath was shaky and erratic. I knew what this was. I had read about it, dreamt of it, and hoped for it. But a Lord, another Worthy? One that likely saw me as a threat to be eliminated?

This can't be happening.

Yet, his eyes pleaded with me as he snarled one word. One word that made my chest twist and shattered those childish dreams.

"Run."

For less than a heartbeat, I hesitated. Then, not knowing what else to do, I did exactly as he demanded—I ran.

My arms pumped and my feet slapped the ground as I ran as hard as I could, pushing myself to go faster and faster. Tears bit at my eyes and I wanted to blame it on the wind, but I knew better. The shadows followed me through the streets, licking at my heels. I shoved through the throngs of people bustling about in the street. Finding my horse, I leapt on top of him. I gripped the reins tightly and dug my heels into the gelding's flank, and he galloped through the town to the outskirts where my senses returned and the shadows finally receded. I pushed my horse faster still until we approached Nikan who was waiting next to Odarum.

The moonslight shone off the Spirit animal, creating a silhouette of his black form against the darkness around him. I jumped off my moving horse and stomped my way to Odarum, glaring at him with a fierceness that made him startle.

"Did you know?" I demanded in a near scream.

"*Know what?*" he questioned.

"*That I have a fucking mate,*" I yelled through my mind. My hands curled into fists so tightly that my nails dug into my palms. Tears streamed down my face in anger or fear or—

"Does he know what? What's going on, Kya? What's he saying?" Nikan rushed over, his face twisted with concern.

Odarum dropped his head to be level with mine, his head so close I could almost touch it.

"*Yes,*" he said in a calm yet lethal voice. "*I know. I have known for some time. It is not my place to interfere. This should not be surprising to you.*"

My body shook, adrenaline coursing through my veins. Of course he wouldn't have told me. He can't.

"Kya?" Nikan prodded.

"Nothing. Let's go," I said, voice clipped.

My mate. My mate is a Lord. And he rejected me. Told me to run.
"Wha—" he started.

I spun on my heel and walked away. I mounted my horse and trotted off through the field, not waiting to see if Nikan and Odarum followed.

Chapter Twenty-Five

KYA

I slept under the stars that night. Too hurt and angry to be under the confines of rock or cloth. I needed to gaze up at the wonder of the universe and let it come crashing down on me. I laid in the lush grass of the plain, my hands clasped behind my head, letting the soft breeze cool me down and calm me. I concentrated on the sounds of the insects, the wind blowing my loose hair, the grass tickling the back of my neck, the soothing swirling inside of me, and the sky above.

It shouldn't have bothered me so much. I should have been stronger. While I may have been keeping myself together on the outside, my soul was cracked, splintering under the weight of it all. My mate's rejection was the final blow, splitting the hard stone of my emotions and allowing them to pour out.

Beneath the stars was where I could go to get away and clear my head. Those little dots of light in the sky promised hope, and it was awe-inspiring to imagine the other realms that could be out there. Ones without diseased land and lost families. Ones without Trials and thieves and denied bonds. Just for a moment, I allowed myself to wish for a world rid of troubles and worries.

I didn't sleep that night. There was too much on my mind. Silence filled my throat the next day. I didn't know where to start, there was so much to say that I couldn't speak at all.

Nikan seemed to understand and let me be, leaving me to my thoughts and leading the way. I didn't even know where we were going as I blindly followed. Odarum stayed close, and I think Nikan had told him that I needed space to work things out in my own way until I was ready.

Once the sun set, we made camp for the night and Nikan spoke.

"We're in Ulrik now," he said softly. An offer to talk and bring me out of whatever this was. He was sitting next to me in front of the fire and looking into the flames.

"Why?" I glanced at him.

I could tell that we were farther north from the cooler temperature. He always knew what I needed. I leaned my head on his shoulder.

"After you bolted from Moury's room to go Gods know where, I met with a contact who said there was word of a Roav in a small village in Ulrik." The corner of his mouth lifted slightly.

"A 'Roav' huh? Wonder who that could be, since there are just *so* many of us." I lifted my head and winked at him.

He looked at me questionably.

"There are rumors that there are at least a dozen Roav out there." I chuckled, remembering the conversation with Njall.

"Really?" Nik asked.

"Apparently." I shrugged.

He shook his head and chuckled. "We should get to the village where Malina was last spotted shortly after morning. We can track her down from there."

I nodded slowly.

"Hey." He elbowed me gently. "You good?"

I smiled up at him. "Yeah. I'm good."

I did feel slightly better about it all. I needed the time to think and clear my head, and Nikan had given that to me.

We left the next morning just as the sun began to crest over the horizon. I spoke to Odarum about training with my magic and shifting, and he agreed that we should start after we find Malina and decide where we were going next. Neither of us brought up the last couple of days. It was done and over with, and time to move on.

Trotting through a small patch of woods, a voice echoed through the trees.

"I never thought I'd be so happy to see someone that I thought was dead."

I stopped my horse. "Doesn't sound like you had a lot of confidence in me."

I searched the dense canopy above me—the leaves were turning from green to red and orange and yellow. Malina was known for keeping to the treetops, using the illusion of the sunlight peeking through the leaves to conceal her. She would get the attention of her victims before blinding them. It gave her the advantage of the high-ground to spy and fight as well as remaining obscured from below. But instead, she stepped out from around the trunk of a tree next to the path.

Malina's hair was twisted into a bun on top of her head. She was dressed in her Roav leathers. Her pack was hanging over one shoulder, and she was twirling one of her daggers between her fingers.

"A mistake on my part." She gave a smirk. "Who would have thought that a Roav could be Worthy."

I hopped off my horse and hugged her firmly. Nikan jumped down and stood next to us before hugging her as well after I let go.

She glanced behind me at Odarum. "Well, it looks like it wasn't quite so unfortunate that I lost my horse. You seem to have an extra. And it's got wings!" She clapped her hands.

"She will not mount me," Odarum huffed.

"I don't know about that. She's never turned down a suitor before." I giggled when he snorted and his skin twitched.

"That's Odarum. He doesn't like to be touched. What happened to your horse?" I asked my sister.

"Ah, damn thing bolted a few days ago. One of those saber-tooths was in the area."

"Did you find what you were looking for?" Nikan asked.

She looked at him and nodded. "Yep. And it's fucking heavy to be lugging around on foot, too. I left this morning to head back to Morah."

She dropped her pack and sat against the base of the tree with her knees bent and her forearms resting on them.

"But enough about me and some old tome. Kya, tell me *everything*."

"We really should keep moving—"

"We have time, Nik," I interrupted as I sat down next to Malina with my legs crossed underneath me.

I told her all that had happened from the beginning of the Trial—leaving out the little details. I told her of each of the Tests, the creatures, being chosen by Kleio and her command for me to find the truth about the Glaev, Odarum, the book being stolen, finding the dead seller, then coming here.

"You have yet to mention your mate to those closest to you. Interesting," Odarum said.

"Watch it. That is none of your concern," I snapped.

Malina took a few moments to take everything in, mulling it over.

"And you didn't discover anything about who stole this book from Morah?" she asked.

"No," Nikan and I responded in unison.

"No other clues about how this Moury male came into possession of it?" She tilted her head to the side and chewed on her lip.

"No," Nikan said.

"Yes," I answered at the same time. He gaped at me as I continued. "I met with one of my contacts and learned that Moury found the book on a beach at the northern end of Dusan."

Umana was my own little Roav secret. We had met on one of my earlier missions and she has been an invaluable asset ever since, not to mention that I paid her well for the information she divulged. But she requested that I keep her identity confidential, not wanting anyone back at Morah to find out. Seeing as we often had to give detailed reports to Eamon about our journeys, I didn't want to put Nikan and Malina in a position to lie.

Both Malina's and Nikan's eyebrows creased.

"There is no beach on the northern end of Dusan. The Rip goes right through it. I think your contact was mistaken or lied to," Nikan said.

"Unlikely. She has never led me astray before." I shook my head.

"There is a small area." Malina blew out a sharp breath. Nikan and I looked at her. "My mother tried to take me there when I was a child. There was a small strip of land just past the Dusan border, at the far end of the Rip, that leads you to an isolated piece of land with a beach. She wanted to visit and stay for a few days with me and my father. I was terrified at the time when we went, being so close to Odes's grave, and we didn't even make it past the Rip before we turned around."

My eyes were as wide as Nikan's. Malina never spoke of her mother and father. Being separated from them after losing our home had been hard for her—hard on both of us—but I had practiced compartmentalization and adjusted to it more easily, while she continued to mask her pain with smiles and sassy remarks.

"So yes, there is a beach at the northern end of Dusan. But I don't know if it's still accessible by land. It was right on Atara's border, and I don't know if the Glaev closed off the path to get to it," she added.

I nodded. "Alright. We can go to Morah and find maps of the area to see if the Glaev barred the path. It would be faster to get there on land rather than going to the coast at the southern end and chartering a boat to get to the northern end."

"Unless you'd like to put those wings to use?" I said to Odarum.

"I would not," he deadpanned.

"This is kind of a big fucking deal. You're all about protecting the balance and everything. Don't you want to help me with the Glaev?"

"That would be interfering," he said.

"We have a plan then. Let's get moving." Nikan stood and walked back to his horse.

"Your mark isn't gone," Malina stated, pointing to my exposed wrist between my sleeve and glove. "I thought it was supposed to disappear when you completed the Trial."

"No." I pulled down the collar of my shirt over my shoulder to show her the extension. "Now that I'm a Worthy, the mark will always remain. It's changed though. It now goes up the length of my arm and bears the symbols of Kleio since she chose me."

Malina and I stood and she gestured to Odarum. "So the flying Spirit pony is like your pet now?"

"I am no pet nor am I some feeble pony!" Odarum shouted through my mind and he reared his head back.

Nikan snorted and I laughed. I was grateful to be here with my family.

A couple of hours before dusk, we stopped to camp for the night. I wanted daylight so that I could start training with Odarum. I was tired of waiting. Malina had ridden with me while Nikan carried our packs to help even out the weight for the horses since Odarum refused to carry anyone and grumbled something about not being a mule when I asked him to carry the packs.

"Why won't you even carry me?" I asked the Spirit.

"I believe that soon you will no longer need to be carried," he replied.

"What do you mean?" I turned to face him after Malina and I dismounted our horse.

"The shift. It is possible, and likely, that you may gain my wings." He lowered his head so that his eyes were level with mine as I approached.

"I'll be able to fly?" My mouth fell open.

"As I said, it is possible. It will not be known until the shifting manifests."

"When will that happen?"

"I do not know. Or perhaps you will only gain my hair."

I scoffed out loud.

Malina startled me when she spoke directly behind me. "Why are you just staring at him?"

"They talk through their minds, and they do it often. It's weird. Get used to it," Nikan yelled from over his shoulder where he was erecting our terra tent.

Malina just blinked slowly then let out an exaggerated sigh. "That is weird."

I rolled my eyes as she walked away.

"Can you help me with my magic now?" I asked when I turned back to Odarum.

He didn't answer. He extended his head and touched me with his muzzle. Before I could protest, we disappeared from the campsite and appeared in a field next to a pond.

Nik is going to be pissed.

My head spun and I stumbled, grabbing the side of my head with my hand before falling on my ass and I nearly vomited. The swirling inside of me was once again burning.

"You have to warn me before you do that," I said out loud. I couldn't concentrate enough to speak through my mind.

"Noted," Odarum said nonchalantly.

"Why did you bring me here? Where are we?"

"Not far. I brought you here so that you could test your new magic without harming anyone."

I hadn't thought of that. I bristled with excitement and apprehension. Some of the magic gifted to the Worthy was dangerous, especially to those that hadn't mastered it.

"The magic the Gods gifted to you is not like that of your birth magic. The wielding of elements is something that comes naturally to your kind, and is a part of you. This magic will feel foreign to you, but it is now also a part of you. You should be able to grasp it and harness its power. It will not harm you, and it will answer when you call upon it."

"How do I do that?" I stood, my vision now back in focus.

"Like the bond of Spirits, and that of your mate as well, it is inside of you. Search for it." He backed away a few steps.

"Okay," I whispered.

I closed my eyes and looked for that tether of Odarum's bond to me. It was there. Like a bright light and no longer concealed by murky darkness. I moved past it where I found another. The chaotic shadows of before now coalesced into an opaque, dark cord that was taut. It had a soft glow and I felt drawn to it, the urge to reach for it stronger than the others.

The mating bond.

A pang of hurt filled my chest as I resisted it. I didn't want to think about that right now. I moved on.

Different from the tethers of Odarum and my mate, like threads extending to them, there were spherical shapes. Almost like orbs. They were scattered within me, all different. One, farther out, was murky and embedded in the darkness with tendrils of whispers whirling out of it, as if softly speaking to me. The one closer was translucent and colorless, like that of glass or a transparent stone.

I reached for it and tried to hold on to it, to cradle it in the palms of my mind and soul. I couldn't grasp it. It was evasive and felt like I was trying to grasp for air in my bare hands. I concentrated harder, sweat beading above my brow, and spoke to it.

Obey.

Odarum had said that if I called to it, then it would answer. I latched onto it, wrapping around it, and it felt more like a thick fluid rather than air. I took a deep breath, refusing to let go, and opened my eyes.

Nothing seemed different. I was in the same spot. Odarum hadn't moved, but his ears were perked forward and alert. Everything was the same.

"It's not working." I dropped my shoulders and sighed.

Odarum rumbled a laugh. *"It is."*

My brows furrowed. I threw my hands up with a scoff and slowly spun in place, looking all around me. The grass was the same, the water was still calm, the ground hadn't changed. Nothing was different or out of place. I even looked to the sky above to see if I was causing a storm or something. I touched my body and felt nothing odd.

"I don't understand. Nothing is happening." I crossed my arms and gave him a pointed look.

"Look in the water and see the magic you harness." He nodded his head forward, gesturing to the water behind me.

Intrigued, I rushed over to the edge of the pond and looked for any changes in the water. Color, consistency, movement, monsters, anything. I reached forward and the cool water rippled under my touch.

"I don't see anything." I said, shaking my head. His steps were muffled in the grass as he came up next to me, and I glanced up at him.

"Exactly."

I turned back to the water, my braid falling over my shoulder, and saw his reflection in the still pond, the black of his hair was stark against the colorful hues of the sunset painting the sky. Next to him, where I should have seen my own reflection, I saw nothing. My eyes widened in realization and I jumped back.

"Can you *see* me?" I asked.

"No. But I can hear you." He turned his head in the direction of my voice.

Interesting.

I placed my hand on his shoulder just above his wing. His skin twitched. To me, my skin shimmered slightly.

"And you can feel me. You can't see me but I can see myself. My skin looks almost shiny." A rueful smile crossed my lips.

I removed my hand from him. I closed my eyes and reached for that bright tether to Odarum inside of me. I wasn't sure if I would be able to hold on to both at the same time.

"If I stayed silent and only spoke through my mind, you wouldn't know where I am." I said, silently stepping around to his other side.

"In theory. But I am able to hear well. I can hear your breathing and your steps in the grass." He snapped his head to his other side and I held my breath, his nose right in front of me.

I poked him right between his nostrils and he squealed, pinning his ears back.

"Stop that."

I chuckled. I could feel myself getting weak and exhausted.

"So how do I make this," I gestured to myself, forgetting that he couldn't see. "Go away? Or come back, I guess."

"Let go of that connection," he stated matter-of-factly.

I closed my eyes and took a deep breath. It was almost as hard to let go of that orb as it was to grab. When I finally did unravel myself around it, I opened my eyes and exhaled.

My body felt heavy, like I barely had enough strength to keep myself standing.

"Well done. Using magic such as this will drain you quickly. It is like a muscle that is untrained. It will tire with use. You are using your body to harness that magic and channel its energy. You must train yourself to build stamina with magic." I felt lightheaded and dazed as he continued. *"But for now, you require rest—"*

I didn't hear the remainder of what he said as I fell to the ground.

Chapter Twenty-Six

KYA

When I came to, I found myself sitting. My back slumped against a warm chest, an arm around my waist, as I rhythmically swayed from side to side. The creaking of leather and sounds of hooves stepping against the dirt roused me further. I squinted at the blinding light piercing my vision as I opened my eyes and lifted my sagging head. I felt like shit, but at least the burning was gone again.

"Damn Kya. You had us scared," Malina said from her horse, next to me.

I turned my head and saw Nikan looking at me with concern, but I could tell that he was infuriated. I looked around and noticed that we were walking along a well-traveled path through sparse trees.

"How long was I asleep?" I asked, rubbing my eyes and stretching my back.

"A day and a half," Nikan bit out through gritted teeth.

I knew he'd be pissed.

Malina pointed her thumb over her shoulder to Odarum. "Pony express here brought you back unconscious. I thought Nik was going to crush him under a rock. I would have paid a good amount of coin to see that," she huffed a laugh at that last part.

"Care to explain what happened?" Nikan asked me.

I sighed heavily, still feeling tired and weak.

"We worked on honing my magic to discover what Kleio gifted me. I found out, but it quickly drained my energy."

"What is it? Your magic?" Malina asked with interest.

"I can become unseen." The side of my lips curved up.

"Unseen? Like invisible?" Nikan chimed in.

"Yeah."

"You mean you can become hidden while in plain sight?" Malina asked in astonishment.

"As if I need magic to do that." I winked.

"True." She shrugged. "So, what does Kleio want you to do with this magic?"

"Uncover the truth about the Glaev," I said.

Nikan and I leaned forward to duck under a low hanging branch.

"And how exactly does she expect you to do that?" Malina asked.

"She said that I already know." I shrugged.

"Why do they have to be so cryptic?" she mumbled.

"The Gods can't interfere. Neither can the Spirits," I said. She tilted her head and gave a questioning look. I sighed as I continued. "Before the war, the Gods used fae as slaves and then during the war they forced magic into them and demanded they fight. That amount of magic in Taeralia was tilting the scales of balance to a dangerous level and the Spirits," I gestured to Odarum who was looking off to the side, seemingly not paying attention. "Warned the Gods that if they didn't stop, then they would destroy the realm. When Odes fell, the balance had shifted so violently that it literally tore our world apart. The Spirits then had to intervene. They made some kind of divine pact or something with the Gods. Part of that pact was the division of the lands, one to each God, with one being neutral in place of Odes, as well as forbidding the Gods to interfere with the natural evolution of fae."

I paused for a moment. "With the exception of the Trial, where they are allowed to grant one fae at a time great magic, the Gods aren't allowed to interact with the fae."

"Wow," Malina breathed. "You need to get out more."

Nikan snorted a laugh.

"You need to read more," I retorted.

"Is all of that true?" Nikan asked over his shoulder to Odarum.

He bobbed his head and said to me, *"A butchered summarization, but yes."*

"You were there during the war?" I asked him.

"I was."

"That was thousands of years ago. How old are you?"

"Spirits do not have an age. We have always existed."

"Like the Gods?"

"Gods and Spirits are symbiotic. One cannot be without the other."

"So did…Spirits die when Odes did?" I asked carefully.

"Many," he said after a moment.

"And if a Spirit dies, do the Gods also die?"

"No. But they do painfully feel the loss."

I thought for a moment. *"You and I are bonded. If I died, you would feel that pain of loss like the Gods feel if the Spirits die. But what would happen if you died? Would I die?"*

He was silent for several moments, and I almost didn't think he was going to answer me. *"I do not know. No Fylgjur has ever died before their Worthy."*

I still couldn't pronounce that damn word. And I had no interest in finding out the answer to my question first hand.

Mentally drained, we made camp that night with another two days' ride ahead of us to Morah. I wanted to practice with my magic but decided against it, not wanting to overdo it and be unconscious for nearly two days again. I felt fully rested and energized and I couldn't sleep. I stayed awake, leaving Malina and Nikan in the tent while I remained outside. It was a warm night and didn't require a fire. Malina created a small orb of light above me so that I could read, now that I finally had some time to do so peacefully, and I was glad for the escape.

It had been a few hours, and I was well into a wonderfully descriptive love scene that made more than just my cheeks heat when I felt a familiar distant thump through my terbis. One that was large and heavy—the same one as that night in Torx. And just like that night, the shadows in that direction were darker than the rest.

Shadows…

My heart plummeted, and my eyes widened with both excitement and dread. The swirls inside of me tugged and I gasped a breath.

My mate has been following me.

The pieces fell into place, and it all made sense. The burning and swirling, that was the bond. If he had been following me, then he wasn't rejecting the bond. But then why would he have told me to run? And the shadows…he was a shadow wielder. It dawned on me then that the calming swirls inside of me were like that of his shadows—the bonds representation of him.

I thought about reaching for it. Reaching for him. But I was…apprehensive. I didn't know if this tug was the bond urging me or if it was him trying to connect with me. Either way, I wasn't ready. But at the same time, I wanted it more than I had ever wanted anything.

Driven by instinct and desire, I stood, facing my mate where he hid in the shadows. Just as I took a step to go to him, I felt him disappear once again.

I waited throughout the night with my palms flat on the ground. Waited to feel him on the terra again. I knew he was near, the shadows inside of me were calm and soothing—comforting. I concentrated my terbis to feel everything around me, searching for him.

I could feel the horses standing behind the stone tent. I felt Nikan and Malina laying on the furs, their breathing and heartbeats steady as they slept. I felt animals slumbering or walking in the distance and I even felt every tree, every rock, everything. But I didn't feel him. Anticipation coursed through me, keeping me awake and alert. But as the night bled into dawn, that anticipation turned to irritation. Irritation at him rejecting me, following me, then vanishing—not to mention bewildered at how he could seemingly appear and disappear.

I was down right aggravated by morning. My past feelings of hurt and disappointment transformed to hot rage at my mate's evasion. I was done waiting for him to appear. Disregarding any politeness, I woke up Nikan and Malina, roughly nudging them with my boot.

"It's daybreak. Let's go," I clipped out, before leaving the tent and gathering the horses. Odarum had kept himself out of sight until now, and followed as we left toward Morah without saying a word.

Nikan sat behind me as we rode and I refused to let him take the reins. I fumed with anger all day, snapping at anyone who spoke to me or ignoring them completely. A few hours before dusk, Nikan's patience wore out.

"That's it. I've had enough of your shit." He ripped the reins from me and kicked the horse into a canter through the trees. I jabbed my elbow into his side and cursed as twigs and leaves smacked me in the face, cutting into my skin. He grunted when I kicked him in the shin, which only caused the horse to run faster.

Once we entered a clearing, Nikan pulled on the reins and the horse stiffened his back legs, sliding to a stop, causing dirt to spew into the air around us as we lurched in the saddle. He jumped off the horse, bending at the knees when he landed. I glared at him.

Malina emerged from the clearing behind us, ducking under a low branch, and slowed her horse to a trot.

"Get off the horse, Kya," Nikan demanded as he removed his sword from its holster on his back.

"Fuck you," I spat through gritted teeth. I was being irrational and I knew it, yet I couldn't help it at the same time.

What in the After is wrong with me?

"Either get down or talk about whatever has you in such a pissy mood." He crossed his arms over his chest and squared his shoulders.

I dismounted. The last thing I wanted to do was talk about anything. My breath shook as adrenaline coursed through my body. Nikan's flicked his eyes to Malina behind me and he nodded his head once. I knew what they were planning. This was what we did with each other. Nikan understood that I needed an outlet for my pent-up frustration and was willing to take the brunt of it.

Malina threw something at me and I caught it before bending down to remove my boots. Stepping my bare feet into the grass toward Nikan, I tied the length of cloth Malina had tossed to me around my eyes and removed each of my daggers from my thighs. I took a deep breath and concentrated on the vibrations through the terra. Through the combination of listening and my terbis, I could detect exactly where they were and their movements—even before they made them, feeling their muscles tensing just before they moved. The blindfold forced me to narrow my focus.

I felt Nikan shift his weight before lunging for me. I side stepped and jutted my dagger out to catch his torso but he blocked, throwing up a rock at the last second. He countered, kicking a stream of dirt through the air straight at me. I jumped then dive-rolled out of the way, bringing my daggers up crossed above my head to catch the blow of his sword.

I pushed him off, feeling Malina coming up behind me, and spun to throw one of my daggers, which she deflected with her own. I could feel her pushing energy outwards and was thankful for the blindfold knowing that she was wielding her light—more for her own practice than for me—to blind her attacker as she came through it.

Nikan had thrown up a rock dome to shield himself from the light. I took the opportunity to sheathe my dagger and quickly drew an arrow, aiming right for her. I released it, and spun to run at Nikan's dome, hoping for the element of surprise when he deconstructed it.

I felt Malina behind me strike the arrow from the air, hearing the crack of the wood as it snapped in half.

"Wrong tip!" she yelled.

"Oops," I whispered to myself.

I didn't understand how she was able to see through her own light, but I knew she could. Within a moment of a step, I felt the vibrations of Nikan coming through the dome as I approached. I crouched down just as he came up and swiped at his feet with my dagger, now back in my hand, my bow still in the other.

He lifted on a mound of rock, and threw me to the side. I landed hard on my back, immediately rolling as Malina's dagger pierced the dirt where I had just been. Jumping to my feet, I nocked another arrow. I could feel Nikan now standing on his rock dome, and I released my bow string, the arrow screaming through the air at him. Malina charged at me from the side and I met her blade for blade, pulling one of my daggers from my back and dropping the bow.

Malina and I went at each other, strike after strike, equally matched. Nikan joined in moments later, and I alternated between blocking and attacking each of them. They were working together to wear me down. And after a long while of fighting the two of them, their plan was beginning to work.

Just as I was about to yield, I felt something in the distance.

"Cease," I shouted firmly. Nikan and Malina instantly stopped mid-attack, an understanding between all of us that we needed to stop at the safe-word.

I quickly removed my blindfold and turned to the other side of the clearing, Nikan and Malina doing the same, following my line of sight. I grabbed my bow and strung an arrow through it, aiming at the tree line. Nikan used his terbis to hold an area of the ground, the equivalent of arming himself. Malina flipped her daggers so that the blades were resting between her fingers, ready to throw them.

On the other side of the clearing, a stocky male strolled out of the treeline down the path, whistling a tune and leading a bull-drawn cart filled with goods. The trader, likely coming from Morah, halted in his tracks when he saw us. His eyes widened.

"Roav..." he whispered with a gasp. He placed a hand over his mouth and mumbled a prayer to the Gods, backing up into his cart. We lowered our weapons, but not quickly enough. It appeared that we had frightened the male, because he yanked on the bull's lead to steer him away down the treeline around us. Odarum was now standing directly behind me.

"Oh I can't wait to see what rumors will come of this encounter. Roav, caught without their masks and fighting each other," Malina said after the male was out of earshot. Her head turned to the side and caught the sight of Odarum. "With a Spirit pony too."

I snorted a laugh when Nikan rolled his eyes.

"Feel better?" He turned to look at me with a smirk.

Now it was time to roll my eyes. "Yes." My face softened, and I looked at both of them. "Thanks."

They gave me what I had needed, let me vent my anger. It wasn't the first time, though it usually wasn't even me who needed the outlet. We all had our own internal turmoil, and sometimes we just couldn't hold it in any longer.

"Any time." Nikan slapped my shoulder and walked to his horse, pushing the rock dome back down into the ground like it was never there.

"Feeling a little frustrated are we?" Malina teased.

I sighed. "I need to figure out my magic, develop the bond with Odarum to manifest my shifting and his magic, complete Kleio's task and stop the Glaev." I didn't mention that I also had to worry about a mating bond with a hot, shadow wielding Lord with silver eyes that made my thighs clench. "So yes, forgive me if I'm a little cranky for it."

"Want to talk about it?" Malina asked cautiously.

I opened my mouth to respond, but the words caught in my throat before they left my lips. I felt it again, off in the distance.

My mate.

Chapter Twenty-Seven

RYKER

B ack in Narh, I couldn't stop it. The bond was impatient. I needed her. I had to control myself. Tried desperately not to reach for her through that glistening tether inside of me, the one representative of our bond—like a precious gem shimmering in the light of the moons.

But after I noticed that low-life stalking her and heard what he was planning to do...my instincts kicked in. And once they activated, I couldn't reverse it. The drive to defend what was mine overpowered any semblance of restraint I possessed.

I hid in the shadows beside a building until he passed by then pulled him in, pinning him to the wall. I put my hand over his nose and open mouth as he began to scream, muffling the sound, and poured fire down his throat until his lungs were nothing but ash. Releasing my hold, his lifeless body dropped to the cobbles.

With the act, the bond within thrummed with the compulsion to claim her and mark her as mine, no matter how much I fought it. I followed her, keeping my distance for as long as I could.

That evening, I summoned her, pleading for her to come to me. I just needed to talk to her. It took everything in me, all of my willpower, to stop myself from claiming her and sealing the bond. When she came into the alley, I parted my shadows for her, concealing us both within a cocoon of darkness, a world of our own.

Then I saw her.

Her brown hair was twisted into a braid, pulling the hair away from her delicate face. My gaze locked onto those perfect eyes. They made me catch my breath, their vibrancy shining straight through my chest. I had never seen such color and expression before. Her irises were a kaleidoscope of green, shifting from one shade to another like the wind tearing through the grass in a meadow.

"It's you…" I strained out.

Her lips parted as she made a small gasp.

Gods, I want to hear nothing but that sound.

The fragrance of lavender and eucalyptus, mixed with the sweet scent of her arousal, filled my nostrils, my mind, my soul. I never wanted to smell anything other than that scent. I braced myself against the wall, trying to prevent myself from snatching her up to take her away from here. Because if I did, if I so much as touched her, I wouldn't be able to resist claiming her.

But the bond was much more insistent than I thought.

It was too much. The instinct to take what the Gods deemed was mine overwhelmed me to an unbreakable point. I couldn't do that to her. I wouldn't do that to my mate. She took a step forward and I nearly lost all control right then. I had to get her away from me, I wasn't strong enough to do it myself. The word tasted like poison as it crawled its way up my throat.

"Run."

She hesitated for the blink of an eye before she spun around and bolted out of the alley and down the street. The bond took over with a primal frenzy, and I chased after her, a predator hunting its prey. I forced myself to slow as much as I could, but my control had finally snapped.

NO!

My shadows snaked through the streets, trailing behind her. I wouldn't do this to her. I refused to treat my mate like property. Not knowing what else to do, I slammed my body into a wall of a nearby building, giving her more time to get away. I needed leave. Even if it felt wrong in every way.

"Theron!" I bellowed down the bond.

A moment later, Theron appeared. He turned his head, taking in what was happening before looking back to me. He lowered his head and softened his glowering eyes, in understanding.

"Get me out of here," I demanded as I touched his shoulder, holding on to him as if my life depended on it.

He Traveled us to the cave within the Eckterre Mountains in Oryn—the one place that always calmed me. My body vibrated with energy as the bond roared in retaliation. My skin tingled painfully, my heart raced, and there was ringing in my ears. Everything about being away from her felt unnatural, and I didn't even know her name… I had fought with my magic to stay out of her mind, and I cursed Xareus for granting me such an *atrocious* ability.

I sat against the cave wall, the chilled rock cooling my heated skin. The air was lighter here and I took deep breaths, filling my lungs with the crisp air to settle the savage beast within. Theron stood on the ledge at the mouth of the cave and lowered his head, looking as if he were ready to set me aflame.

"Why are you resisting? Do you intend to deny the bond?" His voice rumbled in my mind.

"No." Regardless of Theron's near-constant foul mood, he was always there when I needed him, always came when I called. And for that, I was grateful.

"Then why?"

"Because I refuse to claim her like some feral animal," I shouted back, releasing fire around me as I jumped up, my flames unable to burn his body as they licked at his feet. *"And because my Nation will suffer if I do."*

He tilted his head. I released a frustrated sigh and told him of what the Sage had threatened, and the village decimated by the Glaev, along with the panel of Sages and Worthy. He stared at me several moments before responding.

"Your fate has been sealed, as has the females. The Gods bound you two for a reason. It would be unwise to deny them."

"And it would be wise to put her and my people in danger if I did?" I asked. *"I'm bound to protect them and if I bind myself to her, I may be doing just the opposite. The Gods really fucked me over on this one, Theron. So unless you have some magical way to break your vow to intervene and stop the Glaev, I don't really see any other solution at the moment."*

He didn't say anything after that.

We sat in silence for a few hours on that ledge under the moonslight and I watched as the stars moved across the night sky. My thoughts jostled around, weighing heavy on my mind. The Glaev, the Sages, the panel, my people, my mate. I had a choice to make. And one that wouldn't be made lightly.

Unable to stand being so far from her any longer, Theron took me back to Torx before disappearing off to wherever it was that he went. I made sure that my mate would not feel me through the ground, staying up in the trees, as I tracked her down and kept my distance. Watching as she lay in that field of grass all night.

I followed her, the male, and the Spirit the next day as they crossed into Ulrik, where they met up with a female then began to travel southeast toward Riyah. They stopped that night to make camp, and I nearly lost my mind when all of a sudden my mate and her Spirit Traveled away. It wasn't far, but it was enough that the bond was rubbing me raw, like a blister constantly chafing.

Certain they would return soon, I waited out of sight of their encampment and watched the interactions of the male and female—hoping to discover that *this* female had an intimate relationship with the male and not my mate. But all they did was argue and bicker and taunt each other—nothing to indicate that they were involved. I hated waiting. It gave me too much time to think with nothing else to do, and my mind wandered to what was happening back home in Oryn.

Jolting me from my thoughts, the male began shouting obscenities at the now returned Spirit, and my mate lay there unmoving. It felt like a stone had been dropped into the pit of my stomach. I nearly went to her, needing to do something. I needed to know that she was okay. But before I moved to whisk her away to the nearest healer, Theron's voice sounded in my head.

"He has commanded that you not interfere, and trust that he would not allow harm to come to her," he said, sounding annoyed.

"Who?"

"Her Fylgjur."

My mate's Spirit guardian was staring right at me through the shadows I had conjured to conceal me. I didn't know if he could actually see me, but he obviously knew I was there if he had contacted Theron to give me the message.

"Alright." I nodded, though he couldn't see me, and some of the tension eased in my shoulders.

243

I knew he was right. Spirit guardians were there to protect their Worthy's life. Which meant that those that were with her were of no threat to her either. I settled in for the night, resting with my back against the trunk of a tree with my legs stretched across the limb. Even knowing that she had her Spirit to watch over her and protect her, I still wished it were me. But I pushed the feeling away, and let sleep take me.

Nearly two days later, she finally woke. She had been seated in front of the male when they rode. My teeth clenched at the thought of his body touching hers, rubbing up against her backside with his arm wrapped around her. With a snarl, I distanced myself further to where I could no longer see them. But I could still feel her, the bond pushing me to be closer, and was able to follow that feeling.

I continued to keep my distance, not wanting to see her with another males hands on her when I craved her so desperately.

But she came to me…

She'd answered my call. And she hadn't seemed afraid. If she cared for this other male, would she have done that? Or was it solely because of the bond, driving her to me beyond her control?

Well into the night, a feeling of being yanked through the bond, woke me. I sat up, instantly awake and completely aware of my hardened cock pressing into the seams of my trousers.

Is she…aroused?

Excitement coursed through my veins, but for only a moment. I broke out in a cold sweat. My breathing became quick and shallow.

She's aroused. And she's with him.

This had to end. I couldn't take it. I couldn't continue to follow her across the damned continent forever and feel her want for another male. My eyes narrowed and I took off, intending to stop her actions long enough to get her to deny the bond and release me from my misery. I wouldn't invade her mind again. Not without her approval.

I had more control of myself now, the mating bond seemingly pleased with our proximity after our encounter in that alley in Narh. I called to her, gently caressing that glimmering bond as I approached. Then I noticed that she was sitting outside of that stone tent with a book propped up on her folded legs. Alone.

She isn't with him. She's...reading.

I smiled and huffed a breath of relief that she wasn't bedding the male.

I stopped, close enough to see her but far enough away to be concealed by my shadows. But the moment I stepped onto the grass, her head snapped up in my direction.

I had thought that she might feel me, but I didn't know from how far away. My mate knew I was there but ignored my attempt to reach her through the bond. She was sitting in the grass as she leaned against the wall of the tent.

I envisioned her for a moment. I pictured her sitting just as she was then, with a book in her lap and leaning against my chest as she told me of the fantastical worlds and adventures that she lost herself in.

That vision evaporated the moment she stood, facing me. Shaking my head, I knew that I couldn't hear her deny me, no matter how much I needed her to. I wanted to go to her. She knew I was there, she felt me and she wasn't running away even after what I said to her back in Narh.

I couldn't ask her to deny me. I didn't want her to. If she wanted me the way I wanted her, we would find a way without endangering my people. I needed to go back to Oryn and see what Arra had discovered.

I surrounded myself with shadows before calling for Theron to take me back. Leaving now was a small price to pay, to suffer the distance once again, but if she accepted this, it would be worth it. I would remove all obstacles, no matter how challenging they were, if she wanted this. I'd take on the panel. I'd stop the Glaev. If she wanted this, then nothing would stop me from having her.

I couldn't resist the bond much longer. It wanted her. *I* wanted her. And I knew that I would only crave her more and more.

Chapter Twenty-Eight

KYA

We settled in for the night when we finished with our spar. After I had felt my mate near again, I waited.

Once I knew that Nikan and Malina were asleep, I slipped out of the tent and crouched outside by the fire, the remaining embers still glowing red and crackling. Odarum had gone, which I found he often did in the night while we slept, leaving no one else out here but me. My bare feet and hands were firmly planted on the cool ground beneath me. I could feel exactly where my mate was. Close enough that I could faintly feel his heartbeat through my terbis.

Leaving the warmth of the fire, I pulled up my mask just below my eyes, and walked deep into the shadows of the forest, beyond where anyone would see me. The forest floor was nearly pitch black, the canopy above too dense to allow the moonslight to shine through. An advantage for me. While I was able to feel where I was going and didn't need to see, I doubted my mate could.

Once I was far enough out of earshot, I stopped and I closed my eyes, searching for that comfortable swirling thread inside me. Grabbing onto it, I called to it, summoning its other half within my mate. It felt different than when I grasped the tether to Odarum or my magic. This one felt more natural and welcoming.

It took mere seconds to feel him moving toward me from behind, through the forest. He knew I was here, calling to him and waiting. One by one, my senses began to fall away again until all I could sense was him and only him. It was intoxicating. My palms began to sweat, and I rubbed them against my shirt to remove the moisture. My breath began to shake as he grew closer and closer. It felt like an eternity as he slowly and silently approached.

My breath caught, and my spine straightened when I felt the heat of his body behind me, his breath on the back of my neck. His scent consumed me, washing over me in waves. In the corner of my eye, I could see his large hand braced against the trunk of the tree next to me. His sleeve was rolled up to his elbow, revealing the Worthy mark on his muscular forearm.

We didn't speak for several minutes. The only sounds were our heavy breaths and pounding hearts. This had seemed like a good idea before, but now that I was actually here, I started to second guess my decision to confront him. I braced myself and summoned the courage to speak.

"You've been following me." My voice held less bite than I intended and came out as a rasp. My heart was beating so hard against my chest, I was sure he could hear it.

"Hmm," he rumbled. A shiver ran through me.

"Do you know who I am?" I breathed, my voice trembling slightly with restraint as I forced myself to continue to face away from him.

"No. But I know who you are to me." There was a softness to his voice that I didn't expect, mixed with the resonance of power and authority.

My eyes shuttered closed at the sound of his deep soothing voice and I could feel heat building in my core, my body reacting to his proximity. Every part of me was completely aware and focused solely on him. He inhaled deeply before exhaling a sigh, likely scenting my instant arousal in his presence. His own filled my nostrils, clouding my mind from thinking clearly.

"Your name," he strained through clenched teeth.

My eyes opened, and my brows furrowed, reality coming back to me.

"What?"

"I need to hear your name." His voice was a desperate plea, and a gentle caress to my soul.

I took a deep breath, attempting to gain some semblance of myself. Slowly, I turned around to finally face him, craning my neck to look up at him.

My mate.

He removed his hand from the tree and stood fully, towering over me. My breath caught in my throat when my eyes locked with his. Silver irises, shadowed from underneath his hood, bored into me, seeing my very soul. His lips parted, and he released a small gasp before slowly removing his hood, allowing me to see his face. The silver of his eyes glinted through the darkness, as if they contained lights from the stars themselves. I remembered those eyes from the first time I saw them. I couldn't forget. I saw them every time I closed my own.

"You first," I taunted. "Seeing as you're the one who's been stalking me since I left Ilrek." I willed the bite in my voice to return. My eyes hardened in challenge and looked down my nose at him, regardless that he was over a head taller than me.

But I couldn't blame him for what he had done. If he hadn't stayed so close all this time, I most likely would have been driven to find him on my own.

He was the most breathtaking thing I had ever laid my eyes on. He was a vision. A vision made by the Gods just for me. The side of his mouth twitched up into a smirk, eyes narrowing in amusement yet burning with hunger.

"I'd like to think of it more as shadowing rather than stalking." His voice was rough and husky. I was thankful for having my mask in place to hide my smirk at his smart-ass remark.

After a moment of silence, I crossed my arms and lifted my brows, letting him know that I was still waiting for his answer.

"Fair enough," he chuckled then lifted his chin slightly. "My name is Ryker."

"Ryker," I said slowly, testing his name on my tongue. It felt natural, sweet even. Like honey.

His smirk fell and his pupils widened slightly when I said his name. He lifted his hand as if to reach for me, but then stopped himself and dropped it back to his side. Silence sat between us as we studied each other. We were suspended in time, in our own world, as if nothing else existed in the moment except us.

"You still haven't told me your name." His eyes never left my face.

He stopped breathing, waiting for me to speak. I didn't plan to answer him and make him suffer just a little bit longer for telling me to run and hiding in the shadows, denying me what I desired. But I couldn't stop my mouth from moving as my name spilled out of it.

"Kya," I said in a near whisper.

Ryker's eyes darkened and his lips twitched into a small smile.

"Kya." He spoke my name is if it was the most precious word to cross his lips. It was as if my name was made to be spoken by him and his voice alone.

My eyes softened as I looked back up to those silver irises. We stood there, gazing at each other. I didn't know how much time had passed because it felt as if time stopped. There was no awkwardness, no anxiety. My soul knew his and was meant to be with him. The mating bond was gifted to us by the Gods, two halves of a single soul bridged together by the divine.

As difficult as it was, I resisted reaching out to touch him. A deep feeling of doubt washed over me as I thought of our first encounter together in that alley.

He told me to leave, to run. He didn't want this. He didn't want me.

Seeming to sense the change in my emotions, he tilted his head and pulled his eyebrows together in a silent question.

I didn't want to ask. I didn't want to know for certain. But I needed to. I began to shake, with nerves or fear. I glanced away from him, taking in the calm darkness of the forest around us. I took a deep breath, the scent of damp soil and crisp autumn air mixing with the scent of my mate.

"You told me to run," I whispered, looking back to him.

"I did." His lips stretched into a thin, sad line. There was a tenderness in his eyes that opposed his intimidating and dangerous facade.

I looked down at the ground and nodded softly, tears stinging the back of my eyes, and my throat tightened.

"I didn't know what this was until after seeing you in the alley. That burning inside me… I never understood. I thought maybe it had something to do with Odarum at first. Then I saw you and I just…knew." I didn't lift my eyes. Instead, I concentrated on the forest floor.

He didn't respond, didn't move. I glanced up at him and saw that he was still watching me, his eyes roaming over my face in search of something. I lifted my head back up and tightened my arms around myself, chilled from the cool night air. His eyes flicked down to the motion briefly and his body tensed.

"When did *you* know?" I prodded, not able to handle his silence.

"During the Trial. I felt it first when your fate was sealed in the Spirit world."

He'd known that long?

His face looked pained, and he seemed to tense even more and I could see his eyes harden. His chest moved up and down with his quickened breathing. His short answers were starting to piss me off.

Was I so bad that he was in pain to be near me? Was it only the bond forcing him to be here?

"Why did you wait to approach me? Why did you follow me? Why didn't you come up and tell me?" Anger laced my voice, hiding the hurt behind it. I braced myself for the brunt of my stupid childish dream, of one day having a male that was fated to me by the Gods, to be crushed by the Lord before me.

"I—" he stammered.

"Do you want this? If you don't… If you don't want this, then just reject the bond and get it over with."

He flinched. "What makes you think I don't want this? I've followed you across the damn continent. I've abandoned my Nation when it needs me. All so I could be near you because I can't stand being away from you, even before learning your name. I can't get you out of my head. Of course I fucking want this. I can barely control it. It's been killing me not to have you."

My heart lurched and my stomach fluttered. Hearing him admit to the mating bond after dancing around the term hit me hard and made me shiver.

"But you told me to run," I breathed.

"Yes." He huffed in a humorless laugh. "But not for the reason you think."

Ryker let out a sharp breath and closed his eyes for a moment as if to calm himself before looking at me again with intensity in his eyes.

"It's because I know how the mating bond works. And I knew then that I was not in control of the urges. Not enough anyway. The first encounter can be intense and overwhelming, especially for males." He spoke apologetically. "The instinct to claim our mate can completely consume us, no matter how hard we try to fight it. I didn't want that to happen. I didn't want to do that to you."

I knew this. I had read about it time and time again in love stories. It was what drove that private dream of mine to have a mate finally come and claim me, to live happily ever after. But I wasn't completely ignorant about the reality of the mating bond.

Although mates were rare, most instances were recorded and that's where many of the fae had written fictional books about the romantic encounters. Most of the records of the *actual* occurrences were anything but romantic, though. The claiming could be violent, vicious even, the males having little to no control with the strong urges the bond forced upon them, especially if there was another male with his female. Some of these instances had even ended in bloodshed.

A realization came over me and I felt the blood drain from my face as fear took hold. This was my mate, standing at arm's length without having claimed me yet. And I had been traveling with another male. The urge to seal the bond must have been overwhelming for Ryker. Yet he seemed to have control over it somehow. But how long could he hold on to it? And…did I want him to?

His tongue swept out and licked his lips.

Lips that I couldn't stop staring at. I wanted to know what they tasted like.

A wave of heat flashed through me, to my very core, and I thought of that delicious tongue on my body. Something deep inside of me urged to be even nearer to him.

His eyes flicked with a fierce hunger. He tensed and he took a step back as if he could… My eyes widened and the thoughts of what my body yearned to do with his stilled.

"Can you read my mind? Hear my thoughts?" My voice raised an octave, feeling mortified.

"I'm trying not to. But it's so damn hard for me to control everything when the bond makes me so drawn to you." The side of his mouth lifted.

My face paled even more at the admission.

He's been able to hear my thoughts this whole time. And he finds this humorous?

"Not the whole time. And it is kind of humorous. No one has ever discovered my mind abilities since I was deemed Worthy, not even those closest to me until I told them. Yet only minutes with you and you had it figured out. At least my mate is observant," he said with a proud smirk and a shrug.

I glared at him, realizing he was still able to hear me.

"What do you mean 'not the whole time'?"

"I only enter someone's mind when I intend to. But the bond makes me lose control, though I have been able to prevent it the majority of the time. I can feel certain emotions though. I think that's all the bond's doing because I've never done that with anyone else."

"You can feel my emotions too?" My mouth fell open in shock.

I hadn't heard about this, though it was possible that it was entirely unique to us. Some of the mating records indicated that their connections varied. I leaned against the tree trunk next to us and slid down into a sitting position. My arms were resting on my bent knees. It was a lot to take in.

Ryker squatted in front of me, leaning on the back of his heels with his head tilted down so that we were eye level. A slight look of concern was etched into his face.

"Yes," he said softly. "I started to feel you after your Trial, when you returned from Hylithria. It hit me so hard that it nearly brought me to my knees. You were so conflicted…it angered me, whatever it was that caused you such turmoil. I didn't even know who you were but I was ready to tear down the world for you."

I stared into those pools of silver as I became lost in his words.

"I still don't understand, why didn't you approach me sooner?"

He stiffened. "The male you've been traveling with. You've been with him since you left Morah and you share a tent with him. And a horse," he grumbled.

I rolled my eyes. "My *brother* insists on sleeping near me whilst traveling so that we can work together quicker in the event of an attack. He's an overbearing ass, but no threat to you." I eyed him for a moment. "And to put your worried bond at ease, there is no other male in my life that you'd have to challenge."

He breathed a sigh of relief. We stared at each other for several moments before he spoke again.

"Let me see you." He gestured to my face.

I had forgotten that I was still masked. I nodded and pulled the black fabric down, revealing my face. His eyes roamed over it, filled with heat.

My heart was hammering against the walls of my chest, and with that look in his eyes like he wanted to devour me, my core began to heat with desire. My breathing grew faster, and I tried to fight the feeling. Which he could feel. The overwhelming want died down as another question entered my mind.

"How is it that you can feel me but I can't feel you?"

"It's stronger for males. As the bond grows, you'll be able to feel me just as much as I feel you. Until the mating is sealed, our bond craves connection." His lips twitched up.

The tension in his body made sense then. He was struggling to hold back. The fear that he would snap started to creep back into me. I sat up straighter and my hand fell to the dagger sheathed at my thigh. He noticed the movement and his eyes reflected an emotion that I hadn't seen yet—hurt.

"I would *never* harm you, Kya. I promise to never lay a hand on you that you don't want."

But I did want. I only feared the violence that was known to come with mated males. But he was in control.

I leaned in slightly, I couldn't help myself. The pull of the bond was tempting me to reach out, just to touch him, to feel his skin against mine. I was apprehensive of what would happen if I did, but I *had* to.

I reached my hand out and brushed my fingers across his cheek. I ripped my hand away as shock tore through my body, like lightning tingling over my skin. For only a moment, I couldn't breathe. Ryker jumped up and stumbled back, almost falling, as I stood.

"Fuck," he breathed. I could sense how he wanted me in that moment, and it was euphoric to my senses.

"Sorry," I muttered.

At that slight touch, the instinctual urge to have him claim me right then and there, to make me his and make him mine, was almost too great to resist.

"It's alright. But I definitely didn't expect that," he said through gritted teeth. He grunted, forcing himself to take a step back away from me. I eyed the increased distance between us.

"Ryker." My voice was quiet.

His eyes snapped up to mine.

"I want you."

A low growl rumbled in his chest and his body turned rigid.

"You want me." I stepped closer, glancing down at the evidence pressing against his pants.

"I do."

I slowly removed my jacket, watching him track the movement with wide eyes, and dropped it to the forest floor. His eyes snapped back up. Those silver irises clashed with mine in the darkness of the night. I wanted the bond of my mate. I wanted *him.*

"Then claim me."

Chapter Twenty-Nine

KYA

"What?" Ryker choked out, clenching his jaw so hard I thought his teeth might crack from the tension.

"Take me, Ryker," I breathed.

I stepped closer to him until I was near enough to reach out and touch him. His hand flew to the back of my head, gripping my hair at the base but not touching my skin, and pulled me to him. I gasped and put my hands on his muscular chest. It felt warm beneath my touch and I wanted to feel his bare skin against mine.

"Stop," he grunted in a whisper. "I can't control myself."

I tilted my head back to look him in the eyes; the silver in them seemed brighter, glowing almost.

"So don't."

"Gods…this is so fucking hard," he said breathlessly as his face moved closer to mine. I could feel his breath against my mouth.

My tongue swiped across my bottom lip before biting it. His eyes were filled with desperate hunger, and a low growl reverberated through his chest. My breathing increased, each rise of my chest causing the peak of my breasts to rub against his body. Wetness pooled in my core as it throbbed, begging to be filled. His cock twitched against my stomach as I pushed my body against his. His body scorched mine in every place it touched and I wanted more of it.

"Ryker," I pleaded, my eyelids fluttered shut as he moved his lips closer to mine.

"Kya, I can't."

My heart sank and I opened my eyes. He released his grasp on my hair and pulled away from me quickly. I instantly felt the chill of the night, already missing his heat. I gaped at him.

"I thought you wanted this?" I asked. Fighting against myself to not claw my way back to him. Now that I had had him so close, I didn't want to separate ever again.

"I do," he rasped. "But I can't. I'm sorry."

I had thought perhaps that my mind was playing tricks on me in the darkness when wings appeared behind him. But then he turned and I could see the black leathery appendages protruding from his back, his shirt ripped into slits where they had emerged. He spread them out to the sides, the membrane was etched with scars and at the tip of the center of each wing had a curved claw. My eyes widened.

That's why he would seem to disappear.

He glanced back at me over his shoulder for just a moment, his eyes full of sorrow, before he beat his wings once, causing a gust of wind that propelled him into the night sky.

Cold and alone in the darkness, I slumped to my knees on the forest floor and dropped my head into my hands to stifle a sob.

All at once, the veil of the bond lifted and the reality of what I had just done, what I had asked him to do rushed back into me. I had asked him to claim me. I didn't even know it. Then it hit me. *Ryker*, Lord of Oryn and Worthy to Xareus, the God of Chaos.

Gods, I had been so absorbed by him that I hadn't even thought of who he was. Feared for his ruthlessness, he and his

Nation were a force to be reckoned with and, if the rumors were true, had a taste for the blood of his enemies.

Was I his enemy? The Sage female at the Temple of the Fallen God had warned me to watch out for the other Worthy. Not only was I a Worthy with no Nation, but I was also Atarian by birth. I had never sworn citizenship to Riyah, therefore I was still Atarian and technically forbidden. But it would be a cold day in Odes's grave before I let him find that out.

But he didn't seem like he was a threat, and he did say that he wouldn't hurt me. Mates were compelled to protect one another, not harm. But he did deny me.

Again.

He told me he couldn't do it. What was that supposed to mean?

How could I have been so stupid to leave myself so blindly trusting not once, but twice?

I wouldn't let it happen again. I wouldn't leave myself to that kind of vulnerability anymore.

I stood up, feeling a new sort of resolve and confidence, and made my way back to camp. If my mate wanted this to happen, he was going to have to fight for it.

"I think you should get out here." Odarum's voice rang through my head.

I opened my eyes and sat up on the furs. Malina was sitting next to me in the tent with a serious look on her face. When I returned last night, Malina woke up and noted my red, swollen eyes. She never asked why I was crying, and I never said. She just stayed with me until I fell asleep.

I could hear distant shouting outside the tent. Malina and I both stood, she pulled her lips into a tight frown. My eyes narrowed, and my brows creased.

"He was here waiting outside when Nik woke up," Malina said expressionless.

I rushed out of the tent in nothing but my tank and trousers, my hair loose and unbraided, flowing behind me.

Out in the clearing, Nikan and Ryker were standing in front of each other. Nikan, armed with his sword and a firm grip on the terra beneath him, was shouting and Ryker looked like he was about to smash his fist into Nikan's face.

Well, I did say he was going to have to fight for it.

"You need to leave. You have no authority in this Nation, Lord Ryker."

"I don't care where we are. As I told you, I'm not leaving until I speak with Kya." His voice was cold and calm.

Seeing Ryker standing off with Nikan over me appealed to me in a way that I would never admit. I reached for those swirling shadows inside of me as I walked over to them, Malina right next to me. Ryker whipped his head in my direction, and he shot me a brief smile. He didn't take his eyes off me the entire time as I approached and stood before them.

Nikan stepped between me and my mate. I glared at him as Ryker curled his lips back and snarled at the male. Odarum was standing off to the side but alert to the situation. Malina narrowed her eyes at Ryker's reaction. She remained silent but watched our interaction closely.

"Kya, get on the horse and get out of here. He's a Lord and could see you as a threat, just like that Sage said." Nikan's blue eyes bore into me.

"You dare insinuate that I would harm her?" Ryker stepped closer behind Nikan and I could have sworn I saw his eyes flare.

"Kya, leave. Now," Nikan snapped at me.

A ring of fire encircled Nikan. And we all jumped back except Ryker, who stepped through the ring and approached Nikan until there were nearly nose to nose.

"Do not *ever* command her again," Ryker seethed.

"Ryker," I warned and Malina's head snapped to me.

Ryker backed away and snuffed out the fire before locking eyes with me again, and his features softened just slightly.

I felt Nikan grip the rock below with his terbis and I grabbed his arm to stop him from attacking. Just as I was about to open my mouth to protest, Malina spoke.

"No. Fucking. Way," she balked. "You have *got* to be kidding me. Him?!"

I nodded, unsure of how she put it all together.

"What? What about him?" Nikan asked, spitting out the last word like it was acid on his tongue.

I sighed, then removed my hand from his arm. I moved around him and stood next to Ryker, careful not to touch him. Ryker's hand twitched next to mine as if he was doing the same. I felt a deep comfort being in his presence.

"Nik, Ryker is my mate," I spoke softly, hoping to lessen the blow.

Malina smiled brightly at the admission. But Nikan's face remained hard.

"He's a Lord, a Worthy! No two Worthy have ever been mated. How do you know he isn't just playing tricks on you? We've all heard the rumors of his bloodlust. If he sees you as a risk to his status, he would take you down in a heartbeat."

Ryker took a protective step in front of me, glaring at Nikan with malice in his silver eyes. I felt him pull on the bond, as if he needed the reassurance that it was still there and Nikan's words hadn't taken it away, making the bond feel tense and anxious. I moved between them and put my hands up, angry that someone would question my word and insult my mate.

Gods, these overprotective males…

"Nik, Lord Ryker *is* my mate. I know it for certain. Even Odarum confirmed it. And just for the record, he has prevented himself from sealing the bond, even when I asked him to. If he were so eager to eliminate me, he wouldn't have done that."

"Asked him to, huh?" Malina made an amused sound and quirked an eyebrow, but I ignored her and continued.

"He could have killed me on sight. Not to mention, if he truly was a threat to me, do you really think Odarum would just be standing there? Do not question our bond. And you will not harm him." I looked down to the ground beneath us before giving him a knowing look.

With a frustrated grunt, I felt Nikan release his hold on the terra. I spun around to face Ryker and narrowed my eyes at him, his eyebrows raised as he flinched.

"And you," I snapped. "You need to explain your reasoning for last night."

"That's what I wanted to talk to you about." He flicked his eyes from me to Nikan then back. "Could we speak alone?" he asked quietly.

I nodded and turned my head to look at Malina. I jutted my chin toward the tent, and she smiled and winked. She turned and grabbed Nikan's shoulders, spinning him around and pushing on his back to get him to walk toward the tent.

"Get moving, you overbearing brute. The Worthy lovers need some privacy," Malina chipped gleefully, bouncing on her toes.

Odarum walked away with them and dipped his head in acknowledgment.

"Overbearing indeed. And he's your…*brother?*" Ryker questioned.

I turned back to him, and he was staring at the two walking away, no doubt noticing the obvious physical differences. I tried to hide my amused smile as I nodded. This wasn't the first time that people questioned our familial ties.

He nodded slowly before looking down at me. "Is he a half-brother?"

I couldn't hide my amusement any longer, and I chuckled. "Where we come from, blood has nothing to do with family." I turned my head and gestured to them. "His name is Nikan. And the female is Malina, my sister."

"And where, exactly, are you from?"

I turned my head back and found him staring at me with a small smile. I gave him a deadpan stare.

"You're not getting out of this so easily." I crossed my arms. "Why did you leave? Why did you come back?"

"Will you walk with me?" He turned to the side and extended his hand out in front of him.

I gave him a curt nod, and we fell into step with each other across the grassy clearing. He held his arms beside him with a straight posture, the very essence of a Lord. I took him in from the corner of my eye. In the light of day, his broad shoulders were more defined and his face was hardened, with those silver eyes taking in every detail around us without effort. He was the epitome of every description I had read of the Lord of Oryn, but I had never imagined that he would also be as attractive as he was.

"I'm sorry for leaving you last night. The way you were speaking to me was making me lose control, and I was seconds away from fucking you against a tree," he said as we continued to walk.

The thought of us standing in the forest last night flashed through my mind and my skin began to heat. I didn't miss his visible erection either, which only made my skin feel hotter.

He cleared his throat then continued. "I can't seal the bond with you. Not yet at least. I returned to Oryn last night to speak with my advisor about it."

That's…weird.

"You flew back to Oryn to speak to your advisor about having sex with me?" I gave him a questioning look as we crested over a hill, the grass swaying through the breeze tickled my feet.

"Well, sort of, I suppose. But not like you think." He sighed deeply. "I was approached by a Sage after the Trial and was warned to deny the bond with you, otherwise Oryn would suffer. As would we." His voice trailed off.

"What do you mean?"

"The Sages have convened a panel with the other Worthy to decide if our mating is forbidden."

"Forbidden? They can do that?" I gaped.

"Evidently." Ryker shrugged.

"Wha—" I didn't even know what to say. Not only did the Sages and other Worthy know about my mating bond before I did, but they also had already called for a panel to decide if it was allowed. Which was completely unheard of. Not to mention, not a single one of them told me about it. "So, when is it?"

"Our mating trial will happen one month after Nailu. That is if we will not deny the bond or agree to the Raith, stripping both of us of all our bonds and magic." His jaw clenched.

"You agreed to this?" I asked, completely perplexed.

"No," he answered quickly. "Seriously? I was pissed. I didn't agree to anything but they didn't exactly take my opinion into consideration."

"And what will happen if we tell them to shove their panel up their asses and go pound sand then just complete the bond anyway?"

He blew out a heavy breath. "We can't complete the mating or risk them ordering the Nex. But I would *never* let that happen to you."

Great. Just another death sentence hanging over my head.

I stopped breathing momentarily. The bond I had hoped and dreamed for had already been threatened. I shook my head.

"But what does this have to do with your Nation?"

"The Glaev," he grumbled. "That Sage, Vicria, she told me that my Nation would suffer more than it already was. I returned to Oryn to find that her threat was valid. The Glaev had destroyed an entire village—few survived."

"I'm sorry."

Instinctively, and foolishly, I placed my hand on his sleeved arm. We both tensed, fighting the urges to increase that touch. I reluctantly removed my hand.

She...

I wondered if it was the same female who had warned me to stay away from the other Worthy.

"But wait, how would she know the Glaev—" I stopped abruptly.

...is not what it seems...

Kleios words rang through my head. This must have been what she was talking about and it had something to do with the Sage. But I still didn't understand what it meant. Was the Sage controlling the Glaev somehow? Was she causing it? Or did she only know of when and where it would affect?

"Kya?" Ryker's voice interrupted my thoughts. My name on his lips nearly made my eyes roll back. I shook my head to get back to the topic.

"Ryker, do you know how she knew about the Glaev in your land?"

"No. I have people working to find that out right now. Until her prediction, we had always thought it was a disease just like everyone else. But if she knew about it as it happened from across the continent, it has to be something else."

I nodded. "You're right. Kleio told me that the Glaev is not what it seems. I think she wants me to figure out what it is and stop it, restore the balance. That's what we're doing here." I gestured around us. "We're looking for something that could help us find out what it is exactly."

"Let me help you. I can check back in at Voara from time to time until we get it figured out. I can't stay away from you too long, though. The bond will drive us both crazy if we're apart for extended periods of time."

I hid my frown at the thought of being separated from him. I felt foolish for it, I shouldn't have felt that way having just met him. But it was the most logical thing to do. Then, excitement coursed through me at the thought of him being with me as we traveled back to Morah and then to Dusan. My mind wandered to imaginings of huddling close on cold nights and riding together on horseback. My stomach tingled with anticipation and my core heated.

Ryker's nostrils flared. His eyes darkened, and he leaned into me, almost pressing his body against mine.

"And when we do figure this out, together, I'll give you exactly what you begged of me last night." His lips nearly grazed my ear and his breath was hot on my neck. I wanted to melt at the sound of his sultry voice. "I've waited a very long time for my mate, and you can bet that I won't let them take you from me now that I have you. We will get past this, show them we are no threat. Then, I will take you. I will claim what is mine. Because you are *mine*, Kya. I will seal the bond with you and be marked by our mating."

Shivers ran down my spine when he trailed his eyes down my left arm—the arm that would one day bear the mark of our mating bond.

"But until then," he continued. "I can't claim you. I can't risk the people that I have been deemed Worthy to protect."

I swallowed through my panting breaths. "How would they know? What if we just don't tell them and hide our marks? I've done it with my Trial mark." Was I that desperate? Apparently. It was almost pathetic, but I couldn't help it.

"The Sages are spiritually enhanced. Now that they know of our bond, they would sense the shift in the Spirits of two powerful Worthy being mated."

"You think I'm powerful?"

He leaned back and stared into my eyes. "Very."

He stepped away, and I noticed only then that he had surrounded us with his shadows, sheltering our bodies away from the rest of the world so that these moments were just for us. My heart swelled when he smiled at me.

I smiled back, and his eyes seemed to flicker with a faint glow for a fleeting moment.

"We're going to have to find a way to repress our physical temptations in the mean time. And I'd like to get to know a bit more about the one I'm bound to," he said.

"Agreed." I nodded. Though I knew much more about him than he did me. I'd have to be careful with my words if he started asking about my past.

Ryker drew his shadows back as we began to walk through the trees back to camp. It took a significant effort to not touch him, reach for him.

When we made it back to camp, Nikan glared at Ryker with distrust—I understood his apprehension. Nikan didn't speak once as he pushed down our tent and readied the horses.

Odarum was gone and I reached out to him.

"Where are you? We are leaving for Ilrek."

"I will find you." Was all he supplied.

I made a sound of frustration.

Of course.

Two horses, four people. There was no way that Nikan and Ryker would ride together, and there was no chance I'd allow another female, even my sister, to ride with my mate. Without saying anything, Nikan mounted his horse and Malina followed, biting back a smile with a wink towards me.

"If our skin touches again..." he said, shaking his head.

I nodded, understanding, though unhappy with it. "As much as I'd like to essentially sit in your lap all the way back to Ilrek, it's probably best if we don't."

Part of me wanted him with me while the other part still didn't trust him fully. Nikan wasn't wrong. And now I knew that his entire Nation was at risk. If I could have saved Atara by denying a mating bond, I would have.

"Yeah... Besides, I've been gone from Oryn too long. As much as I'd like for you to sit in my lap for the next few days," he said with a wink. "I need to return. I still have a Nation to run." He remained silent for several moments, staring at me with confliction in his eyes.

"I'll meet you in Ilrek then," he sighed. He stepped away from me and I mounted the horse.

Settled in the saddle, I watched as he manifested his wings and took to the skies without another word, and tracked him until I couldn't see him anymore. The bond began to burn as he left. I was torn between what I desired and what was right—whatever that was.

I'd be bound to him for an eternity. The Gods demanded it. They wanted two Worthy mated. Between the mating panel and the Glaev, and the fact that the Gods deemed Ryker Worthy of protecting his Nation... Also, if we mated, perhaps I could convince him to open his borders to the Ataran people and finally give them a home.

Granting one demand meant denying the other.

"What do you want from us?" I whispered to the Gods, before I followed Nikan and Malina into the forest, heading back to Ilrek.

Chapter Thirty

RYKER

I wasn't going to make it. I was going to die. It had been two days since I last saw Kya, since I was last near her, and I felt like the bond was going to burn my very soul.

While in Oryn, I dedicated all of my time and efforts to the matters that needed my attention. It helped keep my mind distracted. Once everything was settled and more manageable for Mavris to handle, I was finally able to go back to her.

Even if it was just for a short while. I couldn't continue to follow her around the continent. Not while I needed to be here. But at the very least, I could get away for a couple of days at a time.

Theron hadn't been able to travel me to her so once again, I flew hard and fast into Riyah letting the bond guide me to her.

She was only a few hours away from Ilrek when I saw her sitting atop her horse riding through the trees. I know I had said that I would see her in the city, but I couldn't wait that long.

I remained a short distance away, observing her as she chatted with the other two. She had a lightness about her that sucked me in and held my attention. The sounds of her soft, breathy laugh while talking with her sister caused my lips to turn upward involuntarily, as if contagious. Infectious.

I quite enjoyed watching her from afar, seeing how she interacted with others, how she held herself with confidence and purpose. Unlike the cheery female she conversed with, she had a seriousness to her demeanor, but also wasn't as intense as the pinched-faced male either. She was a mixture of the two—a perfect balance of light and dark. She was also observant, constantly glancing, taking note of her environment and situation. So observant in fact that she turned her head to look directly at me, as if she knew exactly where I was in the treetops though she couldn't see me through the shadows.

I swooped down and landed between the horses, startling them.

Kya's eyes brightened with her mouth gaped open, and I threw her a wink. I heard Nikan's scoff but didn't bother to look at him. I kept my gaze on my mate whose beauty continued to astound me.

"Mind if I catch a ride with you?" I asked, disappearing my wings.

"What about our skin touching?" She raised a brow.

"I'll be extra careful." The side of my mouth curved into a smile.

Come on. Let me be close to you. I want to know you better.
I hoped my smile portrayed my thoughts.

She pursed her lips and held my gaze for several moments, sizing me up. She was hesitant, and I wondered what had caused her demeanor to change from her eagerness within such a short amount of time.

I sighed with relief when she finally relented and scooted up in the saddle, leaving room for me to climb on behind her.

Both of our bodies were so tense, touching like this, her perfect plump ass rubbing up against me with every sway of the horse's steps. Not a single part of me was able to relax the entire ride, not when I could scent every bit of her.

I hadn't ridden a horse for at least a century. There was no need. Not when I could travel so much faster on my own in the skies. But I wanted this closeness to Kya. The closer she got to me, the more I never wanted her to go. I wanted to curl my body over her and embrace everything that she was. She was intoxicating to me.

"I've been wondering." I broke the silence between us to offer a distraction, more for myself. "Are you able to feel me?"

She slowly turned her head to look at me. Her face blanched. "Erm, what do you mean?" Her eyes darted to my hardened cock pressing against my pants, between us, before quickly looking back to me.

"I know you can feel that. But that isn't what I was referring to." She turned back around and I huffed a low chuckle. "I meant…well, I don't know what I mean exactly. Several times, when I would get closer to you, you could *feel* me."

"How do you know that?"

"I, um," I lowered my voice. Shame washed over me. "I entered your mind before. Only briefly though."

"Hmm," she hummed before she continued. "I don't know if I like that, or if I don't."

My eyebrows scrunched together. I couldn't think of why someone would like that at all.

"But yes," she answered. "I could feel you. Though I didn't know it was you at the time. And I was curious how you were able to seemingly appear and disappear, but after seeing your wings, it all makes sense now." She smiled over her shoulder.

"Appear and disappear?" I asked.

She nodded. "Yeah. From the ground."

My eyebrows raised with intrigue. "You're a terbis wielder."

"Technically." She shrugged.

"What does that mean?"

She sighed. "I'm not strong in manipulation; however I can feel vibrations through the terra and I can sense where and what things are, so long as it's touching the ground."

Manipulation or not, having a unique ability such as hers was something to behold. I smiled down at my mate.

She truly is a rare little gem.

"What about your gifted ability from Kleio? Have you worked on developing it?"

"A bit. But not enough to hold for long without passing out. I need to work on it more, as well as what I've gotten from Odarum. He's supposed to be helping me but he keeps disappearing." She scowled.

"Odarum is your Spirit?" I gazed at her. Those green eyes shone in the morning light, captivating me wholly, and I wanted to taste those lush pink lips.

She nodded.

"Good to know it's not just mine. Has your shifting manifested yet?" I asked.

Kya pursed her lips and shook her head. "No. He said it would take more connection through the bond, but I'm not entirely sure what that means." She twisted her upper body to look up at me. "How did you do it? With the wings and all?"

"Depends on what it is. But from what I've learned, it's equal parts bond and emotion. It took a life-threatening situation for mine to manifest. And my wings aren't the only thing I can shift from my Spirit. It is possible to shift multiple physical aspects as well as a magical ability."

"What ability have you gained from your Spirit? What is your Spirit animal anyway?" Kya asked. Her sweet voice was smooth like silk, and it only caused me to get even harder.

"Get to know your mate later. We're here," Nikan snapped.

Dick.

All three of them pulled up their masks, concealing their faces. I didn't understand why they kept their faces hidden as we approached the city of Ilrek before us.

After depositing our horses at the stables on the outskirts, we quickly passed through the city as dusk approached. I had always appreciated the beauty and peace of the city. I hadn't spent much time in Ilrek, generally busy with matters in my own Nation, but I enjoyed the atmosphere of the culture here. It reminded me of Voara, how harmonious the people were. Nikan grumbled something about running an errand before meeting us back at Morah later.

I walked a step behind my mate and her sister, catching a glimpse of Kya's ass occasionally as we passed through the rings of the city to the center where the great library was. People parted in the streets as we passed through and mumbled low whispers, quickly getting out of the way. I eyed them curiously, realizing that they weren't looking at *us* but rather the two females in front of me. The people in the streets were wary of them. My eyes widened when one such whisper was audible enough to make out a single word.

"Roav."

My mate is a Roav?

How could I have missed it? Had I been so distracted with her presence that I failed to notice? Now that I had, it was obvious. The cloaks and hoods and, for the love of Xareus, they had fucking Roav pins fastened to their cloak.

"Little gem," my voice kept low. "What is your occupation exactly?"

"*Little gem*? That's so cute!" Malina whispered to Kya.

She turned her head and the edges of her pine-green eyes crinkled underneath her hood giving me a wicked look before she winked at me.

"You'll find out soon enough, *shadow*."

Her sultry voice and the mischievous look in her eye had my cock hardening all over again, and I had to adjust myself to make it less obvious after she turned her head back around. And the way she called me shadow had my fists clenching to keep from grabbing her and taking her right then and there. I forced my mind to think about anything else.

We wove our way through the city and thankfully, as we rounded a corner, my thoughts shifted to the great library before us. Even having seen it dozens of times, being in the presence of the towering obsidian building nearly took my breath away as we entered the inner ring of the city. Morah was an incredible piece of architecture, the exterior made entirely of dark glass, shining with the light of the setting sun. Even though the glass was translucent, you couldn't see the interior, but those that were inside could see out.

No one knows exactly how long ago Morah had been built. Some say it was erected by the Gods themselves, but it was more widely believed that it was the work of great terbis, air, and fire wielders. The theory was that the fire wielders heated the rock until it became molten and the terbis wielders manipulated its shape and pressure to form the glassy substance, with the air wielders cooling it quickly. Some have said that it was filled with darkness of shadow wielders, creating the black within the glass, but most doubted that.

Funny how there was no record of how the library was built, when the Scholars who worked inside recorded everything else in the realm.

Home to the greatest collection of knowledge in the world, the library's vast selection was open to anyone in any of the Nations. Any of the Lords, Ladies, or citizens of any kind on the entire continent was able to come here and search through the masses of books and tomes and scrolls anytime they wanted. The Scholars believed that knowledge was something to be shared with everyone, no matter their nationality. I appreciated that about the Scholars. They didn't let the laws of the nations hinder the access to the works of the realm and they weren't loyal to any of the Gods either, their entire purpose dedicated solely to the knowledge contained here.

Kya and Malina walked up the steps, I followed behind, into Morah, their home.

Entering the massive library, I was assaulted with the smell of old parchment and ink and something else—fear. Scholars, dressed in their typical attire, rushed around within the library. Books and paper were strewn over the floor and tables as they attempted to frantically organize them as much as possible.

Kya and Malina froze where they stood, taking in the chaos of their once peaceful home. The two females watched the Scholars for a moment. I reached out to touch Kya, I could feel her worry, but stopped when Malina spoke.

"Where?" Malina demanded. Neither of them breaking their eyes away from the frenzy.

"His study," Kya said.

I didn't have time to ask who they were talking about before they bolted through the library. Kya glanced over her shoulder to make sure I was following.

Of course, I was. I would be nowhere else but by her side given the chance.

I stayed close to my mate as we went to a wide stone staircase and ascended several levels. Malina led the way and Kya was beside me. Though we were in a wide hallway, she was near enough that our hands nearly grazed each other several times, as if our bodies naturally gravitated toward one another.

We stopped in front of a set of heavy oak doors, the dark wood standing out against the washed-out stone of the library's inner walls. I glanced at the two females beside me, taking in their composed state. Even though we had just darted up several long flights of stairs, both Kya and Malina stood as if we had just come from a leisurely stroll. Their breathing was measured and even, which told me that the two must have had intensive training. Malina urgently rapped on the doors with her knuckles, Kya and I stood as we all waited for an answer.

The door swung open, and a slender, older looking male with a tired expression and dressed in beige trousers with a matching top stood in the doorway. Having met the High Scholar on numerous occasions, I recognized him immediately. His face brightened when he saw Malina and Kya, and he wrapped his arms around them both, his eyes glistening.

I didn't feel a threat from this male embracing my mate. Love shone in his eyes, but of purity, like family. The females returned smiles and greeted him. I took this moment to glance at my surroundings, giving them some privacy. He was their High Scholar, and they were his Roav.

"I'm pleased you have returned so much sooner than anticipated. But I'm afraid that we don't have time to discuss pleasantries. As I'm sure you've noticed, something has happened." He lifted his head and looked at me with narrowed eyes. He stepped away from Kya and Malina and bowed at the waist. "Lord Ryker."

"Eamon." I dipped my head in greeting.

"To what do we owe the honor of your presence?" His eyes darted between the females and me.

Kya cleared her throat. "Eamon, he's with me. I'll explain later."

He's with me.

Her outward acknowledgment of us being with each other made my chest swell with a kind of pride that I couldn't keep from my face.

"Yeah, yeah. Pigeon boy has been stalking her for a while and now they're cozy, but what is going on here?" Malina flicked her hand at me in dismissal.

"Stalking?!" Eamon exclaimed, glaring at me.

"*Pigeon boy?* Really Mal?" Kya punched her sister in the shoulder. "Eamon, just tell us what's happening."

My eyebrows raised at her command to the High Scholar who didn't seem to care.

"Yes, alright. Come in and we'll discuss it." He eyed me up and down before giving Kya a wary look.

"He's fine, I can assure you." My mate gave him a sweet, adoring smile and nodded as she spoke. "Right, Lord Ryker?" She gave me an expectant look.

I bristled at the formality and gave a tight-lipped grin. "Of course."

I hated being addressed by my title, and I certainly didn't want to hear it coming from my mate's mouth. But perhaps it was only in the presence of Eamon. I hoped.

The High Scholar nodded and swept his arm out to gesture for us to enter his study. We stepped inside and sat in comfortable cushioned chairs next to an unlit hearth. I made certain to take the seat next to Kya while Malina took the one on the other side and Eamon sat across from us after closing the door. My arms crossed over my chest and my feet planted firmly on the floor, I remained quiet, listening as Eamon explained the events of what had happened within the library.

"We had another break-in last night, but as you have no doubt seen, this time it was much worse," he began.

Another?

I was fully aware of Kya's tensing body as the High Scholar spoke, tightening my arms and fighting myself from reaching for her. I was not a comforting male and the bond was itching for me to soothe her, which was beginning to annoy the shit out of me.

"And before you ask, we don't know who or how many there were, how they got in, or what they took. Unfortunately, four Scholars were killed. Their…their throats were slit. Several others are with healers, waiting for them to wake to tell what they may have seen. The other Scholars are working to sort through the damages and are taking inventory as they do so to determine what might have been taken. And terbis wielders have been requested to assist with the structural damage. They already examined it and have designated it safe enough that we didn't have to evacuate. Where's Nikan? I'd like for him to oversee the repair team."

"Four dead? Who would harm innocent Scholars? They didn't do anything. They can't even fight back."

I instantly closed my mind when the voice of Kya's thoughts entered my head. I hadn't meant to invade her like that again, but it was becoming increasingly difficult to control.

"Structural damage?" Malina asked, sniffling and wiping the wet streaks from her cheeks.

Nothing like this had ever happened before and murder within Riyah, especially of a Scholar, was a crime punishable by Nex.

Eamon eyed each of us. "I assume then that you have not yet seen the eastern side of Morah." We all shook our heads and he sighed. "Come with me."

The High Scholar stood and led us out of his study and down the hall to an open bridge through the center of the building connecting to the other side. He stopped in the middle of the bridge and pointed to the exterior wall, facing east. In the center of the glass was a deep wide crack that extended from the stone floor and snaked its way to the tip of the spire.

Malina gasped, placing her hand over her chest. Kya's eyes widened as her breath caught in her throat. She reached for my arm, grabbing it around the sleeve, and I moved closer to her instinctively, watching as her bright pine-green eyes examined the crack's immense length.

I have to go back to Oryn, talk to Arra, and figure out what the fuck is going on.

After several moments, Kya released my arm. Keeping her gaze on the crack, she spoke to Eamon.

"Was the damage within Morah centralized to any specific section?"

"Yes. How did you know that?" The High Scholar stepped forward with a furrowed brow.

Kya nodded. "Because it means that they were looking for something specific. What section?" She tilted her head to look at him.

"Intake. And histories."

An odd combination.

"They should concentrate their inventories there. My guess is that's where something will be found missing." Her face turned hard.

"Already on it." He gave a curt nod.

"We'll go find Nikan to help with the terbis wielders. Kya, lead the way?" Malina turned to face her.

"Yeah. But Eamon, we need to talk about the book. Our lead was a dead end, and we need an updated map. Can you locate one for us?" Kya said as she started for the staircase on the other side of the bridge.

"Of course," he said. I started to follow Kya but stopped when he addressed me. "Lord Ryker. Might I have a word with you in my study?"

I looked at my mate who gave me a small smile and dipped her head in a subtle nod. I smiled back before she turned and briskly walked away with Malina next to her.

"Don't worry." His lips were set into a firm line as he gestured with his hand to follow him back to his study. "This won't take long."

Chapter Thirty-One

KYA

I watched as Ryker followed Eamon to his study from over my shoulder, and I wondered what Eamon could possibly want to talk to him about in privacy. Malina and I made it down one floor by the time they were out of sight, and I knew that was the perfect opportunity to be alone. The crack had gone up to the top of the building and curled around it out of sight. And I knew how it got there. But I wanted to be alone to confirm it, to be certain of my theory before I told anyone else.

I placed my hand on the warm stone wall as Malina started to descend another level in the library. I paused, sending my terbis through all the different vibrations pulsing within the stone and searching for the one I needed.

Malina had stopped next to me. She understood what I was doing and gave me the courtesy of pausing her movements so it was one less that I had to sort through.

There.

"He's just outside the steps of Morah. Go. Brief him on the situation and find out if he got what he was looking for. I'll meet you in Eamon's study later."

Without question, Malina darted down the staircase. I turned and headed back up and up and up to the top level. I didn't want to be right, but it was the only logical explanation. Except it wasn't logical at all.

Down the darkened hallway, I entered the vacant room and found the hidden doorway to the Roav's ledge. It confirmed my theory right then. The wooden door was hanging askew off it's hinges, open to the chilled breeze with the darkness of the night seeping through.

Whoever got into Morah did so by coming through here. That's why we couldn't figure out how they got in without coming through the only door.

We had been so puzzled as to how the intruder could have entered Morah without coming through the only entrance to the great library. It hadn't hit me until I noticed the path of the damage curving toward this door. The one that we had never told anyone about.

I stepped around the broken door onto the ledge. I glanced over the edge and saw the crack below me, and that it stopped at the opening behind me, cracking the glass ledge right through the middle. I didn't know what this meant but at least I knew how the trespasser entered Morah.

I felt familiar footsteps approaching from behind, and I couldn't help but smile.

Always trailing in my shadow.

"Wow. You can't see this from the ground at all." Ryker stepped onto the ledge and stood next to me.

"Mal's doing. She's good with light illusions." I looked up at him.

The sight of him still took my breath away. His dark hair ruffled in the gentle breeze. His shirt stuck to his sweat covered skin, outlining the toned muscles of his arms and chest. I gazed into the swirling silver of his irises and my heart skipped a beat when I saw the hunger in his eyes like he wanted to devour me.

I'd let him.

But we both needed to resist it. At least until we could figure out what to do about the Glaev.

"So what is this place?" he asked.

I cleared my throat. "The Roav's ledge. Nik built it for us. No one else knows about it but us. And well, I suppose you too, now. But it was a place that was entirely on our own." I sighed and gazed at the darkening sky. A few stars were beginning to twinkle into view. "I'd come out here alone and lay here for hours just looking at the stars. It's my favorite place."

My mate stepped closer to me and glanced up as well. "I understand. I have a place like this too. Somewhere just for me that no one else knows about that I like to go to when I need to be alone. When I need to get away, and I don't have to be a Lord or a Worthy."

"Where is that? The palace in Voara? Or is it too much of a secret to tell me?" I said playfully. I had never been there personally, but I had seen drawings of it.

He slowly moved his head side to side. "No. It's in the Eckterre mountains." He looked down at me, his expression soft. "If you want to go there, I'll take you. It can be another place for you too. And I won't keep any secrets from you. Ask me anything you want and I'll tell you."

I pursed my lips. "Anything?" I asked mischievously, taking a step closer so that our chests were nearly touching.

"Anything." His expression was serious.

I tapped my chin with my forefinger, contemplating what I wanted to know first. "What's your favorite food?"

He raised an eyebrow. "That's your first question?"

"An important one. It matters." It wasn't a lie. But to be honest, I had so many questions I wanted to ask, I didn't know where to start. I wanted to learn about him and what he was like.

"Why?" he chuckled.

"It just does." I shrugged. Food was always important.

"Hmm. Well, any cooked meat, really. I'll eat just about anything. There's very little that I don't like."

"Fair enough."

"My turn," he said eagerly. "What is your favorite thing to do in your leisure time? Other than gazing at the stars."

"It isn't obvious?" I laughed, fully. Not something I did all that often but being near him filled me with a peace and happiness I hadn't felt in…well, I didn't know how long it had been. I blamed the bond for the feeling.

His face fell. "Do that again."

"Do *what* again?"

"Laugh," he breathed.

"Reading." I rolled my eyes and giggled. "I live in a library. It's only natural that's something I'm passionate about, don't you think?"

"I suppose it is." He smiled, leaning down. His scent enveloped me and I wanted to get closer. His lips parted, and all I could think about in that moment was feeling them against mine.

I swallowed.

"Are Mal and Nik back?" I took a step back to keep the temptation of touching him at bay.

"Wouldn't you already know that?" He exhaled deeply.

I felt for them and, sure enough, I could feel them in Eamon's office. I had just been too distracted by my mate and my want for him.

"Right. Yeah I do. We should get back down there and take a look at what Eamon found."

I went back into Morah and walked across the dark room, about to enter the hallway when I heard a slight grunt from behind me. Ryker had lifted and readjusted the door to an imperfect fit, but better than it was. I eyed him after he turned to face me, and he gave me a nonchalant shrug before returning to my side to walk down to Eamon's study together.

"What did you and Eamon talk about?" I asked.

"Just…you and some business regarding Morah and Oryn. He's been after several texts in my possession for decades."

"And you don't want to give them up?" I tilted my head to the side.

"I didn't want to, no."

"Didn't?"

The side of his mouth curved into a grin. "That's related to the other half of our conversation." He winked.

Malina and Nikan were leaned over the large gathering table as Eamon was explaining something to them when Ryker and I entered the study.

"Ah, Kya. Lord Ryker. Nikan and Malina have just informed me of what you learned from the seller and the small beach that was referenced at the northern end of Dusan."

Ryker and I squeezed in next to Malina as Eamon began discussing the details of how this most up-to-date map had been surveyed. But I couldn't hear him. Not with Ryker standing behind me. Not when his hand drifted to the small of my back and rested there. Not when he pressed his body closer to mine in order to get a better look at the map everyone was concentrating on. And definitely not when his thumb rhythmically grazed back and forth. I don't think he even realized he was doing it.

I had never felt so flustered that a simple light touch from a male could completely unravel me and turn me into some dumb-struck adolescent female. But I just couldn't help it. I shook my head and blinked my eyes back into focus, forcing myself to concentrate on the High Scholar.

"—that close to the Glaev of Atara. But, here, shows a small patch of land between the Glaev and the Rip that could be passable."

"It shouldn't take long to get there from here. Maybe three days. We can leave in the morning, with the exception of Nik who's staying behind to oversee the terbis wielders," Malina spoke to the room.

"Actually, I'd like you to remain here, Malina," Eamon interjected and my eyebrows raised in surprise. "I need someone to head the investigation on the intrusion. I don't trust that the Scholars won't be too shaken to put their emotions aside and handle it properly. Use all your channels and resources and find this culprit. And Kya will continue on her journey to complete the task from her God. Lord Ryker and I have discussed that he will travel with her and help where he can."

I guess that's what he meant when he said they were talking about me.

I wondered if he told Eamon that we were mates, though not yet bonded.

"But Eamon—" Nikan glowered from the other side of Malina. I could tell that he didn't like this decision one bit.

"It's decided, Nikan," Eamon clipped, standing fully and conjuring the authority of the High Scholar he was.

Nikan nodded slowly.

"For now, get some rest. You've all been traveling for a long while. And quite frankly, it's late and I'm tired. Let's regroup tomorrow to work out the details."

Eamon ushered us out of his study. Ryker and I followed Nikan and Malina but as we got through the doorway, Eamon cleared his throat and Ryker stopped. I continued walking, pretending that I didn't notice that he wasn't following me anymore.

"The payment?" I heard Eamon whisper.

"I'll send it when I return," Ryker whispered.

Payment for what?

A moment later, he hurried to catch up with me and we all headed up to the residential level.

"More Oryn business?" I asked in a low voice.

"Just a continuation of our previous conversation." He smiled down at me.

I didn't smile back. I wanted to know.

"It's nothing bad, I swear." He held up his hands. "He wanted those texts and I gave him my price."

"And what exactly is your price?"

"That he withholds dispensing your information and status from the other Nations for the time being. The Worthy will know but at least without the Trial announcements, it's less likely for you to be noticed by the general public while on your search for whatever it is your looking for."

My mouth fell open. I didn't even have words to respond but I nodded in thanks.

Once we got to the residential level, Nikan went to his room without saying a word. I would need to talk with him later. The last thing I wanted was to leave things sour again when I left.

"He's welcome to share my room if he wants," Malina crooned, batting her eyelashes dramatically at Ryker.

I snarled at the implication and without thinking I yanked my dagger from my thigh and threw it at her. The blade spun tip over hilt before embedding into the side of the bookshelf behind where she had ducked her head.

She tsked her tongue. "Mating bond grating on your nerves, Kya?" she teased.

I knew that she was provoking me for amusement, but I wasn't thinking straight.

"Thanks for the offer Malina, but I'm staying with Kya." Ryker said from behind me, placing a comforting touch on my back. He understood and was trying to reassure me.

"You're not staying with me, and you're certainly not staying with her. But there might be an extra room since some of the Scholars are out on expeditions." I jutted my chin to a few rooms down the hall from mine.

"Someone broke into Morah and killed multiple Scholars. I'm not sleeping any farther from you than necessary." He squared his shoulders, clearly not backing down.

"I understand." I placed a hand on his shoulder and stuck out my bottom lip in a mock pout. "Don't worry, I'll keep you safe from any intruders."

Ryker rolled his eyes and Malina snorted a laugh, prancing to her room after giving me a wink and a mocking "goodnight", leaving Ryker and I alone.

"My rooms are this way." I gestured to my door.

To be honest, I was nervous about being completely alone with Ryker—not that I didn't want to be—but I wasn't sure if either of us would be able to control our urges. Not to mention, I was allowing a male that I hardly knew stay in my rooms.

Once we were inside, I closed the door behind us and Ryker took in the minimalistic space. While I had lived here for most of my life, I had very few personal items outside of my clothing and gear. The books that were neatly arranged on the shelves belonged to the library and were ones that I had grabbed to place here so that I could read them eventually—though that stack seemed to always get larger, and I didn't get to read as many of them as I wanted.

I didn't have any artwork, or plants, no decorations to make this place feel homey. I didn't want it to. I had always kept the mindset that I was unlikely to survive the Trial, and I didn't want to leave a bunch of meaningless stuff for my family to have to take care of if I didn't. And really, it had never truly felt like home to me. I loved Morah. I loved being here, surrounded by books and quiet Scholars and my family. But I never felt like I would stay here forever.

Ryker moved to the glass wall to look out at the city below, its lights giving a soft yellow hue against the dark night. "This is quite a view you have."

"It's like nothing else." I walked over to stand beside him. My hand itched to touch his, and he must have felt the same because he put his hands in his pockets and stepped away with a deep breath.

"I'll take the couch if you've got an extra blanket. And I could use a bath."

I stopped breathing, thinking of my mate being naked and wet in my bathing room, slick from the soap being rubbed across his muscles. I couldn't help but picture him and wondered if that broad chest that led down to his toned torso had a trail of hair that went past his waist line to his—

"Kya," he warned as he inhaled through his nostrils. I blinked my eyes back into focus from his harsh tone. "If you don't stop thinking about whatever is going through that beautiful mind of yours, I'll be forced to take a cold bath, and I really don't want to do that."

"Sorry," I quietly panted, meeting his gaze. The way he looked at me... "The bathing room is through my bedchamber."

"Thank you." He nodded and took his pack with him as he went to my bedchamber.

I busied myself with tedious chores, doing anything to distract myself from the fact that Ryker, a sexy, powerful Lord, was naked in my bath.

When he finally came out, he had on nothing but loose pants, the sight causing wetness to pool between my legs. Moisture still clung to his bare chest and my mouth parted as my eyes hungrily roamed up and down the length of his exposed skin, riddled with intricate tattoos. I wanted to trace every single one of them. My eyes widened slightly when I did, in fact, confirm a small patch of dark hair that went down his stomach, past his waistband to the obvious bulge of excitement pressing against his pants.

Without a word, I quickly pushed past him and slammed my bathing room door behind me.

I'm the one who needs a cold bath.

After my very long, chilly bath, I finally emerged into the sitting area, dressed in loose sleepwear, to find that Ryker had fallen asleep on the couch, a blanket laid over him at the waist and his arms behind his head. His breathing was even and slow, and I thanked the Gods because I was utterly exhausted and wished for nothing other than the warmth of my bed as my eyes began to droop.

Just to be on the safe side, I slipped one of my daggers underneath my pillow. I didn't think he would harm me, but I wasn't taking any chances. Crawling underneath the covers, it took little time before I was fast asleep.

Chapter Thirty-Two

KYA

Heat enveloped me in the darkness. Ryker's bare skin came down on my own with blissful connection and molded around me as if our bodies were made to fit each other. He nipped and licked at the column of my throat as I moaned breathlessly, grinding myself against the length of his cock.

He trailed kisses down my neck, my chest, taking in the pink bud of my breast into his mouth greedily and kneading the other in the palm of his hand. I arched into his touch as his mouth moved lower and lower, feeling his hot breath on my skin. His hand slowly traced up my thigh, meeting my slickness and pushing a finger into me.

A loud moan escaped my lips.

His heavy gaze watched the pleasure etched across my face, the side of his mouth curved up in a smirk. He spread me wider, adding another finger and pumping them in and out of me slowly, curling them to hit that spot that had me writhing against him. He bent his head down and pressed his tongue against me. My hips bucked against him and my core throbbed as he moved his tongue back and forth, fast enough to bring me close to the edge but slow enough to keep me from toppling over.

"Ryker," I pleaded.

Except I didn't say that. I heard it. In my head.

My eyes shot open, and I was alone in my bed, hot with the intensity of the dream. But I could still hear myself moaning his name in thoughts that weren't my own.

No fucking way.

I ripped the covers off and bolted out of my room to find Ryker still sleeping on the couch, his hardness apparent even from underneath the blanket.

Ayen's ass. He's dreaming about me.

And it had seemed so real and detailed. I ached for his touch that wasn't really there just moments ago. There was no way I was going to be able to sleep if he kept projecting his fantasies about fucking me. And even though I wanted it just as badly as he did, I needed him to stop before I made his dreams a reality.

"Ryker!" I whispered sharply.

His eyes flew open and upon seeing me, he shot up into a sitting position. Tendrils of shadows swirled around us instantly.

"What? What is it? What's wrong?" he said sleepily, eyes frantically looking around.

"Pleasant dreams?" I asked innocently.

"Urm, yes." His words staggered. His shadows began to dissipate.

I gave a not-so-subtle glance down to his pants. He looked down in confusion before his eyes widened, and he bunched the blanket over his obvious arousal.

"Did I say something?" He asked.

I couldn't help the grin sliding across my lips at his embarrassment of dreaming about his mate.

"You didn't tell me that you could project your thoughts to others," I said.

His face paled. "I did?"

"Yes. With visual, audible, and tactile detail."

"I can't do that. Not visual and tactile anyway, just audible. Or at least, I never have before. Not that I know of," he said, shaking his head.

"Oh, you have."

"I have? When?"

"The night before I left for Torx. Except I was seeing through your eyes in my dream. You were flying through a storm," I said.

"I… I didn't dream that. That actually happened," he whispered.

I sat on the couch next to him. "And you didn't know you could do this?"

"Not consciously anyway." He shook his head.

I hummed in thought.

"It may not be my abilities…" Ryker rubbed the sleep from his eyes.

"What do you mean?"

"I've had this…*gift* for nearly three hundred years, and I've never once mentally projected before. And now that the bond has been enacted, you're seeing through my mind. I don't think that's a coincidence. I think it's a part of the bond."

I contemplated this. It made sense. And not everything was known about the connection that mates had with each other once the bond was sealed, or even before it. If it was anything like what I had just experienced, they could have thought it was a dream or didn't tell anyone about it. I knew I wouldn't. I wouldn't have wanted those kinds of details recorded either.

"Well, this should be fun then." I huffed a humorless laugh.

Ryker stood and started pacing the floor in front of me, running his hand through his hair. "I feel like I'm going crazy. I know it's mostly the bond, but I can't stop thinking about you and I want you so badly," he growled.

Mostly.

My stomach fluttered. Was this more than just the bond to him?

"But we can't. We can't risk your people. We can't risk that the council will find out and force the Raith on us or worse, the Nex."

I paused for a moment. I hadn't wanted to say this. It was one thing for me, as I didn't have much to lose out of it, but Ryker's entire Nation was on the line. Even though it would have broken me and been the most unbearable experience of my life, I would have done it.

"Do you want to deny the bond? It would solve so many things and—" I whispered.

"No," he snarled. In the blink of an eye he was bending over me, his nose nearly touching mine and his hands braced against the back of the couch. "You belong to me. And I *will* have you. As my mate, as my wife, as my Lady." My heart skipped a beat. His voice softened, "I've got you and as I already promised you, I will not allow anyone, or any threat, to take away what is mine."

His possessive demands shouldn't have excited me the way that they did. I belonged to him—he belonged to me.

I had to keep my door shut until morning to keep the temptation to seal the bond at bay for the both of us. I didn't sleep much after that. I couldn't stop thinking about his words.

As my mate, as my wife, as my Lady.

Wife? Lady? I knew the whole mate part, but wife and Lady were things we hadn't discussed. To be wed by a Sage through the Spirits wasn't always customary for mates, sealing not only the bond that the Gods gifted but also by binding your soul on a spiritual level as well, as most mates didn't love each other and were driven solely by primal lust.

And I had never heard of both a Lord and a Lady ruling a Nation. While a Lord could have a wife, that did not make her a Lady. Only a Worthy, someone powerful enough to protect their Nation, could be Lord or Lady. Which I technically was. Except I wasn't chosen by his God. I was chosen by Kleio, whose Nation was practically non-existent. Ryker wasn't threatened by me taking his Nation, he wanted me to rule it *with* him. I didn't know how to feel about that. Part of me was excited, while another part was terrified by the idea. Not to mention, if I were to be Lady of his Nation, could I still be Lady of Atara and bring my people back? That's what Kleio meant, wasn't it?

I shook the thoughts from my head and settled in the bed.

I had finally fallen asleep for a few hours, but woke before dawn and everything came rushing right back as I lay there staring at my ceiling. I needed to talk about it, sort out my thoughts out loud, that always helped me.

I placed my bare feet on the ground and concentrated on the vibrations. Sure enough, I could feel Malina moving about in her rooms, she was usually up before daybreak. I quietly but hurriedly got dressed, remaining barefoot, and tip-toed out of my bedchamber into the sitting area. Thankfully, Ryker was sound asleep, and I silently made my way out of my rooms and down the hall to Malina's.

I gently knocked on her door and she opened it moments later, looking behind me before stepping aside and letting me in. We lounged in her sitting area, sipping hot tea, as I told her everything. From the council and the Sage's threat, to the dream, and what Ryker had said after. She remained quiet for the most part, only interrupting to ask a question here or there.

"But you want this? You want the mating bond with him?" she asked softly.

"Yes? But I don't trust him fully, and it seems like it's too much trouble to deal with the consequences." I released an exasperated sigh.

"And if you two can somehow figure all of this out, get past the trial of your bond, and solve the Glaev as your God instructed of you—all while resisting fucking each others brain's out—he wants to make you Lady of Oryn?"

"Pretty much."

She shrugged. "Sounds simple enough. Though *can* you be Lady of Oryn?"

"Which part of this is simple, Mal? And yes, I believe that technically I could be Lady of Oryn."

"I said it was simple, not easy," she said from the rim of her cup. She took a sip and set it down. "Wait… Kya, if you became Lady, that means that you could bring them back. Just like Kleio said."

"Yeah, I thought of that too. But that would only put them in harm's way, wouldn't it? Taking them from the Drift Islands and bringing them to a Nation that could also be destroyed by the Glaev. There wouldn't be anyone left of our people if I did that."

"Which is why you need to figure out how to stop the Glaev so that the main threat to everyone would be eliminated," she said.

"Working on it," I murmured. "But then there's still the issue of the panel for the mating trial. If we go against their ruling and mate, they'll likely issue the Nex. Or force us to endure the Raith, which would take away our magic, and then we can't protect the people anyway."

It's all just so messed up.

"If they find you." She winked. But I wasn't in the mood for that. Her smile faltered. "What are you going to do?"

"Try to find the truth of the Glaev right now. Then worry about the rest later. I can't do much until then."

"What about the Sage female? How did she know?"

"Vicria. Ryker isn't sure but he said he's having people look into it. If I could just get my hands on her then I could get the information," I said.

We remained quiet for several moments.

"Well, you're not fixing all of this right now. But I know what can make you feel better." She rose to a stand and I followed suit.

"And what would that be?" I asked, setting down my tea.

"Hot, fresh pastries from Penny's."

I smiled brightly. "Yes! I haven't been there in ages."

Penny's bakery was a staple of Ilrek. Nikan used to wake up Malina and I early before training and drag us down there, but we hadn't done that in quite some time.

"Come on. Let's get there before all the good stuff is gone." She waved as we left her rooms and entered the common area.

I didn't bother with shoes, I preferred to have bare feet so I could feel. I had done it so often that my feet were calloused and the gravel paths didn't phase me. Satisfied that I didn't feel Ryker moving around in my rooms, we left Morah, down the streets of Ilrek to the outer ring to Penny's.

Malina and I meandered down the empty street, stuffing our faces with tarts and sweet bread. I nearly moaned as the taste flooded my mouth and coated my tongue with the delectable sugary topping. I giggled as Malina dripped sticky goo down her face and tried to lick it away. We took our time strolling around the outer ring watching the sun rise over the horizon, turning the sky from a soft pink to a warm orange tone, having already finished our delightful treats. Shops began to open and people began to emerge from their homes.

"I need to head to the blacksmith before Ryker and I leave to Dusan. I'll meet you back at Morah later after I get more arrows and replace my daggers," I said, eyeing the blacksmith down the way.

"Yeah, I need to get back anyway to meet with the Scholars then go to the healer. But don't take too long or your protective pigeon boy will come looking for you," she joked.

I rolled my eyes and waved her off as she left the outer ring back to Morah. I talked with Fyn, the blacksmith, and picked out my preferred arrows as he added hilts to my choice of metal for the daggers that were lost during the Trial—the ones I left in the Nagasai's head. I wondered about Njall, if he had survived would he still be a blacksmith? I didn't want to think about him, not wanting to dredge up those emotions. I waited while Fyn worked. It took him some time, but once he was finished I paid him, then left.

The streets were bustling with people and traders, and I kept my hood down, thankful that I grabbed Malina's spare cloak before leaving. I had made it to the secondary ring of Ilrek when an arm wrapped around my waist and pulled me into an alley between two stone buildings.

I whipped around and shoved Cade off me. I hadn't been paying attention to my terbis, distracted with thinking of preparations for my journey to Dusan.

"What do you want, Cade?" I said sternly.

"How about 'Hi, good to see you,'" he scoffed.

"I prefer not to lie."

"Don't be like that. I haven't seen you since the Trial. I heard you're Worthy."

"Yep. Now have a nice day," I said coldly.

I turned to leave, but he grabbed my wrist and pulled me back. I looked down at his hand, contemplating cutting it off, before slowly dragging my eyes back up to his.

300

"Kya, wait. Please." He rubbed his thumb over my wrist in soothing circles.

"What?" I sighed.

"Look, I've thought so much about that night. I was a complete ass. Can we just talk for a minute?" he said with soft eyes.

"There's nothing to talk about."

"Come on. I made a mistake. But you and I are good for each other. You know that. And you know you miss the relief that I can give you. I can see the tension." He brushed a strand of hair behind my ear, his fingers softly stroking against my face. "Let me help."

"No." I pushed his hand away slowly.

It was nice to be touched, but I was done with him.

"Why? You're a powerful Worthy with no Nation. We could go anywhere. We don't have to stay in this place anymore. Think of it, you could be powerful enough to take your own Nation if you wanted to." I stepped back and gaped at him. "You can take whatever you want. And I could be by your side when you do." He stepped closer.

I knew he had regretted leaving Gaol and coming here, but I hadn't realized just how badly he wanted out.

"You've completely lost your mind. I don't want that. I don't want to take over a Nation. I don't want to overrule a standing Worthy. And I certainly don't want *you*," I seethed at him.

I started to turn, but he gripped both of my wrists, preventing me from grabbing my daggers. I shoved my knee in his stomach, causing him to grunt but he didn't let go.

"Stop," he ordered. I felt my wrists burning in his touch and I hissed.

I stopped struggling when I felt a tug. That unmistakable feeling deep inside and the shadow that would always find me. A malicious grin crossed my lips when the ground shook as he landed behind me, shadowing us with his spread wings.

A.N. CAUDLE

My mate.

Chapter Thirty-Three

RYKER

Even though Malina had told me that Kya would be back shortly, she had been gone too long for my liking. I needed to be near her, to have her close. I had left Morah to join her at the blacksmith, curious to see what Riyite weapons I could find for my collection.

I hadn't gotten far when I felt something through the bond—rage.

Not giving a shit who was near and who saw, I summoned my wings and took to the air. I relied on the bond to guide me to her. Reaching for it, I tugged on that glistening tether, caressing it gently, letting her know I would come for her. She was only one ring away in Ilrek and when I beheld what was happening, my control nearly snapped completely.

Another male laid unwanted hands on my mate.

I landed behind her with a force that caused the ground to rumble beneath me, spreading out my wings with my lips curled in a sneer. I glanced at the male's hands gripping Kya's wrists and saw the angry scarlet of burned skin. And I did snap.

I was no longer the Lord of Oryn, no longer a Worthy held to a higher standard. I was a feral male seeing his mate harmed by another.

I ripped his hands off her as I stepped between them, putting my mate behind me. My hand shot out and gripped his pathetic throat. He tried to pull it away, using his fire in an attempt to burn me. But like calls to like, and I couldn't be burned any more than he could. His flames singed the fabric around my arms, only pissing me off more. A low growl emanated deep in my chest, and the male glared at me with malice in his eyes.

"Got yourself a fancy Lord now, huh?" he rasped from beneath my grasp.

I couldn't hear if she responded or not, the roaring in my head was too loud. The male's eyes widened and I knew that he could see their glow as I entered his mind.

Repulsive thoughts and intentions, memories of Kya underneath him, bare and writhing for him, flooded my mind before I pulled back.

He wanted her for all the wrong reasons.

I should have killed him right then, and I wanted to, for the vile ideas that plagued his mind. I wouldn't allow someone to waltz around with such revolting thoughts of my mate.

"You bed this male?" I asked Kya, who hadn't moved behind me. My voice was low, edging on the tip of lethal.

"Not anymore." Her voice was cold and harsh.

My blood began to boil, searing its way through my body.

The male in front of me strained a scoff. "Only after she fucked me and got what she wanted." He spat at her. "A cold-hearted *bitch*."

My shadows erupted out of me and snaked over the male, penetrating his nose and mouth. I released his throat, my shadows had a hold on him. The male dropped to his knees as he clawed at himself in a desperate attempt to relieve the smothering hold in his lungs. His eyes bulged from their sockets and pleaded with me to spare him.

I would do no such thing, I was not merciful to his ilk.

I hadn't noticed Kya beside me until I felt the intense shock of her hands cupping my face, turning my head to look at her. The feel of her hands against my skin settled something in my soul. Those bright green eyes bore into mine and the world fell away.

The simple act of her skin against mine shifted everything inside of me. I wouldn't look away from her. I couldn't. At that moment, she was everything to me.

Nothing existed but her.

I hummed a low purr and my breathing slowed, taking in deep breaths. Her lips parted at the guttural sound, and the scent of her arousal wrapped around me.

Without breaking eye contact with Kya, I released Cade from my shadows. "Do not come near my mate again. And if you ever touch her, I will make you suffer a fate worse than death." Not a warning, but a promise.

"Kya…" the male said cautiously.

I snarled at the sound of her name from his mouth.

Mine.

But my mate didn't cower, didn't turn in disgust at my selfish, uncontrollable domination. She smiled ever so slightly and leaned into me. My primal need to claim her and mark her as mine, to wrap her in my scent, to bind her soul to me, was damn near overwhelming in the presence of another male threatening that bond to be taken away from me.

"I belong to *you* Ryker. He will not take me from you." Her voice was soft, comforting.

I understood what she was doing, but I wasn't in my right mind. I was the unhinged beast I swore to never become. She was protecting me from killing him—the consequences of killing someone in Riyah was banishment for life. But her words struck me somewhere deep.

My hand reached around and grabbed a fist full of her hair on the back of her head and my other on her slender waist, pushing her roughly against the stone wall, my hand protecting her head. Her fingers tightened on my face. I could feel the slight scrape of her nails against my skin and I wanted to feel that all over my body as I filled her with pleasure.

One of her hands gripped my arm and I swore she pulled me in further as I pressed my body against hers, my already hardened length against her stomach, shielding her from the male. The bond sang between us. Our heavy breathing and racing hearts matched with each heave and beat.

I leaned in closer, curling over my mate, until our noses touched and I breathed her in, as if I had been drowning and she was my air. I groaned, holding myself back from ripping her clothes off and impaling her with my cock until she screamed my name. But I wouldn't do that to her. Not here at least. Not yet.

"Tell him to leave before I claim you against this wall right in front of him." I shifted away my wings then.

Her breath hitched and she tensed, the scent of her excitement surged and mixed with a tinge of fear. My eyes pleaded, begging for her to heed my request so I didn't do something I would possibly regret. Her features softened in understanding.

Kya turned her head and looked at the male over my shoulder, and I growled, tightening my hold on her. She snapped her head back, meeting my longing gaze once again. I didn't want her glancing at another male, let alone this one, not when our bond was this vulnerable.

"Leave Cade. I don't want you." As she articulated each word, my muscles began to relax. Her thumb stroked over my cheek tenderly, a precious smile spread over her mouth. She whispered quietly so that only I could hear, "Our bond is not endangered by this male."

The shuffling of feet and grumbling of curses let me know that Cade was leaving. Once he was gone, my shoulders relaxed, but I didn't relinquish my hold. We stayed like that, alone and in our own world, and I let myself get lost in her captivating eyes, her sweet scent, her soothing touch. My hand moved from the back of her head to the side of her face, mimicking hers on mine, as I brushed the pad of my thumb across her cheekbone, she leaned into my touch which only made me want to feel the rest of her body under my skin.

My body vibrated with energy, with the drive of the bond to claim her and truly make her mine. I was losing my control, my vision blurred and my grip tightened.

She said in a low breath, "I am yours."

I released a sigh of relief, grateful that she remained patient, reassuring me over and over that she would remain—that she was mine.

I was a Lord, a Worthy of Xareus. And this female had more power over me than I ever wanted to admit.

Minutes or hours passed, I didn't know. Kya grazed her fingertips through my hair, down my neck, across my shoulders, over and over and over, allowing me to ride out my loss of control and rein it back in. She became the calm to my storm.

I finally released her and stepped away, already missing the feel of her against me. I expected her to berate me, to run back to Morah and lock me out as punishment. But to my surprise, she took my hand in hers, interlocking our fingers, and led me back to the great library. I followed her, just as I knew I always would.

Chapter Thirty-Four

KYA

We walked back to Morah, hand in hand, as if it were something we regularly did. I adored every second of the seemingly mundane act. For a few minutes, I let myself pretend that this was normal, and we didn't have the weight of an entire Nation on our backs and that this was how it could be if everything were right in the realm.

We had thought that touching skin to skin would drive us wild, which it did, but we were able to keep ourselves under control. It was almost as if touching kept the urges at bay—a closer connection. At least for now.

When I had first laced my fingers through his, Ryker had simply smiled and caressed his thumb over my hand, looking down at me like I was something precious to behold.

Not that I would have ever admitted it, but Ryker's display of power turned me on, and I had to restrain myself from him as we held each other in that alley. I didn't know how I knew what to do or say to bring him down from his rage. Our souls sang to each other and knew what the other needed most.

But him stepping in and taking over in a situation that I had handled on my own? I didn't know how to feel about that. While I appreciated the gesture, I wasn't some weak damsel who needed saving. We needed to have a talk about boundaries, about space, about him letting me do things my way and on my own.

"About before," I said, breaking the silence between us.

"Kya, I'm sorry about that." His jaw tensed. "I just... I don't know what came over me. I mean I do but... I saw his hands on you and I wanted to rip his godsdamn throat out."

"I'm not upset with you. It was the bond. I get that. But I don't need you swooping in to defend me. Stand by me, support me. Whatever. Just try to let me handle my own problems. I can assure you, I had the situation under control. He's not exactly the worst I've dealt with." I gave a tight smile. From the hardness that settled in his eyes, I could tell that he didn't much care for that, but he was just going to have to get over it.

"And if I can't control it?" he asked, looking straight ahead with a cold expression.

I came to a stop and squared my shoulders. He turned to face me and I looked down my nose at him. "You're just going to have to figure out how. Otherwise, I'll...hug another male just to piss off your side of the bond."

Harmless or not, he didn't like the threat. The narrowing of his eyes made my breath catch.

"A little gem with sharp edges," he said with a dark grin. He leaned in to whisper in my ear. "Don't tempt me."

"Are they tender?" Ryker asked with a look of concern after we made it back to my rooms, gesturing at the redness of my wrists. The burns were already beginning to heal, and I knew that they would be gone by morning.

"It's fine, really. See?" I let go of his hand and held up my wrists for his inspection, turning them back and forth, showing him that they were better than before.

He tenderly grabbed my hand again, holding it closer to his eyes to examine it before doing the same with the other one. Nodding slowly, he released me, taking a step back.

"Right. Well, I just need to change and grab my pack then we can go." I closed the door to my room and quickly changed into more suitable traveling attire. When I came out, I found Ryker waiting by the door. He was holding both of our packs and had a grin on his face as he leaned against the door frame. His eyes lit up and traveled up and down the length of me before pushing off to greet me. My cheeks heated under his gaze, and I couldn't help the small smile that crossed my lips.

"Where to now?" he asked, opening the door for me and closing it behind us.

"The stables. It's a few days' ride, so we'll get new horses for the journey and let the others rest. I reached out to Odarum, but he's *still* gone to wherever he goes."

I wanted to give him a piece of my mind the next time I saw him.

I had thought of Quilla and wanted to take her, surprisingly missing her stubborn demeanor. But this was another long journey, and I didn't want to push the old mare. I was giving her a better life of being cared for in the stables of Ilrek with a nice retirement in the meadows. I made a mental note to visit her, though.

We made our way down the expansive staircase, able to leave the great library without delay. I had already said my goodbyes to Eamon, Nikan, and Malina when we returned before coming up to the residential level.

"If you want," Ryker said, "we could get there in just under a day."

I cocked an eyebrow, and he smiled.

Oh no.

"No." I shook my head.

The idea of flying was exciting but entrusting him to hold me the entire time was daunting. I would be entirely at his mercy. He could drop me and all his problems would be over.

"It's really not as bad as it seems, and it's a lot faster than riding on a horse. Not to mention, I'll need to get back to Oryn soon. If I'm going to help you, we need to make the most of our time. And it'll give me an excuse to touch you for hours." He winked, giving me a sly look. I felt my cheeks heat.

He was right, though. It would be faster, and time wasn't on our side. I couldn't expect him to stay away from Oryn for so long and while I could handle this on my own, I wasn't above accepting help for something this important.

"Okay," I conceded in a sharp exhale. My answer was rewarded with the presence of a wide smile from my mate that made my breath catch. I wanted to see that smile every day.

Ryker followed me up to the ledge, and I could sense his enthusiasm about soaring through the skies with me in his arms. The veins in my neck thudded with my quickened pulse. It wasn't that I was afraid of heights, but I had never flown before. And he would be in complete control of my life, having the capability to end it so quickly. Then again, he could have done that at any point. I couldn't exactly fight shadows.

I faced Ryker as he set down our packs and grabbed the hem of his shirt and started pulling it up.

"What are you doing?" I asked.

"Just switching shirts. My other one has slits in it so my wings don't tear the fabric." He pulled the shirt over his head in one smooth motion, revealing his toned body.

I clenched my fists behind my back so I didn't reach out and touch his deliciously sculpted body. I couldn't stop staring, drinking in the sight of him as my eyes trailed up and down.

When I looked up at his face, his eyes were dark, watching me study him and the side of his mouth tilted up in a smirk.

"Just put your shirt on," I grumbled, turning away and looking out at the city, trying my best to pretend I didn't hear his chuckle behind me.

At my back, his warm breath tickled the wisps of hair beside my ear, and I turned to face him after hearing the material of his shirt slide over his body. His magnificent wings were on display, catching the light of the sun and giving me a full view. I leaned in to examine them closely, grazing my fingertips against the leathery texture. I hadn't really had the chance to take the time to truly admire them until now. He stayed still, allowing me to look as I stepped around him, viewing them from behind.

They protruded from his back, which muscled around the ends of them. The spine of the wings came to a tip with a claw at the top then back down to the other end, filled with sections of scarred leather underneath them. I wondered again how he got those scars, but I felt that if he wanted to tell me, he would do so in his own time. I trailed my finger up one of the spines and he lowered his wing for me so that I could reach the claw at the top.

"They're spectacular," I breathed, my curiosity satisfied. I walked back in front of him with a smile. "Do they hurt when they come out?"

"The first few times, yes. And more so with clothing obstructing it. But you get used to it."

"Are you sure they're strong enough to hold the both of us?" I cocked a hip and raised one eyebrow at him, my smile pulling up at the corner.

His wings wrapped behind me, pulling me against his chest as he created a cocoon around us. A humorous grin splayed on his face when I gave a surprised yelp. "I'm sure."

I bit my lip to keep from smiling.

"Are you ready?" he asked. "You'll have to hold the packs since I'll be holding you."

I nodded, and he unfurled his wings so I could grab the packs.

The thought of Ryker cradling me against him for hours and soaring through the air had my heart racing with anticipation and anxiety. I collected the packs and came back to stand before him.

I just have to trust him.

Scooping me up in one smooth motion, he adjusted me so the packs weren't digging into my chest. "Is this alright?"

"Yes," I said, trying to keep the shaking from my voice. He held me firmly to his body as he stepped to the end of the ledge. I looked down, which I realized was a terrible idea. "Please don't drop me."

"I would never," he said in a low voice, giving me a reassuring smile before he stepped off the edge and descended into nothingness.

My body tensed and squeezed my eyes shut as I waited for the sickening feeling of my stomach turning over as we dropped. But it never came. The swirling wind caught my hair, sending the long strands dancing along the contours of my face. I slowly peeled my eyes open, glimpsing Ilrek below as we glided through the sky. The city grew farther and farther away as we ascended into the low clouds. The view was breathtaking and I realized then that I loved being in the air. It felt so otherworldly yet a part of my very essence.

I relaxed into Ryker, taking in the vast expanse of land beneath us, the different shades of greens and browns creating a symphony of rich textures that sang to my soul. The sky bowed down to meet the earth, touching it in every direction I could see. The light blue of the horizon rising up into a deep azure overhead. I couldn't stop myself from breaking out into a full-hearted laugh, beaming with the thrill and excitement coursing through me—my fear evaporated.

Ryker tightened his grip on me and pressed his mouth to my ear, his warm breath contrasting the chill of the air around us.

"I will never tire of hearing that sound." I could hear the smile in his voice even before looking up at him, seeing pride in the silver swirls of his eyes.

I had never felt so much joy in a single moment. Being in the air, being in his arms, felt as if the weight of everything had been lifted away and I could breathe for the first time. It was an intoxication that I never wanted to come down from.

"You know, your Spirit animal can fly," he said, his lips tickled against my hair when he spoke.

"I do know, but he won't let me ride him. And I'm too pissed off at him anyway for disappearing again."

"That's not what I was getting at. I mean, your shifting hasn't manifested yet right?" he asked.

I shook my head.

"There's a good chance you could have wings of your own. And you could take to the skies any time you wish."

"He told me that. That or I'd get his hair and be warm all through winter." I gave a toothy grin.

"Let's hope not," he chuckled. "Just keep your mouth closed so you don't swallow any insects."

I snapped my mouth closed and looked back out in front of us. I imagined myself flying, feeling the urge to do so as quickly as I could.

After my initial elation, I nestled into my mate and rested my head in the crook of his neck, soaking up his warmth through the chill of the wind, staring out at the world before us. A sound of contentment rumbled through Ryker's chest and he rested his cheek against my hair. We had been close before in that alley but this felt so much more intimate, more than just the bond. My stomach fluttered with excitement, with passion.

I wondered if he felt the same way.

"Were you born in Oryn?" I asked. It was time I got to know a little more about him and while I knew of each Worthy, I didn't know the details of their past. I wanted to know his.

"No. In fact, I was born in Dusan." He looked down at me with a glint in his eye. "Where were you—"

"Well, at least you know the area." I cut him off before he could finish his question. I wasn't ready to divulge my past, but I also didn't want to lie to him. "That could prove to be beneficial while we're there."

He eyed me for a few moments before he responded. "Yes, but even though I lived there for over thirty years before my Trial, I haven't been there much since. Worthy aren't exactly welcome in other Nations. Strictly speaking, it would be best if we encountered as few people as possible."

"Do you miss your homeland?"

He hadn't lost his people, his family, like I had, but I imagined it wasn't any easier to be ripped from the Nation you'd known all your life.

"Oryn is my home, and it will be until I die. I love it and my people. I'd like for you to see it." His lips lifted into a soft smile.

"I have seen it." He raised his eyebrows at me. "Roav. Remember?" I chuckled.

He opened his mouth to speak, but the wind whipped around us faster, and I pressed into him. He didn't say anything else, just held me tighter.

After several hours of being cuddled into his warmth, flying across Riyah and Dusan, my eyes began to feel heavy. The sound of the wind roaring in my ears and the rhythmic beating of his wings lulled me into a dreamless sleep.

When I woke, it was dark and still night. We were no longer flying, but I was still carefully cradled in Ryker's arms. I gently lifted my head off his chest to find that he was asleep, sitting up with his back propped against a tree.

My heart fluttered; even after being exhausted from flying for hours, he still held me.

His black shaggy hair was wind blown, his face slackened in sleep. His wings were wrapped around us, keeping in the warmth, as they rose and fell with his tempered breaths. Shifting slightly, I caught sight of the packs sitting on the grass next to us. It was late, the moons were high in the sky and the stars were in full view above the large deciduous tree.

As lovely as this moment is, I really have to pee.

I carefully crawled off him, pushing one of his wings aside and glancing at his face to ensure that he remained asleep. He stirred slightly and adjusted, but didn't fully wake up.

Quietly, I rushed behind a bush, far enough away that he wouldn't hear me, and finally relieved myself. When I got back, he hadn't moved. I opened my pack and removed a blanket, too tired to bother with setting up a tent, laying it on the soft grass next to Ryker. I touched his exposed arm, rousing him gently, and gestured for him to lie down. He deserved to have a good night's rest.

Once he lay down, I made to retrieve another blanket for myself, but before I could, he grabbed my hand, grunting in protest to my leaving. Without fully waking, he pulled me down next to him, resting my head on his arm, and placed a protective wing over me. Even on the cold, hard ground, I had never felt more comfortable anywhere else in the world than I did in my mate's arms.

What is wrong with me? I shouldn't be snuggled up in a Lord's arms, but here I am. Happy, like a love-struck adolescent.

A smile tugged at the corners of my mouth when he released a sigh and rested his head on top of mine, and we both fell asleep, not waking until morning.

When the sun rose, Ryker flew us to where the narrow path was supposed to be, between the end of the Rip and running parallel along the edge of the decimated lands of Atara heading straight to the sea. We continued to fly to the other side of the Rip, deciding that it would be safer than risking the line between two forms of death.

The eerie grave of Odes was daunting, especially when we reached the other side. Circling around in the air, there was nothing but water below. No land that Malina had spoken of, no beach where the seller supposedly found the book.

"There's nothing here. It doesn't make any sense. Mal distinctly remembers coming to this place, the seller said he came here, *and* there's a map of it," I shouted over the thunder of the crashing waves.

"I don't know. But let's get away from here. I don't like being this close to the Rip," Ryker shouted back.

"Agreed."

He flew us back inland, not stopping until we were a safe distance away from the Rip and the Glaev-stricken land of Atara. I didn't want to think of how close I was to my homeland, having not been there since I was a small child.

Ryker set me on my feet when he landed, and I immediately began pacing back and forth.

"I don't get it," I said with a frustrated snarl. "Umana wouldn't have lied to me, and she wouldn't have given me any information she didn't think was solid. It has to be there."

"Who's Umana?" he asked, tilting his head to the side as he followed me with his eyes.

I inwardly kicked myself for saying her name. I had never revealed Umana's name to anyone. "My contact. She told me that the seller of the book found it on the beach here, which I found highly unlikely, but she insisted. So we came all the way out here for nothing, a dead end." I threw up my hands.

"Hey." He gently grabbed my shoulders to stop me from pacing and face him. "We'll figure it out. What is this book anyway? Why is it so important?"

I sighed and told him everything, from Kleio's demand, to the Glaev theory by Rolim, to the break in, to finding the seller's body, and how this book could help me uncover the truth of the Glaev. Ryker's face morphed into a look of dread as I relayed the information.

"What? What is it?"

He ran his hand through his hair. "Shit, Kya. I'm so sorry." He looked off into the distance.

"Sorry for what?"

He disappeared his wings and held my hand as he quickly stepped us through a small patch of trees before stopping us at the edge in front of a large clearing.

"Ryker," I said cautiously. "Where are we going?"

"Voara," he said softly, brushing a loose strand from my braid behind my ear.

Right then, a massive beast, like nothing I had ever seen, dropped from the sky and landed in front of us. Ryker didn't flinch, only held my back against his chest, keeping me from falling or running. My heart stopped, a scream caught in my throat. As my gaze traveled up to take in the terrifying beast, I felt the blood drain from my face, leaving me shaking in Ryker's arms. Instinctively, I reached for my weapons, but Ryker held my arms down.

The enormous creature towered over us. It arched its neck, tilting its large head to look at Ryker through eyes the color of flames. Ryker seemed unbothered by its presence, but I couldn't tear my eyes away from the sharp dark scales overlapping like chainmail. They covered every inch of its impressive body, only stopping at the base of its wings, which stretched out from its back—like Ryker's. The beast opened its mouth, huffing out a hot breath and revealing a voracious maw lined with serrated, razor-sharp teeth.

"Ryker?" I managed to squeak out, pressing harder against his firm chest.

My words had the unfortunate effect of drawing the creature's gaze. Its eyes shot to me, and it lowered its head, showcasing the horns that adorned its head.

Ryker rubbed his hand soothingly over my arm. "It's alright."

I reached for my terbis out of reflex, but I couldn't feel the beast's huge claws digging into the terra.

Ryker's Spirit Guardian.

He looked down at me, his lips pulled tight, reaching a hand out to touch the snout of his animal. "I know where the book is."

Then we disappeared from Dusan.

Chapter Thirty-Five

KYA

R yker's Spirit Traveled us somewhere so cold my very bones shivered. The moment we arrived, I immediately grabbed my stomach, sickened with nausea from the sudden lurch through space, and hurled up the contents of my last meal onto the smooth, bright-colored stone.

Ryker bent down next to me, pushing my braid away from my face and rubbed his hand over my back in slow circles, until the heaving stopped.

"Are you okay?" he asked as I spit the remaining acidic taste from my mouth.

"Yes," I bit out. I stood fully, feeling faint, and wobbled slightly. Ryker held my arm to keep me from falling, and his beast stared, seemingly curious at our interaction.

Ryker held his gaze for a few moments and I could only assume that he was talking with him through their bond, and I wanted to know what they were saying.

Nik was right, this is annoying.

"Kya, this is Theron, my Spirit dragon." He held his hand out gesturing to the beast who looked none-too-pleased.

"I don't think he likes me," I whispered, shivering from the cold.

"Honestly, I don't think he likes anyone, including me."
Theron growled. Ryker waved him off. "But don't mind him.
He's just a cranky alligator with wings." I snorted at that, feeling
the tension in the air lessen.

"So…you've escalated from stalker to kidnapper. You know
I've killed for less?" I winked.

Ryker leveled me with a flat stare before he rolled his eyes and
the side of his mouth quirked up into a smile.

I finally glanced around, taking in our surroundings, making
sure I kept one eye on the dragon at our side. I had never
personally been to Voara. Mountains towered into the sky all
around us, the distant peaks dusted with snow. Sunlight glistened
off the ivory encrusted slopes with puffy clouds licking at the
furthermost tips.

We were standing on some kind of building that was built
into the side of one of the mountains. No, not built into it, *carved*
from it. Luscious green grass, sparse with trees, filled the valley
within the mountain range, the Eckterre Mountains. The air
was thinner here, and a brisk autumn wind caused my hair to
ruffle and bit at my skin. It was already so much cooler being
this far north. But I didn't pay attention to that. Not with the
awe-inspiring view before me.

Odarum suddenly appeared next to where we stood. I gritted
my teeth.

*"So what, I go off with another Spirit and you get jealous then
finally show up?"* I snapped.

"No. I told you I would be back. We had a gathering in our realm,"
he responded.

"Gathering?" I tilted my head slightly.

"Yes." That was all he offered. He pinned his ears back and
flared his feathered wings at Theron, who bared his teeth. I
watched them curiously as they seemed to converse with each
other silently.

"I told you he doesn't like anyone," Ryker said after a moment.

I pinched the bridge of my nose. "So much is happening right now." I looked up. "Let me get all this straight, you have a Spirit... What did you call it?" I asked, trying not to visibly shake from the cold seeping into me.

"Dragon," Ryker said with a nod.

"Right. You have a Spirit dragon, Odarum has been at some gathering on Hylithria, you know where the book is, and you had Theron bring us to Voara." I gestured to the land around us.

"Yes. We are on the top of the Oryn Palace."

"Well as much as I love the scenery, can we please go inside and you explain in there? It's freezing out here." I wrapped my arms around myself. The side of his mouth lifted, and he placed his arm around my shoulder. I leaned into his warmth as he led us to a spiraling staircase at the other end.

"We'll talk later?" I glanced at Odarum.

"Yes. We have much to discuss." He bobbed his head.

We descended the stairs and came to a balcony with a set of paneled doors that Ryker opened and ushered me through. I was thankful to be relieved of the bitter cold and I relaxed a bit. We stood in a wide corridor lined with large windows on one side overlooking the valley below and the gray mountains around it. Unlit sconces lined the opposite light-colored stone wall and we stood on a beautiful ornate rug.

"It's just a hallway, but welcome to my home," Ryker said, smiling sweetly at me, a smile that made all the cold in me melt away. He placed a hand at the small of my back and I welcomed his touch as he led me down the corridor and around several corners.

I didn't know what I expected Ryker's home to look like, not that I had really given it much thought, but I hadn't expected it to be so bright and warm and open. We passed several rich wooden doors and a few stairs leading down to lower floors.

"Where is everyone?" I asked. I could feel movement several floors down but none up here.

"What do you mean?" He pulled me slightly closer to him, his hand wrapping around my waist.

"I mean, don't you have people here? Workers and servants?"

"There are no *servants,* but yes, people do work here. They will all be downstairs. This is the upper-most-floor, the living quarters. And since it's just me, I'm the only one who comes up here besides those who come up to clean."

It dawned on me that I had only recently ended things with Cade. It was possible that Ryker was involved with someone. He's been a Lord for over three hundred years. I wasn't ignorant to the possibility of it, but we hadn't discussed it.

"So you live here alone?"

"I do."

"No family or…friends?" I was dancing around the question of any females that might have shared his bed before our bond enacted, but I didn't want to outright ask. The last thing I wanted was to run into an ex like he did with Cade.

"No."

"Hmm. And have you always lived alone?"

He looked at me for a moment.

"My father lives in a house farther north in the mountains. He and my mother lived here for awhile, but haven't in years. My brother lives in the city and has never lived here. And no *friends* have ever lived here either." He hesitated for a moment, then pulled me to a stop. "I haven't had any of those kinds of *friends* for some time now, not since long before the Trial. Yes, I have a past just as you do. But I can assure you, you have no one to worry about. Do I?"

"No. There's no one." Something settled in me.

"Good to know." He smiled and we continued down the hallway.

We approached a large set of doors at the end of the hall, and he opened them to reveal a large study, not as large as Eamon's, but still sizable. A beautifully crafted wooden desk sat in the center of the room with stacked papers in the corner.

"This is my private office. Would you mind waiting here for a few moments? I'll be right back."

"Oh, sure," I said with a nod and he dashed out of the room.

I took the opportunity to look around. Shelves decorated the walls with books, and two deep chairs sat before a hearth. But other than that, it was devoid of anything personal. I perused the books as I waited. Most were histories and politics, nothing I would consider pleasure reading.

Ryker returned after several minutes, followed by a male. I straightened. He wore a dark suit and was about the same height as Ryker with broad shoulders and an average build, not quite as muscular. His light brown hair was long and tied in the back. But it was the color of his eyes that drew my attention the most—silver.

Ryker walked over and stood beside me as the male remained just inside the doorway, a hint of a smile on his face. "Kya, I'd like to introduce you to Mavris, chief Advisor to the Lord of Oryn." He sighed, "And my brother."

As if the eyes didn't give that away.

"It's nice to meet you," I greeted.

He smiled warmly. "It's *very* nice to meet you, Kya."

I wondered if he knew that I was Ryker's mate. He walked over and took my hand, kissing the back of it. Ryker growled, tensing his body and clenching his hands into fists. Mavris smirked tauntingly.

Yep. He knows.

Ryker looked at my hand longingly once Mavris released it, like *he* wanted to be the one to hold it. He shook his head, gathering his control. I tugged on the bond and gave him a look I hoped he understood.

He took a deep breath before he cleared his throat. "I'm sure you will be spending quite a bit of time together in the future. Right now though, I'd like to know where the Vaavi are. Have they returned from their mission?"

My eyebrows raised in interest at the mention of this *Vaavi*.

"Not yet. The Ihab pass has been…obstructed." He eyed me warily. "They would have had to go around, on an…alternate route."

"Stop speaking cryptically, Mav. I have no intention of keeping secrets from Kya," he demanded. At that moment, Ryker wasn't just some male who had followed me across the godsdamn continent, he was the Lord of Oryn, a Worthy, regal and powerful.

"Alright." He gave me a tight smile before he continued, "The Ihab pass has been plagued by the Glaev. No losses have been reported, but trade and travel have been affected greatly between the northern and southern ends of Oryn. We'll need to find an alternate solution other than going around the mountain range before winter arrives."

Ryker nodded slowly, eyes distant in thought. Then he walked to the other side of his desk, guiding me by the hand, and bent over the map covering it, trailing a finger over the parchment. Mavris stepped up to the front of the desk to glance at the map as well.

"Hire as many terbis wielders as needed to carve out a new path here." He pointed to one of the southern mountains and traced it directly north toward the valley. "They'll need to tunnel through the mountain, big enough for people and carts to comfortably move in either direction, but small enough to be safe from cave-ins. Hakoa and I had discussed opening this pass before as a safeguard during times of war, and this was the mountain that had the best stability for a tunnel. If our theory on the Glaev is accurate, then hopefully this new pass won't be discovered and can remain free from threat."

"I'll order a team of manipulators right away. For that amount though, it could take some time to construct," Mavris responded before bowing at the waist and departing with a wink toward me. I didn't miss that Ryker rolled his eyes.

Now that we were alone, I spun on him and his eyebrows raised. "You said you had the book, the one I've been searching for."

"I said I know where it is. And I do, sort of."

A non-answer. I gave him a questioning look.

"You'll have it soon," he assured me. Though I was eager to lay my hands on the book, the idea of resting and staying in one place for more than a few hours sang to my weary soul. "But for the time being." He stepped closer, my neck craned to meet his eye, and a wicked smile crossed his face. "We have some time to kill."

"This was not what I thought you meant," I growled at him.

Ryker had brought me to a sparring area outside the palace. It rested against the mountainside, isolated. He had given me thicker leathers, but I was still cold. Odarum joined us, wanting to be involved in me discovering my gifted abilities.

"We need to understand what you've received from Kleio so you can start working on trying to manifest on your shifting, as well as what you have been gifted from Odarum." Ryker thumbed over his shoulder at the Spirit.

"I already know what I have from Kleio. Why are you removing your shirt again? Aren't you cold?"

"I'm a fire wielder. I can heat my body when needed." He tossed his shirt aside, and my eyes roamed his exposed skin, itching to touch him. "I'm going to need you to stop looking at me like that or neither of us will be able to focus."

"Fine," I grumbled. I looked at Odarum, ears perked forward, watching with interest.

"Show me what you've got." Ryker crossed his arms over his chest.

I closed my eyes and reached inward for that translucent orb. I had only done this one time with Odarum, and I wanted to kick myself for not working with it more. Once I had a hold of it, I opened my eyes and gave Ryker a malicious grin before I tapped into that magic. His eyes looked as if they would come out of his head, they were so wide. I silently stepped in front of him, holding my breath so he wouldn't hear, and grazed my fingernail down the rounded ridges of his torso. He flinched, and his muscles twitched beneath my touch.

"Very impressive." His eyes flicked to mine as if he knew exactly where they were. My body heated at the intensity in those silver irises. "Now, let go of that magic. Grab it and release it as many times as you can until it becomes less than a thought."

We spent hours standing there as I came in and out of view, over and over. And sure enough, it had become almost second nature to use that magic. Even in the cold, I was sweating from the exertion. I had become utterly exhausted and my vision was turning spotty, yet I was exhilarated. Practicing in small bursts allowed me to use it longer than I had before, and my reserves were quickly growing. My magic thrummed in my veins and I relished that electrified feeling.

"I won't presume to know how much you can handle, but are you sure you want to keep going?" he asked carefully.

"I think," I panted, "that's enough for now."

"You were incredible." He smiled. "But you need to eat. You haven't had anything since before you emptied your stomach this morning."

As if on cue, my stomach gurgled. Hunger gnawed at my insides, and my throat was dry from thirst. But I was proud of all that I had accomplished today, thankful for Ryker's directions as he helped guide me in honing my magic.

"Well done. You're almost there." Odarum's voice rang through my head, and I smiled at him before he disappeared.

"Thanks." I glanced around my surroundings, then I eyed Ryker while he walked to the other end of the training area to retrieve his shirt. *"Do you trust him?"*

"He won't harm you. I trust that."

"Hmm. You said we had to discuss something?"

"We do. But you require rest. This can wait for now, but not much longer."

Ryker led me back down the path to the roof of the palace and the balcony we had entered through before. I held on to his arm the entire way to keep my legs under me. Too concentrated on keeping myself upright, I hadn't paid any attention to where he was leading me until we stepped through two large double doors and into a bedchamber.

The room was prestigious and substantial in size, adorned with floor-to-ceiling windows with sheer curtains on one side. A crystal chandelier hung in the center of the room, casting prisms of light along the floor. Magnificent, engaging paintings were mounted on the walls, depictions of breathtaking land-scapes with so many colors. In the center of the wall of windows was an exceptionally large bed with posts at each corner, covered with a canopy.

"This is your room?" I breathed, stepping further into the space to drink it all in.

He nodded.

"You want me to share your room?"

The side of his mouth twitched into a smile, and he shrugged. "If you want. We've already spent the last two nights together, and I like the idea of you being close to me."

My mouth parted and I exhaled shakily. "I…" I swallowed. "That's very kind. But I think it would be best if I had my own room."

"I thought you might. I'm having a room prepared for you right now. It's just down the hall." His eyes darkened. "But if you change your mind, I'll have no objections."

I bit my bottom lip and his eyes darted to my mouth. He took a step toward me and I took a step back, holding up my hand to stop him from advancing further.

"I need food. And a bath. Not necessarily in that order. Can you point me to my room?"

Without breaking his heavy stare, he jerked his head to the side. "The bathing room is through there. Yours isn't ready yet."

Before I second guessed myself, I darted for the bathing room, locked the door behind me and leaned my back against it. I felt a seductive caress down the bond.

"Don't tempt me, shadow," I mumbled. But not quietly enough that he didn't hear because I heard him chuckle from the other side.

I pushed off the door and walked to the overly large clawfoot tub made of white porcelain in the center of the room, running the water until steam filled the air, and took a long bath. Missing my usual soaps, I made a mental note to find something that I liked to use while here.

After drying off and getting dressed in clean clothes, loose high-waisted pants and a top that cut at my midriff, I brushed out the remaining tangles from my hair and left it down to dry. When I came out of the bathing room, Ryker was sitting on a wooden chair at a small table covered in delectable-looking foods, their wonderful scents wafting through the room and causing my stomach to grumble.

Ryker eyed me up and down, smiling, and gestured for me to sit across from him. Outside the window, the setting sun's final rays shone off the mountain tops, bursting with warm hues of orange and purple. He continued to watch me while he ate, watching as I devoured the spread, taking deep gulps of the sweet red wine between bites. Rich flavors exploded in my mouth, and I savored each new taste. By the time we finished eating, the stars appeared in the night sky and Ryker lit the sconces with soft flames.

Sitting back in my chair, my hunger finally sated, my eyelids began to droop. The exhaustion truly settled in. My mate, having noticed my drowsiness, led me to the bedchamber down the hall.

It looked almost identical to his, but much smaller. Ryker stood in the doorway as I walked toward the bed.

"When I said I wanted you to stay with me, what I really meant was that I insist. I'd like to keep you close by. The other Worthy…they don't like the idea of our mating," he said.

"You mean to tell me that the palace isn't safe?" I cocked my eyebrow.

"It is. But I can only protect you so much if you're not next to me."

I rolled my eyes and held out my dagger belt in front of his face, dangling it between my fingers. "I'll be fine, Ryker."

Gods, he's like the Oryn version of Nik, only better looking.
As much as I enjoyed his presence, I wanted to be alone.

"Alright." He pulled the door closed behind him.

Tugging the blankets down, I settled into the large bed, resting my weary head on the soft pillow. I wasn't able to keep my eyes open any longer.

Chapter Thirty-Six

KYA

"**A**re you sure you don't need me to stay? I can push my meetings out later." Ryker's look of concern was quite adorable.

"Yes. You have duties to take care of that I'm sure are long past due, since you stalked me across the damn continent for weeks." I knew that he wanted to stay with me in the training area, but I wanted to concentrate with Odarum and not have Ryker as a distraction.

"Shadowed. Not stalked." His eyebrows flattened.

"Whatever you say, *Lord Ryker.*" I let my voice take a sultry lilt.

He narrowed his eyes. "Watch yourself, little gem. Or you'll see just how easily I can abandon my duties again."

My body tensed and my skin heated at the implication. I shooed him away before he huffed a low chuckle and turned to go back to the palace. I rolled my shoulders, releasing the tension.

"Are you near?" I spoke to Odarum. He appeared a moment later. *"I'll take that as a yes."*

"You need to train more," he said sternly.

"*Good morning to you too. And what do you think I'm doing out here? Besides freezing my ass off.*"

"*Train harder. As your Fylgjur, I am requesting that you push yourself to manifest all of your abilities and shifting.*" His voice was harsh.

"*Okay, okay. But you're the one who told me to rest. What's the sudden rush?*"

"*I… I am forbidden to tell you. Most of it, at least.*"

I had never heard him stumble on his words before. He was always so sure spoken. The concern in his tone worried me. "*What is it, Odarum?*"

He hesitated for a moment before answering. "*All I am permitted to say is that something has made itself known. I believe your God knew of it, and now the Spirits do as well.*"

"*But you can't tell me what this is?*" I questioned.

"*No.*"

"*Can you tell me why you can't tell me?*" Maybe if I could have that, then I could understand more of what it was that he couldn't tell me.

"*No.*"

Well that's less than helpful. "*Is it bad?*"

The Spirit lowered his head and stepped closer to me, meeting my eye. "*Devastatingly.*"

"Okay," I breathed, speaking out loud. "Then help me train. Help me manifest my gifts."

Odarum instructed me on how to search for and grasp those orbs of my magic inside of me. The ones from him were…different. They felt shifty and loose, like sand slipping between my fingers. But I could feel them. I had been feeling them since we connected in Hylithria, I just didn't understand what they were at the time.

I had to hand it to Odarum, he had great patience. Every time I would get frustrated and lash out, he would gently offer advice and critique my method. It had been hours, and I wasn't able to do anything more than discern the differences between the orbs. It wasn't as simple and easy as tapping into my invisibility magic.

"Perhaps you need a break," he suggested.

"I'm fine," I snapped, irritated that I was struggling so much with manifesting my new abilities.

"It's only been a few hours. Give it more time."

I scoffed. "You were the one who said I needed to train harder, to push myself. Well, that's what I'm doing."

"Do you know what shifting she will receive?" Ryker strolled into the training area. I turned, and my lips parted as I drank in the sight of him.

His hands were in the pockets of his dark suit, with the jacket unbuttoned and fitted to his body, sculpting the shape of his muscles. His hair was neatly styled and atop his head sat his circlet. A beautifully crafted and simple piece of black metal that was in a twisted pattern, like shadows. It wrapped around his head, coming to a point, like an arrow, down the center of his forehead. He looked magnificently imperial.

Though Ryker spoke to Odarum, the Spirit was unable to communicate back.

Or so I thought.

Odarum flared out his wings and flapped them gracefully.

"I thought you said you didn't know?" I balked.

"This is merely an assumption and the most likely manifestation of myself that you have."

"Have you manifested anything?" Ryker stood beside me. His fingers came up to lightly graze over my back, and he looked at me as if he were seeing me for the first time.

My cheeks heated. "No. Nothing. But he said it would take time." I pressed into his touch.

Ryker hummed in response, seeming to contemplate something. His lips thinned and he looked at Odarum again. "Has she pushed herself?"

The pegasus shook his head slowly, his mane swayed. My mouth fell open in an offended scoff because, of course, I had pushed myself. I had been pushing myself all godsdamned day.

"Would you like me to try?" Ryker asked, still speaking to my Spirit.

Odarum hesitated, looking at me then back to Ryker, then bobbed his head once.

The side of Ryker's mouth twitched with a ghost of a smile before looking down at me. "Come with me. I know of a better place."

He removed his suit jacket and button-up shirt, placing them on the stone. He took off his circlet and set it on top of the clothes.

I furrowed my brows as he manifested his leathery wings.

He held his hand out to me and I took it. His expression was hard, making me feel apprehensive. He swept me up and held me tightly to his body. I relished the feeling of him against me.

With a push of his wings, we were airborne and flying high into the mountains. The air was so much colder up there, and I shivered through my fleece-lined leathers as we continued to go higher and higher to the mountain tops. The wind rustled a few strands of my hair out of my braid. I smiled in delight when Odarum came into view from behind Ryker, wings fanned out and gliding through the crisp air. I had never seen him fly.

His majestic, feathered wings pumped to push his body through the sky next to us. We crested and curved around the mountain, leaning into the wind.

Ryker held me even tighter. "Hold on," he said into my ear.

I squealed as he dove. My stomach lurched, and I tightened my hold around Ryker's neck. He nuzzled his head against me and my heart fluttered at the tenderness.

Ryker landed us at the edge of a cliff overlooking the expansive mountain range. He set me down and Odarum gracefully landed beside us, tucking his wings to his side while Ryker kept his relaxed but still out.

"Take off your jacket," he commanded softly.

"What? No, it's freezing," I protested.

"If we can get your wings to manifest, they'll tear right through it and it won't feel pleasant."

I sighed. Grumbling about the cold, I handed my jacket to him and quickly hugged myself, feeling the wind whip through my thin tank.

"Turn around."

I did as he said.

"Close your eyes. Spread your arms. Relax." He rubbed my arms.

I huffed out a breath and rolled my shoulders, closing my eyes and stretching my arms out to my sides.

"I want you to imagine yourself with wings."

I pictured Odarum's black feathered wings coming out of my back.

"Imagine the feel of the wind ruffling against them, lifting you into the air."

I felt the air all around me, imagining it lifting me from beneath. I tried to concentrate on what that would feel like, but it was difficult.

Ryker leaned in behind me, his lips against my ear and whispered, "Trust it."

"Breathe," Odarum's soft voice rumbled low in my head. I heard his wings rustling behind me, and I imagined they were mine.

Ryker's lips brushed the soft spot below my ear. "Trust *me*." His voice was still a low whisper.

Eyes still closed, my brows pinched together. Before I could open my mouth to speak, two large hands pushed against my back, sending me over the edge of the cliff.

Chapter Thirty-Seven

RYKER

Before the tips of her boots even left the rocky ledge, my wings were out, ready to go after her. I knew that pushing her was a cruel tactic, but I also knew that it was effective—having had the same done to me by a cranky scaled Spirit. Odarum had understood what I meant back at the training grounds and obviously didn't tell Kya what I was planning. It was better if she thought the danger was real.

The gasp of fear that escaped Kya's lips made me flinch. But if this worked, it would have been worth it. This was a test of instincts, hoping to force her shifting to manifest into wings in what she believed to be a life-threatening situation. I wouldn't have let anything happen to her and neither would Odarum—that's why he had come as well. He was her guardian after all and I had planned on pushing his Worthy off a mountain.

I dove after her as she plummeted through the cold air, I could feel her terror through the bond and it left a foul taste in my mouth. But she didn't scream. Odarum had leapt as well and we were just slightly above her, far enough away that if her wings appeared, she wouldn't hit us but close enough that we could catch her before she got too close to the ground. Our wings were tucked, allowing gravity alone to drag us down.

After what felt like the longest minute of my life, Kya's voice howled through the air as two large wings, the color of onyx, ripped from her back. The first time was always painful. Despite the tense moment, pride swelled in my chest.

Kya continued to fall, arms and legs flailing, not knowing how to control her wings that were whipping limply through the force of the wind. I pumped my own as hard as I could, driving myself to get to her before she met the ground. But Odarum had larger and stronger wings than I, and he dove even faster, breaking to the side underneath her and catching her on top of his back in an elegant maneuver. Then they disappeared.

I grumbled the entire flight back to the palace, selfishly pissed off that he was the one that had caught her and took her away. Still brooding, I landed at the training grounds where the Spirit stood. Alone.

"Where is she?" I demanded calmly from him. Though my ego was bruised, I was still grateful that he kept her protected.

Odarum jerked his head toward the building, and I nodded once in thanks before I made the trek to the palace, grabbing my discarded clothes and circlet. I vanished my wings before I entered the palace and felt for the bond to direct me to her back to her bedchamber. Hers, so long as she didn't leave for that stunt I had just pulled.

As I opened the door, an enraged petite body tackled me, wrestling me to the ground and pinning me there. I expected nothing less and I didn't struggle against her hold. Kya's pine-green eyes were fierce and filled with ire as she glared into mine. Her magnificent wings hung limply around us.

"What the fuck is wrong with you?" she spat. "Did you seriously just push me off a cliff and not have the decency to save me?" She hit me in the shoulder, and I tried not to smile in amusement at how little it hurt.

"Odarum beat me to it. I was right above you the entire time. Between the two of us, you were perfectly safe. You can ask him yourself." I spoke slowly and kept my tone calm and even, not wanting to risk angering her further. Though, I did enjoy seeing the fire in my mate. "I'm sorry I scared you. But that was the most effective way to force your shifting to manifest. Odarum knew too. That's why he went along with it."

Her eyes went distant, and I knew that she was confirming what I just said with her Spirit. After a few moments, her vision came back into focus. Her eyes still held a ferocity that I found endearing, but they were slightly softer now. She shoved off me and stood, stomping away across the room with her wings dragging on the stone floor.

She stood at the window and stared out at the mountains for a long while. I sat up and patiently waited for her to sort through her thoughts and emotions. I'd had a feeling that she would be angry with me—I had felt the same when Theron dropped me from the sky to force my shifting.

At least I didn't drop her. She would have never trusted flying with me again if I had.

But it worked. My mate, my beautiful, strong and ferocious Worthy, now had incredible black-feathered wings. I took that time to study them. From the tip to the end meeting her back, they were longer than she was tall. Unable to hold them up, where they would have bent was straightened, displaying every intricate feather, varying in size. They were captivating, just like Kya herself—as if she was born to bear them.

Kya finally turned around to face me, her wings sliding across the floor as she slowly spun. Her features were hard and contemplative as her eyes bored into me. I wanted to reach for her, but I also wanted to give her the space she needed.

"I understand why you did what you did." I held my breath as she spoke. "But I'm still upset with you. I just… I need some time to myself. You really scared me. I truly thought you were trying to…" Her voiced trailed off.

"*—shouldn't have trusted him so easily just because he's my mate—*" I stopped myself from listening further.

Something in my chest sank and I nodded. "I don't blame you. But I promise, I will never hurt you."

"I know," she whispered, not meeting my gaze.

"I'll give you some space," I said quietly and I turned to leave.

"Wait," she called out. "Can you help me make these…go away, for now?" She gestured to her wings.

"Of course." I stepped in front of her and placed my hands on her arms, rubbing up and down. "Try to imagine them gone. Willing them away. Think of how you move your fingers, you don't actually think about it, you just do it. Command your body to vanish them."

With enough concentration, it was easier to shift them away than it was to make them appear the first few times. Kya's face hardened as she focused until, after a short minute, they disappeared.

I left Kya in the bedchamber, giving her the time she requested, and busied myself in my office with neglected duties that had been put off while I had been away. Reports to be reviewed, orders to write, papers to be signed, requests to be accepted or rejected. All the things that were required for a Nation to run.

I had been working peacefully for a couple of hours and night was approaching when a knock came at the study doors.

"Come in." My voice echoed in the large space.

Mavris and Hakoa walked in. Hakoa was a brute in comparison to Mavris. He was the chief of my forces and part of my inner circle along with Arra, who still hadn't returned with the rest of the Vaavi.

Dressed in casual clothing and relaxed expressions, their demeanor suggested it was a social visit, and for that I was grateful. They shoved at each other playfully before closing the door behind them. I shook my head in amusement as I went over to the seating area near the door. Even being over three-hundred years old, Mavris just under that, they still acted like young males not yet having reached their staying age.

"Are you going to tell him or am I?" Mavris said, speaking to the chief of my forces.

"It's not a big deal," Hakoa said with a shit-eating grin. His amber-colored eyes flared from underneath his black hair.

"Tell me what?" I sighed.

"Nothing!" He punched Mavris's shoulder. "Shut up, Mav."

"Hakoa nearly flooded an entire town during a training exercise," he said with a smug smile.

"Kleio's tits, you what?" I wheeled on Hakoa.

"*Nearly.* I didn't though."

I pinched the bridge of my nose. "What happened?"

"I was working with some of the Noavo recruits and I…" Hakoa looked away and mumbled quickly, "partially melted a glacier."

I gave him a deadpan stare of disapproval.

"I re-froze it before any damage was done. I had it under control. The recruits exaggerated. I told you it wasn't a big deal." He shrugged.

"Hakoa, regardless of your exemplary water wielding skills, maybe don't melt glaciers during training exercises," I suggested.

"Yes, Lord Ryker," he mocked.

I rolled my eyes.

"While we're on the topic of issues," Mavris began, directing our attention to him. "We have another report." His face was hard, and I knew that this could only mean bad news. "The Glaev has attacked again. This time, in an…unusual manner."

My eyebrows creased. "How do you mean? And where?"

"It's surrounded the town of Borgara in a near perfect circle," Mavris said, giving me a knowing look.

"I'm more and more convinced that it's Vicria every damned day."

"So it's true then," Hakoa said. "Your theory that the Sage is controlling the Glaev. How the fuck is that possible?"

"I have no idea." I shook my head. It was only a theory, but so far the only one that Kya and I had thought of. There wasn't any other explanation on how Vicria could have known about the attacks without being the one behind it. "Borgara's on the southwestern end, so if she is controlling it, it's not in any pattern that we can predict."

"Perhaps that's on purpose," Mavris offered.

"We need to evacuate them. I can take Theron with me and Travel them to another town nearby with the resources to take them in."

"They've already evacuated," Hakoa's deep voice interjected. "The Glaev wasn't very wide. The terbis and water wielders were able to erect a bridge over it soon after it happened to get everyone out, in fear that it would spread inward. Everyone is accounted for."

I exhaled with relief and rested my head on the back of the chair. "It's just going to keep happening," I whispered more to myself than to them.

"So, how is the future Lady of Oryn? She'll be attending the Nailu celebration in a few weeks right?" Hakoa chimed, changing the subject to a less depressing topic.

The corners of my lips curved into a small smile as I thought about my mate. I still couldn't believe that I had found her, and that she had accepted me. I had forgotten all about the Nailu celebration. The Night of No Moons was celebrated all over the continent with food and music and dancing—a time when souls shone brighter in the darkness and marked the beginning of winter. Though, I wasn't sure if it would be much of a celebration for Kya and I this year, seeing as it signified the approaching date of our mating trial.

"She can't be Lady of Oryn, we already have a Lord," Mavris said pointedly.

My smile faltered into a scowl as I glared at him. "She *can* be if I say she can. But it will be her decision if she wishes to be inducted into the title," I growled. "Since we are mated and she is Worthy, there's no reason she can't be. She's powerful enough to lead and protect the Nation."

"I still can't wrap my head around it," Hakoa said. "Why would Kleio choose someone only *after* her lands were destroyed? It doesn't make any sense."

"I have a theory," I said, leaning forward and resting my elbows on my knees. "Xareus is the God over Oryn. Kleio is the Goddess over Atara. They're mates. Xareus chose me three Trials ago, and Kleio had never chosen before until after *my* mate was born. I think they wanted us to rule together."

Mavris rubbed the back of his neck. "I suppose. But it's just all so crazy."

"And you didn't answer my question," Hakoa said with a knowing look.

I chuckled. "She's doing well. She shifted wings today. But the process…upset her."

Both of their eyes widened slightly.

"You didn't," Hakoa gaped.

I shrugged. "I did. And it worked. But she's pissed."

"Rightly so." Hakoa crossed his arms.

"I don't even want to imagine the temper of a female mated to you. And one as powerful as a Worthy at that," Mavris cringed.

Powerful indeed. She just doesn't know it yet.

"I'm going to leave you to deal with that on your own." He stood to leave and Hakoa followed with a rapid nodding of his head.

Before they walked out, I gave the order for Hakoa to track down the Vaavi. They had been gone far too long for my liking, and I was anxious about their return—I was worried.

I waved them off and after taking care of a few more things, I left as well, heading back to the bedchamber. I stopped at Kya's door along the way.

It was well after dark, so I knocked lightly but when no answer came, I entered to find that she was sound asleep in the bed. She was laying on her side and her loose hair splayed out behind her on the pillow, still wet from a bath, the covers were pulled up to her neck.

Not wanting to risk that she was still upset with me, I didn't wake her. I understood she wanted to be alone, but I couldn't bring myself to stay away all night. I made myself comfortable in a chair across the room and I watched her as she slept, her chest rising and falling in deep even breaths.

As powerful as she would have been, this was a vulnerable time for her. Working to manifest her magic and shifting was draining and left her weak. I wanted her to stay near me so I could protect her if needed. But if she woke and found me hovering, she would have been upset with me even more than she already was. We needed to work together to get through all of this. I wanted her to trust me.

I stayed there for a while, contemplating what I could do to make it up to her. When I was upset, I would either lash out with training while venting with Mavris or Hakoa. But she didn't have anyone here other than me and Odarum. And if his company was anything like Theron, it wasn't much of a comfort.

An idea came to mind, but I needed Theron's help—a gift of sorts that might bring her joy. I walked over and gently kissed her forehead, brushing a loose strand of hair from her face and tucking the blankets around her more. Then, with a smile I quietly left the room.

Chapter Thirty-Eight

KYA

I began kicking and thrashing, trying to get to the surface as I struggled to hold my breath. The water of the river was all around me. Everything was dark. The nagasai was coming for me.

I had to get to the surface.

I had to get away.

I kept telling myself that it was just a nightmare. That I was imagining myself back in the dark depths of the river during the Trial. If I could just get to the surface...

I couldn't hold my breath any longer. My lungs felt as if they were being crushed.

My eyes flew open, and I woke up with a gasp. But instead of sucking down air, water filled my lungs.

It's not a dream.

I was in my room in the palace. I could see the faint glow of the moons streaming through the window. Everything was warped by the water surrounding me. I struggled and fought, lashing out with my arms and legs, but I couldn't move.

Shit. Shit. Shit.

I was suspended above my bed in a sphere of water. It was freezing against my skin and I could feel the faint traces of my hair floating around my face.

A hooded figure stood next to me, his face peeking out from underneath just enough to reveal his hardened features, his arms held out in front of him. A water wielder.

And he was drowning me.

I tried to cough out the liquid as my body began to convulse. I couldn't think about anything other than the need for air. I couldn't even scream or call for help.

Fuck it burns. Make it stop.

Everything happened so fast, but it felt like an eternity as I clawed at my throat, digging my nails into my skin in a primal instinct to do whatever I could to breathe again.

I didn't fear death. But that wasn't how I wanted to go.

A flash of black appeared in my peripherals, but I couldn't see past my fading vision or focus enough to care about anything other than trying to fight my way out.

Suddenly, a body crashed into me and the bubble fell with a roaring crash as I landed on the bed and toppled to the floor. I rolled over and vomited. Water spewed from my nose and mouth over and over to the point that it felt endless.

I could scarcely hear a scream before a sickening crunch and squelching over my heaving. My vision was obscured and my mind was disorientated.

Finally, I choked down the life-giving air into my aching lungs.

I collapsed onto the floor as I gulped down as many breaths as I could. My body violently shook and my muscles contracted. Face down on the cold, hard stone, the outline of a hoof came into view just before everything went dark.

When I woke, I found myself lying alone on the bed in Ryker's room. Odarum was standing on the other end by the wall.

"What happened?" I croaked. My voice was hoarse and raspy.

"You were attacked."

It all came back to me as I recalled the water. *"I remember now."*

I sat up in the bed. I was dry and dressed in, what I could only assume, Ryker's shirt and pants.

I was still upset with him. He had pushed me off a damn cliff. For a good reason, but still. Besides, that hardly mattered to me now.

The sun shone through the windows, casting warm hues across the floors and walls. I looked around the room to find that Ryker wasn't there, and I found myself missing his presence. Placing my feet on the stone floor, I felt for him in the palace. There was activity downstairs, but the upper level was devoid of anyone else as far as I could tell.

"Where's Ryker?" I asked. And why hadn't he come last night?

"I do not know. You are safe for now. He left and I stayed to watch over you. But now that you are awake, I must leave. I will be back." With that, he disappeared.

With all that hair, you'd think he'd be more warm and fuzzy. Ass.

I would have liked more of an explanation about what had happened or who in the After attacked me. Regardless of my wish for solitude the night before, I, once again, found myself not wanting to be alone.

My body had completely healed overnight, as if nothing had ever happened. My mind was crisp and my lungs were clear.

I stepped into the bathing room to get dressed.

Well…not completely healed.

In the mirror, I could see faint red marks down the length of my neck. I must have dug my nails deep into the skin for there to still be evidence of the self-inflicted injury. I looked to the tub and my stomach churned at the thought of being submerged again.

It would take some time before I was comfortable near water. No matter how deep.

I turned away from the tub and found a set of clothes waiting for me. After getting dressed, I decided to head down to find something to eat, and hopefully Ryker. I could smell the food from the kitchen and it made my stomach grumble. Just as I was about to head out the door, I felt someone approaching, multiple someones, with familiar steps that I would recognize anywhere.

I threw open the door to find Malina and Nikan, the former beaming with delight. Malina squealed as she hugged me tightly, nearly causing me to topple over. All thoughts of the night before escaped me in their presence.

"What are you doing here? How did you get here so fast?" I laughed in disbelief. There was so much that I wanted to tell them and show them.

"Pigeon boy came and got us with his cute little Spirit demon," Malina said, nearly bouncing on her toes and clapping.

That explains why he wasn't there last night.

"Theron? He Traveled you here?" I looked between the two of them. Nikan was taking in the space around us, seemingly displeased, but accepted my embrace regardless.

"Yep. Nearly made Nik shit his pants when we saw him." Malina made a mocking scared expression.

"Well yeah, any sane person would. What, you weren't scared that the scaled beast would eat us when you first saw it?" he asked Malina after releasing me. I had missed them both.

"No way. Ryker led us to him, and I knew that he wouldn't have if it was dangerous."

"You trust him too easily. He's a bloodthirsty Lord. You don't know what he would do," Nikan said.

"Watch it Nik," I threatened. Upset with my mate or not, I wouldn't have anyone talking poorly of him. "If Ryker wanted to harm either of you, he would have long ago, and he wouldn't have to use a Spirit animal to do it. You're in his home, and you'll treat him with the respect he deserves as my mate, regardless if you don't approve of him."

Nikan sighed, rubbing his temple with his fingers. "Fine. I can at least appreciate that he came to retrieve us. He said we might be of help to you."

"Help to me how?"

"I don't know. He just said that you might need us, then when we got here he left us on the roof and ran inside. We stood there for a while before someone came and got us and showed us to a couple of rooms," Malina said.

I smiled slightly. He was right, I needed them to talk through my frustrations. But where was he?

I brought them inside the bedchamber and told them everything. From flying to Dusan and what we found, to traveling here with Theron, to Ryker pushing me off the mountainside, and being attacked last night. I was happy that they were here, that I could have someone familiar to talk to. Even though I was used to being apart from them for long periods of time, having them near, having them listen to me, helped me sort all of the chaos in my head.

"He pushed you?" Nikan stood abruptly. Lividity seared from his eyes.

Of course that's all he heard.

"Damn Kya. Are you okay? Who was it?" Malina asked with wide eyes.

"Yes, I'm fine. I don't know who it was. I passed out after and only just woke up. And yes Nik, he did. But it was for a good reason. And he and Odarum were there the entire time. Neither would put me in harm's way. I just had to think I was in real danger in order for my instincts to kick in and manifest my wings. And it worked." I spoke calmly.

"He *pushed* you off a mountain, Kya. How are you okay with this? How are you okay with *him*? He blatantly endangered you and he failed to protect you in his own home. Likely from someone who was trying to kill you *because* you're with him." He was shouting now, throwing his arms out.

"I wasn't okay with it. I'm still not. I told him I needed a little space from him and the next thing he did was leave and bring you back. I'm okay with him because he's my mate and he would never allow me to get hurt." I understood his reservations about Ryker, and telling him about that didn't help. Nikan needed to lash out and I would let him.

"Once again, you put yourself in overly risky situations with little regard for your own well-being." He shook his head.

"Learning to shift my wings was not a risky situation, I had to figure it out sometime." My voice was beginning to show my frustration.

"I wasn't referring to that. I was referring to *him*." I could feel my blood boiling at his words. "Why can't you see that he's a danger to you? An entire Godsdamn panel is being held that could result in you losing all of your abilities and maybe even your life. He's not worth it."

My patience completely snapped then. "What would you have me do, Nik? Reject the gift the Gods have bestowed upon us? Deny the bond? You want me to come back to Morah so that you can constantly keep an eye on me?" I stood in front of him, staring him down. "Because that's not fucking happening."

"Kya, that is not—" Nikan began. But I wouldn't let him finish.

"I don't care who is threatening us. I don't care if you, or the Sages, or the Worthy, or anyone approves. I will be with my mate if I choose to. It is our decision and I don't want to hear another word about it. So either you support me in this, or you don't. Are you going to help me or are you going to cut out and leave?" I wanted him to be with me in this, but if he couldn't...

"Of course I am." His shoulders dropped.

"Then instead of berating me, help me, help *us*, figure out a way around this." The air was tense in the silence, save for our heavy breaths. Then, Malina began cackling.

"What could possibly be funny at this moment?" Nikan asked.

"She just asked you for your help so she can bang her boyfriend." Malina continued to laugh uncontrollably to the point that it became contagious. I couldn't help but start chuckling. She wasn't wrong. My light chuckle turned into a full-hearted laugh, and Nikan joined in with a snicker as well.

This was what I loved about being with them. No matter what, no matter how pissed or annoyed or frustrated we became with one another, no matter how dark things got, we somehow found joy with each other. Our laughter finally died down and Nikan was actually smiling—a rare occurrence.

"You sure you're okay?" he asked, pointing to the fading red marks on my neck.

"Yeah. All good."

"And you really have wings?" He looked over my shoulder as if they were hiding behind me.

"Uh huh. And they're beautiful, just like Odarum's but small-er. I practiced shifting them over and over last night and I think I have the hang of it now, thanks to Ryker. Do you want to see before we go track him down?"

They nodded eagerly, and I smiled broadly as I took off my shirt, leaving only my tank-top underneath.

"Okay, hold on and be quiet. I have to concentrate." I closed my eyes. The first time it happened, I thought my body was tearing itself apart. But Ryker promised that the more I practiced, the less it would hurt.

After a minute or so, I felt the stinging pain of my wings protruding from my back. I opened my eyes after hearing gasps of awe from my brother and sister. I held my wings up and out to the sides for as long as I could—which was only a few moments—but they were incredibly heavy, and my back muscles weren't strong enough to hold them up for long before they hung down to the floor.

"They're stunning," a deep voice rumbled behind me.

At the same moment that I felt him standing in the doorway, the scent of cedar and bergamot filled my nose.

"They're heavy." I slowly spun to face him.

"May I?" Ryker gestured to my wings, which were dragging on the floor.

I nodded, and he approached to stand directly in front of me. His fingers gently ran down the feathers to examine them, and I watched as he moved his hands to the underside, where he lifted both wings off the ground. I sighed in relief and Ryker's eyes flicked to me.

"Better?" he whispered.

"Um hmm," I hummed and nodded.

"Try tucking them. That will help distribute the weight as well as the muscles." He folded them inward and up, pressing them against my back. He still held them but gave me more of the weight. "How's that?"

"Not as difficult to hold in this position." I turned my head to look at my reflection in the window. My wings tucked in this way had the tips just barely above the floor and the peak above my head. I looked formidable.

"Work on holding them like this and stretching them out then back in. That will strengthen your back. Then we can work on flapping and eventually flying. But for now, shift them away, and you can keep them out for longer periods as you get stronger. Which I have a feeling won't take you long." Ryker smirked.

It took much less concentration to shift away my wings and once I did, my muscles were grateful to be relieved of the strain.

"Thank you. For the instruction. And for bringing them." I gestured over my shoulder to Malina and Nikan then turned to face them. "Would you two mind stepping out for a moment?"

"Breakfast has been prepared downstairs in the dining hall if you would like to get something to eat," Ryker told them.

"Don't have to tell me twice." Malina skipped across the room, pulling Nikan with her as they left.

Once the door closed, I scowled at Ryker. "Where have you been?" I snapped.

His lips curled slightly. "Dealing with the male who tried to take you from me."

Chapter Thirty-Nine

KYA

"Who was it?" I asked.

He stared at me for several moments with a cold expression. "An assassin. Hired by Jymar."

The Lord of Gaol. Filthy scum.

"Do you know why?" I asked.

He gave me a knowing look.

I pursed my lips and nodded slowly. "Am I really that much of a threat to him?"

"Not just him. All of the Worthy."

"But why didn't they come after you too? Why only me if it's the mating they're worried about?" I tilted my head to the side.

"I've been a Worthy for centuries and I've mastered my magic. You haven't. You'd be much easier to defeat. Last night only proved that. Not to mention, you're more of a threat to them in the future because, by all rights, you could challenge them. You have no Nation that you'd be risking or leaving unprotected." His words were calm and without judgement.

"I'm not going to do that." I shook my head.

"I know that. But they don't."

We remained quiet for several moments. I could feel the tension emanating from him. He was angry and enraged. My life was threatened. I almost died. What it must have been like for him to come back and find me unconscious...

"How did he even get in the palace? I can feel security all along the perimeter."

Ryker's jaw clenched. "On the lower level of the palace there are refugees, welcomed in after their home was destroyed by the Glaev. The male posed as one of them, biding his time until the opportune moment."

My lips parted slightly in a soft gasp. That made sense now, why I had felt so many down there.

Ryker's mouth twisted into a sneer, displaying his teeth like fangs. "That fucking bastard lied and snuck his way in, slept in my home, and had the nerve to come after my mate." He was nearly snarling the words. "I didn't protect you, and I won't make that mistake again. I won't have any threat to you in my home. The refugees will be taken somewhere else."

"Ryker, don't. Don't punish everyone because of one bad person." I reached out and grabbed his hand. He was shaking with wrath.

"I will *not* risk your safety." His hand reached up as if to go for my throat, but he hesitated. My stomach fluttered and I didn't know what made me step into his gentle grasp with acceptance.

"You have a duty to protect them," I said firmly.

"I have a duty to protect *you*." His thumb grazed along my jaw before he dropped his hand to his side.

Conflict flickered in his eyes—bound to both me and his Nation, by the Gods. But I wouldn't make him choose. His people came first, even if I had to be the one to do it.

"As evidenced, I don't need your protection as much as they do. I can handle myself and when I can't, Odarum will guard me as is his duty." I lifted my chin.

"And that doesn't ease my worries any less." His words held a bite.

What would?

I leaned back from him and held his stare. "I'll stay with you, by your side. But you will not relocate the refugees," I commanded.

He stilled and I could see something swirling in his eyes before he gave a slow nod. I relaxed a little, feeling a small sense of triumph.

"Can you tell me what happened?" I asked as I looked into his ire filled eyes.

I reached for our bond, caressing it gently.

His breaths grew heavy and harsh. "You'll have to ask Odarum for a firsthand account. But when I got back, I instantly felt something wrong with you. When I got to your room, water was pouring out from under the door." His jaw clenched. "Odarum was standing there, on top of your attacker with a hoof buried in his chest. And you…" He squeezed my hand tightly. "You were laying on the floor unconscious, soaked and bleeding from your neck."

My shadow came for me.

I didn't move as he reached up and gently pressed his fingers to my throat, trailing them along the marks.

"I did that," I whispered.

"I know." His hand moved up to hold my face. His thumb brushed against my cheek. "I brought you here and got you dry and warm until you stopped shaking."

"But then you left," I whispered.

"I did." He nodded slowly. "But Odarum stayed with you while I dealt with the male. He almost took you from me."

"But he didn't. What did you do to him?"

He hesitated for several moments, holding my gaze with a cold expression. "I had him taken to a cell while I was tending to you. Then went down there and invaded his mind and found out who he was, how he got in here, and who sent him after you. Then I tore him apart, limb from limb. If any part of my control has ever snapped, it was then."

"You didn't come back."

"I wasn't sure that you would want me to."

"Well, I wasn't sure either, but now I am. It bothered me when I woke up alone." Woke up without *him* there. I wasn't sure if it was just the bond pulling me to want to be with him, or something else…

Ryker's mouth tilted up into a grin. "You want me to be near?" He stepped closer and his hand moved to the back of my neck.

Did I?

"Yes." My immediate answer surprised me.

"Even when you're upset with me?" He pressed his body even closer, nearly touching mine.

I tilted my head back to look up at him. "Yes," I breathed.

"Alright, little gem." He reached around to the small of my back and pulled me against him, my hands on his waist. I leaned into him. I hadn't forgotten what he'd done—pushing me off the cliff—but I'd forgiven him.

His arm tightened around me. Our breathing quickened as he brought his face closer to mine. Heat began to settle in my lower belly and I bit my lip. He eyed the motion and his pupils dilated slightly. His lips parted. I wanted nothing more in that moment than to taste him. To feel his lips against mine, have our tongues clashing, teeth scraping.

As much as it pained me, I pulled away and he released me. "I don't think I'd be able to stop myself," I whispered.

"Me either." His voice rumbled from his chest. "But it's all I can think about." He swept the pad of his finger over my bottom lip, and my breath caught. "To feel my lips against yours. To touch and taste every inch of you. To finally take what belongs to me."

My legs trembled, and my core began to ache with what I wanted him to take. I was tired of waiting. "Let's go find a way for you to finally claim me, shadow."

Ryker and I were both highly motivated and determined to stop the threat of the Glaev. I didn't give a shit about the council or the other Worthy. They could try to take me from my mate and regret it. The Glaev was the real threat. It had already killed hundreds just as a warning, cut off an entire pass, and encircled a small town. Ryker updated me on the recent Glaev outbreak as we went down to the dining hall to meet up with Nikan and Malina for a bite to eat.

"Ryker," I said to him as he was finishing off his eggs next to me.

He looked up from his fork, sliding it into his mouth and slowly pulling it out, groaning at the delectable taste. I never knew that eating eggs could be so damn sexy.

"I...um... I mean, do you know where the book is? You said you 'sort of knew'."

"I do," he said, straightening in his seat.

"What book? *The* book?" Malina asked from across the table as she plopped a berry in her mouth.

Ryker nodded.

"What does 'sort of' mean?" Nikan asked, with genuine curiosity in his voice rather than the bite I'd expected. Hopefully, our conversation earlier had some effect on him.

"At the time, I wasn't sure. But I know for certain now." He reached into my lap and took my hand in his, resting on my thigh.

"Well, where?" I demanded.

Ryker chuckled. "Finish your food, little gem, and I'll take you to it." I gave his hand a squeeze and I finished off my toast and sausage, washing it down with juice.

Once we had eaten enough, Ryker led us out of the palace through the front entrance and down the gravel walkway that lead to the city. Nikan grumbled something about the cold temperatures, but I didn't pay much attention to him. Ryker and I walked side by side, our hands occasionally stealing subtle touches. I would notice him glance at me from the corner of his eye. When I looked at him from the corner of mine, the side of his mouth twitched up.

About halfway down the path, Ryker veered right and continued down another path around the mountain base. We came around the bend to a massive area filled with small buildings and sparring rings and training centers. Ryker left to speak with someone at one of the barracks. There were so many people, wielders of all kinds practicing with their abilities or weapons.

Water wielders whipped the translucent fluid through the air as fire wielders counterattacked with their flames, snuffing it out in a spray of steam. Terbis manipulators flung large rocks as air wielders shifted the wind around them to deflect. I had never seen so many wielders in one place, all using their abilities to train with one another as we passed between the different rings of fighters.

I wanted to jump into one of those rings, transfer the weight of my problems and channel it into aggression. Glancing behind me at Malina who gave me a look that told me she did too. We hadn't had a good spar in a while, not with anyone worthwhile anyway. And Malina battled just as many internal demons—though you would never know it, she hid it behind a mask of a perky personality.

Malina and I stopped in front of one of the sparring arenas and watched a match between two warriors, an air wielder and a water wielder. They were using decently advanced maneuvers, pushing against each other with their elements clashing in a most ungraceful way. Sure, they were strong, but they lacked strategy and tactic, relying on force alone to take down their opponent.

"Awe, they're so cute. I'd give them ten minutes tops with a Roav." Malina mocked quietly next to me, arms crossed, studying the match.

"Eight," I countered. I leaned in closer and whispered, "They're clumsy."

We both giggled.

"Five," Nikan snickered, coming up behind us to watch.

"Are you willing to back that up?" Malina taunted.

"Two jobs," he offered.

"Three."

Nikan contemplated for a moment. "Deal." A wicked grin crossed Malina's face. "But you might want to ask permission before you single-handedly pummel a couple of Noavo warriors."

"I see no problem with this." A broad male in fighting leathers approached with Ryker.

He had shaggy hair like Ryker, but was more muscular and slightly taller. His amber eyes glinted while sizing up Malina and I noticed a scar running down the side of his chin. Mavris and a red-haired female followed them as they approached.

Ryker came to stand next to me. "Kya, this is Hakoa, chief of the Noavo Warriors. This is the central location of Oryn's forces, mainly used for training. Most of the warriors are stationed elsewhere in the Nation." He faced the general. "Hakoa, this is Malina, Nikan, and Kya, Worthy by Kleio and my mate."

My stomach fluttered at the public admission of our bond.

"Pleased to meet you." Hakoa bowed his head and his smile widened when he faced me. "And pleased to meet *you*, Kya."

"Pleased to meet you as well." I bowed my head and smiled in return, enjoying meeting those closest to Ryker.

"And this is Arra, chief of the Vaavi." Ryker nodded toward the female who was eyeing me and my brother and sister suspiciously.

She had pale, freckled skin, and dark hazel eyes. She wasn't much taller than I was and had a toned body with a long ponytail going down her back.

"You have not sealed the bond," Arra said pointedly, staring at my unmarked arm. I growled low at her. "Yet you tell them of the Vaavi."

My eyes narrowed, but Ryker spoke before I had the chance to. "She is to be trusted as I trust you. Her and her family. I will keep nothing from her, and you will do the same, including the Vaavi." A command from her Lord.

"Which is what exactly?" I asked, continuing to glare at the female.

"Perhaps we could take this elsewhere," Mavris offered, gesturing to one of the larger buildings, and we all followed them with the exception of Malina and Nikan. Malina skipped to the sparring ring with Nikan right behind her.

We entered the building, which turned out to be the sleeping quarters for Hakoa, as we stood in what was his sitting area. The two males seated themselves while the female leaned against the closed door behind us.

Ryker leaned against the table, facing me. "The Vaavi are an elite team of female wielders that has remained secret since its induction over one hundred years ago. They complete tasks and go on missions that require swift discretion."

"Unlike the brutes of the Noavo," Arra mumbled behind me.

"Exactly." Ryker stepped closer to me and grazed his knuckles down my arm. "Kya, the Vaavi have the book you've been searching for."

I was taken aback, looking between Ryker and Arra. "And how did the Vaavi get it?"

I already knew. But I needed to hear it from them, and I hoped I was wrong.

Ryker nodded to Arra, prompting the leader of the Vaavi to explain. "When Ryker returned from the Trial of the Gods, he ordered the Vaavi to track down and find this ancient book in an unknown language. The most obvious place to search was Morah. It didn't take much reconnaissance of the library to hear rumors of the book—Scholars get awfully excited about exotic and mysterious texts and like to talk. Once we found its exact location, we took it." She shrugged.

My fists were clenched so tightly I thought my palms might start to bleed from my nails digging in so hard.

"I heard about the Worthy from Morah. Sorry to have missed you, but we're meant to go unnoticed." She winked at me.

Fury flowed through my veins. I couldn't believe what I was hearing. That this bitch, and her band of brats were the ones who broke in. Were they the ones that caused the destruction during the second break-in as well?

Before I could ask, a disturbance erupted outside, dragging our attention. Hakoa, Mavris, and Arra headed out the door to inspect the chaos and Ryker's fingers slipped between mine and led us outside behind them. The crowd was gathered around the training ring, where Malina was taking on four Noavo warriors. I had to bite back my smile at how easy it was for her going against them.

Ryker was quickly swept away by a couple of Noavo with urgent business, and he left me with Arra at the sparring ring.

We leaned against the wall and watched as Malina knocked every one of them on their asses within minutes without breaking a sweat. Nikan stood nearby and rolled his eyes, knowing good and well that she was doing that just to show off. The crowd cheered her on and I noticed several exchanges of coin.

"I'd like to see her fight someone who is actually worthwhile," Arra snipped from beside me.

"You think you could do better?" I taunted.

"Of course. The Vaavi are unmatched."

I tilted my head to the side at her and smirked.

"Against *who*?" I challenged.

"Anyone." Arra narrowed her eyes.

Like Scholars perhaps.

"Hmm."

We all turned as Malina skipped over to us with a smug look on her face.

"Care to take a spin, Kya? It's fun!" she said.

"Maybe some other time. I'd rather focus on the book that was *stolen*." I gave a pointed look to Arra.

"My *Lord* requested it. I will only hand it over to him, and certainly not another Worthy. Mate or not."

Bitch.

Ryker rushed over then. "Sorry, but I need to head back," he said to me with hard eyes and began to usher us all away. "Arra, do you have the book with you?"

She shook her head. "It's back at the Vaavi base."

"Alright, bring the book to the meeting tomorrow."

"Actually, I would feel more comfortable if I had it." I looked up at him.

"Oh, don't worry," Arra said mockingly. Ryker didn't seem to notice. "I'll bring it to my home tonight. It's perfectly safe with me." She put a hand on her chest.

I narrowed my eyes.

We'll see about that.

Malina and I exchanged a glance. She gave me a subtle nod, which I returned. I let Ryker whisk us away, back to the palace.

Once we got back, Ryker flew off to deal with some skirmish along the northern end along the Ulrik border. The bond grew taut as he got farther and farther away.

Malina made herself busy while I took Nik out to the training area, where we met with Odarum. I practiced with my wings just like Ryker had suggested, as well as working with my invisibility and throwing in what little manipulation I could, needing to work on doing both at the same time.

Ryker didn't return until after dark. I lay in his bed and pretended to be asleep when he came in. I could feel him standing at the end of the bed. He stayed there for a few moments before I heard the soft click of the bathing room door shut.

Sometime later, he came back into the room. I felt the brush of lips against my head and a heavy weight sinking into the bed behind me. I nestled into Ryker's warm body when he placed a protective arm around my midsection. His thumb made rhythmic circles over my skin.

"I belong to you," he whispered so softly I barely heard it.

And I belong to you.

I waited until his breaths grew deep and even before I carefully crawled out from underneath him and quickly dressed in the clothes I had stashed under the bed, twisted my hair into a braid, then crept across the room and slipped out the door without making a sound.

Malina leaned against the wall in the hallway dressed in her Roav leathers with her mask up, concealing her face. We didn't speak. We didn't need to. I pulled up my own mask, and we silently left the palace.

Keeping to the shadows, Malina and I watched the house from the other side of the street. All was quiet and deserted at that hour. There hadn't been any movement since we arrived over an hour earlier. Malina and I looked at each other and, with a nod of our heads, we bolted across the street. I followed her lead.

It was where she had been all day and why I had insisted that Nikan come to train with me—so that he wouldn't notice her absence. We needed Nikan to be oblivious, otherwise he would have interfered.

Malina led us to a small window on the back side of the stone and mud house and unsheathed one of her daggers to pry open the window soundlessly. I kept watch while she hoisted herself over the lip of the sill. Once she was in and stepped back, I followed.

We stepped quietly through the house. The halls and rooms were too dark to see well so Malina placed a hand on my shoulder as I navigated our way through to the targeted room she had pointed out to me earlier. When we reached the door, I paused and bent down to place my hand on the stone floor.

No movement from inside.

Slowly, we entered the room. I nodded to Malina and she made her way along the edges while I stalked to the center of the room.

Standing at the side of the bed, I stared down at the female that lay in it. Only then did I use my invisibility. When Malina signaled she had found what we came for, lightly tapping her foot on the floor two times then leaving the room, I pulled out my dagger. I held it against the female's neck and clasped my hand over her mouth.

Arra's eyes snapped wide open as she looked around frantically. She began to struggle until she noticed the blade at her throat. Her face paled and she panted against my glove.

"Is this how you think those innocent, defenseless Scholars felt? Someone invading their home and slitting their throats as they tried to simply stop a thief?" I pressed the blade down until a drop of blood trickled down the column of her throat. "They were slit so deep, they barely had their heads still attached."

I released her mouth.

"We—we didn't kill anyone. We were long gone by the time that happened. I didn't even hear about it until I got back." Her voice trembled.

I had assumed that was true even before I met her. The first break-in was clean and nearly undetected. The second was a gruesome raid. The styles were entirely different and suggested separate assailants.

"I have only one question, then I will let you live." I leaned closer. She couldn't tell where she was supposed to look. "How did you get in?"

She swallowed. "There was a door—a door near the top of the east spire. I air-elevated us up to it."

"How did you know of it?"

"Some female got drunk with one of the warriors and told him. He told us. You can't see it but if you look for it, you can see a small bit of distorted light."

Mal...

"Clever." I leaned in even closer. "But I want you to remember," She flinched at my proximity. "The Vaavi are no match for a Roav."

She gasped and her eyes widened. She didn't see the hand I swung at her head, hitting her hard enough in the temple to knock her unconscious.

Chapter Forty

RYKER

I knew that Kya had been angered when Arra told her they broke into Morah. Guilt washed over me when I saw the fury in her eyes. While I hadn't explicitly told the Vaavi to trespass and steal from the great library, they were working under my command and therefore, it was my fault. Regardless, Kya would have had the book either way and hopefully it would offer some insight into what the Glaev truly was.

If we could figure it out, maybe we could find a way to stop it, and the threat to my Nation.

That was the biggest reason why we couldn't seal the bond. I wasn't worried about the council of Sages and Worthy. And I wouldn't have let them prevent us anyway. I would have burned them where they stood. I would have snaked my shadows into every orifice of their pathetic bodies and smothered them. I would have entered their minds and snapped their sanity or taken complete control until their hearts stopped. Them, I could control. But I couldn't control the Glaev.

Kya was in a surprisingly good mood that day and spent most of it training with Odarum. She was quickly learning to manage her magic from Kleio, and the muscles in her back were getting stronger each time she manifested her wings.

She'll be flying soon.

Kya walked back to me, skin glistening with sweat. Seeing her using her magic so well after only a couple of weeks after manifesting showed me how driven and dedicated she was. She stood beside me, our fingers entwining before we went back to the palace.

When we arrived, Kya went to bathe and change. I had expected her to be apprehensive of water seeing as she nearly drowned, and I felt a slight unease from her, but she surprised me by confronting any fear she may have had with it.

My mate was headstrong and determined. And not just when it came to herself. She had stood up for people she hadn't even known. I thought back to when she had advocated for the refugees, that fiery look in her eyes. Fuck, that look alone could have brought me to my knees. Not to mention her unyielding stature as she lifted her chin to me and demanded I let them stay. She refused to back down, and she was right. And Gods, if that didn't do something to me. Something I wasn't at all prepared for.

I met with Mavris to discuss the border breach from yesterday. Things had been tense ever since the Glaev incident a few weeks ago and when a few hunters from Ulrik wandered just inside our borders, some of the nearby villagers overreacted and attacked them.

"I was surprised you didn't interfere between Arra and Kya," Mavris said while waiting on me to finish writing orders for the Noavo. "They didn't seem to get along."

"There are few Arra does like, and it's not unanticipated that they clash. Both are tenacious and relentless." I didn't lift my head.

"Anticipated or not, you still allowed the leader of the Vaavi to speak to your mate like that. Her future Lady if I'm not mistaken."

I lifted my head up now to look at him. "Exactly."

"I don't follow." He quirked an eyebrow.

"If Kya is going to be Lady of Oryn, she has to earn Arra's, and everyone else's, respect on her own. I can't do it for her. I can't step in for her."

"Very wise of you."

"Says my advisor," I mumbled. I leaned back in my chair and ran a hand through my hair. "Besides, Kya explicitly instructed me not to interfere in these kinds of situations. She can handle herself."

Mavris chuckled. "Maybe she truly is meant to be our Lady. That mate of yours has you showing a kind of restraint *I've* never seen."

I rolled my eyes, but didn't bother to hold back my grin. "You have no idea."

Once we finished sorting out the logistics of ensuring that the border issue didn't escalate into another godsdamned war, I went back up to the bedchamber. I had wanted to find Arra earlier so that we could retrieve the book before the meeting with my chiefs, and I knew that Kya would like to have it sooner anyway. But she had insisted on cleaning up first, so I sent Mavris to have Arra bring it.

Kya was still in the bathing room when I returned, so I settled myself in a chair and waited for her to finish. I listened to the water lapping at the sides of the tub and her sweet muffled humming. I closed my eyes and leaned my head on the back of the chair.

Fingers lightly danced over my shoulder just before I felt the brushing of the most precious lips on my temple. I must have dozed off for a few minutes because I opened my eyes to find Kya standing in front of me dressed in a striking evening gown of green, so dark it was almost black, and accentuated her eyes.

The dress touched the floor and had a slit up one side, giving me a full view of her long gorgeous leg to the top of her thigh. It was high enough to taunt me, like an invitation to run my hand up underneath and see if she was wet for me. The material was snug against her body, shaping every curve and leaving little to the imagination. Her hair was down and swept over her shoulders, covering the thin straps, and the neckline was cut low below her breasts.

Gods, she was beautiful.

The dress was nice, but I knew that it would have looked much better on the floor.

I couldn't help imagining sliding those straps down her shoulders, kissing my way down her chest as I peeled the dress off her body until she was bared to me.

My eyes shuttered when I scented her arousal as I trailed my eyes over her body.

I stood, wrapping my arm around her waist, pulling her to me, and leaned in close enough that our noses touched.

"Little gem, how can you expect me to sit at dinner and keep myself from touching you when you're dressed like that?" My voice was low and guttural.

I'd had some workers arrange a wardrobe for her, but I hadn't specifically told them what to put in it. I was not displeased with their choices.

Kya ran the palm of her hand up my chest and around to the back of my neck, dragging her fingers through my hair with a light scrape of her nails. I shivered, and my trousers suddenly became too tight. Her nostrils flared slightly, and she pressed her body harder against me.

"I guess you'll just have to behave yourself," she whispered.

My hand went to her thigh and slowly slid up the slit of her dress. She bit her lip and I wanted to snatch it up in mine and finally taste her, but I held myself back. I reached around and grabbed her perfect ass. She whimpered softly and moved against me causing me to groan, wanting to feel even more of her and learn what other sounds my touch could bring.

Her head tilted up, exposing her neck, before I kissed and nipped it. She wrapped her leg around me and I held her even tighter. She reached her hand between us and slipped it underneath my shirt, touching my skin.

"Ryker," she breathed.

"Fuck, Kya." Hearing my name in that sultry voice nearly had me taking her to the bed and shredding that dress off of her. "There's so much I want to do to you."

"Tell me."

I grazed my teeth down her neck to her shoulder. "I want to feel all of you." I slipped the thin strap over her shoulder and kissed there. "I want to taste all of you." I trailed my lips down her chest and she arched into me. "I want to claim all of you."

Her breath caught when I grabbed under her thigh and pulled it higher, pressing my cock to her core.

"I want *you*. Do you feel what you do to me?"

She nodded slowly. "Yes. Now feel what you do to me."

She moved my hand up her thigh, up and up and up. The tips of my fingers grazed the outside of her panties, damp with her arousal, and she let out a breathless moan.

So wet…

A low growl rumbled deep in my chest, as I tried desperately to keep a hold of my control. My fingers slid to the edge of the material so that I could move it aside and truly feel what I did to her.

She pulled back suddenly, and I quickly removed my hands. I looked at her with concern that I had hurt her somehow, upset her, but she rolled her eyes and sighed.

"I'll get it."

Then there was a knock at the door.

Kya must have felt someone approaching. I adjusted myself in an attempt to hide my aching cock, but it was pointless. I reached out with my mind to find out who disrupted us and my eyebrows creased just before Kya opened the door for Arra.

"Arra," Kya greeted.

I approached the door and stood behind Kya, grazing my knuckles down her exposed back. Her skin pebbled at my touch and I felt her caress the bond.

"Lord Ryker." She bowed her head.

"Good evening, Arra." I forced a smile. Her timing couldn't have been more inconvenient. "Did Mav talk to you?"

"He did." Arra hung her head. "And I'm sorry to say that…the book was stolen."

My eyes widened and my nostrils flared.

"Oh no," Kya said in a flat tone. "How disappointing seeing as you insisted that it was safe with you."

"What. Happened." I gritted my teeth.

"I was attacked last night. They knocked me out. Some of the event is still fuzzy but I didn't notice that it was missing for some time. We've been searching for it all day but…" Arra's voice trailed off.

"To be robbed in your own home…must have been a worthwhile opponent for the chief of the Vaavi. What a shame. That book was quite important, as you know," Kya said.

She was acting rather odd.

"Well, I'm sure we'll sort it out. But for now, let's go eat." Kya smiled and walked out the door.

Very odd indeed.

It wasn't like her to just let this go, but I had a feeling she was up to something. She was way too calm.

Kya took my offered arm and I escorted her as we walked with Arra down two levels to the informal dining room. This was where me and my inner circle ate when we gathered. It was much smaller than the one downstairs, but had a marble table big enough for eight people. Mavris and Hakoa were seated across from Nikan and Malina. They stopped their discussion when we entered and greeted us. I pulled the seat out for Kya before I took the one between her and Hakoa. Arra took the seat in front of me next to Nikan.

"Where's the book?" Nikan asked, glancing at Arra.

Her face twisted into a sneer.

"Oh, this one?" Malina pulled the book out from behind her and set it on the table.

Nikan clenched his jaw and his eyes shot to Kya, who had a sly smirk on her face.

"You fucking bitch! You broke into my house and stole it! You're the one who held a knife to my throat and knocked me out!" Arra jumped from her seat and pointed a finger at Malina.

All I could do was stare.

You've got to be shitting me.

Malina's mouth curved into a malicious smile. "I liberated the book. But I never touched you." Her eyes snapped to Kya and everyone followed her gaze.

My first reaction was to be angry with my mate, but I knew I had no right. I had let her handle it her way. I just hadn't expected that was how she would do it. Regardless if it worked or not.

Sharp little gem indeed.

Even a little pissed, I was still impressed at how quickly and efficiently Kya put Arra in her place.

"You…you're a Roav?" Arra gaped.

"Shit. Remind me to never piss her off," Hakoa mumbled and sank down into his chair.

Kya and Arra held each others stares for several moments, a standoff.

"Kya…" I said almost in disbelief. I didn't understand what led her to think it was a good idea to go sneaking around at night when she had just had an assassination attempt just the other night.

"Arra and I had a bet to settle. It's done now." Kya shrugged.

"Kya. Mal," Nikan snapped.

I snarled at his tone towards my mate. If he didn't watch the way he spoke, he and I were going to settle things as well.

"We'll discuss this later. Let's get on with it," Nikan stated before sighing. "You sure this is it?" he asked, gesturing to the large book on the table.

"I think so. I haven't had a chance to look at it yet." Kya reached out to touch the leather binding and traced her finger over the raised text.

"It has the notes," Malina said with a nod.

Mavris leaned forward. "Why do you need it so badly? If you don't mind me asking."

Dinner was served and Kya explained the task given to her by Kleio, essentially commanding her to stop the Glaev but not telling her how, and how she learned of the book and the Scholar that had theorized that the Glaev was something other than just a plague. These Gods of ours gave us obscure tasks with little direction.

Despite their shortcomings, Kya somehow remained more driven than I originally had when I received my task. She placed her hand on mine underneath the table and lazily traced circles in my palm with her nail as she spoke and I was transfixed on the motion.

"Ryker?"

I lifted my head to find everyone looking at me. Kya glanced down at our hands and smiled as she intertwined our fingers before looking back up at me.

"Yes?"

"I said, how did you find out about the book?" Kya asked.

"Deres. He's a Sage here in Voara," I said.

"The oldest Sage in Oryn, if not the entire realm," Mavris added.

"How did he know of the book?" Kya tilted her head to the side.

"I'm not sure. I didn't ask, but he's always been loyal to Oryn and to me. I trust him and you can too," I reassured her, knowing that Sages were on her bad side at that moment, given their threat to us.

"I'd like to speak with him. Find out how he knew of the book, and see if he at least knows what language it's in."

"We can go to the temple in the morning." I nodded.

"Well, now that that's settled, I heard that Voara is just *bustling* with brute warriors at night looking for a good time and I could use an outlet," Malina chimed, winking at Kya who just shook her head in disbelief and chuckled. "Anyone want to join me?"

Hakoa stood. "I'll go. I know of a tavern with the best ale in the city and they save their best barrels for Nailu too. Mav?"

Mavris shrugged. "Sure, why not? Anyone else?"

Kya raised her hand eagerly. "Me too!"

I raised my eyebrows at her.

"Don't worry, I'm not looking for any *brute warriors*, but I'd like to explore the city."

"Boo. That's no fun. I'd have loved to see the *Bloodlust Lord* get all worked up over watching the other males drool over you," Malina pouted.

I growled and squeezed Kya's hand, pulling her closer. She caressed the bond reassuringly and looked at me with a soft smile, then glanced back at Malina.

"Mal, play nice. It's not polite to taunt a male over his mate," Kya said playfully and Malina giggled.

"I'll go," Arra said, surprisingly. We all gave her a questioning look. "What? I could go for a good time after having my ass handed to me in my own home last night. Although it would have been nice if someone had told me she was a *Roav*." She gave me a pointed look.

"It wasn't my place to say anything." I raised my hands in defense.

"We're not all that different from the Vaavi. We like to remain discreet," Malina added.

"*We?*" Mavris gaped, glancing between Malina and Kya.
Nikan leaned forward with a smirk. "'We' indeed."

Chapter Forty-One

KYA

Just after the sunset, Ryker and I walked hand in hand down to the city behind the rest of our group. I was thankful to have dressed in more casual clothing before we left. I wore a leather jacket over a tank and tight pants that tucked into my boots while Ryker had on a long sleeved button-up and trousers. Even though I was still exhausted from my exertion of training earlier, I wanted to come see the city.

Everything was bathed in light from the moons and the lanterns lining the busy streets filled with people and life and music. The scent of cooked food and ale came from the packed taverns, combined with roars of laughter. People greeted Ryker warmly, as if he were any other citizen on the streets. Malina grabbed Nikan by the wrist and dragged him into one of the taverns while Arra, Mavris, and Hakoa followed behind and disappeared among the crowd.

"Come on. I want to show you something." Ryker wrapped his arm around my shoulder and kissed the top of my head.

I was glad that he was guiding me through the street because I wasn't paying attention to where I was going—too absorbed in the flourishing city around me. I was amazed at how, even though so much of the Nation was impacted by the Glaev, everyone here was vibrant and lively.

Ryker stopped at a baker's cart and asked for two sweet rolls. The baker insisted that Ryker not pay. When she turned around, he put the coins on her cart and quickly ushered me away.

"I saw that, you know," I said to him as I unwrapped my treat.

"I don't know what you're talking about," he said innocently.

"You paid that baker double the amount."

He shrugged. "Floria's mate died a while back. She struggled for a long time and only recently went back to baking, reopening her shop. I know she still has difficulties and I try to help."

I pressed closer to him. Ryker and I hadn't even sealed our mating yet, and I already didn't want to be without him. I couldn't imagine how devastating it would be to lose him after having been fully connected. He was gaining my trust and making me feel for him separate from the bond. And I didn't want to be alone anymore, so long as I was with him.

I was brought out of my thoughts as I took my first bite of the sweet roll, a fluffy bread with powdered sugar sifted on top. Delectable flavors flooded my mouth as a sweet cream oozed from the center like honey. I moaned at the taste.

"I've heard of this!" I exclaimed with a mouthful, making a mess on my face as I devoured the treat.

"You have? Floria is the only one I know that makes it."

"I know, I heard about her too. Not her name, but the baker in Voara and the sweet bread with the most delicious cream inside. One of the contestants told me about it during the Trial." I licked away the sticky remnants in the corner of my mouth.

"Who was it?" He tilted his head at me as we neared the end of the street where the crowd was thinning.

My lips flattened. "His name was Njall. He was a blacksmith from Oryn, I don't know where though. He... Well, he helped me. We helped each other solve the riddle and he even saved me a couple of times." I had been so preoccupied lately that I hadn't thought of him in quite a while.

"Was?" Ryker threw away the wrappings and curled his arm around my waist. My eyebrows scrunched together at his question. "You said his name *was* Njall," he clarified.

"Yeah. Was."

"How do you know he died?" He glanced down at me.

"That Sage, Vicria, told me he never came back when I asked about him," I sneered as I thought of that wretched female.

He hummed in response and I was glad for it, not really wanting to dampen the mood thinking of Njall.

Ryker brought us to the northern outskirts of the city. The valley lay open in front of us, and I took in the peacefulness of the chilled night. He tucked me closer against him, extending the warmth of his fire abilities, and led me through the grass toward a patch of trees.

"Where are we going?" I asked.

"You'll see." He smirked.

We walked into the trees and after a couple of minutes I saw light emanating up ahead. I squinted to better focus my eyes on the origin of the light giving off a bluish hue through the trees. We walked closer and closer until we came upon a small clearing in the middle of the sparse forest. Right there in the opening, a single large tree sat.

It glowed with soft light, shimmering, like moonslight over the surface of water. I smiled at the pure beauty of it. It felt like a beacon, drawing me nearer until I could see that the entire evergreen, from the exposed roots in the soil to the tips of the leaves, was covered in the light.

"What is it?" I marveled in complete awe, I had never seen anything like it and it was captivating.

"It's some kind of bioluminescent moss that's usually found at higher altitudes, but for some reason, it also grew here on just this one tree. It glows brightest during the Nailu, not having the light of the moons to dampen its glow. It's considered to be sacred and, legend has it, that it was touched by Xareus as a gift for his mate, Kleio."

I glanced up at Ryker. He was looking down at me with something in his eyes that I had never seen before and it made my stomach flutter.

"That's sweet that he gave his mate a tree."

"I will give *my* mate so much more than that." He brushed his fingers lightly over my face, tucking a stray strand of hair behind my ear.

Gods, I wanted nothing more than to kiss him then. To feel his lips against mine in that magical moment. I lifted to my toes to do just that, thinking that just one kiss wouldn't drive us too far. Just one…

But I stopped when I thought of Nailu and what would come after it—our mating trial. The threats, the Sages and Worthy, the Glaev, all of it came rushing back to the forefront of my mind. On the off chance that one of us would lose control, we couldn't even taste each other.

I looked back toward the city, to the people we were protecting by preventing our mating bond from being sealed. We couldn't risk their lives. I slowly lowered back on my heels.

They were being targeted. No other Glaev attacks had been reported outside of Oryn. Not since the Trial. Not since Vicria warned Ryker that he would regret not denying the bond. It was too much to be a coincidence.

So many of Oryn's people had been killed or forced to abandon their homes simply because we were together. Was that selfish of us? To toe the line, risking their lives just because we couldn't stay away from each other?

Ryker's face fell when a single tear streaked down my cheek. He wiped it away with his thumb and my lower lip trembled.

I was so tired. So exhausted from my fate always being closer to that of death rather than life. Especially now that I wanted one.

He pulled me into him, pressing his lips to my forehead for a long moment with his eyes shut tight. We could feel each other's anguish through the bond. The hurt inside me howled down that swirling tether. I wrapped my arms around him and buried my face into his chest.

Unable to hold it together anymore, tears flooded down my face. Ryker held me tighter, laying his cheek against the top of my head. A choked sob burst from my lips and I couldn't stop the heaving cries that followed.

I barely noticed when Ryker lifted me into his arms and shifted his wings. And I barely noticed when he thrust us into the air and over the city back to the palace. I blinked through bleary eyes when he continued to carry me to the bedchamber to find a tear falling down his cheek.

He sat on the end of the bed and held me in his lap, resting his chin on the top of my head and rocked gently while brushing his hand down my hair soothingly.

"Little gem…" he whispered. "Everything will be okay."

"It's not fair. I finally found you, *my mate*, and I can't even have you." My whimpered words were barely discernible through the sobs.

"No." He held my face and carefully pulled my head back to look at him. His expression was so open and every emotion shone in his eyes. "I am already yours, bond or not. I was made for you and you were made for me. I've waited three hundred years for you, and I will wait for the rest of my life—so long as it means that I get to spend every moment of it with you." He wiped away my tears. "Nothing will keep me from you. I belong to you. I have *always* belonged to you."

I pulled my head back slightly and gave a soft smile. "And I belong to you, my shadow. Always."

I was still disheartened by everything, but through it all I knew that I would have him with me. But why did it have to be so hard? Why did fate have to be so cruel?

"Kya…" He curled his fingers through my hair. "Let me make you feel better. Even if it's for a short while. "

He bent his head down and lightly brushed his lips down to my neck, just below my ear. I tilted my head in answer, giving him better access to my throat. He turned me around on his lap so that I was facing away from him, languidly nipping and licking at my soft skin.

He trailed his fingers down my neck and chest, then unbuttoned my jacket. Heat flooded me. I let out a gasp when he moved his hand to my breast underneath my shirt and pinched my peaked nipple before he rubbed it with the pad of his thumb, drawing out pleasure after the pain.

His touch was hot against my skin and the world melted away. Everything in me lit up and I felt a fire in me unlike anything I had felt before. Nothing existed outside of him.

His cock hardened beneath me and I ground my ass against him, eliciting a groan from him.

"You better stop that or I'm going to claim you right now. This is about you. Let me do this." His voice was guttural and pleading.

My skin pebbled as his fingers traced my stomach, down and down to my waistband. I lifted my hips when he stopped there in a silent question for permission, making it easier when he slipped his hand underneath. He continued his slow movements down, under my dampened panties. My hips bucked when he brushed his fingers over my swollen clit, craving his touch. He tightened his arm around me to hold me down.

I spread my legs apart. My lips parted in a gasp when he slowly slid a finger into me. My hand shot up and gripped the hair at the back of his neck and leaned my head to rest on his shoulder. He pulled his finger out to the tip then slowly pushed back in.

"Fuck," he purred. "So wet for me…"

He pulled his finger out again, fully this time, and circled that sensitive bud of nerves. He pushed two fingers back inside me, dragging a moan from deep in my throat when he curled them to hit that perfect spot.

"Gods, I'm going to come just from that sound alone," he sighed against my skin, pumping his fingers in and out of me.

Ryker plunged his fingers deeper and harder. I panted, feeling the pleasure building higher and higher.

My breath caught when he started moving his thumb in circles over my clit in time with the pumping of his fingers. My body began to tense, feelings of pleasure tingling from my head to my toes. I exposed my neck to him as he continued to nip and lick at my throat. All I could think of was him, his mouth, his tongue, his fingers plunging in and out of me and swirling his thumb over my clit.

"Ryker," I pleaded breathlessly. I shamelessly ground myself against his hand.

He felt so good, I never wanted it to stop. And that was only his fingers. I wanted more, *needed* more. Of him.

"That's right, take what you need from me," he groaned.

He moved his other hand from my stomach and kneaded my breast. My eyes nearly rolled to the back of my head. I turned my head and watched him watching me, riding his hand with darkened eyes and parted lips.

His eyes flicked to meet mine, glazed with raw need.

Ryker kissed his way up my neck to my jaw slowly, as if he were memorizing the shape of me with his lips.

His fingers whispered across my chest and up to my throat and wrapped them around the base in a gentle possessiveness. His thumb brushed along the column of my neck.

My stomach fluttered when his mouth drew across my cheek until he was almost touching my lips.

"What I would give to taste you right now…" His voice was guttural. "But even the taste of your mouth would have me driving myself into you."

I wanted both equally.

My vision began to turn spotty as my release neared. He pumped harder, deeper, circling faster and faster until pleasure shocked through me. My mind spiraled with stars as ecstasy flooded my veins. I clenched around his fingers, trapping his hand between my thighs, and screamed his name. He continued to stroke me through my release until I was limp against him.

He removed his fingers and I whimpered, missing being filled with him. "I want more."

He chuckled.

I looked into those silver eyes and found that heart-clenching gaze again. He had taken my pain and turned it into pleasure.

Ryker stood and carried me to the side of the bed and laid me down before removing my boots for me while I removed my jacket and my pants when he walked to the other side. The amount of control he displayed impressed me, having been touching me in that way but taking nothing for himself.

Tucking myself under the covers, I placed extra pillows behind me so that Ryker and I wouldn't touch. I didn't want to tempt either of us. I heard his boots and clothes clatter to the floor and waited for him to get in the bed.

After several moments of not feeling the bed shift under his weight, I turned my head to look at him. He eyed the pillows as if they had personally offended him and wanted to set them on fire.

"No," he snarled before wrenching the pillows away and throwing them to the floor.

"Fine, but behave," I scoffed a laugh and turned my head back and settled to go to sleep.

I finally felt him climb under the blanket, and I yelped when he yanked me by my hips until my back rested alongside his warm body. His arm wrapped around me and I placed my hand atop it.

I almost wanted to scold myself for being so hesitant with him before. I had been missing this the entire time. It felt right being in his arms, like it was where I belonged. Our bodies fit perfectly against each other, as if we were made for this.

We were. We were made for each other. We were mates.

He delicately brushed my hair behind me and kissed my neck with a tenderness that made my heart clench. I nestled against him, running a gentle caress down the bond. His lips turned upward in a smile against my skin as he returned the gesture with a caress of his own. I fell asleep with a contented smile in the safety of Ryker's embrace.

Ryker shifted behind me, pressing his hips into my ass as he moved to adjust his position.

My eyes snapped open. I could feel the bare skin of his chest against me, moving up and down with heavy, even breaths of deep sleep. I wondered just how much of his body was exposed. Thinking of the possibility of his naked body against me, a warm feeling tickled in my lower belly. I could feel my arousal pooling between my thighs.

The pillows should have stayed.

Now that I had felt part of him inside me, I became unhinged. I was losing control. I wanted him. I needed him. I had to claim him as mine.

I turned to face him and found myself slightly disappointed when I discovered that he was dressed from the waist down, yet still appreciative that he was. My emotions about everything with us were conflicting. I wanted him in sinful ways, and at the same time I knew I shouldn't.

Except right then.

Right then, my judgment was clouded with uncontrollable desire, the logic of reasoning left behind and overpowered by my divine need for him.

I told *him* to behave, as if he was the one who needed to get a hold of his control. But at that moment, *I* was the one who lost control. Driven by something greater than either of us. The bond roared inside me, demanding to be sealed.

And I wanted it. *Desperately.*

I studied his immaculate body, lightly running my fingers across the muscles of his torso, tracing the outlines of his tattoos. Caressing the column of his neck with the tip of my nose, I inhaled his scent, taking in the very essence of him. His lips twitched and I wanted to taste them.

I knew I should stop. But I couldn't. I needed more of him. All of him.

But I needed him awake to do so. I wrapped my leg around his waist and pushed him onto his back, straddling him with my thighs around his hips.

I leaned down, my hair falling to the side of his face. Gently touching my lips to the shell of his ear, I spoke in a soft and low, sultry voice, "Wake up, my shadow."

He opened his eyes, squinting with sleep, before they flew open and locked with mine. His heart started to race, I could see his pulse pumping faster beneath the skin of his throat. His hands braced my hips and his breathing became erratic, matching mine.

I studied him, watched his features turn from confusion to understanding, debating.

He didn't say a word. He held my stare with heated eyes and his jaw clenched.

I felt him harden right under where I craved him, the heat in my core building at the feel of his cock throbbing. My mouth parted when he took in my body sitting on his.

I ripped my shirt off, tossing it aside and leaving only the thin linen wrapped around my breasts, which did nothing to hide my peaked nipples. His eyes trailed up and down my exposed skin, releasing a shuddering breath through his nose when those silver irises met mine.

Unable to stop myself, I rocked back and forth across his length, the thin material of our clothes allowing me to feel the ridges of him. I moaned softly, causing him to tighten his grip. His face was hard, almost pained with restraint, but he wasn't stopping me. My heart raced in time with his.

I rode him shamelessly, it felt too good to stop. I could feel the evidence of my arousal soaking into our clothes.

Ryker groaned deep in his chest. The sound had me grinding myself on him harder and faster. He sat up and gripped the hair on the back of my head in his fist, pulling it gently until I was looking at the ceiling. I gripped his shoulders, digging my nails in to give me more leverage to go rougher, needing more friction.

His hot breath on my throat sent a shiver down my spine and straight to my center. He sucked and licked and kissed my neck hungrily, moving his hips in time with mine, giving me what I silently asked for.

His hand came up to cup my breast and pinched my sensitive nipple between his fingers before rubbing his thumb over it soothingly. I arched into his touch, but it still wasn't enough.

"Ryker," I breathed. "Claim me. Please." I was aching with the need to be filled with him.

"Kya…" he moaned pleadingly. "Don't. Don't ask that of me. I can't tell you no."

He pulled back to look into my eyes, resting his forehead on mine.

"We—fuck," he grunted when I started moving myself in circles over him.

In the next breath, he flipped me over on my back, pinning my wrists above my head. I trembled with anticipation.

His body was on top of mine, and we froze for a moment. Our faces were close enough that our panting breaths brushed against each other's lips.

I held his stare before I wrapped my legs around his waist and started grinding against him again. As if he couldn't stop himself, he moved with me, and the pressure in me built higher and higher.

I let out a loud, breathy moan.

His pupils dilated and he pressed himself against me harder, growling.

"Kya, we can't," he rasped. "I need you to stop because I can't. I can't stop myself. I want you too fucking badly." Yet still, he continued to move.

"I don't want to stop," I whined, pleaded. His muscles tensed.

"I don't *want* you to stop. But I *need* you to." He pushed his cock against me hard and my breath hitched.

"I want to claim you." Again.

Yes.

"I want to bury myself inside you." His head burrowed into the crook of my neck.

Please…

"I want you to bear the mark of our bond, to show the realms that you're fucking mine—that you belong to me." He licked up the column of my neck and brushed his lips over my jaw.

I wanted those lips in so many other places.

"I do belong to you," I panted.

He raised his head and I could see the tendrils of his control drawn so taut, they were about to snap. His beautiful silver eyes begged for me to take the control he was so close to losing.

Something inside of me cracked and the back of my eyes stung. I stopped my movements.

What was wrong with me? I was endangering his people. His home. *Him.*

A tear slipped down my cheek. Ryker's eyes tracked the drop before wiping it away, then rested his forehead against mine. I closed my eyes and inhaled deeply, scraping for the remnants of my self-control and piecing it back together before opening them again.

He released my wrists and gently held my face in his hands as we gazed into each other's eyes that spoke what our lips didn't. *I know.*

We stayed like that for a long while, until the sun's rays began to lighten the sky over the mountains, trying to fight the inevitable. He stroked my hair soothingly the entire time.

"I want to show you something." His gravelly voice was quiet. "Will you come with me?"

"Yes," I said with a small smile. "But I should probably dress first."

He smiled back and got off the bed before extending a hand to help me up, holding it for a moment before letting go, and I made my way to the bathing room.

"Kya."

I turned back to face him and hummed a response.
He stared into my eyes. "You're beautiful."

Chapter Forty-Two

KYA

R yker took me down to the bottom level of the palace. I hadn't been to this part yet. The place was impeccable. Bright stone walls gave the space a warm feeling, so different from the darkened glass of Morah. And I loved it.

The open area of the hall was bustling with people, and I stopped to watch them. I had felt them when we arrived here, but I had assumed they would leave at some point. Families were gathered together, children playing on the floor next to piles of blankets and scarce belongings. Older fae sat on chairs, conversing with one another and telling exaggerated stories about great adventures. Tables lined one of the walls covered with food and pitchers of water.

They seemed content enough, but I could taste the mournfulness in the air. I could hear the weariness in their voices, smell their worry, feel their souls deflated and broken.

"Who are they?" I asked, still staring out at the people.

"Survivors." His voice was filled with hurt. "They're from Mirren, a town on the southeastern end of Oryn. Or at least it was. It was destroyed by the Glaev during the Trial, the one Vicria threatened about, and those that survived and had nowhere else to go came here. "

"But that was weeks ago. Why haven't they had homes erected for them? Why do they stay here?" I didn't understand. I had never expected that a Lord would allow the common fae to reside in his home.

"Because they're always welcome here. And those that remain haven't decided where to go next. They lost everything. Lost their loved ones as well. They're welcome to stay as long as they wish. They're safe and cared for."

"Is this what you wanted me to see?" I whispered, looking up to him to find that he was already looking at me.

He nodded and I felt a great sadness, for him and his people, wash over me—as well as shame.

"This is who we're protecting. We're fighting the Gods' wills to keep them safe. I wanted you to see them." His words caused a pang in my chest.

I thought of my people as well, and how I wouldn't put them at risk if I could help it. He grabbed my hand and smiled sweetly. He kissed the back of it and tugged for me to follow.

"Come on. I want you to meet them too."

I talked with nearly everyone. Ryker greeted every single one of them by name and introduced me. I tried my best to remember them all but that wasn't my strong suit.

He went off to help someone and I continued to listen to the survivors' stories. They told me of the ones they lost, their torments and troubles, and I listened intently. If I was able to help them in any way, I would. I understood them, their pain of being torn from their home by the Glaev—not that I shared my story with them. It wasn't about me.

I hadn't paid attention to what Ryker was doing, but I was constantly aware of where he was. I gathered blankets that needed to be washed with some of the women, held and read to a small child on my lap so that his mother could have a moment to herself. Even though they had little to nothing, they smiled and laughed. I swept and cleaned and gathered more food and water.

And it wasn't enough. Not near enough. I needed to do more. My heart tore for them.

I stood back by the table, getting a drink of water and wiping the sweat from my forehead with my sleeve. I found Ryker in the bustle of people as I watched them.

I needed to stop this from ever happening again—to stop the torment from happening to any more of Oryn's people. I needed to stop the Glaev.

Ryker and I made the trek alone to meet with the Sage, Deres. I had attempted to bring Malina and Nikan with us, but Nikan only grumbled sleepily from behind the door saying that Malina didn't come back the night before. Ryker had gone to collect Mavris and Hakoa, but he returned alone as well with a smirk, saying that they were hungover from the night before and weren't alone in their rooms. Since it was just the two of us, he lifted me into his arms and flew us to the temple on the southern end of Voara.

The temple was small in relation to other temples around the continent. This one was simple and welcoming, cozy even. Its taupe-colored stone exterior had faded after centuries of weather and the wooden doors creaked when we entered. The walls, while worn from age, held a feeling of antiquity that was to be honored. The air was heavy with the feeling of an otherworldly presence that was comforting.

It reminded me of Hylithria.

The dais, at the other end of the temple, held a table with several bowls and burning incense. I had never really understood what the Sages did or why—I had never really cared.

"Deres?" Ryker called out.

A few moments later, a male came through one of the inner doors, wearing the typical Sage robes with the sash across his waist. He was tall, very tall, at least a head taller than Ryker. He had dark skin with matching brown eyes. But it was his hair that caught my eye the most as he approached. It was completely grayed, which was very rare among fae, and it indicated that he was exceedingly old.

"Kya," Ryker's voice brought me back and I snapped my mouth shut, not realizing it had fallen open as I rudely stared. "This is Deres. Deres, I'd like to introduce you to Kya, my—"

"Mate. And a Worthy, chosen by the elusive Kleio herself!" His deep booming voice echoed off the stone walls. He smiled widely.

I offered a smile in return before my brows scrunched together. I looked down at my arms, my skin hidden underneath my sleeves.

Deres chuckled. "I don't need to see your marks to sense the strong bond between you. The Spirits have granted you great powers." He looked at Ryker. "Possibly greater than yours even."

"I have no doubt, Deres." A look of pride crossed his face as he glanced down at me.

I smiled awkwardly at the comments, not really knowing what to say in response.

"So, what brings you all the way down from the palace? I'm sure you two are very busy. Well," he paused, looking between us. "Not *that* busy."

My eyes widened. "You can tell that we're not mated? Without seeing our marks?"

"Yes. Any Sage that is attuned to the spiritual balance can. We can feel the shift when mates seal the bond."

"You were right then," I said quietly, glancing at Ryker. "Vicria would know if it happened, if we completed our mating."

"Yes. Vicria has a deep enough connection to the Spirits that she would be able to sense it. Specifically you two, though? I wouldn't know about that. It's possible. Your bond to each other is powerful." He stepped forward and held out his hands in front of me. "May I?"

I glanced at Ryker and he gave a subtle nod. I looked back to Deres and gave a tentative nod of my own. He placed one hand on my head, his thumb pressed to the center of my forehead and the other over my heart and closed his eyes. He stayed like that for several moments before he opened his eyes and removed his hands. He took a step back, wide eyes sparkling with intrigue.

"Fascinating," he whispered. He rubbed his chin and looked at me curiously. "Kya, how many other connections do you feel? Besides the ones to Odarum and Ryker, how many magical ones?"

I had so many questions, he wasn't supposed to know about the bond to Odarum, or even his name. But I answered his question first.

"Like the orbs? I don't know. A few. I haven't counted them. There's the one that gives me invisibility from Kleio, but the others are faint and I haven't tried to hone them yet."

"But there are more than two?" He pressed.

"Yeah," I said slowly. Deres and Ryker looked at each other. "What? What does that mean?"

Ryker ran a hand down his face. "It means," he breathed in disbelief. "That you have more than one magical ability gifted to you from Kleio. You only receive one from your Spirit."

"They can do that? The Gods can give more than one gift? What about that balance? Has that ever happened before?" I asked, incredulous.

"They can. And they have before, just not in a very, very long time. They usually only grant the ability or abilities that you would require in order to fulfill their purpose for you." Deres spoke knowingly. His confidence made me believe him. "What was the task that Kleio gave you? Her exact words."

I took a deep breath. "She said I was to serve her Nation." My eyes went distant as I thought back to my conversation with the Goddess. "That the Glaev is not as it seems. And her command for me to restore the balance, I asked her how, and she told me to listen. That I would learn, and to seek the truth. When I asked how to find it, she said that I already knew." I shrugged my shoulders.

I didn't already know. I had no idea what I was doing.

"Which brings us to why we're here in the first place," Ryker added. "Kya has some questions about the book you told me to find."

A rueful smile crossed Deres's lips. "You were successful." Not a question, but a statement.

He gestured for us to follow him through one of the doors and we all sat in a small sitting area. Ryker and I sat with each other on a settee, our knees touching. Deres took the seat across from us.

"What did you want to ask?"

"What is the book?" I leaned forward.

"The book is ancient, a tome written in a language not of this realm, and rumored to have shown up just after Odes's death thousands of years ago. It is said that the book is about dark magic and perhaps its origin."

"But what is dark magic? Eamon mentioned it before but no one seems to know what it actually is." I glanced at Ryker.

He shook his head, not knowing either, and looked at Deres skeptically.

"Magic is energy. And, as I'm sure you know, having lived among Scholars, that energy has equal opposites in order to balance each other out. Light and dark. Day and night. Good and bad."

"Like the Spirits," Ryker offered.

I listened intently as Deres continued.

"Yes, exactly. The two are not so different, as you might think. It is why the Spirits intervened with the Gods in the first place. There was such an imbalance after Odes fell, that the world tore itself apart, threatening ultimate destruction. Such as it is again, now."

"Wait," I interrupted.

Is not what it seems.

The memory of Kleios voice rang through my head.

"Do you mean to tell me," I said slowly. "That the Glaev is this dark magic? Magic not of this realm?"

Deres shook his head with a shrug. "I don't know for certain. I only know that it is disrupting the balance. I can feel it every time it grows. Every time it kills a little more of our world, threatening to destroy the realm. And I know that the book I told you to find might have something to do with it."

"It definitely will. Have you heard of Rolim Fawarin?" I smiled when Ryker gasped in understanding.

"An old friend. I was the one to originally tell him of the dark book that led him to his theory about the Glaev. But he died before he could complete his theory and his work was lost to time. Until it wasn't." Deres gave a sad smile.

"Do you understand its language? Obviously Rolim did." Ryker asked. He reached over and laced my fingers through his.

"No. I never learned, and I'm not sure that Rolim did entirely either."

I nodded and contemplated that information for a moment. Everything that Deres said matched what Eamon had heard as well. I needed to translate that book and figure out this dark magic.

"One last question, Deres." He nodded for me to continue. "Did Rolim say how to control dark magic?"

If Vicria was somehow controlling it, she must have figured it out. *Someone* was controlling it.

"No. Unfortunately, I never learned that either, if he did. But perhaps his work will tell you."

Ryker and I stood to leave. My head was a jumbled mess of thoughts. I needed to go over Rolim's notes and see if I could decipher the book myself. And I wanted to find that Sage. It was most logical to think of Vicria as the dark magic wielder. She knew about it. There was no other explanation. She needed to be stopped and now that I knew she was using magic, as a Sage, her life had a death sentence on it.

We thanked Deres and began to leave before he stopped us. "Kya," he began. Standing to approach. "Hone your gifts. They were given to you for a reason."

Chapter Forty-Three

KYA

After we returned from meeting with Deres, Ryker and I went up to meet with Malina and Nikan in one of the larger rooms on the upper floor. It was the palace's own library, and while it wasn't close to the extensive collection of Morah, it was still impressive.

Beautiful dark marble shelves extended from the floor all the way up to the high ceiling, filled with books from every subject you could think of. The center of the large room held several tables, one of which Malina and Nikan were leaning against, waiting for us to arrive with the dark book safely tucked under my arm. I sat down across from them and placed the book on the table.

"I will leave you to it then. I have a few things to take care of, but I will rejoin you when I can." He leaned down and whispered next to my ear, "Will you eat with me later?"

"I'd like that," I said with a smile.

Ryker walked out of the room, leaving the three of us alone in the library.

"Well it's not home, but it has the same feel. Let's get into it then." Malina gestured to the book.

"Kya, what did the Sage say?" Nikan asked. "Did you learn anything useful that could help us?"

I sighed and rubbed my temple. "A lot."

I proceeded to tell them of our conversation with Deres, before we dug through the book and poured over Rolim's notes as best we could—most of which didn't make sense.

"I don't understand any of this," Nikan mumbled after hours of reading over the note pages inserted into the book. He ran his hand through his hair and blew out a sharp breath. "Kya, I know you want to stay here, but doesn't it make more sense if we take the book back to Morah and let the linguist Scholars sort through this? I mean, this *is* their area of expertise." I looked up at him. "I'm not just saying that to get you to leave. Ryker can come too for all I care. But we've been at this for hours and neither of us even know what we're looking for."

"He's right Kya," Malina said with one of the pages in her hand. "Just look at his writing. It's like he used both languages but didn't explain what the words meant. Even the context doesn't help."

I knew they were right. It did make the most sense for us to use the best resources possible for something this important. No, I didn't want to leave Ryker, but I wasn't opposed to it if needed. Not if it meant that I would ultimately understand what the Glaev was and learn how to stop it. That was more important.

"Yeah, okay. Why don't we take a break from this and meet up later to discuss. We can leave in the morning. I'll talk to Odarum and see if he's willing to Travel us back to Morah," I offered, thankful for the break myself.

"Thank the Gods. My head is killing me. I need a hot bath. And tea. And sleep," Malina whined.

"With the amount of ale you consumed last night, I'm surprised you're able to stand at all," Nikan said before we both busted out laughing at Malina's suffering.

"You're just jealous that I didn't end up sleeping alone last night. Or that I barely *slept* at all," she crooned with a wink aimed at me.

"And exactly which of the dozens of males that were drunkenly drooling over you last night did you wind up going home with?" Nikan crossed his arms and leaned back in his chair.

I was silently enjoying the bickering, trying to bite back a humorous grin.

Malina tapped her fingers on the table in contemplation before she leaned in and whispered, "Let's just say, I climbed a mountain last night—and I wasn't disappointed when I reached the peak."

I snorted a laugh. Nikan grimaced and shook his head before we both stood, the chair legs squeaking against the floor. Nikan and Malina left as I bent over the table and collected the papers, placing them back in their respective places in between the pages of the book, closing it and leaving the palace library.

"Are you near? I want to talk to you and I need to train." I reached out to Odarum. I wanted to speak with him and see if he would take us back to Ilrek. And if I was being honest, I just missed his presence. He had been so absent recently.

"I will meet you at the training grounds outside the Oryn palace."

My steps were quick as I made my way down the corridor, eager to meet with him. I was on the opposite side of the palace so I tried to hurry. I wanted to get in as much time as I could before meeting up with Ryker. I fumbled with the book as I tried to get my jacket on before coming around the corner where several corridors intersected, not paying attention to my surroundings.

Someone barreled into me as I turned down the hallway. I dropped the book as a large body crashed down on me, taking me to the floor under its weight. The air was knocked out of my lungs when my back hit the floor and I groaned under the heavy figure. The male lifted his head after having smacked it on the floor next to my shoulder.

Hakoa's eyes widened when he realized who he had toppled over.

I felt it then through my terbis, those familiar steps that I could never forget. If he saw another male on top of me…

"Get off, get off. He's—" My wheezed voice was cut off by a snarl.

Blinding rage rippled down the bond and I knew that Ryker's primal instinct would snap seeing another male on top of his mate, pushing all logic aside and clouding his true nature.

Hakoa's eyes bulged from their sockets. This situation looked very, very bad.

Hakoa tried to push himself off of me, but Ryker had lost all sense of control of himself. I could feel the writhing chaos through the bond as he ripped his friend off me and threw him against the wall. I jumped to my feet just as Hakoa grunted from the impact. Ryker immediately gripped him by the throat and held him against the wall, his toes barely touching the ground.

Hakoa didn't fight back, even as Ryker manifested his wings, splaying them outward in threat. He knew that Ryker was not in his right mind. What Ryker saw when he came around the corner panicked his bond, making him think that another male was trying to bed his mate.

Ryker's shifting didn't stop with his wings. Before my eyes, his skin turned dark as scale after scale appeared until his entire body was covered with swathes of rounded plates, each layer overlapping the one below to create a thick leathery hide of impenetrable armor.

I didn't have time to marvel at his transformation. He was going to kill Hakoa over an accident, and it wouldn't be *him* doing it. I leapt forward, ducking under Ryker's arm, putting myself between him and Hakoa, and looked up into his eyes, the vibrant silver glazed over with fury.

"Ryker, I've got you." I grabbed his face and the tether of our bond as tight as I could, hoping to reach through to him in more ways than one.

Hakoa tried to gasp for a breath.

But still, Ryker didn't look at me, his face was twisted with ferocity. Smoke and shadows pulsed from his body, encompassing us in near darkness within a second. I could feel his body trembling with ire through the stone and my fingertips. He was fighting with himself. Trying to prevent an irreversible mistake that he would regret.

Not knowing what else to do, I hoisted myself on him, wrapping my arms around his shoulders and my legs around his waist, filling his line of sight. Leaning my head forward, I brushed my lips across his ever so slightly.

It wasn't a full kiss, but enough to get his attention. I knew it was wrong at that moment, but I couldn't help the urge any more than he could control himself.

His entire body shivered and he blinked rapidly. His silver irises, free of the haze, glowed.

"He tried to claim what is mine," he growled into my mind.

I took a deep calming breath, soothing the bond. I spoke back through my thoughts. *"I belong to you and no one will take me from you. What you saw was not what you think. It's—"*

Ryker was flung back away from me.

Hakoa's arm held me steady against him so that I wasn't hoisted across the corridor with him. He placed me down as he coughed heaving gulps of air back into his lungs.

Ryker's body was tense where he lay against the wall, his chest rising and falling heavily while glaring off to the side where I felt someone standing. I turned to find that Mavris had his hand held out toward my mate. Muscles strained, sweat beaded at his brow that was furrowed in intense concentration.

He was controlling Ryker.

A blood wielder.

"Mavris…" I said cautiously as I slowly approached. "You have to let go, you could kill him."

Blood wielders were forbidden for a reason. With a simple thought, wielders could kill someone within seconds without leaving a trace. When fae came into their abilities during adolescence and were found to be blood wielders, they were either killed or sanctioned under the control of the Sages in Bhara with the use of elixirs that tempered their abilities. How Mavris had gone all this time without being discovered was beyond me.

"Mav," Hakoa choked out a warning.

"I'm not going to fucking kill him. I'm slowing his blood flow and lowering his heart rate until he calms and can come back to himself," Mavris gritted out through clenched teeth.

I looked to Hakoa who nodded in reassurance that Mavris would not kill his brother. I rushed over to Ryker and held his rigid, scaled hand. His pulse felt unnatural, and I cringed but refused to let go while he rode this out.

After several minutes, Ryker's pulse slowed and the tension in his body eased. The scales across his body began to shift back into his normal tanned skin. Mavris breathed a sigh of relief and braced a hand against the wall as he let go of Ryker's blood. Ryker hung his head, shaking it back and forth, and I squeezed his hand.

"Hakoa…" he whispered. "I'm so sorry. I didn't mean it. I saw you on top of her and I just…"

Hakoa stepped forward and offered a hand to Ryker, helping him to a stand. I stood and stepped back to give them space. He patted Ryker on the shoulder.

"I get it. No hard feelings. If it were my mate, you would have been drowning in your own fluids."

"And I probably wouldn't have stopped him," Mavris huffed a laugh which caused Hakoa to laugh harder with Ryker following.

I gaped in confused astonishment at how they could find anything about this situation humorous. Ryker turned toward me. Noticing my expression, he pulled me into an embrace.

"I'm sorry to you as well," he said into my hair.

"It's okay," I whispered. I wasn't even remotely upset that he had entered my mind. I tilted my head back to look at him. "And I'm not the one that almost died over a clumsy run-in."

"No. But I did lose control when I tried so hard not to." He brushed a hair behind my ear. "And you had to find out about Mav's abilities in such an abrupt way."

"I had planned to speak with you about it after you two were fully mated, hoping that you'd like me enough by then to not have me killed," Mavris said.

Ryker turned so I could look at his brother.

"How have you kept it hidden all this time?" I asked.

Mavris just shrugged. "It's a long story. And one for another time." I took the hint and let the matter drop.

"And how many people know?" I looked between the three of them before settling back on Mavris.

"Just us plus Arra and my father." Mavris stepped forward and placed a hand on Ryker's shoulder. They both nodded to each other before he and Hakoa walked away down the corridor I had come from, leaving Ryker and I standing alone.

"Are you alright?" He traced his fingers down my arm, looking into my eyes with concern.

I smiled up at him. "Yes. I'm fine."

"I was coming to find you to see if you were hungry yet. Where were you headed?"

"To meet with Odarum then to speak with you. But now may not be the best time."

His eyebrows creased. "How come?"

"We'll talk later. During dinner," I said as Ryker bent down to grab the book from the floor, checking it for any damage before tucking it under his arm.

"I can go with you."

"No. I'd like to talk with him first, then you."

He stared at me for a few moments. His lips were pressed into a thin line.

"Alright. I'll see you soon then." He kissed me on the forehead, then we turned and went our separate ways.

"That took much longer than expected," Odarum said with his ears perked forward in interest as I entered the training area outside the palace.

"Sorry. Ran into some trouble along the way."

The sun was just beginning to set over the mountains and I could feel the temperature dropping in the air, the sky turning a burnt orange color with hues of pink. Despite the cold, I was starting to love being here. Which brought my thoughts back to the matter at hand.

"I need you to take me and the other Roav back to Morah in the morning. Would you mind?" I asked.

"I do not mind." Odarum relaxed his ears and lowered his head in a slight nod. *"But first, I request that you practice more with your shifting. You assured me that you will work faster in honing your gifts."*

He had every right to call me out. I had promised him that I would work on it. He warned me that he learned that I needed to do it quickly. I was struggling to find the time for it all. But going back to Morah and getting the help from the Scholars would have freed me up so I could train more.

"Now," he demanded.

"Cranky ass," I accidentally said through the bond rather than thinking it to myself.

"We have had this discussion before. I am a horse. Now shift."

I removed my jacket. My skin pebbled from the cold just before my wings emerged behind me.

Odarum walked around me to examine them, sniffing and nudging them with his muzzle before walking back in front of me. *"Can you flap them?"*

"I can try but the feathers—"

"What's wrong with feathers?" He shot his head back in offense, ruffling his own wings.

"Oh nothing! They're just...heavier than I thought."

"Well, when they are all together they are, even though individually they are not." He walked around me one more time, making a full circle. *"Beat your wings up and down, like this."* He extended his to demonstrate.

I struggled to hold mine out to the sides like him, my muscles screaming as I slowly moved my wings up and back down, slumping them to the ground.

Odarum nodded. *"Again."*

For the next hour, I tried and tried again, pushing my body harder in order to continue to beat them against the air. Despite the cold, sweat covered my body, dripping down my forehead and stinging my eyes.

"I have an idea," he said as he extended one of his wings forward and craned his neck to the side, gently biting one of his feathers and pulling it free from his plumage.

"What are you doing?" I asked curiously.

Odarum placed the black feather, as long as my forearm, on the ground in front of me. *"I want you to beat your wings hard enough to lift this single feather off the ground. Once you have done that, I will allow you to retire for the night,"* he said before he disappeared from sight.

"Godsdamnit," I muttered under my breath.

I closed my eyes and allowed my wings to slump to the ground, resting my back muscles for a few moments. Taking deep breaths, I willed what strength I had left. In and out. In and out. I opened my eyes and concentrated on the feather before me. Cringing from the strain, I lifted my wings and thrust them forward and down as hard as I could.

Nothing.

Over and over for nearly an hour, I tried to pump my wings as hard as I could until I felt like they would fall off. I decided to give it one last shot before I went back inside. I lifted my wings again, at a different angle this time, and thrust them down.

For the briefest moment, I felt nothing through my terbis as my feet left the ground then landed back to the stone again. I breathed a laugh of disbelief as the feather slowly glided through the air, in front of my face. Holding out my hands beneath it, the feather landed in my palms. I tenderly held it between my fingers with a wide smile.

Shifting my wings away, I squealed with glee, hopping from one foot to the other in celebration of lifting not only the feather from the ground, but myself.

"Well done," Odarum spoke through my mind from wherever in the realms he was.

I was so elated in that moment that I didn't feel the aching pain of my muscles as I grabbed my jacket and ran back to the palace with a new-found wind in me, feeling exhilarated and awake, with Odarum's feather in my hand.

By the time I got back to the bedchamber and bathed, it was dark. I quickly got dressed and rushed to the informal dining area, bringing the feather with me, to meet up with Ryker.

One of the Noavo warriors rushed out of the room when I arrived with a look of dread etched on his face. I saw Ryker as I walked in. The sight of him made my heart flutter. He was dressed casually, in a shirt and loose pants standing at the window looking out over the city below.

Smiling mischievously, I tapped into my magic and became invisible. Slowly, silently, I stepped closer and closer, creeping up behind him. Once I was close enough to touch him, I reached my hand out—

"You should really work on your heavy breathing, you know," his tone was flat.

I scoffed, disappointed. I'd have loved to see the great Lord of Oryn jump out of his skin. I released my magic.

"Yeah, I guess I do," I laughed. I craned my neck to the side to look at him, and my smile fell when I saw the sullen expression on his face as he read some kind of report in his hands.

"Ryker, what is it? What's wrong?" I had hoped he still wasn't upset about earlier, with Hakoa. His friend understood, we all did.

His eyes remained fixed on the single piece of paper. He took in a deep breath and I could feel his anguish through the bond—my worry only worsened.

"Helerie is gone. The Glaev took it."

Chapter Forty-Four

KYA

Helerie was the third largest city in Oryn. Thousands of citizens had resided there when the Glaev hit. It spread from the center, voraciously consuming life after life until it reached just past the last remnants of the settlements. Males, females, and children, all lost within minutes. A few dozen had barely escaped with their lives and fled to nearby towns for help. But there was no one else left to save in the city. There was no city. Not anymore. Not according to the report that Ryker and I were bent over.

We had opted to eat in his study so that we could go over the reports while he later coordinated operations with his chiefs. I remained in the corner, seated at a small table with my legs folded underneath me, keeping to myself and staying out of the way as Ryker's study became a bustling of people coming and going. Tuning out the roar of the chaos, I concentrated on the reports as they came in, looking for any mentions of the origination point for the Glaev and its exact path, while simultaneously creating a timeline map to break it down for better reference.

Well into the early morning hours, the throngs of people began to dwindle until it was just Ryker, Mavris, and Hakoa standing around his desk and discussing something. I wasn't paying attention to what they were saying, too concentrated on pouring over the recounts of the attack from the remaining survivors. When I finished, I stared at the parchment before me for a long while, astonished at the map I drew.

"Hi." Ryker's voice brought me out of my thoughts. He crouched down next to me, cupping my face and rubbing his calloused thumb over my cheek. His eyes were heavy from exhaustion.

"Hi back." I offered a smile and he returned it.

Mavris and Hakoa were excusing themselves, leaving and closing the double doors behind them.

"I think we've done all that we can do for now tonight. We'll meet again in the morning to assess further." He gestured to my makeshift map. "How's that going? Learn anything useful?"

I turned my head back to my drawing. "Only that I know for certain that the Glaev is controlled by someone. Someone who calculated the highest population points and attacked in three strategic areas to inflict the highest damage possible." I sighed. "But I do think I found out something else as well."

I pulled over another page. This was an actual map, marked with the areas over Oryn that had been attacked by the Glaev since the Trial, along with the dates. Pulling out the notes from the book, I laid it all out in front of us.

"Even without understanding most of Rolim's notes, I think his theory was correct on it being magic. Here he listed out numbers, I think it's some sort of measurement of the Glaev."

"Like its…intensity or damage or something?" He pulled a chair over and sat next to me, resting his hand on my back as we both leaned over the table.

"Your guess is as good as mine. But here's what I do think I understand: he listed them all in a timeline, just like I did over here for the attacks on Oryn and one thing in particular correlates."

"And what is that?" he asked.

"The longer the spans between attacks, the larger the affected areas are and vise versa, the shorter the time between them, the smaller they are." I turned my head to look at him.

"Power," he said after a moment before those silver eyes met mine. "Rolim's numbers are power. If Vicria is honing this dark magic, she may only be able to use so much at a time until it needs to be restored. Probably similar to that of our own magic reserves. Maybe that's why there are smaller attacks. The dark magic hasn't had enough time to replenish from the previous one."

My mouth fell open in astonishment. Listening to his deductions about my findings was one of the sexiest things I had ever heard, and if it wasn't for the impending doom that hung over us, I would have had him claim me right there.

He smirked and leaned in to whisper in my ear. "You haven't even scratched the surface of what I'm capable of."

My mouth snapped shut, and I reared my head back. "Did you just listen to my thoughts?"

"I told you I can't always help it, especially with you and that beautiful mind of yours," he chuckled.

"Once we are fully bonded, you will be able to freely speak into my mind as well. Just as you are able to do with Odarum," he said into my head.

"How do you know that? I've never heard of that before," I thought, knowing he was listening.

He held my hand in his. "It's not known to anyone other than mates. My parents were mates and my father told me."

"If it's known only to mates, then why did your father tell you?"

"He only disclosed it to me after I had told him of *my* mate." He smiled.

"Hold on, why is it that I've met your brother but not your parents?" I asked.

Ryker's shoulders dropped slightly, and his smile was tight.

Were. They were mates.

"Oh. I'm sorry. What happened?"

He shook his head. "Another time. Right now let's get to bed, and we can revisit this later and continue our findings on the Glaev in the morning. Which is in…" he paused to look at the clock. "Two hours."

I nodded in agreement, feeling the drowsiness hit me. But I wanted to know about his mother, his past. I supposed I couldn't entirely blame him. I still hadn't told him I was from Atara and I didn't plan to until I knew that I could bring my people back.

Ryker gathered the papers and book from me and tucked them under his arm, pulling me to him and walking us out of the study down to the bedchamber with his other arm around my waist. We got to the room and Ryker began to unbutton his black shirt and I couldn't peel my eyes off him. It was late and I was tired, *we* were tired, and I still needed to tell him that I was leaving to go back home to Morah in the morning. But right then, all I wanted to think about was him and his bare chest.

I stepped closer and ran my hands up his stomach to his bare chest, around to his back, and suddenly I wasn't quite as tired anymore. Ryker wrapped his arms around me so that we were completely entwined. I didn't want to think about all the problems weighing on us, I only wanted to get lost in him as I looked into those bright silver eyes, breathing in the scent of him.

Our bond was getting stronger and stronger every single day, every moment we spent together. We could feel each other's emotions as if they were our own. And at the moment, what I felt from him, what I saw reflecting in his eyes, was something I never thought that I would feel in return. But I did, I knew it. And from the rising smile of my mate's lips, he knew it too as I flooded the bond with what I had yet to put into words.

We let go after a while and crawled into bed, facing each other with his arm around my hip, holding me close to him. I lightly traced the tattoos on his chest with my finger as my mind wandered. And as much as I wanted to forget the troubles surrounding us, I couldn't. Running it over and over in my mind from Kleio's command to the Glaev attacks, from the mating trial to the dark book.

Ryker drowsily brushed my hair behind my ear and kissed my forehead, drawing my attention up to him.

"What are you thinking about, little gem?" His voice was deep with grogginess.

When I didn't answer, he peeked an eye open. "I can always find out for myself if you won't tell me," he said teasingly.

I rolled my eyes, eliciting a chuckle from him. "Just…everything. I can't clear my head, there's too much noise," I said softly.

"What do you normally do to quiet your mind?" He propped his head up on his fist and rubbed his hand down my unmarked arm.

"I usually read, but I haven't done that in awhile."

He raised his eyebrows. "Yeah?"

I nodded.

"Well then, let me find something to read to you." He threw off the covers and jumped out of bed.

He returned a minute later with a few books in hand, crawling into the bed to lean against the cushioned headboard. I giggled and sat up to rest my head against his chest.

"I don't know what you typically like, but here we have," he held up the first book. I doubted he had anything close to the books I read, full of romance with happy endings, but I was pleased with his efforts regardless. "*Histories of Oryn - Biographical Appendix Volume two.* Riveting stuff right here."

I snorted a laugh.

He glanced at me from the corner of his eye with a playful smirk as he continued, "No? Well how about *Strategic Studies for Noavo Warrior Combat?*"

I shook my head with an amused grimace.

"Damn, I was *sure* that was the one. Alright, if those won't do, then how about I bore you to sleep with mispronounced ancient words from a mysterious realm. Sounds intriguing already." He held up the dark magic book and squinted at the faded title. "The divi...divination of dar...dark con...jugation."

I shot up in the bed with wide eyes as I stared at him with disbelief. "What the fuck, Ryker? You could read that this whole time?" I looked down at the strange, unknown language.

"What? No. I just sounded out the letters, I have no idea what I actually said."

"No. You just said 'the divination of dark conjugation'."

His eyes narrowed and he shook his head slowly. "That's not what I said, Kya."

I scoffed. I threw back the covers and sat on my knees, flipped open the book to a random page and pointed to a random word.

dauði

"Read this word right here."

He looked at me skeptically before he fumbled with the word. "Dea...death."

"You just said 'death'." I sat back on my heels.

Listen and you shall learn.

The memory of Kleio's words replayed in my head over and over.

"Oh shit." My voice was barely a whisper. I looked up at Ryker and grabbed his face before leaning forward to kiss his head, smiling when I pulled back. "I know how to translate it."

"You mean to tell me that one of your abilities, given to you by Kleio, is being able to understand languages when they're *spoken* to you?" Nikan rubbed the sleep from his eyes the next morning. He stood from his large bed in one of the guest suites he had been occupying just down the hall from Malina's.

"Yes. That's exactly what I'm saying."

I walked over to the window and pulled back the drapes to let in the morning light, which brightened the room enough that I could see the symbolic tattoos of the Atara Nation across his back. Nikan went to the wardrobe and pulled a shirt over his head.

"Well, that's awfully fucking convenient," he mumbled under his breath.

"What is that supposed to mean?"

He closed his eyes and sighed deeply. I could tell he was holding back. "Nothing. Never mind. If you really think you can understand it and translate it, then I'll take your word for it. But don't you think it's a bit odd that you can understand this one particular language?"

"It's not just this one. Ryker and I tested it with other languages that I don't know, earlier this morning, and when spoken to me I hear them as if they were spoken in the common tongue."

"You're an aligist? You can understand any language spoken to you?"

I nodded. "Another one of Kleio's gifts."

"Then I suppose our work here is done." Nikan leaned against the wardrobe with his arms crossed.

"Who?"

"Mal and I. Our mission was to help you find the book and help you to get it translated so that you could solve the Glaev. You've been successful, without our help, might I add, so Mal and I will still go back to Morah."

"But you can still stay here to help me. I haven't solved it yet." A pang of sadness knocked in my chest.

"We're still Roav, Kya. We swore a life oath. I think you get a pass on it since you're Worthy now and mate to a Lord, but that doesn't apply to me and Mal."

"I know that, but Ryker would let you—"

"We're not citizens of Oryn. We're not citizens of *anywhere*. We made the oath and we will not break it. We're going home."

"Morah has never been home and you damn well know it." My voice began to shake with fury and agony. The word *home* never elicited anything other than bitterness from me.

"How can you say that? You've lived there practically your entire life. Your nightmares are your only memories of—"

"Do not compare the longevity of our lives there as justification. Just because you were there longer than I was doesn't make it any less mine than it does yours—" I was yelling.

"Kya…" Malina's voice cut in. I felt her and Ryker behind me but I ignored them. Tears began to stream down my hot cheeks.

"—or maybe you just don't care anymore because *you* have no one left from there whereas Mal and I do."

"Don't you dare say that I don't care! The Glaev took my entire fucking family, and I've had to live with that every day since. But I've moved on, I found a new family, a new home.

Why do you think I'm so godsdamn protective of you and Mal and Eamon?"

"Enough." Ryker's deep voice rumbled through the room.

"Nik. Let's take a walk," Malina said from the doorway behind me.

We continued to hold each other's stare until Nikan reluctantly stepped around me and walked out the door.

"Take her to a sparring ring." I heard Malina whisper before I felt her follow Nikan down the corridor to the staircase.

That argument was just as bad, if not worse than the one we had before. I didn't understand what it was about us, but Nikan and I always found a way to get under each other's skin and turn a simple conversation into a heated fight.

Atara was always a sensitive subject with any of us. We rarely talked about it with anyone, even each other. But I hadn't really thought about why Nikan was so much more accepting of Morah, so content and happy there. I had always assumed that he had adjusted more easily than Malina and I because of his age, and he was planning on leaving Atara anyway. That's why he was gone in the first place when Atara was destroyed. He had left his family, who lived in the center of Atara, to visit Ulrik, considering taking citizenship there once he reached his staying age. The Glaev had hit before he ever made it to Ulrik, taking his parents and his sister.

His sister.

Gods I was so stupid. I never put two and two together.

He wants to protect Mal and I because he couldn't protect Tsirra.

I turned around to face Ryker who was standing just inside the room dressed in his usual Lord attire, with a black button up with the sleeves rolled up and his hands tucked into his pant pockets. He waited patiently for me to speak, but I didn't want to talk.

"Let's go."

Chapter Forty-Five

RYKER

K ya's anger pulsed through the bond as she stood before
me with her fighting leathers and weapons in the sparring
ring inside the training area. Even without feeling her rage
through the bond, I knew that she was furious. Her body was
red hot in only a shirt and leather pants, and she didn't shiver
when a cold blast of wind cut through. I was able to use my fire
to keep myself warm, but she wasn't. Despite the midday sun,
the temperature was near freezing up in the mountains this time
of year, as winter was nearly upon us. I had offered to be the one
to spar with Kya. Malina had told me to bring her out here, and
I was willing to be an outlet for her temper.

"No elements." The lethal calm of her voice had me hesitating
for a fleeting moment.

I had never heard her sound like that and I liked it more than
I should have. My powerful, formidable mate. I was eager to see
her truly fight with emotion fueling her. Not only was she a
trained Roav, but she was Worthy. She had to be good to have
survived the Trial.

She barely gave me the time to get into a stance before she
came at me with her blades drawn. I had opted for no weapon,

she wouldn't harm me. She couldn't. No more than I could harm her.

I had been falling for her for weeks. Her ferocity and passion, that beautiful fucking mind, her smart witty comments and stunning body, I loved it all. Even though I didn't know much about her, I knew who she was. I knew her soul and her heart. It called to me. I would voice how I felt, but now wasn't the time.

She threw her outrage toward me, blades slashing through the air as I blocked with my arms and ducked out of the way but didn't counter. She was stronger than she seemed and just as swift as the wind as she spun and jabbed. Over and over and over.

I had to put in quite a bit of effort blocking her, more than I had anticipated.

Maybe she would hurt me. She certainly could. *Such a sharp little gem.*

Taking away the risk of serious injury, I grabbed her out-stretched wrists and twisted them until she was forced to drop the daggers. I grinned at her vicious snarl, her fierceness excited me, that sound and the fire in her eyes made my cock twitch. My hands still gripping her wrists, I held her stare and stepped closer to her as I caressed the bond to calm her overwhelmed soul.

But she wasn't ready for that.

She took that opportunity to drive her knee into my side. Grunting and letting go of her wrist, she used her free hand to push me and swept her leg out, causing me to fall flat on my back and pulling her down on top of me. That seemed to snap her out of her enraged state.

She blinked down at me before slowly lowering her head to rest on my bare chest. I released her wrist and brushed my hand down her braid, my other wrapped around her waist. Taking the daggers from her back, I tossed them aside. Just to be safe.

Her panting breaths were cool against my hot skin as we lay on the stone in the sun. Being in this position only excited me further and I hardened underneath her. If she noticed, she didn't say anything.

We didn't speak for several minutes while her heart rate came down—mine having only increased. She lifted her head off my chest and reached up to cup my cheek.

"Thank you." The edges of her lips curved into a small smile.

I bent forward to kiss her forehead. "Of course."

"You already think it's Vicria so why don't you just go grab her? We could put her—" Hakoa cut off when Kya interjected.

"If it's not her, then we could risk whoever it is lashing out. We don't have confirmation, but we're certain that she's involved somehow."

Hakoa came to my study to continue to look over the reports from the last Glaev attack in Helerie and determine where some of the forces might be best distributed. Reports were still trickling in from the Noavo and Vaavi with recounts of the events from survivors and witnesses.

"And if she's working alone?" Hakoa asked.

"Then it won't be an issue to stop her and stop the Glaev." I nodded.

"You can't kill her, you know." Kya crossed her arms and leaned back in her chair. "Not unless you can prove that she's using the dark magic. She's a Sage, their lives are protected under the laws of the Council. I won't let you die for that vile bitch."

But I wouldn't be dying for her, I'd be doing it for Kya and Oryn. Not that I'd let it happen anyway. I wouldn't allow anyone to take me away from my mate or my Nation.

Before I could respond to tell her just that, I heard the incoherent shouts of a familiar voice coming down the corridor toward my study.

I looked at Kya, who was staring at the door with a concerned look on her face. She looked up when I took her hand in mine. Hakoa lowered his head with a resigned look on his face.

"Kya, I'm sorry about this," I said.

Her eyes widened slightly. "About what?"

"Him."

The doors flew open as Mavris followed behind the upset male who burst through them, trying to calm him down. He had that same crazed look in his eyes that had taken over his once-charming face. I stood and approached him while he continued his delirious babbling.

"Father," I greeted with a short bow of my head.

"Sorry Ryk. He just showed up. I didn't even know he was coming," Mavris said.

"Of course you didn't, because I hadn't told anyone." My father looked like he hadn't slept in days. I needed to talk to the healers about giving him something to help him sleep again.

His light brown hair was unkempt and longer than the last time I saw him. His clothes were filthy on his strong body and looked too big for him. He normally would be just as tall as Mav and myself, but with his slumped posture, he looked smaller. The mental frailty of his mind took an enormous toll on him. It tore at my heart to see him this way, so unlike the rugged, kind, and patient male that had raised me.

He started arguing with Mavris and I took a deep breath to calm myself. His state wasn't his fault but he had become impossible to deal with and dangerous to those around him. It was why I had sent him to live away from the city.

I noticed Hakoa whisper to Kya briefly before he slipped out the door and left.

"—and you can't tell me I'm wrong!" He was still yelling.

"Hi." Kya's voice was sweet, and she had a pleasant smile on her face when she came to stand next to me and greet my father.

"You're the Worthy, then?" he demanded, spitting his words.

Her eyes squinted when her smile grew wider. "I'm Kya. It's very nice to meet you."

"Kya, this is our father, Cadoc." My lips thinned into a sad smile.

"Enough delays!" He stepped closer and grabbed Kya's shoulders. She didn't flinch or even try to step away from his grasp. Instead, her eyes softened. "You saw her, didn't you?!"

"Father!" Mavris and I exclaimed in unison. I reached to take his hands off her.

"It's alright," Kya said gently.

"I'm sorry. I promise he won't hurt you. He's just…" I spoke into her mind, not wanting my father to hear.

"I know. It's okay." Even her thoughts were soft and understanding.

"Did I see who Cadoc?" She placed her hands on his and tenderly removed them from her shoulders.

"I know you did! Now where is she? Why didn't you bring her back?"

Mavris dropped his head back and sighed. I didn't blame him. We had been dealing with this for decades, but no amount of answering his questions helped when he got like this.

"Who?" she prodded.

"Who?! How could you not remember her?" He was near screaming in Kya's face but she didn't balk. "Her name is Leysa! She has brown wavy hair and eyes that sparkle like the moons!"

I pressed my eyes shut. These moments were the hardest with him. His desperation was so palpable, you tasted it in the air.

"Our mother," I told her.

"She had to have been there with you! You went into the Rip. I know you saw her. Now tell me where she is!" Father continued. He was breathing heavily, and his eyes frantically darted back and forth between Kya's.

"Will you sit with me?" She led him to the chairs, and they sat down across from each other. Mavris leaned against the wall and dragged a hand down his face.

"Where is all this coming from?" I asked in Mavris's mind.

"He heard from someone that the contestants went into the Rip to get to the Woltawa Forest. He's now convinced it's some kind of entrance to it and thinks that's where Mother is. At least that's what I gathered from him downstairs."

"It's possible but unlikely. That was a completely different situation."

"Cadoc, there was no one inside the Rip. There was nothing there. It was devoid of light and life and time. It was the Gods who sent us to the Woltawa Forest. Otherwise, there's nothing but death inside."

"Did your mother go into the Rip?" she asked.

"From what we know, yes."

"Why do you think she's alive?" Kya spoke to my father. There was no judgment in her voice.

"The bond still lives and so does she," Father scoffed. "She's not dead. I would know if she was. She's just…lost."

He broke down and began sobbing into his hands. Mavris went over and pulled him to a stand before taking him out of the study to get him some rest in one of the rooms on the upper level.

Kya came over and wrapped her arms around me. "I'm sorry about your mother. And your father. His anguish over losing his mate…"

"I know." I held her to me.

"I don't want that to happen to either of us."

"I won't let that happen." I kissed her head. "I promise."

Chapter Forty-Six

RYKER

W e went back to the bedchamber, and she bathed while I ordered some lunch to be sent up to the room. I quickly ran down the corridor and met with Mavris. He had called for a healer to give our father a calming elixir while he rested. We discussed what to do when Father left and agreed that both of us would visit, as well as a healer to attend to him daily.

The run-in with my father was not something I had planned to introduce Kya to for a while.

Back in the room, I sat on the end of the bed with my elbows resting on my knees. I tried to think of anything that would distract me. Like sparring with Kya earlier. The memory of her sweaty and panting on top of me.

Gods, I wanted nothing more than to flip her over and bury myself inside of her, claiming her as mine for eternity and watching the mark of our mating emerge on our arms. A permanent symbol of our inseparable souls, worthy of fate itself. And thinking about that had me remembering about the other night with her sitting atop me and rubbing herself along my cock, looking regal and magnificent. It took everything in me to not taste her then, knowing that if I did I would snap entirely—and nothing would stop me from claiming her.

When Kya came out of the bathing room, she was wrapped in nothing but a towel that came down just past the curve of her ass. Her wet brown hair was hanging over her marked shoulder and those green eyes sparkled in the sunlight streaming in from the windows. My already hardened cock throbbed with want, with *need*.

"Sorry, I forgot to grab my clothes before going in there. But if you want to go ahead and wash up, I'll just get dressed out here."

I jumped up and stormed past her into the bathing room so I didn't rip that towel from her and take her against the damn wall. Turning on the water to muffle my grunts, I stripped my clothes off and gripped my shaft, pumping hard and fast, imagining I was fucking my mate rather than my hand. A low grunt reverberated from my chest with my release, spots of black filled my vision for a fleeting moment of euphoria. It was just enough to temper my urges but far from satisfactory, and I was growing tired of not having her.

I quickly bathed then dressed before going back into the bedroom to find that our food had arrived and Kya was already piling a plate with cooked meat and warm bread, the book open on the table.

"You know what I don't understand?" she said without looking at me. She must have felt me coming up behind her. "When I read it, even out loud, I don't hear it in the common tongue, but when someone else does, I do. *Listen and you shall learn.* Stupid."

I couldn't help my grin at her mocking rant. "The Gods are mysterious in their reasoning," I uttered before taking my seat across from her at the small table.

We ate in silence. I watched her as she continued to read the Scholar's notes and muttered to herself through mouthfuls of food. She finished well before I did, and I was impressed with how someone so small could eat so much. But she was in a much better mood now that she had a full stomach.

"Who gave you which gifts?" she asked. She sat back in her seat and looked up at me.

I hesitated for a moment before answering. "I was born with the shadow element and received fire from Theron. The mind manipulation is from Xareus."

It wasn't something I was proud of. The gift of mind manipulation was repulsive, and forbidden for a reason. It was wrong to enter someone's head and fuck with their thoughts, their memories. But I was a Worthy, a Lord. And since it wasn't something I was born with, I was able to keep it hidden. Other than those closest to me, no one knew, and I refused to use it unless they gave me explicit permission to do so. Mavris and Hakoa had agreed that I could talk to them through their mind freely and that has proven to be useful over the years, having been in several situations where we needed to speak privately while in the presence of others.

Arra had never felt comfortable with it so I never did it with her.

Unless I needed to—like with the assassin—the only times I have done it without someone's permission was when it first manifested, and I didn't know how to control it and when I was first near Kya. I still struggled with the latter, and it took considerable concentration to stop myself from hearing her thoughts.

"Hmm. Have you discovered why? What was his task for you?" she asked curiously. She was so damn cute when she tilted her head to the side like that.

I shook my head with a shrug. "No, I don't know why. And his task was cryptic, just like they all are."

"But what was it? Your task."

"'Reveal the darkness.' I have no idea what it means."

I thought back to when I was in Hylithria, covered in blood—a mixture of mine as well as some of the other contestants—as I stood before Xareus and he deemed me Worthy of protecting his Nation. His task was three fucking words.

Kya hummed in contemplation. It wasn't as if I hadn't spent centuries mulling over his words, trying to decipher what his task truly meant, which I was sure she was doing now.

"I guess we'll find out eventually."

I smiled at 'we'. "Yes, *we* will."

We spent the next several hours of me sounding out the words in the dark book while she translated and wrote it down, word for word, hour after hour. We had agreed to stop at the end of the next page when someone rapped on the door. I walked over to answer it while Kya continued with the notes.

Arra stood with another Vaavi, Ragna, when I opened the door.

"Arra. Ragna," I greeted.

"Lord Ryker. Ragna just returned from Helerie and is here to deliver her report," Arra said. Her face was hard and emotionless.

I nodded. "You can divulge your account down in my study. The warriors are handling them and sorting through them."

"Actually, I thought you ought to hear this yourself," Arra said quickly. "And your ma—um Worthy Kya."

My eyebrows raised, and I stepped aside to let them in. Kya stood and bowed her head in greeting.

"Ragna, tell them what you told me," Arra commanded.

Ragna cleared her throat. "I was stationed just outside Helerie to keep watch on an organization we've had our eye on for some time. Just before the Glaev occurred, I noticed a female in robes walking sluggishly along the perimeter of the city. It wasn't unusual until she made her third round. I followed her as she made her fourth round, staying out of sight. She made two more rounds and each time, she stopped at what looked like some kind of markers, would stand there looking at the city for a moment then move on to the next one. She eventually left, venturing away from the city, and I went back to my post.

"It wasn't until after the attack, and I had joined up with the Noavo recovery forces, that I learned that there were specific points outside the city where the Glaev was concentrated to form a ring around the city. I did confirm that those points were where the female had stopped at the markers."

No one moved. No one breathed as we listened to Ragna.

She looked to Arra who gave a nod of her head in permission to continue. "The female had white hair…wearing Sage robes."

"And there's only one female Sage with white hair," Arra stated.

"Vicria," Kya spat.

Arra and Ragna nodded.

My body began to tremble with rage. That was all the evidence we needed to prove that she was the dark magic wielder.

"I… I think I know how to stop her," Kya whispered. She rushed over to the book and I followed. "Read this word right here. I think I know what it means by context alone but I want to confirm."

"Ræna," I said.

She jotted in her notes and I remained quiet while I watched her sort through her thoughts. She slowly raised her eyes to me, her mouth curled into a wicked grin. "Tell me, Lord Ryker, how exactly did you get your wealth?"

I leaned forward and gave a wicked grin of my own. "Because I'm more like my dragon than just wings and fire."

"Good. Then I need you to retrieve this." She pointed to a particular phrase.

I read her notes.

**...prismed jewels deprive dark magic so that it cannot be
maintained by the possessor.**

I nodded once. "And what will you be doing?"

"Meet me on the roof in an hour," Kya clipped before storm-
ing out of the room and slamming the door behind her.

I landed on the roof an hour later, when the sun had nearly
set. I was met by Kya, Malina, and Nikan. All dressed in black
leathers with cloaks and masks covering the bottom half of
their faces except Kya, whose mask was pulled down, and each
of them was fully armed. Nikan had a sword strapped to his
back. Kya and Malina both had daggers on their thighs and
bows with quivers across their shoulders. Odarum was standing
behind Kya, wings tucked in tight. He bobbed his head to me
in greeting. Kya turned her head to look at him and I could tell
that they were speaking with each other before she turned back
around to face me.

"Do you have it?" she asked in a tone that sent a chill down
my spine.

"I do. I brought one for each of us."

"Us?" She raised an eyebrow.

"You really think I'm letting you go without me?" I knew
what her plan was. I wouldn't stop her, but Gods be damned if
she thought I wouldn't be coming along.

"No," Malina and Nikan said in unison and I tried not to sneer
at them.

"I didn't ask you," I said to them through gritted teeth.

"Ryker, they're right. This is what we do. We know how to
remain undetected." Kya stepped forward and I shifted away my
wings.

"I have shadows. I know how to remain hidden as well and I can provide additional cover if needed." I crossed my arms over my chest.

"He's got a point," Malina said.

"Yet he's not Roav," Nikan said sternly.

Kya paused for a moment.

Come on, little gem.

"Nik, it's not a bad idea. He can stay outside the wall while we go in and if we need assistance, he can help. Not to mention that solves the problem of crossing the river. This way we can take the safer route through the city," Kya said to him.

Nikan sighed, pinching the bridge of his nose. "Fine. But he needs to keep his control in check. If he senses you in distress, he can't just come busting in there to come to your rescue." He looked up at me. "Trust that we know what we're doing."

"Done."

Odarum Traveled us to the outskirts of Bhara, the City of Sages in Riyah, beyond the two-story wall that surrounded it. Having been to the city several times for official Nation business, I knew my way around well, as did the others. We stayed hidden within the trees until it was completely dark, watching the city quiet down for the night.

Before we left, I had tried to convince Kya to allow the Vaavi to do this, I didn't want her to be in danger. But she shut me down quickly with a snarl and a roll of her eyes.

Kya stood in front of me, my arm wrapped around her waist, and leaned back against my chest while tracing circles on the back of my hand with her fingertip. I don't even think she knew she was doing it, her full attention solely on studying the city before us.

Taking a silent step forward, Nikan nodded his head toward Bhara. Knowing it was time for them to leave, I bent down so that my lips were touching Kya's ear.

"Come back to me." I kissed the sensitive spot below her ear and I felt her shiver.

She glanced at me from the corner of her eye and whispered, "Even if I didn't, I know my shadow would always find me." The side of her mouth tilted up into a smile.

"I'll stay in your mind, but only to listen for your call when you need," I said through my thoughts to her.

"*Good,*" she responded before turning away and following Nikan and Malina. Then, she became invisible.

I was genuinely surprised at their ability to remain unseen, I hadn't even seen them as they crossed the open field between the trees and the wall. I only caught a glimpse of them as they climbed to the top. I sent shadows after them to provide extra cover, and they disappeared from sight to the other side.

Odarum had remained perfectly still as the hours passed. Pacing back and forth, I waited for her to return. Kya had remained silent the entire time, which I supposed was a good thing but it drove me mad having to just wait around while my mate was out there without me.

The moons had risen high in the sky, and I was growing impatient. It shouldn't have taken that long. Just to ease my worry, I gave a slight tug on the bond, not wanting to distract her by speaking into her mind, just enough to portray my concern. A moment later, I felt a gentle caress across the shimmering tether, and I instantly felt better knowing that everything was fine. Her mind, as well as the bond, had remained calm and I supposed I shouldn't have been surprised. This was what she did. So I continued to wait.

Another hour passed, and I had kept my eyes on Bhara's wall, searching for a glimpse of the Roav when I heard the snapping of a twig off to the side of me in the trees. I cast my shadows around me and Odarum, concealing us from anyone who might be near. It was then that I felt the bond settling as my mate emerged though the shadows with Malina next to her and Nikan behind them. Vicria unconscious over his shoulder, a diamond embedded in her sternum.

Nikan dropped Vicria on the ground and pulled Malina and Kya aside. He whispered to them for several minutes. When they finished discussing, Nikan strolled back into the darkness of the trees. Malina and Kya walked back to me. I tilted my head to the side and furrowed my brow when Kya looked at me.

"Nik's going back to Ilrek so that he can continue his work with Eamon. Malina is coming back with us. Let's get out of here."

Chapter Forty-Seven

KYA

O nce we made it back to Ryker and Odarum, with Vicria in tow, Ryker told Odarum to Travel us to a specific place just outside the Noavo station where Hakoa and four other warriors were waiting for us. No one spoke as we arrived. Ryker and Hakoa exchanged a nod before Ryker handed Vicria over to one of the warriors, and they all turned and walked toward the mountain.

"Where are they taking her?" Malina asked and I didn't miss the slight glance that she shared with Hakoa before he and the other warriors left.

"Voltaryn," Ryker answered.

"It's real?"

Even with our extensive network, we had never been able to confirm the rumors of the prison within the Eckterre mountains. Prisons were forbidden. Hundreds of years ago, the council of Sages, Scholars, and the Worthy of the Nations voted to have them eradicated and opted for harsher punishments—either the Raith or the Nex. Both options removed the threat of the criminal. They would have their abilities removed, or they would face death. As harsh as it was, it was effective.

"It is real. The Noavo guard it and its occupants."

"What's the plan with the Sage then? Just hold her there forever?" Malina asked.

"Somewhat. But that's not entirely what Voltaryn is for," Ryker said.

"What else is it for?" I tilted my head to the side.

"Interrogation."

After leaving Vicria in the hands of Hakoa and the Noavo, we spent the next two weeks transcribing the dark book, which was proving to be more difficult than anticipated since the pronunciation was complicated. In the early mornings, I would freeze my ass off outside with Odarum, working on strengthening my wings to eventually be able to fly. Ryker would help also, when he had the chance, but mostly he had other tasks to take care of.

Malina and I would train in between stints of translating, keeping our bodies in shape and working on relying on her other senses while I was invisible to better herself and allowing me to practice with my magic. I had been able to increase the amount of time that I could use it, going longer and longer each time to build my endurance.

No new attacks had occurred since Vicria had been taken and that eased my worries but it didn't feel right. Something was off, especially as I continued to learn more and more from the dark book. But until I could fully understand it, it was all we had to go off of, and we could breathe for a moment.

Odarum continued to push me to manifest his gift but to no avail. He would leave for hours or days and come back just to urge me to try harder. All he could tell me was that a presence had made itself known, and I needed to hurry. Which led me to wonder if the Sage wasn't the end of it after all.

"Come in," Ryker's deep voice called out after I knocked on the door to his study. We had been busy all day and hadn't seen each other since last night.

I pushed open the door to find Ryker behind his desk writing. The days were getting darker as winter approached, and the study was lit with warm hues from the sconces lining the walls. His hair was messy, like he had been running his hand through it over and over. The top buttons of his shirt were undone, and the sleeves were rolled up. His face was set in hard seriousness as he concentrated on his work. I closed the door and approached his desk when he glanced up at me.

The tension in his shoulders relaxed a bit, and he smiled wide enough to show his teeth. He stood and strolled over to me, grabbing my face and brushing his lips on my forehead.

"Do you have a moment? I hope I'm not interrupting." I gestured to the desk behind him.

He waved it off. "Never. I'll always have time for you. Have you had anything to eat yet?"

"No." I shook my head. "I just got back from speaking with Odarum and I think Mal went to the city for the evening. She's been going out almost every night after sitting with me all day."

He chuckled. "Would you like to come eat with me? The kitchen staff will have gone home by now, but I'm sure we can find something."

"Gods yes. I'm starving."

He placed his hand on the small of my back and led us to the kitchen. I perched myself on the counter and watched as he went through the cabinets and gathered food on a platter.

I snickered when he set it down next to me. I picked up an apple and took a bite.

"What's so funny?" he asked, taking a bite of my apple as I offered it to him.

"I just never imagined that a Lord would ever serve me food."

"Little gem, once we are mated, I'll be serving you in many ways."

I felt my cheeks flush. Ryker put his hands on my knees and spread my legs. He stepped between them. I bit my lip and his eyes flicked down to the motion. He leaned forward and kissed up my neck.

"Ryker," I breathed. "I thought you wanted to eat." His calloused hands moved up my thighs making my breath catch.

"There's only one thing I want to eat right now."

And I wanted nothing more than to satiate his appetite. We were both starving for each other.

"We can't." My voice was a pained whisper.

He stopped his languid motions along my neck and raised his head. His silver eyes darted between mine.

"There hasn't been an attack in weeks. If she were going to attack again, she would have done so by now. If you're worried about the mating trial, I'll take care of it. Unless…you no longer want—"

"Stop." I pressed my finger against his lips. "I will always want you, want *us*. So don't say that."

He nipped at my finger and smiled. "Alright."

"But I'm still worried. It just feels too…easy. What if we're wrong, and it wasn't her after all?"

He stepped back and crossed his arms. I tried not to pay attention to his hardened length pressing against the seam of his pants.

"You think we should wait a bit longer to see if another attack happens?"

I nodded. "Has she said anything?"

"No. Nothing of use at least. She's only demanded to be released."

I looked off to the side. "Can you not go into her mind and figure it out for yourself?" I glanced back at him.

"I tried." His face revealed no emotion. "Something is off about her mind and I don't know what it is. While I can hear her active thoughts, everything else is…blocked off somehow." His jaw tensed. "I attempted several times, pushing and trying everything I could but," he shrugged his shoulders, "I couldn't get access to her mind."

"How is that possible? Has anything ever happened like that before?"

"I don't exactly do it often, but no, I've never encountered a mind I couldn't penetrate." He swallowed. "My guess is it has something to do with that dark magic but I honestly don't know."

Dark magic is really starting to piss me off.

"Did she at least confirm or deny that she was behind the Glaev? Or that she was present in Helerie?"

We need something to work with.

He shook his head and that didn't make me feel any better about it. At the very least, I expected her to lie and deny the allegations against her. "What about the book? Has it said anything about the Glaev or how to stop it? Or how it's wielded?"

"Not specifically. But some of the Scholar's notes are starting to make more sense. He talks about power retention, conduits, and adaptation, but I don't know what all of that means yet." I hung my head and sighed. "I'm trying. I really am. But I don't want to risk us being wrong and be the reason that Oryn suffers even more."

He gently grabbed my chin and lifted my head. "Then we'll wait until we're certain."

"Okay."

"Finish eating. We'll worry about this again in the morning. But for now, there's somewhere I'd like to take you."

"Where?" I asked with a mouthful. I had pretty much lost my appetite, but I forced myself to eat a few more bites.

"Saabha. It's one of the smaller towns in the northwestern region of the mountains. It's not that far from here."

I had never heard of it, but I was intrigued and up for a late night trip. I swallowed my food and pushed my plate away. "And how will we get there?" I had a feeling I already knew and I wasn't looking forward to it.

Ryker's lips spread into a wide grin. "Well, you need to practice feeling the wind on your face."

I groaned.

It's going to be so cold.

I was right. It was freezing this high up and the chilled night air cut right to my bones. I was thankful for the warm clothing while flying. Ryker held me as we soared over the mountaintops, gripping me under my knees and back. The night sky was sprinkled with soft clouds, illuminated by the waning moons on the horizon and the stars. Regardless of the cold, I loved it up there. I felt free from everything.

Ryker was right, it wasn't far when flying, but I couldn't imagine how long it would take to travel on the ground, winding through the mountainous terrain. By the time we landed on the outskirts of Saabha, I felt frozen. Ryker shifted away his wings in the darkness of the night before he took my hand and led me into the town. Though the nights were growing longer with the winter season, it was still relatively early in the evening. People were still bustling around shops and other businesses along the gravel streets.

"Where are you taking me exactly?" I asked, pressed into his side for warmth as we walked, and he put his arm around my waist to hold me closer. I could feel the heat emanating from him and I stopped shivering.

"I wanted to get you something, so I had some new daggers and arrows commissioned for you."

"Really? You didn't have to do that. But why all the way out here? Aren't there blacksmiths back in Voara?" I looked up at him.

"Yes, there are. But the wielder here… Well, lets just say that I wanted a special touch for these," he said with a smirk.

I didn't know what that was supposed to mean, but I took the hint that it was a surprise and let it be as we continued our leisurely stroll through the town.

We approached a building with a metal sign outside that said 'Brathir's' with two crossed axes below it. Ryker opened the door and I could feel the sweltering heat on my face. It was small, as far as forges went, but beautiful metalwork and weapons of every kind were mounted on the walls. The wooden door slammed shut behind us and I began to sweat from the heat of the place.

I looked around and all the breath released from my lungs. Not from the heat. But from who was hammering at a stick of hot metal. Shirtless, his Trial mark was missing and he looked stronger. Sweat dripped from his head as he worked. Tears threatened to burst from my eyes.

"Njall…" I whispered in disbelief.

At the sound of his name, Njall turned his head to look at us. His face lifted into a smile and his eyes began to glisten. He set down whatever he was working on and rushed over, stopping in front of us.

"Lord Ryker," Njall bowed his head.

Ryker bowed his head back with a grin on his face. He knew. He did this. For me. My mate had tracked down another male for me.

"Kya!" Njall's large frame wrapped around mine as he lifted me off the ground and spun me around, making me giggle.

Ryker made a noise somewhere between a growl and cough.

Njall set me down with the biggest smile I had ever seen and braced his hands on my shoulders.

I noticed Ryker's hands curl into fists out of the corner of my eye, before he shoved them into his pockets. While he did this for me, I knew it took great strength for him to watch another male touch his mate. I mouthed 'I belong to you', and his tension lessened a little.

"I heard you were Worthy, but I wasn't able to find out where you had gone," Njall said.

"I just can't believe you're alive." Tears streaked down my cheeks and I quickly wiped them away.

"I'm alive, Roav. All thanks to you."

"And I'd be dead if it wasn't for you." I hugged him tightly. I pulled back from him and stepped closer to Ryker.

He put his hand on the small of my back, unable to help himself.

"What happened?" I asked, shaking my head. "The last thing I saw before being taken by the Gods was an arrow heading for you.

"Ah yes. Well, the arrow struck true." He pointed to a scar on his shoulder, just above the collarbone. "But that was something else though, seeing you just disappear into thin air."

"You're telling me," Ryker mumbled under his breath.

"And you," I nudged Ryker with my elbow. "How did you find Njall? The Sage told me he never came out of the Trial."

"I didn't trust her word." Ryker shrugged. "And it took some digging with the help of Arra to find him, seeing as Njall isn't his name."

My head whipped to Njall, who raised his hands in defense at my gaping mouth.

"He's right. It's not. Njall is what everyone calls me, though. A nickname given to me by my parents. But you do know my actual name now, it's on the sign outside."

"Brathir?" I asked.

Njall nodded. "Would you like to come up for some tea?" Njall's eyes lit up. "I have so many things I want to tell you, and I bet you have a story or two to tell of your own!" He wiggled his eyebrows in Ryker's direction.

I looked to Ryker to make sure we had time, and he nodded once with an approving smile. I nodded my head eagerly. Grabbing Ryker's hand, I led him behind me as we followed Njall up the stairs to his living quarters on the level above the forge.

"So how did you get out of the Woltawa Forest?" I asked, as Ryker and I sat at the small metal table near the front window.

Njall went to the kitchen and lit a fire with his fingertips before placing the kettle atop it. He turned to face us, leaning against the counter with his arms crossed and a grin on his face.

"After the Gods took you, and the arrow struck me in the shoulder, the male came for me and we brawled. I took the arrow out and stabbed it through his eye before stepping through the arch. The next thing I know it's dark, pitch black, and it felt like nothing existed, like when we went into the Rip.

"I appeared inside the temple after that. The Sages were outside waiting for the contestants to return. They told me that I had passed the Trial but that I was not deemed Worthy, and then they removed our Trial marks. I searched for you, but they said only one female had returned and it wasn't you. I knew then that you had been chosen.

"I rested for a while. I have no idea how long I slept but when I woke up, you still hadn't returned, but everyone else who had completed the Trial had. I left in the morning and came here." His smile was one of pride.

"Where you opened your own forge," I said.

He nodded. "I did! And isn't it wonderful! It's small, I know, but the previous owner moved so I was able to buy it up cheap and it's all mine. Now that the Trial is behind me, I can have a real future." The tea kettle whistled and Njall stood to remove it from the fire, then poured tea for each of us.

"And he's a talented blacksmith. I saw his work when I was here last, and the townspeople have been raving about his work. They're pleased to have him here," Ryker said, taking two steaming cups from Njall and handing one to me.

"Now," Njall started, sitting across from us, "I would really like to hear about this." He gestured between Ryker and I.

I spent the better part of an hour summarizing everything that had happened since the Trial. From the Sages and the panel, to the book, meeting Ryker, coming to Oryn, and how Ryker and I were mates but hadn't sealed the bond yet. Njall had asked a few questions as I recalled everything over the past months, but outside of that, he sat quietly and listened.

"Wow," Njall sighed, leaning back in his chair. "And to think, it was stressful when I *pretended* to be your mate. I can't imagine the stress that comes with being your actual mate." He huffed a nervous laugh.

Uh oh.

Ryker stiffened, sucking in a sharp breath through his nose. "What?"

"No, no. It's okay." I placed my hand on his. "It was only pretending during the Trial, it got our attackers distracted enough to not kill us. Don't worry, I yelled at him for it."

"That she did." Njall nodded enthusiastically.

"Did you…" he asked in my mind.

"No. Nothing like that happened."

Ryker relaxed, but not by much.

Njall and I shared our story from our time during the Trial. Njall particularly lingered on the time he was dragged by the lurvinea. Ryker listened with a smile, but I could still tell that the bond was tense, irrationally telling him that this other male was a threat.

I leaned into him and whispered in his ear, "He won't take me from you."

He smiled gratefully and gave my hand a firm squeeze.

We left shortly after, but not before Njall presented me with a set of lightweight metal arrows and two new daggers. The blades were made of a strong steel, yet light and perfectly balanced with beautifully crafted hilts. I thanked and hugged him, promising to come back to visit.

Ryker and I flew back to the palace. We went back to the bedchamber and immediately got into bed, it was well past midnight.

As we laid in the bed, with Ryker's arms around my waist, he whispered against my shoulder. "The Nailu celebration is in a week."

"Celebration?"

"Yeah. You never celebrated it in Ilrek?"

I shook my head. "No. Nik, Mal, and I would usually go out on the ledge of Morah and look up at the stars all night. The city would put out all the lights and without the moons, you could see every star in the realms." I turned around to face him. "Is that similar to what you do here in Voara?"

"No. All of the citizens gather outside the city. They dress up and sing and dance through the night in the darkness."

I chuckled. "That sounds like fun. And I think it's a good idea. Especially for the people. They could use hope and happiness to get through these hard times."

"Mav said the exact same thing."

"Did he now? I guess he and I are attuned to each other so well," I said playfully.

"Don't test me, little gem," he growled and I giggled, kissing his cheek. He breathed a sigh. "You're the Lady our people deserve."

My stomach flipped at the idea of being Lady of Oryn. I had never thought I would be Lady of anything. Even after being deemed Worthy. And I still worried about being Lady of Oryn and Lady of Atara. I needed to bring my people back.

Chapter Forty-Eight

KYA

A couple of days later, Malina and I were sitting in the library in the palace doing more translations of the dark book. We were both dressed in casual clothes—loose pants and long sleeved shirts. We had gotten well over half of it done by now, and it was starting to make more sense, but nothing that directly related to what the Glaev was or how it was conjured or stopped.

"So what we know so far is that one: Rolim was a fucking genius," Malina stated.

"No shit," I mumbled as I continued to write and not looking up as she continued.

"Two: the Sage bitch had to have had some serious power to be able to manipulate this kind of magic. But then there was that thing awhile back about using some kind of mechanism to concentrate it right? So she could target certain spots."

"I don't think it's a mechanism exactly. It's like…it's funneled somehow, through something else. I think that's what it meant when it said that there is some kind of reserve that holds all of the built up power. I think she stored her power then released it through this 'conduit' onto a specific place. I don't know. That's just a theory. That's not even mentioned in Rolim's notes."

Her eyes went distant. "Funnel the magic? Through what, and is there a limit?"

"I have no idea. A limit to what?"

"The reserve. You said it was a retention of some sort as if she's storing power. So is there a limit to how much power she could retain before it has to be released?"

I thought for a moment, tapping my finger against my chin. "I don't know. I don't remember it saying anything like that. But I do know that the more power that is stored, the more damage the Glaev can do. But that could also be a restoration of some kind over time."

"Didn't you say something about energy too?" she asked, leaning back in her chair.

We had been at it for hours, and it was getting late in the afternoon. We would stop soon and go out to the training area to spar.

"Yeah, but it was more like a passing phrase. Deres is the one who mentioned the significance of energy."

"Right. Magic is a form of energy or whatever he said." She rubbed her temples.

"Something like that." I started stacking the papers. "I want to go talk to Vicria."

"What for?" She sat forward and closed the book, resting her arms across it.

"I want to ask her how she did this shit and what all of this means. And by Gods, I want to know if she knows how to reverse it."

"And what makes you think she's going to tell you anything? Hakoa has had her for weeks doing Gods-know-what to her and she hasn't talked."

I shrugged. "Maybe since she has some sort of vendetta against me and Ryker, she'll speak to one of us. And we both know that if Ryker goes in there, he'll likely kill her for what she's done to his Nation."

"*His* Nation?" Malina gave me a pointed look and my brows creased. She sighed. "You keep saying *his* Nation, *his* people. But from how I see it? It's yours too. Or will be. Not only are you Worthy but you're mated to it's Lord."

"Not yet. Not fully."

"Explain that to me. Why haven't you fucked him yet? I'd kill to bang a Worthy!"

I snorted a laugh. "There's an entire panel who have threatened our lives if we do. And, because there's still the chance that we're wrong about Vicria, and we don't want to risk, oh I don't know, the death of his people."

"*Your.*"

"Shut up." I smiled.

We fell quiet for a few moments.

"Do you think he'll let them in?" Malina asked softly. She was looking out the window.

"I'm not sure. I'm hoping I don't have to risk asking. If I'm successful in my task, I won't need to." I glanced down at my lap.

"Is that what you want?"

My head shot up and I stared at her in disbelief. "Of course it's what I want," I said in a raised whisper.

"But you'll have to choose. Won't you?"

"I don't know, Mal. It's not like there's a manual for this kind of situation. And right now, I only have one option so I don't have to worry about choosing at the moment. I can't solve a problem before there is one."

"Wrong. You plan for every contingency. You've at least thought of it and played out the various ways this could go. It's one of the annoying things I adore about you." The side of her mouth quirked up.

I rolled my eyes and tried to hide a smile.

"Well, I heard about this Nailu party thing and I didn't bring anything worthwhile to wear. We're done with translations today, so let's skip out on sparring and go into the city to do some shopping." She stood from her chair.

"Mal, you hate shopping," I chuckled.

"So do you but that doesn't solve my problem. Come on. Let's go find something that's going to get us both laid." She skipped to the door and I followed as we giggled down the corridor.

"I'll meet you out front. I'm going to let Ryker know I'll be in the city," I said once we got to the staircase.

She rolled her eyes. "Ugh. Mates."

She went down the staircase and I placed my hand on the stone wall. I could feel him up on the upper level in his study with others in there that I thought could be his brother and someone else I didn't recognize the feel of. I dashed up the stairs, taking two at a time, and down the corridor, eager to meet back up with Malina and explore more of the city. The door to Ryker's personal study was open, and I slowed my pace as I entered. Mavris was standing next to Ryker, patting him on the shoulder with a broad smile next to Arra.

"Hi," I said in greeting.

"Kya," Ryker said, leaving his brother's side and walking over to me.

He smiled down at me and brushed my loose hair behind my ear. Being apart from him all day made the bond tense but the proximity settled it and I released a silent sigh. His silver eyes held a look of longing that made my heart swell.

I smiled brightly at him before looking over at the other two. "Hey Mavris. Arra. How are you?"

He smiled warmly. "Hi Kya. I'm doing well. And please, call me Mav. I just came by to—"

"To tell me that he's looking forward to Nailu in a couple of days," Ryker interjected.

Arra rolled her eyes. He and Mavris shared a look for a moment and I was sure that Ryker was speaking into his brother's mind. But I didn't give it much thought.

"Actually that's what I wanted to talk to you about," I said.

"Sure. What about it?" he asked. His fingers lightly brushed the inside of my wrist.

"Mal and I are going into Voara to look for something to wear to the celebration."

"That's a great idea. You should take Arra, too."

"I'll just excuse myself," Mavris chuckled as he made for the door.

It was just Arra, Ryker and I. I still wasn't the biggest fan of Arra, but I knew that she was important to Ryker and to Oryn. If he liked her enough to have her in his inner circle, I thought I at least ought to give her a chance. "Uh, yeah."

"Really?" she asked skeptically.

"Sure. Maybe you could show us around and point out the good shops." I shrugged.

She eyed me up and down. "I don't really like shopping."

"Neither do I and nor does Malina. So this could make for an interesting adventure." I smirked.

She nodded slowly. "Alright. But I don't know what the good shops are. I really don't get out much, other than to the taverns Mav and Hakoa drag me into."

"Go find Lorotte," Ryker chuckled. "She has a shop in the western district. Tell her I sent you and she'll take care of all three of you."

"I'll see you after then." I gave his hand a firm squeeze before Arra and I left his study and met with Malina.

My sister was sitting on the steps outside the palace doors, her shiny black hair swayed in the gentle breeze. She stood when

I approached and raised an eyebrow when she noticed Arra behind me.

"Pigeon boy give you an escort?" she snarked.

"Pigeon boy?" Arra asked.

"Ignore her. No, Mal. It's fine. *Be nice*," I said sternly.

Malina looked Arra up and down before she shrugged. "Whatever. If you're fine with it, then so am I. Do you know what we should be looking for, Arra?"

"Not really, but apparently Ryker does," Arra said. "And I know where he's talking about. Come on. I'll show you."

Arra led us to the western district of the city, weaving through the streets until we came to a small boutique with clothing displayed in the front window. The wood door creaked as she pushed it open, revealing an open room with dresses and skirts of all shapes and colors hanging on bars that lined the walls. Malina and I followed Arra inside. When Arra used a gust of air to close the door behind us, a female voice came from a back room at the other end of the shop.

"I'll be with you in just a moment."

"Take your time, please. It's not like we have all day," Arra muttered under her breath.

"Are you always this cranky?" Malina asked.

"Only when I'm sober," she grumbled.

Malina leaned toward me and whispered, "I'm starting to like her."

"You barely know her. How can you have an opinion so quickly?" I scoffed.

"Well she doesn't talk much, she can kick ass, and she likes to drink. Just my type. Oh look at that one!" Malina walked over to an extravagant dress hanging near the front of the shop.

A moment later, a tall, lean female sauntered in from the back. Her curly blonde hair went down to her waist, golden skin peeking from a short blue dress that came just below her knees with matching heels. Her lips were painted a deep red that nearly matched her eyes.

"Welcome. My name is Lorotte. How can I help you?" Her voice was like silk.

"Lord Ryker sent us. We need to dress for Nailu and he assured us that you would help. This is his mate, Kya," Arra said formally, and I wondered if she ever loosened up. Maybe that's why she liked to drink.

"Kya. It is an honor to meet you. Lord Ryker is truly blessed by the Gods to have received a mate. And a beautiful one at that." Lorotte bowed her head.

"Thank you. And this is my sister, Malina." I gestured to Malina who was skipping back over to us.

"Hi!" she chimed.

"A pleasure," Lorotte said. "Now, the Nailu celebration is only two days away so I will need to get your measurements and get started on your pieces. Take a look around and let me know if you see something and I can work on the customization to your liking."

I looked around the room. "Do we not just...pick one?"

"Only if you feel strongly about it. But if Lord Ryker said I would take care of you, then I certainly will. I've known him since he was young. His mother and I were friends. I would do anything for him."

Were.

I gave a grateful nod, and we began to look around at the selection. A moment later, a hand grazed my arm.

"As the mate to Lord Ryker, I was wondering if you would like to wear the traditional dress of Oryn. Although you certainly don't have to," she offered with a grin.

"No, I would love that. I believe that traditions are important to uphold." I smiled back.

"Wonderful! Let me grab some materials from the back." Lorotte briskly left the room.

Malina came to stand next to me. "You could make some modifications, you know."

"Such as?" I asked.

She gave me a sad smile.

I shook my head. "No. This is Oryn. And besides, I never earned that honor," I said softly. It wouldn't have felt right.

"Kya, you were deemed Worthy by *Kleio.* I think if anyone has earned that honor, it's you."

I didn't say anything, and Malina's lips thinned before she went back to peruse the rows of clothes.

Lorotte came back a few minutes later with several swaths of fabric. Her features were hard in concentration as she held each one up to me.

"Oh now this one is perfect. Yes. I think this will do very nicely," she said, nodding.

Malina and Arra approached, each with a dress draped over their arms. Malina's was a beautiful burgundy color and Arra's was a deep rich blue that made her red hair stand out. I had to hand it to them, for not liking this sort of thing, they sure knew how to pick out what accentuated their features.

"Well, that will most definitely compliment the eyes." Arra said looking at the material Lorotte was holding. And I could have sworn there was the slightest hint of a smile on her face. At least it wasn't her usual scowl.

"Indeed. I love it. You'll look like a walking jewel," Malina said, clapping her hands.

"Lord Ryker does like his gems. And you will be his most precious treasure," Lorotte said.

I laughed. "Okay, I'll take it."

"Good." She tossed aside the swaths and spun me around. "I'll get all of your measurements and have these delivered to the palace by tomorrow night."

After we left Lorotte's shop, we explored the city for a bit before Malina and I went back to the palace. Arra had gone her own way back to her home. I was beginning to like Arra, water under the bridge and all that. She still scowled the entire time, but I think she had enjoyed herself as well.

Just as we were approaching the steps of the palace, Odarum appeared beside us. I was getting used to him showing up at unexpected times. *"I need to speak with you."*

"I'll meet with you later, Mal," I said.

Once she was inside I turned to face Odarum. *"Where have you been the last few days? Having secret Spirit meetings in the Hylithria again?"*

"As I have told you, time is different. What you perceive as a few days is only hours in comparison in Hylithria. But yes, that is where I have been."

"Can you tell me anything this time?" I crossed my arms and leaned against the stair wall.

"A little. I must warn you that the…presence is nearing. You need to prepare yourself." He stomped his hoof against the gravel.

"Prepare myself for what? What is it? Is it a thing? Or a person?"

"I cannot tell you more than I already have. If I could, I would have by now but it would be interfering. But I need you to heed my warning."

"Odarum, I'm trying. But it's kind of hard when I don't know what I'm preparing for or when to expect it." I closed my eyes and pinched the bridge of my nose. *"I will train with you all day tomorrow, but other than that, I don't know what more you expect me to do."* I looked back up to my Spirit guardian. I knew he

was doing everything he could and that he was likely telling me more than he should have.

He bobbed his head. *"Thank you. I will see you at dawn."*
Then he disappeared.

Chapter Forty-Nine

KYA

O darum worked me into the ground for two days straight. But I could see the results from the past few weeks of near constant training. I was getting stronger and stronger every day, with my magic and my wings. I could disappear from sight without a second thought, and I was able to get airborne so long as I had a running start. And now, I could combine them.

As I took my final run for the day, I honed my invisibility, thrusting my wings out and taking to the sky. I climbed higher and higher in the air, feeling the crisp breeze across my wings.

No view could compare to what I saw. The mountains, the *world*, were beneath me.

I looked over my shoulder when I heard a whinny, just in time to see Odarum soaring past. Right as he was beside me, I became visible again. He jolted and flapped his wings back with a roar. I threw my head back and laughed.

Odarum chuckled. *"Well done Kya. You have improved greatly."*

"Does this mean I get the afternoon off? It's Nailu tonight." We banked to turn back toward the palace.

"Yes."

"Are you coming? Do Spirits even celebrate Nailu?" I tilted my head slightly.

"In our own way. It is the night of mating," he said.

I tried not to grimace at the mental image.

I closed my eyes, feeling the wind against my face and the peace and freedom of being in the air.

"Kya?" Odarum said after a few moments.

"Hmm?" I kept my eyes closed. I loved this feeling.

"You should pay more attention."

My eyes shot open, in fear that I was about to fly straight into a mountainside, but there was nothing but the skies before me. The next second, I was being pulled upward and spinning. Odarum's deep laugh sounded in my head—I had never heard him laugh before—as a scream ripped from my chest and turned into a thrilled squeal.

My shadow.

Ryker had come from beneath me and was holding me against him with the biggest smile on his face.

"Shift your wings away, little gem," he whispered against my ear.

When I did, Ryker readjusted his hold of me so that my legs were wrapped around his shirtless waist and my arms around his neck, tangling my fingers in the hair on the back of his head. The feel of his bare skin beneath me made the bond thrum. I looked back down to where Odarum was, just in time to see him Travel away. Ryker began to slowly descend, beating his wings just enough to keep us from dropping too quickly.

I lightly smacked Ryker on the shoulder. "You scared the shit out of me." I was grinning widely.

"I've hardly seen you for the past couple of days. When I saw you appear out of thin air in the sky, you were absolutely breathtaking, and I couldn't stand to be apart from you for another moment." His arms tightened around me.

My stomach fluttered, and I grazed my nose along his. "I'm glad."

His chest rumbled a sigh as he rested his forehead against mine and closed his eyes briefly before staring right into mine, into my soul—just as I could see into his.

I was wrong. There was one view that could compare.

"Hold on tight," he said with a wicked smile.

I squeezed him with every bit of my strength. He folded his wings and angled us down as we dove through the air, eliciting another screaming laugh from me at the sudden drop. The wind roared in my ears as it rushed past but it was thrilling.

He landed us smoothly on the roof of the palace and set me on my feet. He bent down and kissed me on my forehead. Gods I was so ready to feel those lips against mine. As much as I loved his tender kisses, I wanted to taste him. I wanted him to ravish me.

"I saw that Lorotte came by late last night. Are you happy with the dress?" he asked, grabbing up his shirt from the floor and slipping it back on after shifting away his wings.

"I am. It's beautiful. Have you seen it?" I laced my fingers through his as we made our way down the steps to the balcony.

"No. Lorotte would beat me if I looked," he breathed a laugh.

"Good. I want to see the look on your face when you see it on me first, rather than hanging up." He held the door open for me as I walked through, still holding my hand.

"Kya, please remember that I'm not yet a fully mated male."

"Are you worried that you'll lose control when *you* see me or when *others* do?" I smirked at him playfully. I felt the bond tense.

In the blink of an eye, he had me against the wall, the stone was cold through the wing slits in my shirt. He grabbed my ass and pushed me up the wall, my legs instinctively wrapping around him as he pressed his body against mine and my breath caught.

"Don't tempt me, little gem," he growled. He released my hand and grabbed my hair in his fist, tilting my head to the side and roughly kissing my throat. "Say it."

"I belong to you," I breathed. "I always have. I always will."

He sighed and rested his head on my shoulder. "I belong to you," he whispered. That swirling tether between us relaxed, contented.

For the time being.

I kissed the top of his head, then he set me down. "I'm going to start getting ready with Mal. I'll be in her room so don't come down there. I'll meet you at the celebration."

With that, I darted through the corridor, down the stairs and to Malina's room where she was already bathed and waiting. I quickly bathed and noticed that it was nearing dusk. I had just wrapped a towel around me when I heard a knock on the door to Malina's room.

"Yes?" she called.

"Lord Ryker asked for this to be delivered for the two of you." A male voice that I vaguely recognized.

Malina looked at me and I shrugged. I hid myself behind the door when she opened it and thanked the male before closing it again. She held a platter of delicious fresh pastries.

"Being Lady of Oryn has its perks!" she exclaimed, setting the tray on the desk by the window. She didn't wait before picking one up and stuffing her face.

"I'm *not* a Lady." I rolled my eyes and picked one up too.

"Fine. If he keeps this up, I'll gladly be his Lady," she said with a mouthful.

My eyes cut to her and I snarled. "Fuck off, Mal. I'm already on edge as it is."

She ignored me and continued to eat.

When we were both finished, we did our hair, hers up on her head and mine half up on one side, then changed into our outfits.

My mouth fell open. "Damn, you look like sex with legs."

Lorotte had said that she would provide us with the custom attire for Oryn, but I had never imagined that it would be so beautiful. Malina's burgundy skirt was thin with a slit going all the way up to her hip, exposing her entire leg. Her top was of the same fabric. The straps were narrow over her shoulders, and it came to just below her breasts, leaving her midriff bare.

She spun around, the bottom of the skirt swirling around her slippered feet. "I know! And look at you!" She bounced over on her toes and led me by the shoulders in front of the mirror. "You *look* like the future Lady of Oryn."

I smiled and slowly spun to get a good look. The style was the same as Malina's with small differences. My straps wrapped around my neck and the fabric was beaded with small jewels at the hem of the top, underneath my breasts, as well as the waistband of the skirt. And Lorotte was right. The color was perfect. It really did match the eyes.

"Oh, one last thing," Mal said, reaching into a drawer and pulling something out. She walked back over and stood behind me. "Close your eyes." I did as she said. She messed with my hair for a few moments. "Open."

Tears pricked the back of my eyes and my chest tightened. Malina had braided a feather into my hair. A custom for those of Atara. It was subtle enough that no one would likely notice since I didn't have the paint across my eyes and temples. People would probably just think it was in honor of Odarum.

"And now you look like a Lady of Atara too," she whispered.

A tear slipped down my cheek. I saw hints of my mother in my reflection. The feather was a symbol that she always donned.

"I miss them," I said.

"I miss them too. But let's honor them tonight."

I nodded my head. "In that case." I manifested my wings. The design of the top allowed for them without tearing the fabric, and I wondered if that was intentional. I plucked a single feather, before shifting my wings away. "You'll need one too."

She turned around and allowed me to braid it into her hair. The last daughters of Atara.

The air dome in the valley outside the city was held by air wielders and warmed with fire manipulation. For which I was grateful. The lack of coverage on my body did little to warm me on this first winter's night. The sky was lit with the mass amounts of stars now visible without the moons to outshine them, but nothing else outside of that. Every light in the city was out.

It was my favorite night of the year, as all the realms and stars shined down on me.

Malina and I walked through the near silent city to the northern end of the valley. And when we made it inside the dome, it was like another place entirely.

People were everywhere, nearly all of Voara was there. The females were wearing skirts and tops, just like we were, or dresses. The males wore loose pants and tunics, most cut down to expose the chest, or just button up shirts that were left open. Some had no shirts at all, and Malina wasn't the least bit disappointed about it.

Music thrummed in the air. The stringed instruments and beating drums moved my soul in a way that I never thought possible, so loud and deep that I could feel it in my veins. Several people were along the perimeter of the dome, standing with friends and family, laughing and chatting over the music. But mostly everyone was in the center. A mass of people dancing, moving and swaying to the beat of the drums. Lines of people, holding hands and stepping in time with the song, moved about. Others were coupled up, their bodies flushed against each other and grinding and moving as one to the beat. It was sensual and intimate.

Malina darted off when she saw something of interest, as I stood there, taking in the view of an entire city coming together to live and prosper in the darkness.

I gave myself tonight. This one night to forget everything, the past, the Glaev, Sages and Worthy and unknown dangers that awaited. For just one night, none of it mattered, none of it existed.

Mavris stepped from the crowd, I hadn't noticed him among the mass of people, and approached me.

"Kya, you look beautiful." He grabbed my hand and kissed the back of it. "And might I say, that is a good color on you."

"Thank you, Mavris." I smiled warmly. He looked so much like his brother. Speaking of… "Where's Ryker?" I could feel through the bond that he was near. Usually, I was able to sense him through my Terbis, but there were too many vibrations so close together that I couldn't separate them.

"You're my brothers mate. Call me Mav, please. And he's somewhere around here. I'm sure he'll find you soon enough." He shrugged, still holding my hand. He gestured to the crowd. "Would you like to dance?"

"Actually, I would." My smile widened, and he pulled me into the throng of dancers.

We merged with one of the lines and danced around and around. Spinning and weaving and dipping and laughing. We would switch partners for a stint before coming back together. My hair whipped through the air and my skirt swayed.

Out of nowhere, Hakoa suddenly jumped in to take Mavris's place, pushing him out of the way with a smug grin and whisking me into a spin away from him. I threw my head back and laughed. I heard Mavris shout playfully in protest as if he were offended but the smile on his face said otherwise as he jumped back into the dancing with someone else.

Surprisingly, Hakoa's large frame moved with grace through the steps of the dances. He had on dark pants and a matching tunic that exposed his chest, and I could just make out some of the tattoos in the darkness.

"You shine brighter than any star in the sky." Hakoa smiled down at me.

My cheeks blushed, and I opened my mouth to thank him, but then I felt it. That unmistakable feeling of being watched.

Hakoa's eyebrows furrowed when I stopped dancing. I smiled knowingly at him. Hakoa lifted his head, looking out through the people before his eyes locked on someone behind me. I could feel him standing just outside the crowd as they continued to move around us.

I wrapped my arms around Hakoa, his arms wrapped around me in return. "Thank you for dancing with me," I said as I released him.

He bowed his head and returned to the dancing.

I turned on my heel. Ryker's silver eyes shone in the starlight, standing out against the crowd. I used them as a guide through the swarm of dancers.

My mate.

Emerging from the crowd, Ryker's eyes swept up and down my body. He wore all black, his shirt unbuttoned, revealing his tattooed chest and torso. His shaggy hair was unstyled and swept to the side, just touching the tops of his brows. His eyes hungrily trailed over me, making my skin flush under his stare. Just a look from him had me hot and wanting.

My tongue swept across my lower lip as I took him in with just as much hunger and desire in my eyes. Gods, I wanted him.

He gave me a knowing look and gripped my hips, pulling me against him. His nose grazed up the length of mine and I shivered.

"Do you like the color?" I gazed up at him from underneath my lashes.

"Silver." His voice was thick and husky.

I placed my hands on his chest and lifted to my toes to whisper against his ear. "It goes with your eyes. A match to my mate."

A low growl rumbled in his chest, and his hands tightened on my hips when I kissed just below his ear. A sound greater than any music.

"Dance with me, shadow." I dropped back down to my heels.

He brushed his hand down my hair and fiddled with the feather braided into it, looking at it curiously before meeting my gaze. "Always."

He grabbed my hand and led me into the crowd behind him. When he stopped, he turned around to face me, placed his hand on my lower back and pulled me in close against his body. My hands were up behind his neck, and his other hand gripped my waist. He rested his forehead against mine.

We swayed and dipped to the beat. The music never stopped. The beating of the drums would shift and transition smoothly in a constant rhythm, like the beats of a heart. I became lost in his eyes.

Somehow, in the middle of all of those people, it was just the two of us. Our bodies, the music, the darkness and the stars above. The world fell away and nothing else existed.

"Do you know the legend of the moons?" he asked softly.

I shook my head.

"They're lovers. It is said that they're Spirits that loved each other so much but couldn't be together. They wanted to live in peace among the stars forever so they became the moons. Always with each other in the skies and gracing us with their light to guide us." He kissed the tip of my nose and I blushed. "They were the first mates, and they take one night a year to love each other away from the world."

"Like we're doing now," I whispered.

"Only I'll give you every night, every day. Until time itself comes to an end."

The dynamic in the air changed. My heart was so full, so free.

Ryker spun me around so my back was against his chest. My hand came back up behind his head and my fingers grazed through the hair at the nape of his neck. He bent his head down and ran the tip of his nose up the column of my throat. I tilted my head back to rest on his shoulder. His hand splayed across my bare stomach, and I intertwined my fingers with his. His other hand was still gripping my waist. My ass was against his hardened length. Heat pooled in my core.

We rocked and swayed against each other, in time with the beat of the drums, with the beat of our hearts. Everything was passionate and electric. Our bodies moved together as one.

I lost track of time, focused solely on the feel of his body guiding mine to the music, the beat in my chest, the bond thrumming between us. I never wanted to leave this moment, this perfect moment with us in the darkness. It didn't matter that we were surrounded by thousands of people dancing in the same way. It was only us.

I tilted my head into him and kissed up his neck to his jaw. His arm tightened around me and his hand traveled from my waist to my thigh, exposed through the slit in my silver skirt.

His hand was hot against my skin, tingling from his touch. I wanted this to last forever.

Ryker's movements slowed, his trailing hand, his body against mine. Until he stopped moving and lifted his head. I could feel his heart racing, hammering against his chest. I turned around in his arms to face him, searching his eyes and trying to understand the emotion in them. His hand cupped my face, the other on my lower back, brushing his thumb over my bottom lip and his eyes darkened, pupils dilated.

His shadows came around just the two of us, concealing us in his darkness.

"I have to," he whispered before his mouth crashed into mine.

Electricity zapped through my body and soul as I finally had his lips against mine. His tongue licked against the seam of my lips and I parted them. He invaded my mouth and our tongues danced against each other. His fingers gripped my hair and he tilted my head back to go deeper, to taste more.

My hands gripped his shirt, pulling him closer to me. I had waited long enough.

"Ryker," I said against his mouth. "Claim me."

That was all it took. One kiss made me lose control and I had to have him. All of him.

And my mate didn't hesitate.

He shifted his wings and lifted me up by my ass. I wrapped my legs around him, our mouths never parting and still devouring each other as if our souls had been starved our entire lives. He held me tightly against him and carried us into the air and toward the mountains.

Chapter Fifty

RYKER

E verything about tonight drove me mad with desire. With want. With *need*. From seeing her wearing the dress of my Nation, made to match my eyes, to the way our bodies moved perfectly against each other, to the sweet taste of her mouth. Her scent of lavender and eucalyptus mixed with her arousal.

I couldn't take it anymore. I couldn't wait.

Vicria had been secured, the threat to my people gone. And the moment Kya said those words, when she begged me to claim her, what remaining control I had snapped.

I wouldn't deny the bond any longer. I wouldn't deny her.

I shifted my wings, ripping them through my shirt. I lifted her into my arms and she wrapped her legs around my waist, her skirt bunching up at her hips, before I took to the skies.

The palace was close enough but I wanted us to have complete privacy, so instead, I flew us to my cave on the other side of the mountain. She would see the one place that was sacred to me and that I could truly be myself. A place all to my own that no one, not even Mavris, knew about. Her mouth never left mine even as we banked around the mountain. Those soft lips and voracious tongue would be the end of me. And I would have gladly accepted it.

It wasn't until I gently landed us at the cave opening that she broke our kiss. But my mouth was instantly on her again, lapping and nipping at her throat as I walked us inside the tunnel and she took in the cave. With half a thought, I lit the sconces lining the walls and the hearth in the alcove that I was heading to.

"What is this place?" she asked, swiveling her head to glance around the space.

"My cave. *Our* cave," I corrected myself. Nothing was solely mine anymore. I would give her everything of mine. I wanted to give her every part of me.

When we entered the chamber, she let out a gasp. I lifted my head to see her gaping mouth and I had to hold myself back from taking it in mine. The chamber was lined with precious gems of every color, size, and shape. The light from the sconces made them sparkle. But it was nothing compared to the sparkle in her green eyes.

"It's beautiful," she breathed. I didn't stop walking, too eager and desperate to take her to the bed.

"All the gems in the world wouldn't be as beautiful as you," I said.

She looked at me with hooded eyes and bit her bottom lip. And gods damn me if that wasn't the sexiest little thing she did.

I stole her lip from her bite and sucked on it, eliciting a groan from her. The sound went straight to my already hardened cock.

I quickened my pace to the alcove near the back of the cave. Kya pulled her lip from me and crossed her arms over her chest, grabbing the hem of her top and ripped it over her head, baring her breasts to me. My breath left my lungs.

I took her breast in my mouth. She tossed her head back, releasing a moan that echoed off the walls. I smiled inwardly, wanting to learn every little thing that I could do to earn such glorious sound from her again and again.

"Take me now," she snarled.

So eager.

"I've had a long time to fantasize about this moment. I'm not just going to fuck you against the cave wall. I will properly bed you. But first, I'm going to fuck you with my fingers, and then my tongue, before I give you my cock."

Kya shivered from my words and my hot breath against her skin.

A moment later, I crossed the threshold into the alcove that held the bed. The fire in the hearth was warming the chilled room. I laid her on the bed and stood up straight. She gestured to my shirt. I shifted my wings away and removed my shirt, tossing it to the cave floor.

She sat up and licked up my stomach and chest, trailing her hands up and down my sides like she couldn't touch me enough.

I pushed her back against the bed and leaned over her, bracing my hands on either side of her head, caging her in. Something raw and primal surged through me—a hunter who had cornered its prey. I watched with hungry eyes as she untied the string of my pants.

My mate was in need, craving to seal our divine bond. But I had no intention of rushing this. We would only have our first time once.

I grabbed her wrists and pinned them above her head, lacing our fingers. Our mouths crashed together in a passionate kiss of tongues and teeth. I held both her wrists in my hand and moved the other one down to cup her breast, flicking her peaked nipple, before moving it down her stomach, over her skirt and to the slit at her thigh.

Her skin pebbled beneath my touch. I inched my hand up under her skirt.

"Kya," I said dangerously. "Did you dance with me wearing *nothing* underneath your skirt?"

She whimpered and nodded, and Gods if that didn't make me even harder.

I released her wrists and grabbed the waistband of her skirt. She lifted her hips off the bed and I slid the garment down her legs, tossing it to the floor.

Grabbing her behind the knees, I pulled the swell of her ass to the edge of the bed. I knelt down before her and spread her thighs, baring her slick cunt to me. Her clit was swollen with need and utterly soaked.

"Little gem," I whispered. "You're so wet for me."

I slid a finger into her.

So tight. So warm.

I leaned forward, watching her face as I brushed my lips against her. Her body twitched, and her mouth parted in a soft gasp.

With the first lick of my tongue, she moaned from deep in her throat and plunged her fingers into my hair. My pleased growl rumbled against her, causing her to shiver.

Fuck, the taste of her.

I licked and sucked on her before sliding another finger inside, stretching her and curling them to that spot that made her writhe beneath me. Plunging them in and out and licking her, I felt her muscles tense as her pleasure built and she pleaded my name in a breathless whisper.

I removed my fingers and gripped the backs of her thighs before I ferociously fucked her with my tongue, burying my face in her. I was starved for her and if this was the last thing I ever did, I would die happy.

Carefully watching her face, I licked up to her clit, stroking back and forth, circling, and diving my tongue back in. I needed to know what drove her mind to oblivion. Where she liked to be licked most. How hard and rough she wanted it.

"Ryker…" she panted.

She rode my face shamelessly. And I watched every moment, every expression, until I ruined her completely. The sounds that came from her perfect lips were like a symphony resonating off the walls of the cave.

Ever since she came around my fingers, I had imagined the moment she would come on my tongue. It was better than I had ever dreamed.

She clenched around me as she came and I stroked and licked her through her climax.

I stood and she watched through hazy eyes as I removed my pants and freed my cock. Her eyes grew wider with a flicker of something dark and hungry.

Slipping one arm under her knees and the other behind her back, I lifted her and set her down on the pillows at the head of the bed. I climbed on top of her, between her legs, and took her mouth in mine again, letting her taste herself.

She traced her fingers across my stomach and my muscles twitched. She continued down and down until her hand gripped me, moving up and down my shaft. I groaned and she smiled against my lips. Her thumb traced along the tip, gathering the bead of arousal there and spreading in stroking circles that had my cock throbbing.

Gods, that feels so good.

I raised up, one arm braced on the bed. She guided my cock to her entrance and circled there, coating me with her. She held my stare the entire time.

My lips spread into a grin as I spoke in a low guttural voice, "You belong to me."

"Yes," she breathed. She gasped when she stretched around me as I slowly thrust myself into her to the hilt.

The feeling was unlike anything I had ever experienced before. The bond snapped into place, sealing our mating, our fate, and our souls joined just as our bodies had. We had truly become one. What I had been waiting for, what I had wanted and prayed for for centuries.

I had her. She was mine. And she was more than I had ever imagined I would be worthy of.

"I love you, Kya," I whispered the words that had been lingering on my tongue. A tear streaked down her face. "I love you beyond the bond. I have loved you since you accepted me back in Ilrek and I think I loved you even before that." My hand came up to her throat. I tenderly wrapped my fingers around the base and stroked the sensitive skin there with my thumb. "I will follow you to the end of time and protect you until my last breath. I will stand beside you even if the realms burn. And I will love you until they are nothing but ashes amongst the stars."

She choked on a sob and my mouth crashed into hers, swallowing the sound, as tears leaked from her eyes.

She whispered against my lips, "I've loved you since that night in the forest, when you stopped yourself from claiming me, fighting against the will of the Gods for me. Since you fought against fate for your home, for your people." She deepened our kiss. "And I will love you until the stars die out. My mate."

Staring down at her, holding her gaze, I pulled out and pushed back in slowly.

"My mate..." I thrusted. "I claim you." Thrust. "As my mate." Thrust. "As my wife." Thrust. "As my Lady."

"Yes. Fuck me, Ryker." A breathy demand.

And I would not deny her again. Raw instinct had me grabbing her hip and I pounded into her hard and fast, over and over. I never wanted to stop.

She clenched around me and arched her back as she shattered and climaxed again.

With one final thrust, I slammed into her. Release tore through me with a roar, and my muscles tensed as I spilled myself inside her.

We gasped a breath in unison and looked down at our arms. The slight stinging sensation drew my attention as our mating mark appeared, glowing with a soft light. Kya's mark appeared at the same time, identical to mine with the same lines and swirls on the inside of her forearm from her wrist to her elbow.

Our mating was complete. We were bound to each other for eternity. A unification that was pure and unbreakable.

I kissed her with a soft tenderness so unlike the moment we had just shared, running my fingers down the feather in her hair. I could feel the remaining ebbs of her pleasure through the bond. We were connected in every way.

Without me being inside of her head, she spoke to me through her mind, through our bond. *You belong to me.*

"Always and in every way."

She had my body, my heart, my soul, my everything. She had all of me and I had all of her.

Mine.

With her legs still wrapped around me, she flipped us over so that I was on my back. She braced her hands on my chest. Seeing her marked by my claiming had me hardening inside of her again. Her lips spread into the most seductive smile and she rode me, rocking her hips back and forth.

Even as she came, screaming my name and trembling with pleasure while my teeth were sunk into her breast, I still hadn't had enough of her and I wasn't sure that I ever would. I fucked her over and over again. On the bed, on the floor, against the cave wall. Now that we had started, we couldn't stop. Our desire for each other had become an insatiable pit we were desperate to fill. And we didn't hold back.

Chapter Fifty-One

KYA

R yker lay asleep beside me in the bed when I woke, our naked bodies tangled together underneath the blanket. Our clothes remained discarded on the floor, and I had put my feather on the table by the bed. His hair was tousled from my fingers, having run through it so many times last night as he plunged into me again and again and again. Pushing us over the blissful edge into euphoria so many times I had lost count. But I still wanted more.

The mating bond was so much more than I had ever imagined it would be. Apart from the near constant need to be filled with him, we were connected on every level. We could share thoughts, memories, and speak to each other. I could feel his emotions, his pain, his pleasure, as if it were my own. I could feel his power, thrumming under his skin. His soul called to me, and mine to his.

It was an unbreakable union that not even death itself could fracture.

I held out my arm to gaze at my mating mark. The sight was dazzling and unreal. It wasn't at all like the Trial mark which was filled with strange unknown symbols of the Gods. This mark was something else, something completely unique to us. It was such a beautiful design.

The swirls reminded me of Ryker's shadows, and I was sure that's exactly what it was meant to represent. There were also lines and something that resembled flames or waves that intertwined with the swirls, all of it as black as ink. The glowing had stopped shortly after it started.

I had dreamed of this, fantasized about it for as long as I could remember. I had read every story I could find, and I would picture myself being whisked away by someone who was bound to me for eternity and going off on adventures and making love until the end of time. No matter how unrealistic my fantasies were, I couldn't help them. Except the fantasies couldn't compare to the real thing.

My mate, who lay beside me, holding me in his arms, was so much better than any of the fictitious males I had ever dreamed of.

I snuggled against him, getting closer to his warmth in the cool cave room. Ryker stirred at my movement and tightened his arms around me, but didn't wake. We hadn't stopped touching since last night. I needed to feel his skin against me, to breathe in his scent while the bond was so newly forged. Tracing his tattoos with my finger, I remained in his comforting embrace while he slept for a bit longer.

His breathing changed and, although he hadn't moved, I knew he was beginning to wake up. I pressed light kisses to his muscled chest. The tracing of my finger turned into long languid strokes up and down his torso and I felt him harden against my leg. I smiled against his skin before I looked up at him to find his silver eyes gazing down at me.

"Good morning, mate," I spoke through our bond.

"It is indeed." He cupped my face with his hand and stroked my cheek with his thumb, his eyes still heavy with sleep. "I was

afraid to wake up," he said out loud. "Terrified that it was all a dream."

I held up my arm, displaying my mating mark. "It's real. We're bound by fate for an eternity."

I crashed my mouth to his and climbed on top of him, straddling his naked body and resting myself on his cock. I leaned forward to position him at my entrance, our mouths devouring one another. But before I could slide myself down his shaft, he sat up, broke our kiss, and flipped me around so that my back was to him. He got to his knees and put his hand between my shoulder blades and pushed my chest down to the bed. I jerked when he pressed his tip to my wet core.

In one smooth motion, he slammed into me. I moaned at the feeling of being filled with his considerable length.

His arm wrapped around me, hand lightly holding my throat, and lifted me until my back was against his chest. My head leaned back to rest against him, my fingers tangled into his hair. He was buried so deep in me in this position. Ryker licked up the column of my throat to my ear.

"This is exactly what I envisioned last night, what I couldn't get out of my mind when we were dancing and you were grinding your ass against me," he whispered.

The thought of last night heated my skin.

"Say it," I breathed. I needed to hear it. I could never hear it enough.

His voice was low and lethal. "You belong to me."

We danced, grinded, and fucked each other until we were both limp on the bed from pleasure. He got off the bed and walked over to a basin filled with water. He touched it with his finger to heat it, steam rising into the chilled air. He wet a cloth, ringing it out, and came back over to the bed. He cleaned me gently before tossing it aside and resting against me again.

"I love you. Beyond the bond."

"Beyond the bond." Ryker kissed my shoulder with such tenderness as he held me to him.

We lay there in comfortable silence, soaking in each other for a long while.

"Do we have to go back?" I broke the silence. I knew we needed to get back at some point but for just a little while, I wanted to stay here with him, in our place away from the rest of the world where it was just the two of us.

"Not today, little gem. I need at least today with you all to myself."

Normally, mates would hole up somewhere for weeks or months after sealing the bond. It was the primal instinct for the males to impregnate the female, which could take quite a long time. I didn't have to be concerned with that. I had already taken my yearly elixir in the summer. But that didn't make the instinct to be isolated with my mate any easier to overcome and only have a single day with him. We couldn't afford to ignore our responsibilities any more than that.

A different kind of hunger had us getting out of bed. The only clothing I had was what I wore last night and my top was somewhere in the chamber of the cave. Ryker pulled out one of his shirts from a wardrobe for me to wear and he put on a pair of loose pants before we left the alcove to find something to eat.

He didn't have much food in the alcove where he had a small kitchen, but enough to tide us over. We ate bread, cheese and fruit at a wooden table. He only had one chair, so I sat perched on his knees and I mentioned to him that he would need to get another one if we would be spending any amount of time here, to which he protested and said that he enjoyed me on his lap, and we both laughed.

Ryker held my hand as he gave me a tour of the cave, showing me all the different alcoves, most of them filled with gems embedded in the walls.

"I see you have a thing for gems," I said with a wry smile.

He shrugged. "I think I took on more of my Spirit dragon than I was intended to. I've come to love hoarding precious treasure all for myself."

"So this," I gestured to the glimmering stones around us. "Is how you got all your wealth?"

"I suppose. It's all natural and native to the mountain. Theron dug out the cave for me after I had become Lord, when I needed some place to get away, and it was then that I discovered that the mountains are filled with them. Terbis wielders mine some of it, in moderation, and while that seems like Oryn is keeping the precious jewels to itself, it's so that we don't damage too much of our lands."

So misunderstood.

Even as a Lord, he was still just a male, one who had spent his life protecting his Nation and its people. When he was at the cave, he didn't have to be Lord of Oryn, Worthy by Xareus, he could just be Ryker.

"Do you like being a Lord? Ruling over Oryn," I asked as he led me down one of the tunnels deeper into the mountain. A roaring sound was getting louder and louder and I could feel the rumbling through my terbis.

"Most of the time, I do. But there can be difficult decisions to make, and those are the days I wished I wasn't. But I have never strived to *rule* my people, I want to *lead* them. I want them to willingly follow me rather than cower in submission,"

My response was taken from my mouth when we came down into a large cavernous opening on the other end of the tunnel. The sound was deafening as it echoed off the rocky walls from the waterfall that came from the top of the cave. A magnificent cascade of rushing water gushed from within the mountain into a sparkling river. The water was so clear you could see straight to the bottom.

I breathed easily. It wasn't the water that scared me, but the unknown of what lurked within it. I was fine so long as I could see through it and reassure myself that there weren't creatures hiding in the depths.

My face brightened into a wide smile. The water looked refreshing and I was utterly filthy. I made my way to the edge of the water and I started to take off Ryker's shirt from my body.

"What are you doing?" he said in a husky tone from beside me. His pupils dilated as the hem of the shirt crept higher and higher up my body.

"I need to bathe. I smell like sex and sweat." I pulled the shirt over my head and let it drop to the damp floor. His hands gripped my waist.

He inhaled deeply. "You bear *my* scent. I don't wish for you to wash it away."

With nothing underneath, I was completely naked. I bit my lip as his eyes traveled along my body. Heat pooled in my core at the hungry look in his silver eyes.

I leaned in to whisper in his ear, "Then you better stop me."

Ripping myself from his grasp, I ran down to where the waterfall was dumping into the river. I dared a glance over my shoulder to see Ryker tearing at his pants and a wicked look in his eyes.

I leapt into the water, submerging myself completely before I broke the surface and looked back to where he had stood on the edge. But he was gone, likely already in the water, coming for me. I made myself invisible and dunked back under, swimming behind the waterfall.

A little game of hunter and hunted.

I resurfaced behind the waterfall and pressed my back against the cave. My heavy breaths were drowned out by the roar of the water. Adrenaline coursed through my veins from the primal play.

Ryker's dark frame emerged in front of me, the water beating against his body as he prowled forward with glowing eyes. Excitement bubbled in my stomach.

My shadow had come for me.

I knew he couldn't see me, but through our bond, he could sense me, just as I could with him. Never again would either of us not know exactly where the other was.

His silver eyes cut right to mine. His darkness seeped from him, swirling over the water toward me, licking at my wet skin. Ryker's lips curled.

"You can't escape your shadow, little gem. No matter what, I'll always find you," he said, his tone much softer than the features on his face.

"Good."

I let go of my magic, appearing right in front of him, and his mouth was on mine in an instant. He pressed his body against me, pushing me harder into the wall, his arms braced against the cave around my head to cage me in. My arms circled his neck and I tilted my head back to deepen the kiss, opening my mouth for him to invade. Our tongues were desperate and vicious, clashing against each other.

His hand reached down to grab my thigh and hiked it up over his hip. My breath caught when the tip of his hard cock touched just where I wanted it to.

"Say it," he growled against my lips. And I knew. I would always know.

"I belong to you." He pounded into me hard and fast. "You belong to me," I cried out, the pressure in my lower stomach building higher and higher with each thrust.

"*Fuck*, Kya," he groaned. And Gods, hearing him say my name nearly sent me over the edge.

His hand left my thigh and came up to cup the back of my head. I could feel his pleasure building through the bond, and it mixed with mine. My stomach tightened and with the next thrust, I threw my head back, protected from the wall by Ryker's hand. I clenched around him with each wave of pleasure washing through me. My mate's body tensed, his cock pulsing inside me. His moan was swallowed by the roar of the water, and he buried his face in the crook of my neck.

We remained there, trembling in each other's arms, while we came down from our sated state, our hunger for each other quenched—temporarily. Afterward, Ryker brought over the soaps that he kept in the cavern, where he would bathe whilst here. He began to wash me, lathering the soap through my hair and dipping me back to rinse it. We grabbed our discarded clothes, and he carried me from the watery cavern back to the alcove with the bed where I put on one of his clean shirts.

Ryker and I spent the rest of the evening talking and laughing, sharing memories and past adventures. Just being with each other with none of the worries of the world outside our cave.

But our blessed time away was nearing its end.

I laid my head on Rykers chest while flipping through one of his books on history. He traced his fingers in slow circles on my back, reading a book of his own. That moment was just as perfect as the rest of them during our stay here and it made me fantasize about a simple life with him away from the rest of the world.

"Your book selection is terrible," I grumbled humorously.

A low chuckle rumbled in his chest. "You don't approve of what I read?"

"I don't care what *you* read, but we're going to have to make some serious changes to our collection. There's nothing in here that *I* care for."

He stilled beneath me, and I glanced up at him. The corners of his mouth were turned up. The bond purred with adoration.

"What?" I said with a smile.

"I just love hearing you say *our*." He kissed my forehead. "We'll get you whatever you want, little gem."

I nestled into him further and continued to read the horribly dry history text. A few minutes later, Ryker cleared his throat.

"I wanted to ask you something."

"Hmm," I hummed without looking up.

"I've mentioned before about…about you becoming my wife."

My stomach fluttered. I tilted my head back to look at him, meeting his gaze. "You have," I said quietly.

He kissed my temple lightly. "Kya, would you do me the honor of being my wife and allow me to bind myself to you through the Spirits?"

My heart skipped a beat, pure love pouring down the bond between us. "Yes, Ryker."

He released the breath he had been holding in a shuddering exhale. His hand came up to cup my face. "And will you, Worthy of the Goddess Kleio, lead and protect our people, by my side as Lady of Oryn?"

I searched his eyes, unsure what I was looking for. Being Lady of a Nation, under a God that didn't choose me… Uncertainty flooded through me. And Ryker felt it. A pang of hurt crossed his features and came down the bond.

"If you don't want to—" He shook his head.

"No. That's not it." I closed the book and set it aside, then turned to face him. "I don't think I should. Xareus didn't choose me to lead Oryn. He chose *you*."

I couldn't be Lady of a Nation by a God that didn't choose me. The Nation I was deemed Worthy to protect didn't exist anymore.

He smiled brightly which caused me to bunch my eyebrows in confusion.

"*They* chose *us*," he breathed. "We are two Worthy. Mated. And we *love* each other. I think that they, Xareus and Kleio, want both of us to lead. Together."

I sat up and grabbed both sides of his face. "Do you really mean this?" I whispered.

"Yes." His voice was sure and steady.

He reached down and grabbed something from the floor, then grabbed the wrist of my arm with our mating mark. He brushed his lips in a feather-light touch against the unmarked skin of my wrist, and unfolded a cloth to reveal four half circles.

Marriage bands—an unbreakable band of metal, forged around the arm between the mating mark and the palm of the hand, a representation of the spiritual coupling. I picked up the two smaller ones and studied them. They wouldn't be secured together around my wrist until a Sage performed the ritual. The other two were for Ryker.

"You will be bound to me through the divine and the Spirits and the Nation, where even death will not break them," I whispered.

"Until the stars die out." He leaned forward and kissed me deeply. *"I will have you in every way. My mate. My wife. My Lady. For eternity."*

I stared into those irises of swirling silver. *"Yes. My mate. My husband. My Lord."*

He claimed me again. And I lay there in blissful contentedness, heart full, and bond fully sealed, feeling the rise and fall of Ryker's even and heavy breaths while he slept. Relishing these last few hours of the night alone with my mate. I soaked in the short time of isolation with him, knowing that come morning, it would be time to return.

Chapter Fifty-Two

KYA

Deres was waiting when we arrived at the temple before dawn, hand in hand, bearing our mating marks. He was, in fact, expecting us, having felt our merging of souls through the Spirits. Theron and Odarum had appeared without us having told them. They knew it as well. While it was unusual for others to be present during a marriage ritual, it had felt appropriate for our Spirits to be present during such a spiritual moment.

Deres performed the marriage ritual, reciting the sacred words, and our guardians bowed their heads. Then our bands were placed around our wrists and sealed seamlessly—unable to be removed or broken. Not even in death.

Ryker flew us back to the palace, holding me in his arms. I wore the top and skirt that I wore during Nailu and wrapped a blanket around my waist to stave off the cold bite of the wind, nestling into his body for warmth. My hair was twisted up into a bun, the whipping air causing strands to come loose. I glanced at the marriage band around my wrist and smiled. The black metal was surprisingly warm against my skin despite the cold as it rested comfortably at the edge of my mating mark.

Ryker continued to carry me even after he landed on the balcony, through the corridor of the upper floor, and into the bedchamber. He sat me on the edge of the bed and kissed me softly, longingly, lovingly. My mate. My husband. Forever bound to me by the Gods and Spirits, through our hearts and souls.

Our sweet, gentle kiss turned into something more, and he took me. Then again in the bath before we washed each other. And I still couldn't get enough of him.

"Will we tell everyone?" I asked as we dressed in the bedchamber. I pulled on my loose pants and tied them at the waist.

"Our mating is not meant to be hidden, and I have no intention of doing so. Regardless, it would be near impossible to hide it. Not only do we bear our mating marks and marriage bands, but for a while, it's unlikely that we will be able to keep our hands off each other," Ryker said, buttoning the shirt to his suit and rolling the sleeves up his forearm.

I huffed a laugh. "I've noticed. But I was talking about an announcement. To the people. Or do we just let them find out by word of mouth?"

He put his hands in his pockets and leaned against the wardrobe next to me. "They'll be told. I'll have Mav handle informing our people of our mating as well as our marriage. As far as the rest of the world, they'll find out in due time."

"I'd like to tell Nik and Eamon." I laced my boots.

"Do you want to travel there or send a letter?"

"A letter will do for now. I'll write one up and send it later." I looked up at him.

"Whatever you want is fine with me." He brushed my hair behind my ear. "I have a few things to take care of today. Are you still planning on meeting with Malina?"

"Yes. We'll continue our translations of the book and see what else we can figure out about the Glaev. I'm hoping that we can find some way to reverse it but so far nothing has come of that."

Ryker kissed me before he left the bedchamber. I twisted my hair into a braid and made my way down to Malina's room. I didn't feel her in there, but that didn't mean she wasn't in there. She could have been on her bed, still asleep. When she didn't answer her door after several knocks, I felt for her around the palace and still felt no sign of her. I decided to go to the library without her and review my translations alone.

After reading over some of my translations and Rolim's notes, something stood out about channeling the dark magic that didn't make sense to me, no matter how much I tried to understand it. But I knew at least one way to find out.

Ryker will not be happy.

Deciding that I would deal with him later, I quickly left the library, making my way down the stone staircase and out the front doors of the palace. The sun had just crested over the horizon, and lit the sky in hues of orange and yellow. I followed the path that Ryker had taken me to the Noavo command station. When I arrived, I asked one of the passing warriors where I could find Hakoa's barrack. He pointed me in the direction and informed me that he was likely still asleep. I was too eager to speak with him to care about that, and I rapped on his wooden door. A few moments later, I could feel the footsteps of two people from inside.

He wasn't alone. I concentrated my terbis on the lighter footed person and my jaw dropped, awestruck at the feel of the familiar female's steps.

Hakoa opened the door with groggy eyes, pulling a shirt over his head. His eyes widened when he saw me standing with a smirk on my face.

"Kya. This is an unexpected visit." He glanced behind me as if looking for someone else. "Is everything alright? Where's Ryker?"

"Everything is fine and Ryker doesn't know I'm here. May I come in?"

"Sure. Let me just make sure that—" He glanced sheepishly over his shoulder.

"She's my sister. I don't care if she's dressed or not. It's freezing out here, please let me in," I said curtly.

He stepped to the side to let me pass and closed the door behind me. Malina came in from the other room, half dressed in an overly large shirt that I could only assume was Hakoa's. It wasn't shocking that she had found someone to keep her warm at night but I hadn't expected that it would be Hakoa.

"I thought I heard your annoying voice. What are you doing here?" she asked.

"I could ask the same of you," I said dramatically with a wink, noticing Hakoa's cheeks redden slightly.

"We haven't left the bed since Nailu." She leaned in to whisper, "I told you Orynians had stamina."

I opened my mouth to respond with a quip but was cut off by a screech.

"What is that on your arm?!" Malina yanked my arm forward by my hand and pushed up my sleeve. I couldn't hide my grin as her face lit up in realization and she screamed, jumping up and down and hugging me.

"You're married? And mated?" Her shrill pitch made me wince. At least her reaction to this mark was better than the last.

"Yes, we wed this morning."

"Oh shit," Hakoa grumbled.

Malina and I both turned our heads and scowled at him.

"Is there a problem, *Chief*?" she asked through gritted teeth.

"Udon's balls... Yes, there's a big fucking problem," he said, running his hand over his face. "You're recently mated, to a *very powerful* and possessive male might I add, and you're in another male's home. If you wanted me to die, there are more merciful ways."

I waved him off. "It's fine. He's busy right now anyway. It'll be some time before he realizes I'm gone."

Hakoa leaned his head back against the door with a thump. "I do *not* like this."

Malina and I giggled. I knew that Ryker would have lost it if he found me here, but I wasn't worried since I didn't plan on being here long.

"I came here to ask a favor of you actually, Hakoa," I said.

He nodded for me to continue.

"I need you to take me to Voltaryn," I stated.

He blinked slowly at me. "Why?"

"To speak with Vicria."

"She hasn't said a word except demanding to be released, despite our...best efforts. Why do you think she'll talk to you?" Hakoa tilted his head to the side.

"For one, she has something against me, I don't know what, but now that Ryker and I are mated, she would have felt it and that may just make her angry enough to talk. And two..." I glanced at Malina out of the corner of my eye.

Her lips spread into a wicked smile. "We have ways."

He blew out a sharp breath and mumbled, "Ryker is going to kill me."

"So you'll take us then?" Malina asked eagerly.

"Us?" he balked.

Malina and I exchanged a look of confirmation before we said in unison, "Yes."

Hakoa glanced from me to Malina and back again. "Fine. If it will get you out of my barracks, then yes."

Once Malina and Hakoa got dressed, he led the way toward Voltaryn, our boots crunching against the gravel path heading east, away from the warrior command station. Malina pressed me for details of my mating with Ryker. Hakoa had protested about hearing such details but I ignored him and continued to lay out the specifics and only left out certain descriptions for Hakoa's sake. Malina's mouth gaped open farther and farther as I continued. I didn't miss when Hakoa's eyes would dart to her when she displayed excitement about a specific detail. Then I told her of the marriage ritual at the temple with Deres.

It was hard to believe how much had happened in just the few months since we had talked like this back in Morah before the Trial. I was Worthy, mated, and wed.

A pang of hurt rang through my chest—I missed Eamon and Nikan. Eamon would be happy for me and while Nikan would likely have never said it, he would be happy for me too. I shook off the thought of them.

"When were you planning on telling me about you banging the Noavo chief?" I leaned in to whisper to my sister with a smile. Malina and I had dropped back a few steps behind Hakoa.

The side of her mouth lifted. "It started as a one time thing when we got drunk that first night in the city but then…it wasn't."

"You have feelings for him?" My eyebrows rose and my mouth fell open in genuine shock. I had never heard of Malina sleeping with someone more than once.

She stopped walking, staring at the male walking ahead of us. I stopped next to her. The serious look on her face was rare when she wasn't being a Roav.

"I don't know. I don't *not* feel something but we haven't exactly talked about what this is or isn't."

We continued to follow Hakoa.

"What do you want this to be?" I asked carefully.

She shrugged and her long black hair fell behind her shoulder. "I'm not sure. All I know is that I like what it is right now and I'm not ready for it to change. He may look serious and cold all the time but when it's behind closed doors, he's actually very sweet and a big softy." She smiled. "Even on the first night, when it was supposed to just be some fun after getting hammered in the tavern, he never treated me like a quick fuck."

Our conversation came to an end when Hakoa stopped at the edge of a small body of water.

"We're here," he said.

I gasped when I felt it. And Malina's eyebrows bunched together, looking around. "There's nothing here."

"Oh but there is," I breathed.

Beneath the water, I could feel a vast system of tunnels underground. Deep below my feet, the rock had been carved out and I could sense that it went underneath the city. The tunnels led to various chambers where I assumed one held Vicria.

Hakoa manipulated the water in front of us, parting it and exposing an opening to the tunnels into Voltaryn. He held the water apart so that we could enter. Once he was inside, the sound of crashing water above us roared through the tunnel as he released its hold. It was pitch black. I had no issues seeing where I was going, using my terbis to guide me, but Malina and Hakoa needed light.

"Mal?" I pressed, my voice echoing against the rock.

"Yep."

An orb of light appeared and floated above us, illuminating the rounded tunnel walls dripping with moisture.

"You can create light." He marveled at my sister. I focused my attention elsewhere to give them some semblance of privacy.

"I can do so much more than that," she said teasingly.

Hakoa growled and the scent of arousal filled the tunnel. "This way," he said in a low, quiet voice that still echoed.

We followed Hakoa farther and farther down underground, at a slight decline. I could feel us coming up to a large chamber, around a bend that connected to half a dozen tunnels, and footsteps filled the area. We came to a wall of fire that blocked our path, encircled in metal embedded in the tunnel walls and floor, with four Noavo guards stationed outside.

"The Gate of Elements," Hakoa said to us as we inspected the wall. "The gate is composed of a layer of each of the elements and laced with lethal toxins so that no one may try to pass through. The gate is inside of these metal rings here." He gestured to the dark metal lining the tunnel. "One of each of the elemental wielders is stationed on either side to allow passage and if anything were to happen to one of the guards, one element is pulled and causes the metal ring to collapse inwardly. Like tumblers to a lock, the entire thing would come down. It keeps anyone from entering or leaving that is not permitted. This is one of three gates into Voltaryn as well as the smallest."

It was smart. Metal was the only form of terra that couldn't be manipulated with wielding. And with each element present, it would take four different kinds of welders at once to open the gate.

"So why couldn't a terbis wielder just tunnel their way around the metal?" Malina asked.

But I already knew. I could feel the metal extending out in all directions, surrounding the prison within the mountain.

"By the time anyone would be able to dig far enough around the metal within the mountain, we would stop them. The metal is embedded around the entire structure, just not the tunnels," he said.

Hakoa nodded to the four guards in front of us, and they each manipulated their part of the gate simultaneously, pushing and compressing the elements against the metal ring so that it didn't collapse and allowing us to pass through. They closed the gate behind us with a wall of air at our backs.

Inside the chamber, guards were stationed at each of the tunnels and spaced down each of them as well as at the openings, where the prisoners were held. We continued to follow Hakoa as he headed down one of the tunnels on the right, the guards bowing their heads as he passed by.

"Where are you?" Ryker's concerned voice rang down the bond.

"I'm fine. I will be back soon." I planned on telling him of my whereabouts when I returned, not wanting to worry him before I had the chance to talk with the sage.

"Kya," he growled in warning.

"It's okay, Ryker. I know what I'm doing." I caressed soothingly down the tether. *"I love you beyond the bond."*

There was a pause.

"Beyond the bond." His tone was far from happy, but he returned the caress.

Deep down the tunnel, we stopped in front of a small opening with two guards stationed outside the metal door. They moved aside for their chief, and we stepped inside.

Chapter Fifty-Three

KYA

V icria sat on the thin pad with her back pressed against the wall and her hands flat against the pad at her sides. The diamond was still embedded at the top of her sternum. She still wore her robes, which were filthy with dirt and blood and other things I didn't want to guess at. There was a stench to her as well from lack of bathing, mixed with that of the bucket. Hakoa nodded to one of the guards who unlocked the cell door for us, creaking with the sound of metal against metal as it swung open.

Malina and I shared a knowing glance before I looked at Hakoa. Malina stepped inside the cell as I spoke to him.

"Would you wait out here please?"

With his reluctant nod, I entered the cell. Malina threw up a wall of light, obscuring the inside of the cell from the outside and bending her light on the inside so that we could not see the outside, giving us privacy.

Malina backed against the wall and remained silent as I stepped toward the Sage, crouching down in front of her. The putrid odor of her filth invaded my nostrils.

"Hello Vicria." My voice was poisonous.

"Well if it isn't the Worthy with no lands. Oh wait, I'm mistaken. I suppose being mated with the Lord of Oryn grants you a ruling over his Nation as well. One can only hope that the other Worthy won't see this as a threat to their positions of power." She rolled her eyes, keeping her gaze from meeting my face.

So she could tell. That means the rest of the Sages could too.

I tilted my head to the side. "You don't truly care about that now, do you?" I felt a familiar set of heavy steps that I would know anywhere in the tunnels we entered through. I ignored it.

She sighed exaggeratedly.

"She's yet to be broken." Malina's voice was calm and lethal.

Whatever interrogation techniques the guards used, it was far too merciful. Simply holding her here, and maybe a few beatings, wasn't enough to crack her.

"We can fix that," I said with a lilt.

Vicria scoffed and mumbled something under her breath.

Too quickly for her to react, I pulled my daggers from behind my back and stabbed my blades through the back of her hands, into the thin pad beneath and the floor below. She wailed and tried to pull back, but I held them steady.

"Now," I said with a low voice once her screaming turned to cries through gritted teeth. She trembled from the pain. "I have some questions I need you to answer, and I want to make sure I have your undivided attention." It felt good to slip back into the skin of a Roav once again. "If you answer honestly, I *might* just take out my blades when I leave here. Do you understand?"

"You vile *bitch*," she spat. I pressed my blades forward slightly and she screamed. "Yes! Yes! I understand!"

"Oh good!" I said mockingly.

Malina chuckled quietly from her corner.

Ryker spoke through the bond then. *"What are you doing?"*

I could feel him standing just outside the cell and sense his emotions, a mix of anger and worry and longing for his mate.

My shadow would always come for me.

I thought for a moment while Vicria was still screaming.

Maybe Ryker being here could prove to be beneficial.

I knew how he felt about using his magic, and I hated myself for asking him to use it.

"I need answers. Some things are not adding up from what I read. I know you said her mind is blocked but you also said you can still hear her active thoughts. My shadow, can you enter her mind and see if she's telling the truth?" I asked carefully.

He hesitated for a moment before responding with a sigh.

"Yes, little gem. I would do anything for you."

Vicria had stopped screaming and I spoke. "First question: were you the one controlling the Glaev attacks?"

"No," Vicria bit out.

"Not a lie but not the complete truth," Ryker said to me.

"Tell me more. Explain it to me," I demanded.

"I would find a location and it would be destroyed by the Glaev."

"Truth."

"What is the Glaev?"

"It's some kind of dark magic. It absorbs the energy of life until there's nothing left," she said.

"Truth."

"How does it work?"

"I..." she stumbled. "I don't know."

"Truth."

"How did you learn about it?"

She paled. "From...a book."

"Lie," Ryker growled.

A cruel grin crossed my lips. I pressed the blades forward again, with more pressure this time.

"Try again!" I shouted over her wails.

Malina bristled behind me.

"It was him! He's the one controlling it! Stop, stop!" she screamed.

I lessened the pressure on the blades.

"She's telling the truth..." Ryker sounded agitated.

"Who is *he*?" I demanded, my heart rate increasing.

What she said made sense. It seemed so unlikely that she was the one doing all of this on her own with no explanation as to how she was able to hone magic at all, as a Sage. But to hear her confirm another...

"He calls himself Daegel," she sobbed. "He's a dark wielder from another realm."

"Explain," I hissed.

"He's behind everything!" Vicria screamed. "Someone stole a book from him and he needed it back desperately. He's been hunting it for years. It's his...guide or something. He's killed so many for it, and he went to personally find it in Morah after he had some drugged up low-life killed. And he cursed me after I made a deal with him a long time ago. He used me to find the places for him to attack. I couldn't be released from my deal until my task was complete."

He really was behind everything. The murders of the Scholars and the seller. That was him.

"Which is what exactly?" Ryker asked.

"What is your task?" I relayed Ryker's question.

"To serve him."

"How? Why you? You're a Sage with no abilities."

"I'm more...sensitive to the Spirits. It allows me to detect where there are greater amounts of them." She curled her lips. "He had me determine which places for him to attack based on how much he had of his reserves at the time."

My breath left my lungs. I shook my head, clearing my thoughts from my readings of the book. "What is his ultimate task? Why is he doing this? What does he want?"

"I don't know. He doesn't tell me anything. He only gives commands," she said. "However, he has been particularly fixated on finding something recently. Something other than his book. A precious diamond."

"No... Kya, let me in," Ryker requested carefully. I ignored him.

"A diamond?" I asked with a raised eyebrow. It couldn't be that simple. That's what stopped the dark magic from being wielded. It didn't make sense.

"Kya. Let me in," A demand.

Vicria lifted her head to look at me with a malicious smirk. "He's been gathering information on finding someone specific. Someone he calls the Diamond. That's the only one who can give him the amount of power that he needs in order to complete his ultimate task..."

"Malina, let me in!" Ryker shouted.

"...found within the darkness of fate..."

I looked back at Malina. She glanced between me and the light wall at the doorway with furrowed brows. I narrowed my eyes on Vicria as she continued.

"...a female. One of the last daughters..."

A conglomeration of shouting voices and commotion ensued behind me, but I kept my focus on Vicria, now wheezing and gasping for breath.

"...a Worthy with no Nation."

My face paled and everything went silent in the room.

Vicria leaned in closer, pulling against the blades of her own will, our faces nearly touching. She whispered in a strained rasp, so that only I could hear, with a scowl on her face, "He's coming for you. I held him off as long as I could, but the moment you sealed your mating, your power grew and he could sense you. I tried to warn you, but you just wouldn't listen."

"Warn me? Why didn't you just come right out and say it?" My mind was all over the place with the amount of information.

"The curse mark on my chest. Go ahead and look," she croaked.

My eyes widened when I ripped down her robe to see a black mark right over her heart like a blot of ink, spreading out across her body.

Ryker gripped me around the waist and lifted me up, holding me against his chest and backing away, leaving the daggers in Vicria's hands. Malina came up in front of Vicria. I pushed off Ryker and whipped out my bow with an arrow aimed at the Sage.

"How do we stop him? How do we stop the Glaev?" Malina demanded, her hair was now a mess.

"Answer her," I snarled when she didn't say anything, pulling the arrow back farther.

"The Rip." She hacked a cough, the curse starting to consume her. Her body began to convulse strenuously as she gasped desperately for air, hunching over with her head against the floor.

One of the guards behind me gasped when the black curse spread along her body, webbing out along her skin, through her veins. We all stepped back, pressing to the other end of the cell. She arched and threw her head back violently with her mouth gaping open in a silent scream. The whites of her eyes began to turn black.

Malina breathed, "It looks like—"

"The Onyx Kiss…" I finished. Ryker's arm came back around my waist.

Vicria thrashed so violently that she ripped her hands from the daggers, slicing straight through the flesh and bone. She fell back, grasping and clawing at her chest and throat, the blood pouring from her hands staining her robes, and the blackness continuing to spread along her pale skin.

Then suddenly, she stopped. I felt her heart beat one last time.

No one said a word as we stood there, appalled at what we had just witnessed. I turned to face Ryker, noticing the cuts on his face that were already beginning to heal. I looked to Hakoa and the other guards to find their faces, arms, and chests cut as well. I eyed them all curiously then noticed the blood on Malina's blades at her thighs.

"That wasn't the Onyx Kiss. That was dark magic," Malina said quietly.

I nodded.

"Kya?" Ryker whispered. His eyes met mine with a sad smile.

I felt his overwhelming emotions of longing, worry, and anger. The same as before. "Take me home."

Chapter Fifty-Four

RYKER

I escorted Kya out of Voltaryn, hissing as I touched the cuts on my face.

Malina had kicked my ass when I broke her light barrier with my shadows trying to get to Kya, and used very little effort to do so. She came at me with a rage that I had never seen from her before. She sliced at Hakoa, and I, and the guards all at once, though we did little to stop her, refusing to attack her in retaliation and only trying to defend ourselves. I never expected someone so cheerful and bright to be so vicious and dark.

The Roav are violently protective of one another.

And Kya didn't even bat an eye when she saw the damage her sister had inflicted. The look on Kya's face was one of a Roav—cold, hard, and lethal.

Once we emerged from the tunnels, my mate came back to me, the mask of the Roav fallen away to leave the female that had every bit of my heart and soul. Her face lightened, and her features softened with the sun on our skin. Her braided hair hung over her shoulder, swaying slightly with each step.

Aching for her touch, I took her hand and held it firmly in my own. She leaned into me as I heard the crash of the water over the entrance. The adoring look in her eyes as she looked up at me made my heart swell.

She was all mine, in every way.

Without a second thought, I shifted my wings and swept her into my arms. Dirt kicked up from the thrust of my wings as I lifted us into the air and flew back to the palace, leaving Hakoa and Malina on the gravel path. Kya nestled into me and I could sense her erratic emotions flowing through her—a jumble of confusion and concern. I remained quiet during the flight, letting us sort through all of the information we had just learned.

When I noticed earlier that Kya had left, the bond yearned to be near her, and irrational fear filled me that she had left for another male—though I knew better. I felt exactly where she was and immediately flew there. Furious with Hakoa for bringing her to Voltaryn, I was also distressed. Not because of her, but *for* her. And the Sage's words…*his precious diamond*…

I was terrified.

Fury surged through my veins. Someone was trying to take my mate from me.

I hadn't noticed that my grip had tightened on Kya until she squeezed my hand and kissed my neck. Holding her gaze, I couldn't help the images that flooded my mind of her being taken away from me by another. As much as I tried to keep her from feeling my anguish, I couldn't stop it.

"It's okay. I'm right here. No one will take me from you." Her soft voice soothed as we landed on the balcony of the palace.

I placed her feet on the ground, and she grabbed my hand and led me inside. But it wasn't enough. I turned her and pressed her back against the wall, grabbing her ass and lifting her. Kya's legs wrapped around my waist, pulling my body against hers. I kissed her roughly, and she only pulled me closer, gripping my shoulders with her fingernails digging into my skin. I had to have her.

"Ryker," she gasped breathlessly against my lips as I rolled my hips into her. "Take me to our bed."

I pushed off the wall and carried her to the bedchamber.

Slamming the door shut behind me, I spun around and pushed her back against the door. The bed was just too far. I needed her right then. I needed to feel her pleasure, her connection as my mate.

Mine.

She tore her mouth away and ripped off her jacket and shirt. "Yes, my shadow, I'm yours. Touch me. Take me."

I took her breast in my mouth and sucked hard, flicking her peaked nipple with my tongue. Her fingers gripped my hair and she let out a moan, tossing her head back against the door. I spun around again and went to the bed.

Kya began to unbutton my shirt but I grew impatient and ripped it apart causing the buttons to snap off. Her hands roamed over my chest and down my stomach and my muscles tensed from her touch. She lifted her hips off the bed as I yanked her pants off before quickly removing mine and she rubbed her thighs together.

As much as I needed to be inside her, I needed her pleasure more. I needed to *be* her pleasure.

Pushing her knees apart and kneeling on the floor, I bared her pink flesh. My pupils dilated at the sight of her exposed clit, glistening with her arousal. I growled deep in my chest before my mouth was on her. I licked and fucked her with my tongue, lapping up her arousal like a starved beast. And *fuck* if she wasn't the best thing I had ever tasted.

From beneath hooded eyes, I watched her face, etched with pleasure, as she cried my name, begging for me not to stop. I gently bit her swollen clit when she closed her eyes, eliciting a gasp, the sound going straight to my throbbing cock.

I needed to see those green eyes and watch them roll in the back of her head while I devoured her and sent her over the edge. She clenched around my tongue with her hands fisting in the sheets.

Kya whimpered when I stood, still wanting, still needing.

Her eyes darkened as I crawled over her and settled between her trembling legs. She wrapped herself around me, melding her body against mine. The sunlight from the windows made her brown hair shine and her skin sparkle.

I kissed her deeply, plunging into her mouth as she tasted herself on my tongue. I groaned when she sucked on it hard with a moan of her own.

She gasped when I hilted myself into her. Gods, she was so warm and wet and tight around my cock.

"Kya," I growled. "You belong to *me*."

She nodded rapidly.

"Say it," I demanded, pulling out and thrusting back into her. "I need to hear it."

"I belong to you," she breathed a moan.

Mine.

"I will always belong to you."

I buried my face in her hair, the scent of lavender and eucalyptus filling my senses. I groaned against her neck as I continued to pump in and out of her. My balls tightened as my release began to build.

"Even after the stars die out and the last embers of the realms flicker through the skies."

I held her shoulders to keep her from moving while I slammed fast and hard into her. I roared with my release. My hot cum spilled into her. She threw her head back, and I took her mouth, swallowing her cries of pleasure as she came. She clenched around my cock each time it pulsed inside her.

When we came down from our intoxication, I rolled us over onto our sides and pulled her to me, holding her and kissing her softly. Her body was relaxed. Something primal inside me raised its head with pride.

I gazed down at her and traced my fingers languidly down her arm. Her skin pebbled, and she curled her body into me. I shifted my wings and laid one over her to keep her warm, while using my fire to heat my skin.

"I'm sorry for making you angry." Her breath tickled the skin on my chest.

"Little gem, I was never angry with you. I was worried about you. I still am," I whispered against her hair. *"I love you, beyond the bond."*

Her lips tilted up. *"Beyond the bond."*

Kya fell asleep as I held her in my arms and I must have too, but not for long because it was still daylight out when I woke up with her on my chest. I kissed her on the forehead and she stirred, blinking away the sleep from her eyes before meeting mine with a soft smile.

We sat up and I moved off the bed to retrieve our clothes, then went to the wardrobe to find a new shirt that still had buttons. Kya crossed her legs under her and pulled her shirt over her head. Lifting her gorgeous hips, she pulled on her black skin-tight pants that shaped her ass so perfectly.

Just as I was lacing my boots, Kya placed her feet on the floor to stand when her entire body stilled. The color drained from her face and the feeling of dread washed down the bond. Her eyes widened and her breathing increased with her rapid pulse.

"Kya, what is it?" I asked carefully as I approached.

"The Glaev."

509

We rushed out of the bedchamber and down the corridor to the balcony. A pit formed in my stomach at the sight of a black ring of pure death encircling the city of Voara below. It was slowly growing inward, and would soon be too large for the bridges—and escape.

Kya and I were frozen in horror for only a moment.

My city was under attack. Thousands of lives were going to perish if I didn't do everything I could to get them out quickly.

"Hakoa! Get warriors to the city and get as many people out as you can. The Glaev is surrounding Voara. Do it fast before it gets too large to form bridges." I commanded in his mind. His barracks were close enough that I could still speak with him from the palace. It was why it was there in the first place.

"On it," he replied tersely.

I ripped off my shirt and shifted my wings, readying to jump off and fly down there to get as many people as I could out. My heart sunk when Kya began to do the same.

"No," I snarled. I put my hands on her shoulders. "I need you to stay here."

"If you think I'm just going to sit here while I'm one of the few capable of flying people out—" she snapped.

"You can't fly people out. Your wings aren't strong enough yet, and you could fall over the Glaev. I won't be able to con-centrate on saving them if I'm worried about protecting you."

She shifted her wings.

"You're just going to have to deal with it then." She kicked me hard in the stomach, pushing me away enough to break my hold on her so she could run to the edge of the balcony. She leapt off without a moment's hesitation.

I growled in frustration and instantly followed her.

"Do not carry more than you can. Get the children first. They'll be smaller," I demanded.

I saw her nod her head below me.

Tucking my wings, I soared past her and dove down towards the city.

"Theron!"

He appeared in the air a second later. He looked to me, then to the ensuing chaos below. He didn't need to be told what to do. In the next instant, he disappeared and I saw him appear in the city below.

The Glaev was getting closer, already touching the buildings on the outskirts and turning them to ash in seconds. I pumped my wings to fly down even faster. When I reached the city, I flared them out to soften my landing as my boots rumbled against the ground. I glanced around as people were scattering away from the Glaev and toward the elemental bridges.

Kya was still in the air, coming down as fast as she safely could. She at least knew that if she pushed herself too hard, she wouldn't be helpful.

"Touch the dragon! He will travel you to safety!" I roared over the sounds of panic.

I leapt into motion, grabbing those in closest proximity to the Glaev and too far from bridges and flying them safely past the edges of the Glaev so they could be escorted by the warriors. Theron Traveled as many people as he could, disappearing and reappearing alone, over and over. Bridges fell when the Glaev touched their edges, and warriors re-manipulated bridges farther away until it was too wide to build across. Some of the stronger wielders were able to manipulate their element in a way that allowed them to launch people over the Glaev and be caught by someone else. Until they couldn't even do that anymore.

I kept my eye on Kya as much as I could, as she flew the smaller children across and handed them off before going back again. I saw Odarum appear. He was Traveling as many people as he could as well.

Buildings came crashing down all around the city before being completely consumed. The Glaev crept closer to the center. There were still too many people to get out in time.

Just before one of the buildings on the far end of the street was being decimated, a male rushed out holding a sick-looking female in his arms and a young child in hers. My eyes widened, and then I was airborne in the next blink, flying to them as fast as I could.

"Theron. Theron! Get to them!" I bellowed.

I flew harder and harder, as fast as I possibly could. The Glaev was faster than the male and I wasn't going to reach them in time. But I pushed and pushed. My wings screamed with the force. It wasn't enough.

"Ryker!" I barely heard Kya through the bond.

The male glanced behind him just as the Glaev was on his heels. He saw me rushing for him. He kissed the female on the head before he launched her through the air away from him—just as the Glaev touched him and his body turned to ash. The female rolled to the ground, protecting the child in her arms. She looked back and began screaming for the male that was no longer there. The child was crying. I was so close. But even as the female began weakly running away with the child in her arms, I wasn't close enough. I was nearly touching her outreached hand when she and the child were consumed.

"Fuck!" My roar echoed across the decimated landscape as I flew back to get more people.

"Ryker," Kya called for me.

I found her and landed next to her in the middle of the city.

"He's here," Kya said with an eerie calm.

Her eyes were set in a hard stare with a composition that I knew to be that of a Roav. Her bow was drawn with an arrow with black tipped feathers.

My heart dropped for a moment before she backed up against me, comforted by her proximity and touch. I instinctively splayed my wings out in a primal threat to protect my mate. My eyes darted around, looking for the dark wielder.

I reached out to Mavris and Hakoa, speaking in their minds to ask where they were and hoping that they were able to get the people to safety. They both responded, thank the Gods, and said they were ushering people within the city.

Theron and Odarum appeared next to us silently. The air was still and stale, so unnatural, like the calm before the storm. I fought every instinct in my body against taking Kya away from here and to safety the moment I saw the figure emerging from behind one of the buildings.

He was nearly as tall as me, with dark pants and a hooded cloak over broad shoulders. His eyes were a deep blue that shone with malicious intent in the setting sun. He strode closer, and I felt Kya's body tense and straighten. He stopped within a building's length and looked between us before staring down at Kya and revealing white teeth in a cruel grin. My hand came around Kya's waist and pulled her against me.

Mavris and Hakoa ran up from behind us, standing between me and Theron and handing me a sword.

"Ryker, listen to his mind. What is he thinking?" Kya asked.

I reached for his mind. His thoughts were erratic, so unlike the calm demeanor he displayed on the outside. But before I could make sense of anything, he put up a wall around his mind, shielding him from my grasp. His cobalt eyes cut to mine.

"Your little tricks won't work on me." Daegel's strange, accented voice carried through the air. "My request is simple. Give me the Diamond and I will leave your people in peace." He held out his gloved hand to her, holding my stare.

My grip on her tightened to the point of bruising. I would give my life before I ever let him so much as touch her.

The dark wielder looked at Kya. "Come. There's no need for more death today," he spoke softly to her.

My body vibrated with fury, and my shadows began to snake out around me, reaching for the threat against my mate. Kya squeezed my arm in reassurance, but I was already seeing red. I would rip his fucking head from his shoulders.

"Easy, my shadow. No one will take me from you." Her voice was a calm whisper in my mind.

"No? Perhaps you need a little incentive, then." Daegel smirked.

He said something in a language that I didn't understand, yet sounded familiar. He reached out like he was holding something above the ground and clenched his hand into a fist.

Bound and gagged and clearly beaten, Nikan was pulled from some kind of dark blue smoke from the ground.

Kya lowered her bow and I felt pure terror from her. She made to go to him, but I held her tightly. I entered Nikans mind. As much as I hated doing it without someone's consent, certain times were necessary.

"Nikan. It's Ryker. Stay calm. We'll get you out of this. What happened?"

"Ryker! Don't let him get to Kya! Leave me! Tell Kya that I—" Nikan was gone, taken through the smoke in the ground.

"Wait! Bring him back!" Kya demanded.

Daegel chuckled. "I will return him once I have you. So what will it be?"

Theron and Odarum stepped forward, blocking us from Daegel. Flames licked Theron's nostrils and mouth, seeping between his teeth, and Odarum spread his wings with his ears pinned back. I could still see Daegel in the space between them. His smile fell to a disgusted sneer, his eyes darting between the two Spirit Guardians before locking with Kya's.

"If you will not come willingly, then I will take you by force," he roared.

Before I could blink, he moved and Theron's fire blasted forth, creating a river of red flames following him as he went for Odarum. Kya pushed off me and aimed her bow at Daegel, with an arrow dripping with black liquid. My skin shifted to scales.

That same blue flaming smoke met Theron's fire, fighting it back with greater force, and it threw Theron back. He made to move for Odarum then, and Mavris stepped in front of us holding his hand out at the dark wielder. Daegel stopped and looked to my brother whose face paled, glancing at his hand with a furrowed brow.

"My blood runs black. You have no power over me," he thundered.

Mavris had to jump out of the way of his flaming smoke, as did we. Kya dove in the opposite direction of me, Odarum constantly keeping his body between the dark wielder and my mate. The Glaev grew closer.

How were we supposed to fight against this, against him?

"Stop this!" she pleaded, her voice filled with desperation.

I was airborne within the next heartbeat, afraid that she would try to surrender to him. I had to get her out of there. I felt her terror before I landed next to her and looked at the dark wielder.

Odarum was fighting against him with a glowing light, tinged jade, erupting from him with the beat of his wings. I had never seen anything like it, but it was effective. Daegel was struck by the light, and he bent over with a grunt from the impact.

I took advantage of his vulnerable state, and blasted out my fire as well as my shadows. He blocked them with his blue smoke, equally matching the power of my elements. I wielded more and more. Between darting away from Odarum's magic and countering my abilities, and dodging Kya's arrows. Daegel was becoming less controlled.

"No, I'm not leaving you!" she shouted at Odarum, tears streamed down her face.

Kya raised her bow and pulled back the string, the feather of the arrow brushing against her cheek. Before she had the chance to shoot, inky darkness exploded violently from Daegel's hand, aiming straight for my mate's Spirit guardian. Odarum reared up with his wings flared out, blocking it with his body to protect Kya.

With a howling roar, Odarum fell.

The world seemed to darken. The force of the dark magic pushed him over his hooves and tail. With the tips of his wings aimed for the heavens, his lifeless body struck the ground.

Chapter Fifty-Five

KYA

I felt my heart tear apart in agony. The moment Odarum's body hit the ground, I fell to my hands and knees. Tears streamed down my face. I couldn't hear anything over the deafening sound in my ears, not realizing it was me as a blood-curdling scream ripped from my throat, my heart, my soul. I couldn't move, I couldn't think, I couldn't *breathe*.

He had begged me to flee but I refused to leave him as he fought. It was my fault. All my fault. And his death was on me.

His last words to me had been drowned out by the sound of his pained roar. The sound was so unnatural and raw. The Glaev's darkness spread across his chest, devouring him.

Theron landed over his body with a heartbreaking screech and a mournfulness in his eyes as he wailed for his fellow Guardian. In the blink of an eye, they were both gone. Disappeared. Away from this realm.

Ryker towered above me, putting his body between me and Daegel, the murderous bastard. Smoldering flames and shadows erupted from my mate as he protected me. I didn't see when Hakoa appeared beside him, wielding water above him in a whirlwind with a power I had never seen, spikes of ice flying from it toward the dark wielder.

I didn't fear death. I feared pain and suffering and loss. And I wouldn't lose anyone else. No one else would die, not when I could stop it. No more death. No more darkness.

No more.

I gripped the ground beneath me through gritted teeth and searched inside me for that orb that Odarum had tried so hard to show me. It was like air, wispy and loose. I grasped it with everything I had in me. Burning seared through my entire being, but I refused to let go and it thrummed through my veins as I finally wielded Odarum's gift to me.

When I opened my eyes, jade-colored torrents of light blazed in my palms—the same as what my Guardian had, what he unknowingly gave me all those months ago.

I lifted my gaze to Daegel, ignoring Rykers attempt to push me farther behind him and telling me to run as the dark wielder advanced against the magic and elements striking him. Calling to my terbis and manipulating it like I never had before, I shook the ground beneath me, forcing it to sink and enclose around Ryker and Hakoa's feet before dragging them away.

Ryker bellowed, clawing at the rock and dirt to get to me. I could smell the blood from his hands as he tore them against the ground. I slowly stood and took a step forward.

A malicious grin spread across my lips as I locked eyes with Daegel, lifting my bow and pulling back the arrow that was dripping with the poison of the Onyx Flower. I wrapped the glowing jade swirls in my palms down the length of the arrow and released the bow string. The arrow screamed through the air with the jade-green light wrapped around it.

Daegel was unbelievably fast and caught the arrow with his hand and howled, looking at his palm with shock on his face.

This power harms him.

He spun around on his heel and flung the arrow back to me. I made to dive out of the arrow's path, aimed for my chest, but I wasn't quick enough. I grunted as it caught me in the stomach.

With the last bits of my strength, I released as much of my new-found power outward at Daegel, striking him in the chest. He recoiled back from the force. He began chanting in a foreign language, too low for me to hear, gripping his chest where it glowed with the jade light.

I watched him as I fell, too weak to stand from the poison seeping into my veins. I felt Ryker pulling me up to him. My vision began to turn spotty and everything seemed to spin and contort. The sound of thunder was so loud that I heard a pop in my head before everything went silent with nothing but a constant buzz. My head lolled back against my mate and I closed my eyes, unable to fight against the slowed pounding of my heart before everything went dark.

Chapter Fifty-Six

RYKER

The Glaev kept spreading, it was everywhere, except around her—as if it shaped around her. Everything had happened so fast from the moment we landed in Voara. I couldn't wrap my head around it, only acting in the moment.

Hakoa used his water to fill underneath the rock dragging us away from Kya and Daegel, seeping into the cracks and expanding it to the point of breaking. I scrambled to my feet and ran to her as she had shot her arrow with green light surrounding it. It looked like what Odarum had used earlier. I had to jump and weave before taking flight to keep from touching the plaguing land. But I didn't reach her in time.

The arrow had pierced her stomach and she lashed out one last time at Daegel. He bellowed from the pain and released a shockwave so powerful that it caused the buildings, all the way to the palace up on the mountain to crack and rumble. Dust filled the air, obstructing my view of him. Then, I heard a snarl and when the dust cleared, he was gone.

I looked around to find that the Glaev had stopped advancing. But I couldn't think of that.

Kya…

I couldn't take her to the palace. I could still see it crumbling in the distance.

I called for Mavris and ordered Hakoa to get all of the refugees out of the palace with the help of the Noavo warriors who were coming up from the command station.

"Theron!"

He appeared moments later. He was blurry, and it wasn't until then that I realized that tears were welling in my eyes, dripping down to my dying mate.

"Take us to the cave." Mavris and I both touched his lowered snout before appearing at the mouth of the cave.

Kya's gasping breaths tore my heart out as I held her against me, rushing through the tunnel of the cave to the nearest alcove that had a table and medical supplies. Mavris was right behind me. I laid her on the stone table and grimaced when I saw her body covered in black veins, the poison spreading through her body. Soon, it would reach her heart.

She began to convulse.

"Hold her down," Mavris ordered. Being a blood wielder, he was one of the few people who could draw the poison from her blood. I just hoped there was time.

I held her shoulders down and put my head against hers. *"Hold on. Just a little longer."*

Mavris grabbed her blood soaked shirt, tinted with the black of the poison, next to where the arrow was embedded in her stomach. He ripped it open, exposing the wound. He grabbed the arrow with one hand and placed his hand on her onyx colored skin next to it.

"This process will hurt her, and she will likely thrash from the pain and fight against me. Do not attack me. I am helping her. Remember that," he commanded.

I nodded without hesitation and tightened my grip on her shoulders.

With a sharp inhale, Mavris pulled the arrow free, tossing it aside and placed his tattooed hands over the wound. The black-tinted blood seeped through his fingers. With a deep breath, he began to pull the poison from her blood through the tear. At first, she stilled, and I held my breath, but then her body arched off the table in an unnatural contortion. Her eyes widened so far I thought they might actually pop out of their sockets, and her mouth opened in a spine-chilling shriek.

I had to fight myself to keep from stopping Mavris, to stop her pain. I kept telling myself that she would survive this, and it would be over soon. She had to survive, because if she didn't, neither would I.

"Shh. It's okay. You'll be okay." My voice broke, barely audible over her shrill wails.

Mavris pushed her body back down to the table with force, his muscles straining to hold her down as he whispered apologies over and over. He pulled and pulled more of the tainted blood from her veins.

Kya gasped through broken cries as she begged and pleaded, "Sto-stop! Pleeeease!"

My tears dripped into her sweat covered hair and I tried to hold her head down to keep her from smashing it against the stone.

"It will be over soon," I promised, then looked at Mavris. "Right?"

The pained look on his face told me all I needed to know. "I'm sorry, but it takes a while."

We were torturing her, and it ripped my heart and soul to shreds as the minutes or hours passed. I continued to hold her down as she suffered through violent, constant tremors. But it was working.

The blackness in her veins slowly dissipated and her skin returned to a more natural yet still pale color. Finally, the poison had been fully pulled out of her system and she stopped thrashing, her eyes fluttering shut with hushed, raspy whimpers.

Mavris sighed and removed his hands from her stomach. The venom of the Onyx Flower pooled on the floor, mixed with her blood. He backed away from the table.

I moved to Kya's side and pulled her trembling body to me, cradling her in my arms. The wound was beginning to heal but her body was still cold and covered in her sweat. I placed soft kisses on her cheeks, her closed eyes, and her cracked lips.

"You're alright." I glanced over to my brother, who was sitting against the wall with his arms on his knees. "She'll be okay, right?"

He nodded. "She'll be fine. I got it all. But she's still lost a lot of blood and she needs to rest."

I could tell that he had overexerted himself, and that he was drained. His face had a gray tint and was covered in sweat.

"Thank you Mav. Thank you for saving her."

By the time Mavris had the energy to move again it was dark and I pointed him in the direction of an alcove with a couch that he could rest on. Kya still slept in my arms and I carried her through the chamber down to the lower alcove with the river.

With our clothes still on I waded into the water. And still, she didn't wake, too exhausted from the toll that the poison had taken. Her wound had healed, but it was still red and scarred, and likely would remain a permanent mark on her body. I gently removed her shredded clothes, leaving her in her undergarments as the water began to wash away the blood and sweat from her skin. Carefully dipping her head back, I ran my fingers through her hair and undid her braid. Her brown hair cascaded in the flow of the water like a sheet. I held her suspended in the river and rubbed her body with a soft cloth until all of the blood was gone.

This shouldn't have happened. I should have taken her out of there. The dark wielder was far more powerful than I had ever imagined, yet he hadn't used his magic against her.

He wanted her alive.

I pondered that as I took her back to the alcove with the bed and changed her into one of my shirts before placing her in the sheets. She stirred when I crawled in next to her and she rested her head on my bare chest with a sigh. There were so many questions running through my mind while I rubbed circles on her back.

Where did Daegel go? Is he injured? Will he come back? How did he get to Nikan or even know who he was to Kya? How does the magic work?

We needed to know more. He had chanted in another language, similar to that of the book. I needed to find it. I needed to go back to the palace to find the book, talk with Hakoa, check on the refugees, and assess the damage. But I didn't want to leave her...

"Are you awake?" I asked Mavris through his mind.

"Yeah. Just reading one of your shit books about history. Seriously, you really need some better reading material here. This is boring as fuck. Nice cave by the way. Very dragon of you."

The side of my mouth ticked up. *"Come down here. Past the chamber and down the tunnel on the right."*

A few moments later, Mavris came in and sat on the edge of the bed.

"What's up?" He still spoke through his mind so he didn't wake Kya.

"I need to go back to the palace. Can she handle the travel?"

He shook his head. *"I wouldn't. She needs to rest. She'll be out for a while. I'm certain she'll still be asleep when you get back. Likely a full day at least, if not longer."*

"I'm not leaving her," I clipped.

"Ryker, she'll be fine. I'll watch over her until you return. Go do what you need to do." Mavris gave a small smile.

He was one of the few that I trusted fully. I knew she would be safe with him. And he was right. I needed to take care of things, and I couldn't do that here. With a shallow nod, I grudgingly agreed to let him stay with her.

Carefully, I slid out from under her and kissed her forehead.

"I'll be back soon, little gem," I whispered and traced my thumb over the marriage band on her wrist.

I called to Theron and he met me at the mouth of the cave. Snow had begun to fall, the sign that winter had officially arrived.

"I need to go back to the palace," I said as I placed my hand on his scaly shoulder. He transported us and my heart sank when we appeared on the front lawn.

Facing what should have been the Oryn Palace, there was nothing left but crumbled ruins. The palace had fallen. The place that had been home and refuge and a symbol of my Lordship to my people, their protector, lay in a pile of broken stone. For nearly three-hundred years, I had lived in the palace. Memories flooded my mind. Of the first night I had stayed here after completing my challenge, dinners filled with laughter and chattering with Mavris and Hakoa and Arra. My father and mother walking the halls with their heads held high at the success of their son. My people coming and going, seeking help and guidance. My nights with Kya, warming the bed beside me.

Noavo warriors were all over, clambering over the rubble, cleaning up and assisting others, carefully weaving around the areas infected with the Glaev. A few children gasped at Theron's menacing presence. A hand on my shoulder startled me out of my thoughts and Hakoa stepped next to me, looking at the broken palace.

"Some of the wielders tried to mend it before it fell but we had to concentrate on getting all the refugees and workers out first." He turned his head to me. "The palace can always be rebuilt, but lives can't be brought back."

"Thank you. Where is everyone?"

He nodded and pointed down the hill toward the Noavo command station. "Temporary structures are being erected for shelter until the palace can be rebuilt. The ones we saved from the city will stay in the encampments or go elsewhere."

Hakoa trailed off, burdened that we weren't able to save everyone. My throat tightened. I hadn't protected them.

"How many?" I croaked.

"We're still counting. But at least three hundred from the city are missing or dead...so far." His voice was filled with sorrow.

I took a deep breath. "We'll give them a proper ceremony tomorrow night. Summon Deres to see off their souls."

We were silent for several moments.

"Is anyone still in the city?" I asked.

"No. After you left, we gathered everyone in the Mosun district. Theron came back immediately and Traveled everyone out."

"Good. I want you to bring in the warriors stationed at the Dichara Sea to help with the displacement."

I hoped it was enough. With all the recent attacks and displacements, our resources were beginning to thin.

He nodded, and we were quiet for a moment, taking in all the destruction around us before he cleared his throat. "How's Kya?"

"She'll be fine. Mavris is with her while she rests. I'll check in on her later, but I'm honed to his mind in case he needs me."

"What are you going to do? We can't just let that bastard roam free and hold Nikan prisoner. He has to be stopped. Look at what he did. Look at all that he's capable of."

"I'm going to stop him. I'll send his soul to the depths of the After," I growled. Then I thought of my people and all they were capable of. I needed to learn about Daegel. How and where he operated, if he had any weaknesses. The side of my mouth curved up. "Track down the Vaavi."

Hakoa bowed his head and walked away to speak with some of the other warriors. I turned to face Theron.

"What is he?" I demanded.

"A powerful being from another realm, and an atrocity in this one. He does not belong here."

"And you couldn't have warned me about him? You couldn't have said anything at all?"

"I could not before. Now that you know of his existence, it is not considered interfering if I discuss him now."

I lifted my head slightly to urge him to continue.

"We do not know where he comes from or how he came to be here, but he did not get here on his own. And the darkness he possesses is a foul magic, one of corruption. It is unnatural to this realm and is disrupting the balance. What your kind calls the Glaev." He lowered his head beside me.

"And that's why it…" I didn't want to say it. I had never heard of a Spirit guardian dying while their Worthy was alive. *"Where did you take him?"*

"I left what remains of him in Hylithria, where his soul will rest."

"What is Odarum's magic? It seemed to be the only thing that affected Daegel. And I think Kya has it too." Seeing her manifest her gifts from Odarum filled me with pride, even though it came too late to save the Spirit.

"It is Waalu, energy. Pure energy."

Deres's words came to mind, *"magic is energy"*. If Kya possessed energy and Daegel possessed dark magic then—

"I have to get back." But first, I needed to find the book in the rubble. Assuming it survived.

I shifted my wings and flew over the palace to the other side to one of the terbis wielders helping to clear the rubble.

"Warrior Zeá." I dipped my head in greeting.

Her head bowed. "Lord Ryker. I'm sorry about the palace. But don't worry, we'll get it fixed up in no time—"

I lifted my hand. "My only concern is that everyone is safe. It's just stone. And my home is with the people, not the palace." She smiled at that. "However, I do require your help."

"Of course. Anything." Zeá straightened, her brown eyes bright and eager.

"I need help in finding a book. One in particular. It would have been in the library and where we're standing is about where it would have been. I'll need you to move the stone out of the way so that I may find it." It was going to be a long and hard task, trying to dig out a single book, buried within the remains of an entire library.

"Lord Ryker," Zeá shouted.

She had been moving the broken stone of the palace out of the way for hours in the dark, creating a hole down to where the library would have been, without complaining about the cold despite the harsh wind and snow building up. I had kept a fire going near her, but with her getting closer and closer to the books, she insisted I put out the flames in fear that I would burn the parchment.

I crawled my way back up the pile of rubble where I had been moving what pieces I could and placing items that could be reused on the ground below.

"What is it?" I asked when I approached.

Zeá was crouched down in a hole of her own making. She stepped aside to reveal that she was standing on a pile of books. We continued to move the stone away. Other warriors tried to help, but I insisted, and ultimately had to order, that they attend to the citizens and do what they could to help.

Finally, after pulling up hundreds of books, Zeá pulled out the dark book and handed it up to me. I thanked her before heading back to the cave with the book tucked under my arm as well as a couple of others that we had pulled from the pile. The wind and snow obscured my vision, but I had flown that way so many times that I could practically do it with my eyes closed.

Mavris had fallen asleep and was resting in a chair that he had pulled up to the side of the bed. Kya looked as if she hadn't moved, and I was grateful that she was still sleeping while her body healed but I had hoped that she would be awake when I returned. I desperately wanted to hear the sound of her voice, her laugh, to see her smile, needing to replace the last sounds of her screams of agony and pain. After waking Mavris and escorting him to another alcove to sleep, I returned to the bed and fell asleep with my mate safely tucked against me.

Chapter Fifty-Seven

KYA

E verywhere hurt when I woke up in Ryker's arms. My head, my muscles, my veins, and my heart. For a blissful moment, when I first opened my eyes, I didn't remember the day before. I didn't remember seeing the bodies being consumed. I didn't remember Odarum dying to protect me. I didn't remember being struck with my own poison-tipped arrow. I didn't remember wishing I would die rather than endure the pain to live. In that fleeting moment, it was just me and my mate, warm in bed. Until it all came crashing back down on me, and I felt like I was drowning under the weight of it all.

And I could feel everything, more than I had ever before. I could sense everything around me in a new way. I could sense the flow of the river through the mountain, the heat of the walls around me, the power of the storm outside. It was almost overwhelming.

I needed some air so I slowly slid out from Rykers embrace, careful not to wake him, and headed for the mouth of the cave. I walked through the chamber and into the tunnel, the padding of my bare feet echoed off the walls and the air felt cooler the closer I got to the cave opening. Snow piled on the ledge of the cave mouth and even in the darkness of the storm I could still see flurries of snow drifting past through the mountains where I had learned to fly. Where Odarum had taught me.

With a shaky exhale, I reached for him through the bond.

"Odarum?"

Silence.

A tear rolled down my cheek.

"Odarum… I'm so sorry."

I pressed my side to the wall and slid down to the floor, hugging my legs to my chest. I rested my head on my knees and watched the storm pass by, replaying the night before over and over in my head. The people's screams of terror, Ryker scrambling to save everyone, Nikan being pulled from darkness with his sunken eyes and bruised face, Odarum standing between me and Daegel. I hung on to every word that the bastard had said, watched in my mind every moment as if it were in slow motion until the slightest bit of light from the sun made the white clouds of the storm glow.

The vibrations of soft steps pulsed through the rock as I felt the approaching figure come to a stop a ways behind me, as if hesitant to come any closer.

"I can feel you standing there, you know."

"I forgot that you had a special kind of terbis. That's an amazing ability," Mavris said from behind, coming up to the mouth of the cave.

"Yeah I suppose."

He handed me a blanket, which I accepted with a grateful nod and wrapped it around myself. He was barefoot and in nothing but a thin shirt and pants. His loose hair was a mess and there were dark circles around his silver eyes. He sat beside me with his arms resting on his thighs.

"Aren't you cold?" I asked, turning my head to face him.

"No. I can control my blood flow and when I increase it, it warms my body," he said with a shrug.

"You can control your own blood?"

He nodded with a small grin. "I can. It's very helpful in stressful situations when I need to remain calm. I think it's one of the reasons I can handle being Ryker's advisor and function under all the pressure."

"Now *that's* an amazing ability."

He chuckled. "I'm certainly grateful for it. Sometimes I have to rely on it to keep me from snapping under the stress of it all. I don't know how Ryker does it all the time."

"I don't either. I certainly don't know how I will." I shook my head. There was already so much going on, and I wasn't even a Lady yet.

"I think it'll be easier because you two will do it together."

I smiled at that, and we were quiet for a few moments.

"Thank you for what you did. For saving me. I hope it wasn't too exhaustive for you."

"Of course, I'm just glad I was able to get it all before it was too late. I've only ever had to do that a handful of times, and it does take a lot out of me but it was worth it." He paused for a moment. "I could feel it though." He gestured to me.

"Feel what?"

"Your power. It fought against me."

"It did?" So much had happened in so little time that I hadn't had the chance to take the time to truly understand my gift. I felt guilty for having it.

"Yeah."

"I'm sorry it fought you. I don't even know what it is."

"Energy," Ryker's spoke through the bond, and I couldn't help but smile at the sound of his voice.

A moment later, I felt him walking up to us and I turned my head to look at him from over my shoulder. He wore nothing but loose pants. He sat behind me, his legs on either side, and kissed the top of my head. I leaned back against him, grateful for his warmth and his presence. He wrapped his arms around my chest with a contented sigh.

I felt him harden against me. I turned my head around and gave him a stare. Now was not the time.

"I can't always help it when you're around," he laughed. "I'm happy you're awake. How are you feeling?" he said softly against my hair.

"Like I was shot with a poisoned arrow," I huffed. His chuckle rumbled against my back. "So what about energy?"

"Your magic, the gift you received from Odarum, is energy."

My brows creased. "How do you know?"

"Theron told me. One of Odarum's abilities was raw energy. He called it Waalu."

"Energy? But Deres said—"

"I know. I thought the same thing."

"Do you two want to fill me in? What does Deres have to do with energy magic?" Mavris asked, rubbing his eyes with his palms.

"Essentially, what he said is that magic *is* energy. So if Kya has energy—" Ryker started.

"What, she has all magic?" Mavris balked. He leaned into me and whispered, "Can you make me read minds too?"

I giggled.

"Mav! You really want *two* forbidden abilities? One isn't enough?" Ryker shoved him in the shoulder playfully.

Mavris crossed his arms and shrugged. "I would just like to know who keeps stealing the sweets from my desk when I'm not around. I still think it's you, Ryk."

"I'm the *Lord of Oryn*. You honestly think I would need to steal sweets and from you of all people? Besides, I told you already, my coin's on Arra." Ryker leaned in to whisper against my ear, "She's the sneaky one of the group anyway. It's just logical."

"Says the male who sleeps in the same building," Mavris grumbled.

I snorted a laugh. Their interaction reminded me of Nikan and Malina.

"Sorry Mav. I don't think I can give you mind abilities. All I have is this green stuff." I lifted my hand and pulled that energy from within me.

Swirls of glowing green tendrils streamed from my hand, snaking down my arm. Not having had the time to study it before, I observed my new magic. I had never seen Odarum use this ability before yesterday, and I didn't understand what it did, what it was capable of. Now that I had used it, it came so naturally to me. But it felt different from the magic I had from Kleio. And it felt more...powerful. I could feel it thrumming with vibrancy as it danced along my skin. It was warm and bright like li—

"Wait... I need the book. We need to go back to the palace." My words were rushed and I quickly stood.

"Hold on." Ryker stood also and put up his hands. "I already got the book and brought it back here while you were asleep."

"You left?" I blinked.

"I didn't leave you alone. Mav stayed here while I helped the warriors with some of the cleanup of the palace."

"The palace?" We weren't anywhere near the palace.

Ryker glanced to the ground and his shoulders slumped before meeting Mavris's stare, then back to mine. "The palace was destroyed."

I felt the blood drain from my face. "But the people inside. Mal—"

"They're fine. No one was crushed in the palace. The terbis wielders there were able to hold up certain areas long enough to get everyone out. When I got there, Hakoa already had wielders working to sort through the wreckage. And Malina had been helping those from the city."

"And Voara? Did everyone get out?" I dreaded the answer.

"No. Hundreds were lost. But the Glaev stopped when Daegel left." He spat his name. "His magic isn't from our realm. It's why no one can counter it, and it's throwing off the balance. But we still don't know why he's doing this or why he wants you specifically."

I shook my head slowly. "We have to get Nikan back. Daegel has to be stopped."

"He will be. I promise you that. And…I think you might be the one who can do it," Ryker said with a sigh.

I looked at him skeptically. "You do?"

He nodded and stood, extending a hand to lead me back inside the cave. I followed him back to the alcove where we slept. He gestured to the corner where he had left the book when he returned last night. I walked over to pick it up and noticed other books piled with it as well.

"What are these?" I asked. He was putting on a shirt he pulled from the wardrobe.

"Oh. Um, books. For you. I know you said that you like love stories, and I found a few while I was sorting through the rubble and thought you might like them for when we stay here." He smiled as I started to flip through the pages.

They were indeed stories filled with romance and adventure, just what I loved. I looked back to him with a wide grin. The small notion of picking out books for me in the destruction of his home made my heart flutter.

"Thank you, Ryker. I really appreciate this and yes, this is exactly what I like."

His chest puffed out slightly. I placed the novels down and brought the dark book to the bed and crossed my legs underneath me with the book between Ryker and I as he climbed on the bed as well.

I opened the book and was surprised to find that all of the notes from me and Rolim were still safely tucked within the pages. We delved into my notes and continued some additional translations.

"Look at this. Right here." I pointed to one of the notes and Ryker leaned over. "This is what I didn't understand but after hearing Daegel recite some of these words, in the manner that he did, I think he was…summoning this magic to do something specific. Because he said some of these other words and it did something entirely different from his magic. And this one here specifically says something like assimilation."

"Assimilation of what? Why is that significant?"

"It's what Vicria said. She said that the Glaev *absorbs* the energy of life. And remember when I said that there was that thing about some kind of reserve?"

"Yeah. It's like his own personal power reserves. She confirmed that. That Daegel could only do so much damage at one time and wanted maximum spiritual life dependent upon how much he had," he said with a nod while jotting a few things down himself.

"Yes but I don't think that's all of it. I think he has only a certain amount of reserve for his magic but I also think that the energy being absorbed is assimilated somewhere…else."

"For what? And what about the prism? That stops the dark magic from being wielded. So we could do to him what we did to Vicria." He leaned forward.

"I don't know what the energy would be stored for or how. And I don't think a physical diamond was what the book was actually talking about and Vicria wasn't even the wielder so really it was all pointless."

"Good to know," he mumbled.

"I think the jeweled prism was translated incorrectly. When I read with Mal, we came across what we thought was a conduit but there was also something about adaptation. I think it was referring to that." I shrugged.

"With your energy…it seems to be something that truly affects Daegel, hurts him even. And there's something else too." I lifted my eyes to him. "I think you can reverse the Glaev."

The side of my mouth lifted in a smirk. He was coming to the same conclusion that I had earlier when I realized that my magic, my energy, was like the opposite of dark magic, just in a different form.

"How much do you know about energy?" I asked, leaning in closer.

"Not much I suppose. Just that energy is in everything."

"Exactly. And it isn't something that can ever be destroyed either." It was times like these that I was thankful that I had lived among Scholars and spent countless hours learning from them. "Energy can take every form you can possibly think of, and it will change from one form to another. The Glaev, dark magic, is just a form of energy that is consuming other types of energy. And I think that's what Daegel wants me for. To adapt my form of energy to create more Glaev and assimilate more of the life energy to the reserve he's building up with it. But," I paused and took his hand with a smile. "I think that I can use my energy to shift the Glaev to another form so that it isn't decimating the land anymore."

"Kya, this could change everything. Our world won't be dying anymore," he said with a bright smile before grabbing my face and kissing me.

I pulled back and chuckled before my face fell. "It could. But Daegel has to be stopped first."

"I already sent for Arra and the Vaavi. They'll find him. And I'm betting they could use the help of a couple of Roav too, but we'll have to wait out this storm first."

I looked to the gems embedded in the walls, shining against the soft light of the fire. "He called me Diamond."

Ryker released a heavy breath. "Yeah."

"And with Vicria, when she started talking about the diamond he was looking for, you begged for me to stop." I continued to gaze at the walls.

"Yeah," he said again.

I turned to look at him. "You knew that the Diamond was me. Before she even said it."

"I did." His face remained neutral.

"How did you know that?" I asked softly, shaking my head.

He hesitated, glancing away for several moments before sighing and looking back at me. "Because your name means Diamond."

We spent the rest of the day waiting out the storm in the cave. Ryker and Mavris watched as I experimented with my energy. Though I didn't admit it out loud, it was fun. I was able to do things and find energy in places I never thought about. The sound of the waterfall crashing into the river, the force of the wind at the mouth of the cave, the heat emanating from the flames in the hearth. Which led me to an idea.

I sent out my tendrils of swirling energy to the crackling logs and watched as the flames began to die out, but I continued to push it further. We all gasped as we watched the logs turn from black to brown. But still I pushed. I wanted to see just how far it could go. Small twigs began to sprout, and I couldn't help the wide grin that spread across my face as little green leaves grew at the ends.

"Life," Ryker breathed. "You can restore life."

By the time it was dark outside, Mavris had gone to rest, still not fully recovered from using so much energy on me the night before. The storm had died out and Ryker and I decided to wait until morning to return to Voara. Thoughts of Odarum came back to me. And though I was utterly spent from using so much magic throughout the day, I wanted to clear my head.

I went back to the mouth of the cave and lay on my back with my head resting at the edge of the cliff, watching the stars appear in the inky black sky. Ryker joined me, and I held his hand in mine. We were so high up on the mountain that I felt like we could just reach out and touch the sky.

"This is what you would do back in Ilrek right? On the ledge in Morah?" he asked as we gazed up at the twinkling lights above.

I smiled. "Yeah. I used to do it all the time. One of the Scholars taught me about the constellations, and I would spend hours and hours finding them in the sky. More just out of fascination than anything."

"Can you show me some of them?" He pulled my hand up to his mouth and kissed the back of it before resting it against his chest.

"Really?" I asked enthusiastically. Malina and Nikan never had much interest in it and I was happy to finally share it with someone, especially my mate.

"Of course."

"Well that one there, the one that looks like two squares laid over each other," I pointed up to a cluster with my other hand. "That's Onvera, The Crates of Time."

He hummed and nodded as I continued.

"And that one there, that's Braegia, the Warrior of Night."

"Oh, I like that one."

I giggled. "And this squiggly one that goes across the sky is Xala, the River of—"

...what has a river that does not flow...

The task of the Trial came rushing back to me as did Kleio's words.

...seek the truth...restore the balance...

Her task for me.

...what light brings to life yet dies in the darkness...

"A shadow," I whispered.

"Hmm?" Ryker said.

I leaned over and pressed my head to Ryker's, sending him my thoughts so that he may also understand.

...where the land meets the sky...

The mountain.

...The Glaev—Is not what it seems...

...only its death will bring forth the path...

Darkness. Night.

...How do I find it? You already know...

The riddle.

I pulled back from him, and we sat up as my thoughts and memories continued to pour into his mind. Ryker gasped when he finally understood. Kleio had provided me with everything I needed to complete her task. I looked back to the sky and followed where the river constellation led.

"What direction is that?" I asked.

"Southeast. It leads right to..." He sighed. "Right to the Rip."

Chapter Fifty-Eight

KYA

"What does that mean?" Malina asked.

Theron had taken us to Hakoa's barrack at first light, and we were now in his sitting area. Ryker and I were sitting next to Mavris, sipping on hot tea with Malina and Hakoa across from us, both of which were still dressed in what they had been sleeping in. Malina was wearing loose pants and one of Hakoa's shirts, and Hakoa wore only pants, leaving his tattoos on display. While they rubbed the sleep from their eyes, we told them what we had discovered about my magic and how everything was coming together to stop Daegel once and for all.

"What does what mean?" I leaned back against the couch and Ryker put his arm over my shoulders, pulling me against his side.

"The star river and the Rip. What does that mean?" she asked again.

"We think it's leading us to Daegel's location." It was the only reason we could think of, at least. And I hope we aren't wrong.

Malina's eyes widened, darting between Ryker and I. "You are seriously not thinking of going after him, are you? Fuck,

Kya. Look at what he did. He captured Nik. He destroyed Voara and tore down the palace for Nox's sake." She glared at Ryker. "You're really going to allow her to confront him again? He killed her Spirit. He's after her. What makes you think he won't kill her? He already tried to with her Kiss laced arrow."

"Which I doubt he knew was poisoned. No fae would die from just a simple arrow," I added.

"That's not the point. He tried to kill you, and your mate is going to just take you right back to him."

Ryker's arm tightened around me. "This is her decision. I won't stop her. And if she is going, you can damn well expect that I'm going to help her in any way I can. Regardless if I'm happy with it or not."

"You disagree that I should go? I'm the only one who can stop him."

"No, little gem, I don't disagree. But that doesn't mean I like it." He kissed my temple.

Malina just stared at me for several moments. I could see her mind working. Running through scenarios and variables. Until finally coming to the conclusion that it was better that I have as much help as I could get rather than no help at all.

"Well…shit. Then I'm going too," Malina said.

"So am I." Hakoa crossed his arms.

"Ayen's ass…" Mavris pinched his nose. "Yeah, me too."

"No," I stated. I would not put any more lives in danger than was necessary. I knew that no matter what I couldn't keep Ryker from coming, he'd just find me anyway.

"Excuse me?" Malina barked. "Why the fuck not?"

"Because you don't need to be there. I'm not putting you at unnecessary risk." And I didn't want to worry about her. She could handle herself just fine, but against Daegel? I wasn't sure she'd be any help.

"Don't," she said through gritted teeth, and everyone stiffened at her tone. "You think that just because Nik is gone you have to be like him?"

I met her stare before announcing to the room. "Can you give us a minute?"

Everyone quickly stood and went outside, closing the door behind them and leaving Malina and I alone.

"I'm not being like Nik. This is completely different," I said trying not to get worked up.

"Oh? And how is that? You're trying to stop me from *my* decision for the sake of what you think is best for me. It's no different from how he is." I could feel the bite in her words.

"It is different." My voice grew louder.

"How? How is this any different?"

"Because if something happens and I don't make it back with Nik, you'll be the only one left…" I squeezed my eyes closed and exhaled. "I don't think you'd be able to do anything anyway. No element seems to have an effect on this male. I'm not going to lose the last family I have left."

"Oh boohoo." My eyes snapped open just in time to see her rolling her eyes. "You know, for someone who's so godsdamn smart, you're pretty fucking stupid sometimes. It doesn't matter if any of us are left. If *you're* gone, then there's no chance that anyone else can come back. That's your task, isn't it? Restore the balance and bring them back? How are you going to do that if you're dead?" she whispered. "This is bigger than any one of us. This is for them."

I didn't respond. I couldn't say anything against that.

"What exactly do you have planned anyway? You're just going to go find this male and hit him with some green light, all by yourself, and hope that he brought Nik along with him?"

"No." Malina narrowed her eyes suspiciously. "I…I don't know. I don't have all the answers. I'm going off of very little, and most of that is just based on guesses." I hated not being certain. Not having a plan. There was so much that was unknown, and that left too many possibilities.

Her eyes softened. "Kya, it's alright to not have all the answers. But let us help you. Let us decide for ourselves what to risk, and let me help you sort through this. Come on. " She got up and came to sit next to me. "Let's work it out!"

The side of my mouth lifted. Maybe she was right. Maybe this time, I needed to work with others rather than alone.

"Alright." I nodded.

"Well, tell pigeon boy to get back in here!"

"I heard that," Ryker grumbled and I could practically hear his eyes rolling.

They all came back in and sat back down. Ryker sat on the other side of me, and I reached for his hand, pulling it into my lap. Hakoa and Mavris sat across from us. Mavris leaned forward with his elbows resting on his knees.

"Right then. So Daegel is somewhere near the Rip according to stars, correct?" Malina started.

"Yes." I nodded.

"And Kya's energy magic harms him to some effect," Hakoa said.

"All we really need to do then is distract Daegel enough so that Kya can get in a good shot. That seems simple enough," Mavris said with a shrug.

"Easier said than done," Hakoa muttered.

"Except we can't kill him if Nik isn't there. We need him alive to find out where he's keeping him," I said, and everyone's heads turned to me.

"She's right," Ryker agreed. "But if he is there, then yes. We just need to make sure that we get Nikan away from Daegel first. Then Kya can hit him with her energy."

"Let's say that we are actually successful. What do we do after? Just go back to living our lives like nothing happened?" Malina slumped back with a sigh.

I tapped my chin and contemplated. I had thought of what my energy could truly do. "Well, first I need to see if what I think can happen *will* happen."

Ryker looked at me questioningly.

I chuckled. "Come on. Let's go find out."

We all stood and left Hakoa's barrack and made the trek to the edge of the city, where the Glaev surrounded what was left. I shivered, partly because of the cold and partly because of the sight before me. It was the first time I had seen the extent of the destruction.

I broke away from Ryker's arm around my shoulder and walked over to the Glaev, standing before it and staring at the decimated terra. I hated the sight of it, the empty black hole that I could feel, the reminder of the mindless destruction it brought by simply being.

Without a second thought, I called my magic to me and swirling tendrils filled my outstretched palms, tingling across my skin. I concentrated on what I wanted it to do, and pushed it to the Glaev-infected land in front of me. Ryker approached and stood behind, watching and not disturbing me as my magic spread across the blackened area. But then people had started to gather and were whispering amongst themselves. My magic started to dwindle, my concentration diminishing.

What if this didn't work? What if I was wrong or worse, what if this did more damage than good?

I started to pull back my magic, but then shadows enveloped all around me and I felt the heat of Ryker's body at my back. His breath brushed against my ear as he spoke.

"Shh. Clear your mind. Don't think about anything else. It's just you and me here."

I nodded and took a deep breath. "Okay."

I pushed my magic out again, with more force this time. It took several moments and sweat started to bead above my brow from the effort, but then, the darkness, the Glaev, began to dissipate and what looked like white smoke rose into the air.

The back of my eyes pricked with tears and I gasped quietly, continuing to push out more and more of my magic, causing the land to glow. I was healing the land, ridding it of the plague that had assaulted the world. Once a small area was filled with lush green grass, I stopped.

All this time, Odarum had had the ability to fix all of this. But because of their interference restrictions, he couldn't. But I could.

"It worked," I whispered under my breath.

"My powerful mate." I could hear the smile in his voice.

He pulled his shadows back to him and gasps sounded from the surrounding people as they took in the sight of the healed Glaev with a slight glow around the edges, like it was still slowly growing and working on its own.

I wasn't waiting another moment to fix more. I pushed forward and out, spreading the tendrils of energy as far and wide as I could.

Hours passed. And I pushed and pushed more and more of my energy to restore the land around the city. The buildings didn't miraculously reappear, but they could be rebuilt. I had made it halfway around the city before I nearly collapsed from the exertion.

Shouts and clapping and hooting erupted from all around from the people. The Glaev was gone. Not all of it, but where I had touched it with my energy.

My head felt hazy, and my body was weak. It didn't help that I had just suffered poisoning only days earlier. Ryker noticed my fatigued state. He came up next to me and placed a supportive arm around my waist.

"Let's all part ways here and get some rest so that we can leave at dusk," Ryker said. "Kya and I will go to the cave and try to get some sleep. I have a feeling that we have a very long night ahead of us, and we'll need our strength to go against Daegel."

"Why do we have to leave at dusk? Why don't we just leave now?" Hakoa asked, and I couldn't help but notice that he leaned slightly closer to Malina.

"Because we need to be able to follow the River constellation for a more accurate location. The Rip is huge, and it does make sense that he would be near there, but it's just unclear as to where exactly. The constellation will give us a better guide."

"Because of your Trial riddle?" he asked skeptically.

"Yes," Ryker and I said in unison.

"You must have a lot of faith in the Gods," Hakoa huffed.

I shrugged with a small smile. "I have to."

We all went our separate ways then. Ryker flew us back to the cave, I was too exhausted to even summon my wings, let alone fly. Once we were in the cave, he took my hand and led me to the kitchen alcove.

"Let me get you something to eat," Ryker said, guiding me to sit at the small table near the corner.

As if on cue, my stomach gurgled. "I am pretty hungry."

He chuckled as he took out a few things from the cabinets and lit a fire with a pot of water over it. "Do you like stew?"

"Who doesn't?"

"Stew it is, then," he said with a wink, then turned back around to the ingredients on the counter in front of him.

I watched him prepping the food, cutting up vegetables and dumping them into the pot of boiling water. All the while, I could hear his thoughts and I'm not sure he even realized it.

He can't have her.

I can't stop her, I won't.

Maybe I should just leave while she's asleep and take care of him myself.

No. I couldn't do that to her. She would resent me for it. I care about her brother and I want to stop the dark wielder, but I care so much more for her.

I don't want to risk her.

How can I keep her safe?

His mind was spiraling. He was worried and anxious, and I hated that he felt that way, but I didn't know how to make it better. I came up behind and wrapped my arms around his waist and held him tightly. It was all the comfort I knew how to give in that moment.

I caressed down the bond. "No one will take me from you."

Chapter Fifty-Nine

KYA

We spent the day in the cave, in our own world, eating and resting in preparation for what was to come. Ryker and I had lay in bed to get a couple hours of sleep. I closed my eyes and quieted my mind until I heard his heavy, even breaths.

I watched him sleep, trailing my eyes over his face, memorizing every part of him in that moment. The way his hair flowed over his forehead, the slight movements of his eyes beneath his lids, the way his mouth was shaped into a straight line as he slept.

His thoughts from earlier came back to me. That he wouldn't leave me here, that I would resent him for it.

I hoped the same couldn't be said for him.

But I had lost enough people I loved. I wouldn't lose anymore. I wouldn't allow any more of Oryn's people to die because of that bastard. Not Ryker, not Mavris, not Hakoa. None of them.

I lay there awake while my mate held me in his arms, and his warm embrace made me wish I could stay there forever. Our bond purred with contentment. But I had made my choice. It would fight me, I knew it would. It would pull and thrash against my soul, begging me to stay. It was unnatural, wrong, to be away from one's mate. I had never imagined that I would ever find my mate and when I had fantasized about it, I hadn't imagined that I would have to leave him.

At least at this distance.

Slowly and carefully, I crawled out of his arms, already missing the warmth of his body, and out of the bed. Quietly grabbing my clothes and my weapons, I left the alcove and went into another to dress.

I'd had to make sure that I hadn't actively thought of any of this while Ryker had been awake.

This is a bad idea. What am I thinking? This will hurt him. He will just come for me anyway. My shadow will always come for me.

No. I need to go. I'm the only one who can do anything against Daegel anyway. There's no point in putting others at risk. I just need to take care of him then get Nikan.

I knew that Malina would be pissed when she found out that I left her behind too. Nikan was just as much her brother as he was mine. No matter what, no one would be happy. But at least they would be alive. I would rather them hate me than be dead. I couldn't live with myself if anything happened to him.

I kept my steps silent as I went back to the alcove where Ryker was asleep. I stood at the side of the bed, watching the rise and fall of his bare chest, and bent down to gently kiss him on his hair, running a loving caress down that swirling tether.

"Beyond the bond," I mouthed.

I turned to leave but stopped when I noticed Odarum's feather on the bedside table where I had left it during Nailu. Picking it up, I twirled it in my fingers. Carefully, I removed my jacket, hanging it over my arm, and shifted my wings quickly to pluck a feather from them. Then, I went into the jeweled chamber to pry one of the gems from the cave wall, and left both on the table beside Ryker.

After one last glance at my mate, I left the alcove and headed down the tunnel to the mouth of the cave. My heart ached with every step.

Theron was there at the opening. He had stayed, waiting to take us when we were ready. The setting sun created a silhouette around him, making him look regal and formidable as I approached. I stood beside him, looking out over the snow-covered mountains. I was dressed in my tight black leathers and armed with daggers. My bow and quiver of arrows with the different colored feathers were strung across my back and my braided hair moved up and down over my shoulder with the slow rise and fall of my breaths.

"I need you to do something for me. For Ryker," I said to the Spirit dragon.

He tilted his head and I turned to face him.

"I need you to take me to the Rip."

Theron growled with his lips curling up, showing his teeth.

"Just hear me out." I put up my hands. "You want to protect Ryker. It's your purpose as his Spirit Guardian. And I want to protect him too. This is how I can do that, how *we* can do that. Let me do this."

Theron rumbled a sound in his chest, like a mix between a purr and a growl.

"Please, Theron. Take me to the Rip. I understand your reservations. If anything happened to me, as Ryker's mate, it would hurt him. But he would still be safe," I begged.

He looked down the tunnel of the cave then back to me, contemplating. Then he lowered his massive head, his yellow eye level with mine.

"Thank you," I whispered. I placed my hand on his muzzle then everything went black for a moment as he Traveled me away.

But not to the Rip.

He took me just outside of Hakoa's barrack. I looked around then back to the dragon.

"What are we doing here?"

Theron jerked his head toward the barrack, toward Hakoa, toward Malina.

"You want me to take Mal?" I deadpanned.

He narrowed his eyes and growled.

I rolled my eyes and scoffed. "The whole point was so that no one else would be at risk."

"I think his point is that *Ryker* wouldn't be at risk."

I whipped my head around to find Malina coming out of the barrack, dressed in her leathers and armed with her daggers. Hakoa stumbled, half dressed, out of the doorway after her.

"What are you doing, Mal?" I snapped.

"Coming with you, obviously." She stepped off the porch and walked toward me. "Don't worry. I already cleared it with the lizard. And apparently he agreed with me."

"Malina, stop." Hakoa grabbed her elbow. "You're just going to leave?"

"Hold on." I shook my head. "Theron agreed to what?"

"To take me with you, dumbass. You really think I didn't know what you would do? You can go without your mate, but you're not going without me. I have every right to help Nik just as much as you do." She snapped at me then turned her head to Hakoa. "And yes, I am leaving." She gently pulled her elbow free from his grasp and her eyes softened.

She wasn't wrong. I glared at Theron from the corner of my eye, but what was I going to do? Argue with a temperamental Spirit dragon and my sister? I hated this, I hated that she knew me so well that she was able to plan this.

Hakoa looked at me then back to her. "Let me come with you. I can at least help."

Malina cupped his face, and I realized then that what they had between them was more than I had thought. The look they shared held something much deeper than they had let on, deeper than I think they knew themselves. It made me hate this even more.

Crossing my arms, I turned away to give them some privacy while they whispered quietly to each other for several moments.

My impulsive plan was already going to shit. I hoped that Hakoa would convince her to stay, but ultimately she was right. She had every right to help Nikan just like I did. He was her brother too.

"And Kya," Hakoa said louder. I turned back around to see him glaring at me. "You really think Ryker would be okay with this? Does he even know you're gone?"

I didn't answer.

"So you just left." He shook his head in disbelief at both of us. "You're both just…leaving."

Malina started to walk away from him with a hard look on her face. "We're Roav. Get used to it."

"No. Stop, just—" he started to reach for her but Theron lowered his head between us and Hakoa, then snarled with his teeth bared at the chief, smoke billowing out of his snout. Hakoa jumped back with his hand up. "Fuck! Alright!"

I gave him a tight-lipped smile. "Sorry, Hakoa."

Malina and I placed our hands on Theron's shoulder. The last thing we saw before we left was Hakoa running off, cursing up to the skies.

Chapter Sixty

KYA

We appeared in an open field of grass. The air was warmer and it was darker than back in Oryn. The bond tugged at me, urging me to be with my mate, but I pushed that feeling aside.

Malina hurled over herself and emptied her stomach. I cringed at the sound and the smell of the acid spilling onto the ground.

"Shit." She spat on the grass. "I forgot what that felt like." She kept her hands on her knees taking deep breaths.

"You good?" I handed her a canteen of water from the pocket of my cloak.

"Just give me a second."

I looked up at Theron. "Don't bring him here. No matter what. Ignore him if you can."

With the dip of his head, he disappeared, leaving Malina and I alone. After a few moments, she stood and wiped her mouth.

"How far away is it?" she asked.

"Not far. Just beyond those trees." I pointed to the small patch of forest ahead of us.

"How do you know he's there?"

"This was where the book was found. The river points to here. It was just the most logical place I thought he would be."

I pulled out my bow and strung an arrow, then led the way through the trees, using my terbis to navigate us in the darkness. Malina's boot kicked something, and she grumbled a curse under her breath before she manifested a small orb of light above us, just bright enough to see the ground. She kept her hands near her blades, ready to grab them if needed, and trained her eyes on the trees. We remained silent as we trekked through the small patch of forest.

Just past the tree line, I held up my fist for us to stop. Up ahead, we could see the edge of the Rip on one side and the Glaev touching the end of it on the other.

The destroyed Nation of Atara.

It never got any easier seeing it, knowing just how many had died that night in a matter of minutes. Our home. Our people. While our families still lived, they were suffering more than if they had died too.

Malina stepped up and stood next to me, both of our arms crossed over our chests. We didn't speak. We just stood there for several moments, staring at the vast wasteland before us.

"For them," I finally broke the silence.

"For them. And for us," she echoed softly.

Then I turned and headed toward the edge of where the Glaev met the Rip. I took a deep breath, grasping my magic, and the swirling tendrils of energy filled my palms and ran up my arms. Without hesitation, I thrust my energy out on to the decimated land, turning it from black to gray, to brown, to green. I made a path wide enough for the two of us to cross without having to worry about the Rip or the Glaev on either side.

I made a promise to myself that when this was all over, I would restore our Nation's lands, restore the balance. Just like Kleio ordered me to.

As the path grew, I walked forward onto the restored land, extending my magic farther ahead. I could feel myself weakening with the exertion, not having fully recovered from earlier and still unused to the amount of power I was wielding. Malina could tell too.

"Kya, slow down. You're going to strain your reserves," she said.

"It's fine," I panted and sweat began to bead on my brow.

I clearly wasn't. I was becoming exhausted quickly, but Malina wasn't going to push me on it, she had to trust that I knew my own limits. But she remained close, following me as we passed between the deadly Glaev and the depths of the Rip until we came up on the beach Ryker and I had tried to find before.

When the Glaev was cleared enough for us to reach the other side, I collapsed, falling to my hands and knees on the sandy beach. My head spun and my vision was spotty. I dug my fingers into the shifty substance, focusing on that instead. I knew I was pushing it, but it was necessary. I couldn't have flown over it while carrying Malina, and we needed a quick getaway in case we were ambushed by Daegel.

Taking a deep breath, I turned to find a beach. The one that wasn't there the last time Ryker and I had come. But I hadn't thought of the sea. The low tide having receded, exposing more of the land. Slivers of moonlight reflected off of the water's surface. Large boulders were visible as well, smoothed from thousands of years of the water's erosion since the Rip's formation.

"Kya?" Ryker's voice sounded through the bond. *"Kya, what's wrong?"* I knew that he could feel just how weak I was, just as I could feel his panic before a wave of understanding washed over him. *"Little gem...where are you?"*

I squeezed my eyes shut, hating the pained sound of his voice. He knew. He just didn't want to believe it. We couldn't hear each other's thoughts from this distance, but we could still communicate from anywhere in the realm and feel each other's emotions.

"I'm fine. Ryker, I'm sorry. But I need to do this." I kept my inner voice calm, soothing down the bond to let him know that I was still with him.

"No…no, no, no. Please, come back. You promised I would be with you."

"I know. But I couldn't let anything happen to you. Oryn needs you. Your people need you. I need you. Safe and far away from here." My vision started to come back with my slow deep breaths.

Malina gave me the water and I drank nearly the entire thing.

"This isn't one of your Roav jobs. This male is after you. He's dangerous." His voice was desperate.

"And I won't endanger you!" My voice was raised. *"I will not risk your life, not if I can help it."*

"I'm coming." It wasn't a question, but a promise.

"You won't make it. It's a two-day flight."

"Fuck! Theron won't answer me." I could feel his adrenaline surging.

"He's protecting his Worthy," I said apologetically.

I took Malina's offered hand and stood. I tried to block out the sound of his voice in my mind. I concentrated on the sound of the ocean waves, the sound of the wind skating across the shifting sand beneath my boots, the eerie silence of the Rip directly behind me.

"You good?" Malina asked.

I gave a shallow nod. "Ryker's awake. He's pissed."

"Do you blame him?"

"No."

She pursed her lips. "Well, tell him to be quiet. You're already weak and the last thing we need is for him to distract you."

I nodded in agreement and was about to speak to him when he beat me to it.

"You took Malina...but not me."

He must have found Hakoa. And quickly. It was the only reason he'd have known Malina was with me.

"I did. It wasn't entirely my choice and I will explain everything later," I said quietly to him. *"But please trust me."*

"I do trust you, but it's not about trust. He is trying to take you from me!" The bond rumbled with fear and anger.

"No one will take me from you," I stated firmly. *"Ryker, I love you beyond the bond. But please shut up. I need to focus."*

He was silent for a moment before he responded. *"I'm coming for you."*

And I expected nothing less from my shadow.

"Kya," Malina whispered.

I looked at her. Her eyes were trained on the water ahead as she slowly pulled up her mask before unsheathing her daggers.

My head snapped in the direction of her stare, and my eyes widened in disbelief. There was a sandy path around a bend that was visible due to the low tide on the other end of the beach, right where it met up with the edge of the Rip. But what nearly made my heart stop was the island at the other end. One that hadn't been there before.

A Drift Island.

Following Malina's lead and mostly out of habit, I pulled up my mask and drew my bow. I couldn't help but wonder if this was one of the islands that our family had been stranded on. I hoped it wasn't, seeing as it was dead, rotted with the Glaev.

The boulders obscured the entire sandbar and island from us. Malina gave me a knowing look and a nod. We both ran, keeping low to the ground, toward one of the large rocks and crouched behind it.

"Can you feel anything?" Malina whispered. The roar of the waves drowning out her quiet voice so much that I struggled to hear.

"No. Not through the sand or the Glaev." Another reason I hated the dark magic.

"Let's get closer then. See if we can spot any movement on the island."

I looked at her like she was crazy. "No one can be on it, Mal. It's the Glaev."

She shared the same look of astonishment. "He can. He stood on it, back in Oryn. I saw him."

Well shit.

"Alright, let's get closer," I conceded.

We darted across the beach to the next boulder nearer the Drift Island, pausing to glance around for movement, then sprinting to a space between two boulders next to each other at the curve of the bend. We pressed our bodies against the rock before leaning over to peer around the side of it. I could see where the sandbar met with the beach. The path itself was narrow and unaffected by the Glaev.

My spine shivered as an accented voice came from behind us.

"Hello, Diamond."

Chapter Sixty-One

KYA

I had never feared staring into the face of death. I had always walked alongside it. But when those I loved were on that line with me, I was terrified.

At the sound of his gruff voice, Malina and I whipped around, our weapons raised, to find Daegel standing at the edge of the Rip. He didn't have his hooded cloak this time, so I was able to see him more clearly. The blonde of his hair was short in length. It was cropped close to his head on the sides, while slightly longer on top. Those cobalt eyes, like the dark waters of the sea, were striking against the paleness of his freckled skin.

I blinked in wonder at how someone so alluring could be filled with corruption, rotted to the core.

We hadn't seen him when we had darted from boulder to boulder, not when he was behind one himself. And beside him, with labored breathing and a bloodied face, Nikan stood with wide blue eyes filled with dread. His hands were bound, but he wasn't gagged this time. My heart dropped at how close to the edge he was. One slip, one small push, and he'd be lost to the depths of the chasm forever.

Through the bond, I felt Ryker's anxiousness at feeling my own trepidation.

My eyes flicked between my brother and the dark wielder. Daegel's lips spread into a rueful smirk. He opened his mouth to speak, but Nikan beat him to it.

"Mal, get Kya out of here. You don't understand what he is. What he's capable—"

Daegel struck Nikan in the jaw, and blood spurted from his mouth as his head was whipped to the side from the impact. Malina and I advanced. I drew my magic to me, snaking it down my hand to my arrow.

"Now now. There's no need for that." Daegel held his hand up to us, the blackness of his dark magic swirling around his palm and fingers. We stopped but kept our weapons trained on him, my arrow, glowing with the energy, aimed right at his heart.

"Let him go," I demanded. I would kill him where he stood but he was too close to Nikan. If he started to fall back into the Rip, he could take Nikan with him.

"Surrender yourself to me and tell your friend to drop her weapons, then I'll release him."

I didn't believe him for a second. Even if I did surrender, he would just kill them eventually anyway. I didn't say anything, just narrowed my eyes in challenge. I could hurt him and he was outnumbered.

Daegel huffed. "I would expect nothing less from a fierce little thing like you."

He placed his hand on Nikan's shoulder, not breaking eye contact with me. With a wink, he squeezed and there was a crack right before Nikan's howl. Even with how strong our bones were, Daegel broke his shoulder like he was cracking an egg.

"Let's make sure you behave," Daegel said with a malicious grin. He pushed Nikan backwards until the back of his feet were at the edge of the Rip, the rocks chipping away beneath his heels down into the endless abyss.

"Wait! Stop!" Malina screamed as we both advanced.

"Ah ah ah. That's far enough." He held his hand out and we froze. The dark magic from his hand billowed down to the ground. It blackened the sand in a semi-circle around him and Nikan, expanding out toward us.

My breathing quickened and my heartrate spiked.

"Godsdamnit. What's happening?" Ryker's voice demanded. I ignored him, too focused on what was before me.

Malina and I leapt back, away from the Glaev as it slowly crept outward, until it stopped. It had created a barrier around Daegel and Nikan, too far for any of us to jump across. Nikan was trapped between the Glaev and the Rip. My mind quickly reeled on solutions to this new problem.

I could use my energy to counteract the Glaev so we could get to him or I could shift my wings and carry him across it.

But I didn't trust that my wings were strong enough, since I was weak from using so much of my magic earlier. It would take more time for me to replenish my reserves. Odarum was right. I should have listened to him. I should have worked harder.

"Talk to me," Ryker pleaded.

"I'll make this easy for you, Diamond." Daegel stepped on to the Glaev, walking slowly toward me with his arms held out to his sides.

I eyed every step, every motion. I quickly glanced at Malina and in a blink, we shared a knowing look. She started to move away from me.

"Come with me willingly, and I might let your friends live." I bared my teeth as Daegel continued. "Or you don't and I'll take you anyway and kill your friends where they stand."

I pulled my bow back a little farther, adjusting the position to keep it trained on his heart. He noticed this and stopped just at the edge of the Glaev barrier.

"What's it going to be?" he gritted through his teeth. "Hurry up. I don't have all night and neither does he."

My eyes snapped to Nikan when he yelled. The Glaev around him was slowly closing in. He had minutes at best before he either backed up off the side of the Rip, or was consumed by the Glaev.

"Fuck. You." I whipped my head to Malina who was on the other side of the Glaev circle. "Now!"

I released my arrow and slammed my eyes shut, turning my head away. Malina wielded a beam of light aimed for Daegel, bright enough to blind if looking straight at it. Nikan knew this too, he would have shielded his eyes as best as he could but I hoped that Daegel was distracted enough that he would look directly at her. I thrust out my hand and poured my magic into the Glaev, trying to create a small path through it from Malina to Nikan.

Daegel grunted and cursed. Malina's light dimmed enough for me to open my eyes. Daegel was holding a hand over his eyes and the other gripping the wood of my white feathered, non-laced, arrow that had struck his shoulder. I pushed more of my magic out as quickly as I could, but I felt myself weakening even more.

"Kya!" Ryker shouted down the bond.

"Busy!" I snapped, and he remained silent but I could feel a wave of frustration.

Daegel snarled, and I turned my attention back to him. He glared at me, ripping the arrow from his muscle like it was nothing more than an inconvenient thorn and tossed it to the blackened ground.

I threw my hand up toward him, redirecting the energy just in time to block the magic he wielded at me. The two magics collided with one another in a fantastical eruption of equally opposing forces that flared out from the epicenter, blocking my view of Daegel on the other side.

Out of the corner of my eye, I saw Malina dive and roll out of the way of the dark magic launched at her, landing right where she had stood. Dropping my bow, I thrust my other hand toward the enclosing Glaev around Nikan, trying to give him more time.

Malina grunted as she leapt out of the way of another attack, and I closed my eyes again as she wielded another beam of light toward Daegel.

His magic sputtered against mine, and I took the opportunity to turn invisible and jump out of the way before his magic came at me again. My vision was beginning to turn spotty from utilizing so much of my magic. Sand sprayed up from the impact of my boots sliding across the surface, the sound giving away my location—another thing Odarum had warned me about.

I couldn't hold both, the invisibility and the energy, so I switched back and forth between the two. I zig-zagged through the sand, attacking Daegel with my energy and creating the growing path through the Glaev while I was visible, and disappearing from sight to jump out of the way of his own attacks.

With him concentrating on me, Malina was able to make headway toward Nikan while using her light to blind Daegel as best she could, but that meant that I had to constantly use my magic—draining what little reserve I had left.

I blinked away unconsciousness, trying desperately to hit the dark wielder. If I could just get close enough, I would be able to land a blow but I couldn't, not while he remained on the Glaev beneath him. It took everything I had to concentrate on my magic. Nikan and Malina were shouting and screaming, but I couldn't hear over the roar of Ryker's distressed voice filling my head and tearing my soul. I couldn't see between Malina's light beams and the bursts of mine and Daegel's magic. I couldn't feel Daegel through the Glaev.

It was too much. Everything was shutting down.

I had to let go of my invisibility, needing to save as much strength as I could to use my energy to create the path and fight against Daegel. But it wasn't enough.

I had to concentrate all of my magic, my energy gifted to me by my Spirit Guardian, at the dark wielder, leaving Nikan stranded at the edge of the Rip with the Glaev closing in. I pushed forward. With one final surge, the last of what I had left, I thrust it at Daegel.

The remnants of my depleted magic trickled from my fingertips. I tried… I tried so, so hard to keep standing, to keep pushing forward, to reach the Glaev where Daegel stood.

But he got to me first, just as the last swirling tendrils of my magic died out.

Daegel leapt through the air and tackled me as we rolled on the ground in a frenzy of strikes and kicks. I managed to stand but I was too weak. He stood, pinning my back to his chest with his arm around my neck in a hold that I couldn't break free from.

I fought and thrashed against him with the last bits of my strength, pushing us back and back and back.

"What is he doing to you?" Ryker screamed.

"Malina! The kiss!" I bellowed into the night.

I didn't fear death.

"Shh, my shadow. It's okay." I caressed down the bond, sending every piece of my heart and soul to my mate.

Malina appeared a moment later. My bow and an arrow with the black feathers of the poison-laced tip aimed at us.

"Back off! It's over!" Daegel roared. With his hands occupied, he couldn't use his magic.

I pushed back with a grunt, using all my strength. Our feet stumbled on the rocky ground beneath us. Malina's eyes were wide, her face pale with dread.

"*Say it, Ryker,*" I whispered.

I pushed again.

"*What?*"

"*Say it.*" It was a plea, begging to hear it one last time. Daegel and Malina and Nikan were still screaming, but I couldn't hear them.

Daegel's arm tightened around my neck, and the rock crunched under my boots.

Push.

"*You belong to me.*" His voice was apprehensive.

I stared into Malina's wet brown eyes, saying all that I needed to say with a simple look that I knew she would understand.

"*I promised that no other would take me from you,*" I said to Ryker.

Push.

"*I meant it.*"

"For them." I mouthed silently to my sister with a small loving smile. "For us."

"*Little gem…*" Ryker's voice trembled.

Push.

"*And I'm sorry that I'm the one who's taking me from you.*"

"*Kya—Kya please!*" he begged.

Push.

"*I love you Ryker—*"

"*KYA!*" he bellowed.

Daegel's boot caught against the crumbling rock at the edge.

Malina pulled back the bow string, a tear streaked down her beautiful, olive-skinned cheek. Her mouth was moving, but I had tuned out everything except the sound of Ryker's voice.

"*—beyond the bond.*"

I nodded to her subtly.

Malina let go. The arrow soared, singing through the night air.

"NO!" The last thing I heard was Ryker's voice roaring down the bond.

The arrow pierced through my chest and right into Daegel's.

With one final push, our bodies fell over the edge. I silently prayed to Kleio that she would save the ones I loved. I had completed her task. I looked up to the river in the starry sky one last time before the mists of the Rip took us.

No, I didn't fear death. I feared fate.

Epilogue

I look down at the fight ensuing below. Daegel has served me well over the years, fulfilling my demands and capturing the Diamond as I commanded. But he spares the others, and my lip curls in a sneer at the male's mercy.

I feel my cheeks lift, drawing the edges of my mouth upward with delight. The soft skin of each curved lip peels apart, exposing the glossy whites of my teeth when he pulls her to him. The female hasn't even realized that she is pushing him right to where they are destined to go anyway, right where I want them, falling into Odes's grave and ripping them from the realm.

My plan is falling into place. Without the Worthy female's Spirit to guard her, there is nothing keeping me from fulfilling my ultimate goal. Soon, I will have my revenge.

Acknowledgements

Before I get into thanking all of the amazing people who helped me get this story out into the world, I just want to say that I never thought that this would happen. Being an author was a dream that I never knew I had. My life will never be the same, and I wouldn't have it any other way. And not only did I write one book, but I have an entire series coming and likely more after that.

Worthy of Fate started as one simple idea. One thought. I couldn't get it out of my head for weeks, and it was driving me crazy. So I decided to just jot it down, to get it out of my head, and leave it be. Three months, and many words later, Worthy of Fate was a full novel. And it all started with a winged horse.

This has been an incredible journey with so many late nights, frustrations, tears, laughs, and discovering an amazing community within the book world.

First and foremost, thank you to my husband for taking on the extra load in our already chaotic life and giving me the guilt-free opportunity to lock myself away and dive into my fantasy world. Simple words on a page can't express my gratitude for your endless support and equal enthusiasm. Thank you for listening to all the late-night ramblings, holding me through the emotional waves, and helping me with the *research*. And thank you for pushing me to see this through. I love you so much, handsome.

Thank you to my boys. If you ever read this one day, I hope you know that I'm so thankful for you being so supportive and being okay with hanging out with me while I had a keyboard on my lap. Mommy loves you more than you will ever know.

Marie. Girl, I don't even know where to start. This whole thing wouldn't have even started if it wasn't for you urging me and constantly being my hype, dragging me out of my own darkness. I know this wasn't what you signed on for as my life-twin, but I couldn't have done this without you.

To Mallory, thank you for being there from the beginning and reading all those atrocious first chapters. You helped me find my style and encouraged me to keep going. All those suggestions and long phone calls paid off. Your help and advice have been invaluable, and I'm forever grateful.

Laura and Rachel, you guys stuck with me and have been my rock. With our constant chatting and brainstorming, word help, and continual support, you two gave me the foundation to bring the book to its fullest. I can't thank you enough, and I love you both! (One of these days, we'll go on that retreat, I promise.)

Thank you to my family for all of your support. I've instructed most of you not to read this, and if you did, don't come at me if you're scarred. You were warned.

To my beta team: Colleen, Courtney, and Elyse. You guys were absolutely incredible, finishing in such a short amount of time with such a long book! You brought WoF to the next level, and you did it with style. Ryker and Kya wouldn't have turned into who they are if it wasn't for you.

To Kirsty, thank you for your dedication and time to take on my atrocious manuscript and guide me to turn it into a story worth telling.

To Noah, thank you for going above and beyond. Not only did you exceed my expectations, but you also explained and taught me how to be better. About the commas, I promise I'll do better next time, but I'll probably still mess it up.

To everyone who read it and gave me feedback, thank you! Doug, you read it more times than anyone else and gave amazing insight to help me bring Ryker to the male he was meant to be.

To the wonderful authors that I've met, your guidance and advice helped me to get this beauty successfully published. Melissa K. Roehrich, Charissa Weaks, Melissa Kieran, Emily Grey, H.L. Hamilton, Mallory Benjamin, R. Lynn Hanks, Laura Elizabeth, Kris K. Haines, and all of the other amazing authors who answered my endless questions, from the bottom of my heart, thank you and I hope to meet you all one day!

And thank you to you, readers, for taking a chance on this debut novel from a baby indie author. I hope you enjoyed it, and if you did, stick around for the next book in the Realms in Peril series. Strap in because it's about to get darker.

About the Author

A.N. is a dark fantasy romance author. She loves spending time with her husband and kids. She's a homebody who enjoys escaping into other worlds, either through reading or writing.

Website: www.ancaudle.com
TikTok: tiktok.com/@ancaudleauthor
Instagram: instagram.com/ancaudleauthor
Discord Reader Group: https://discord.gg/NBPgtRapg5

Printed in Great Britain
by Amazon

47957580R00330